Y0-EKP-523

ACKNOWLEDGMENTS

The writing of Bridgebuilders happened in spurts and starts, and while this was a little hard on the author (me), it was even harder on those loyal people who offered time and opinions to help me get it right. They are a persistent bunch.

Special thanks to Amy Raby, Darke Conteur, Patty Jansen, David Fortier, and Rhonda Garcia for their online support. They saw the early chapters and gave honest criticism and constant encouragement. I'm especially pleased to know we are all still mucking around in each others' lives and writing.

Lani Longshore, Jordan Bernal, and Ed Miracle have nurtured this book from its first toddling steps through to this graduation moment. Without their merciless slashing, there would be far too many adverbs in this story.

And always, thank you to Rick, husband extraordinaire. He never gives up on me. I love you, darling.

Marlene Dotterer
2012

THE TIME TRAVEL JOURNALS

BRIDGEBUILDERS

MARLENE DOTTERER

ISBN: 0985957417
ISBN-13: 978-0985957414

Also by Marlene Dotterer

Novels
The Time Travel Journals: Shipbuilder

Short Stories
The Farm

Anthologies
Pagan Writers Presents Samhain: "Webs"

THE TIME TRAVEL JOURNALS

BRIDGEBUILDERS

SECOND UNIVERSE

Chapter 1

1977
Comber, Ireland

Sam Altair didn't believe in life after death, but even as Casey Andrews' flower-lined casket inched lower into the ground, he knew that she would never release her hold on him. He had known the old lady for only five years, yet his wire-rimmed glasses had fogged several times as he stood behind her family at the gravesite. Was he crying for himself, or for the older version of Sam Altair who had stolen Casey from an alternate timeline when she was just twenty years old?

The present Sam Altair stood at the gravesite, the thirty-one-year-old inheritor of a lifetime of someone else's sins. He was surrounded by Casey's children and grandchildren, along with a plethora of grand-nephews and -nieces. A wail from the side reminded him there were also a couple of great-grandchildren. The woman had become a matriarch.

The seventy years since her abrupt move backwards through time had brought her love and family and friends, something that he suspected would have happened to her no matter where she was. Casey Wilson Andrews had been that kind of person. He had grown to love her, too.

Her last request burdened him. He doubted that she had asked anything of anyone else, other than to live in peace and happiness. But Sam Altair had debts to pay and Casey had not been reluctant to demand he cover them.

Even though he wasn't *that* Sam Altair.

The casket rested at the bottom, and Casey's daughter, a pixie-like woman with short white hair, stepped forward, her black skirt and blouse flowing like water along her thin body. She tossed a single daisy, Casey's favorite flower, onto the casket. Her gesture released the others, who moved to toss their own offerings into the grave. Casey had often said she wished to die in the spring, when the flowers were blooming, so they could do this very thing. She wanted flowers in her grave. It was true, somehow, that Casey usually got what she wanted.

When they were all finished, a few of them looked to him and he stepped forward to place his own offering, an acorn from the oak tree that grew in the Belfast Botanic Gardens. The tree had come back in time with Casey and Sam in 1906, the result of a time travel experiment gone haywire. Casey would have laughed in delight if she'd known he was going to do this. Sam rather hoped the oak would take hold in this place. He could think of no greater legacy for her.

The graveyard workers began to fill in the hole, and Sam's gaze wandered to the waiting headstone. Like all the others in this part of the church's graveyard, it was dignified and simple, but with a message chosen years ago by her husband:

Casey Ashley Wilson Andrews
May 16, 1885 - June 4, 1977
Beloved Wife of Thomas Andrews of Dunallon
and Mother of His Children
"The Reason I Lived"

Of course, she had been born in 1985, not 1885, and the truth behind the quote was a story known only to three of the people here. And to any in the future, who might have access to the time travel journals.

∞

At the entrance to the graveyard, Sam caught up with Casey's granddaughter, Sarah. The early summer day was bright, and the green hills of Comber wandered away to the blue sparkle of Strangford Lough. The moment might have been awkward, but Sarah favored Sam with a mischievous glance.

"The flowers are bloomin' everywhere," she said. "Just like she requested."

His lips twitched as he noted the blanket of color covering the hills. "Casey's inside track," he said, and Sarah laughed.

"Atheists aren't supposed to have inside tracks," she told him and he had to smile, because she had leaned close to whisper it. He hoped she did that because she wanted to be close to him and not just to keep Casey's well-known secret from being heard by other family members. Her chin jerked back to the graveyard. "Not going to pay your respects to ... you know?"

Sam shuddered and linked his arm through hers to guide her to the car. "I'll pass." In truth, he'd never once stopped by the grave of the first Sam Altair. He knew, that as Casey's guardian-of-record, the man had earned a spot on the edge of the section devoted to the

Andrews family. There was just something indefinably creepy about it though, and Sam couldn't bring himself to visit.

Besides, Sarah was here. There was no time to waste.

"It's good to see you again, Sarah." *Ah. That was original.*

But she smiled. "I missed you too, Sam." She leaned against her car, hands in the pockets of her cardigan, the breeze blowing strands of her chestnut hair across her nose. She regarded him with a tincture of amusement. Her eyes were as green as her grandmother's had been.

He returned her smile. "How long can you stay?"

"Hopefully, several years."

"What? What do you mean?"

She shrugged. "I could stay in Galway and work at SpaceSystems for the rest of my life. But I thought I'd see about the family business."

Harland & Wolff Shipyards. Not officially the family business, but there'd been an Andrews or close relative at the helm practically since its inception. Sarah was the latest in the Andrews line of shipbuilders that had started with her grandfather. When he was Sarah's age, Thomas Andrews was building the grand ocean liners of the early twentieth century. Sarah built spaceships, but Harland & Wolff had expanded to include the new mode of travel.

Sam didn't bother to question his heart's rapid beating. He wanted her to stay. He gripped her shoulders. "No sense letting all that talent going to the competition." He kept his words light, but his smile would have made the flowers grow.

She bit her lip, examining his face with a trace of uncertainty, but made no effort to move out of his grip. "I want to be home," she said. "I hope we can get ... reacquainted."

Now, *there* was a word fraught with meanings. Sam was all set to explore some of them, but the presence of so many family members hindered him. That, and an approaching voice pitched to brook no nonsense.

"Sarah, me love. You'll be takin' a load of the wee ones in your car. Can you fit five of 'em?"

Sam dropped his hands from her shoulders, though not before a final squeeze. He turned as Sarah stepped out to face her father, Casey's third and youngest child, as he approached with a line of children trailing behind him.

"I only have seat belts for four, Da'," she said. "As ye know."

Tommy Andrews shrugged. "It's just to Ardara. You can squeeze 'em in."

The children didn't seem to mind, although there was yelling for "shotgun" as they scrambled in, the little car bouncing with their efforts. Sarah nabbed a collar and pulled one out. "Ye can go with Sam there, Jeffrey. I drove this thing from Galway and it's needin' tires. No seat belt, no ride."

Sam was more amenable to this than Jeffrey, although the reminder that it was "just to Ardara," a drive of less than five minutes, provided one didn't run into a flock of sheep crossing the road, placated him enough. Jeffrey managed to convince a cousin to come along. With the boys safely belted in and making loud scatological noises in mimicry of his car, Sam endured the ride to the Andrews ancestral home on the banks of the lough.

The commotion in the house and yard was in inverse proportion to the solemnity of the funeral. A large group had already assembled out back, past the rose bushes, to continue the ongoing intra-family football match: Montgomerys versus the Andrews, currently two-up for the Montgomerys.

"Sure to be put right, now that Sarah's back," Sam heard as he approached the field, and Sarah's loud protests were roundly ignored as she was pulled into position and the ball was off. Sam watched, amused and frustrated. But honestly, there'd be no way he'd get to talk to her, anyway. Not today.

This would be all right if he could play too, but the family competition was a serious thing. "Only blood allowed" was the rule, and not even Sarah's brother-in-law, a defender for Ipswich, could play in this game. So instead, Sam kept score, joining in the general observation that poor Sarah had not managed to make too much of a difference.

∞

His laboratory at Dunallon was dark, and Sam didn't bother with lights when he entered later that night. He sat on the nearest stool and sighed, removing his tie with relief. The stillness reached into him as he sat, his thoughts lazy and jumbled. He wanted to think about Sarah, but Casey kept intruding, her bright green eyes laughing at him from a wrinkled face. Her eyes had been bright practically until the moment she died. Such a funny old lady. He'd had no experience with old women before being summoned to her presence five years ago, and he was surprised as she became a friend and confidant. She was close to ninety when he met her, yet her frail body housed a sharp wit and a sense of humor honed from decades of exposure to her husband and his brothers. She offered him a career and a nearly endless supply of funding, as well as the chance to work with one of the most respected physicists of their age, her son, Jamie. Dr. James Andrews had been trained at the knee of the original Sam Altair. He had learned early that time travel was possible, and that he and his family were living in the resulting universe of an experiment gone awry.

A universe they were determined to make a good one.

Sam wiped a tear from his cheek. *Damn, I'm going to miss her.*

"I'll miss her, too," a voice said, and Sam started, turning to the door. Sarah stood outlined in the light of the hallway lamp. Sam gasped out an embarrassed laugh and reached for a Kim-wipe. "What are you doing, here? Aren't you staying at home?"

She rolled her eyes and stepped into the room, letting the door close behind her. Before it shut, he heard voices in the background. Jamie and Alicia were home, as well. He suspected they'd brought a gaggle of out-of-town relatives to stay. Not even Ardara House could hold the entire clan, anymore.

"I am, of course. Mum won't have it any other way, you know," Sarah said. She stood before him for a moment, a looming shape against the darkness. He heard her grab a stool and drag it closer. "Lights, dim," she commanded, and even at that strength, he blinked against the brightness.

She grinned. "You're such a sentimental slob, Sam. Sitting in the dark, crying over my grandmother."

He laughed and tossed the Kim-wipe into a receptacle. "And she's deservin' of it, lass. She was my friend, in spite of all the ways I was a disappointment to her." He smiled at the countertop, shaking his head a little.

Sarah snorted. "In what ways are you thinkin' you were a disappointment? She never mentioned any."

He shrugged. "Subtle things, I guess. I wasn't 'her' Sam, after all. When she met him, he had thirty-five years of physics research behind him; I was a wet-behind-the-ears postgrad. Time travel was just an amusing, not-very-possible side effect of my hypothesis. I'd never even given it serious consideration. And she wanted me to read his journals and be ready to jump universes in just a few years."

"And here you are, five years later, ready to start building a prototype," Sarah said. "I don't think she was disappointed."

He lifted his shoulders in mute acknowledgement, then blinked, staring at her in surprise.

She looked over her shoulder in confusion, then back at him. "What?"

"Who told you we're ready to build a prototype?" Silly question. There was only one person who could have, but why ... ?

She propped her elbow on the counter and rested her head on her upraised arm, smiling at him. "Uncle Jamie had a chat with me after you left the funeral. That's why I came over before going home. To talk to you. He offered me a job."

Sam gaped, horrified and hopeful all at once. "He did? What job? He never mentioned he was going to do that."

"He didn't know I was planning on moving back to Belfast. He said you need an engineer."

"Yes, but Sarah ... " Sam snapped his mouth closed, not at all sure what to say to her.

Her face darkened. "You don't want me to work for the consortium?"

The cold in her voice chilled him and he reached to touch her face. She jerked away, but just a little. His finger brushed her cheek. When she didn't move again, he stroked upward along her cheekbone, then cupped his hand behind her neck. "I would be ecstatic to work with you every day," he whispered. Her eyes filled with tears, but she didn't say anything. "And honored," he continued in a firmer voice. "We'd be fortunate to have you. But if you work on our project, what about your career? You won't be building spaceships. I'm concerned it will be a setback for you."

She squeezed his hand and stood up, moving away from him. He watched her, desire licking him with flame. *I shouldn't have touched her.*

She leaned against the wall, arms folded, and regarded him thoughtfully. "Obviously," she said slowly, as if thinking it through, "if I spend the next few years building your time machine and other equipment, I won't be building spaceships. I'll be years out of the loop. Yeah, I suppose it would hurt my career, if I went back to spaceships. But you tell me, why would I do that?"

"Go back?" Sam glanced around the lab. "Where do you see my work going in a few years, Sarah? Even if we're successful, I frankly cannot figure out a use for time travel. I suspect it will be more trouble than it's worth. And infinitely more dangerous."

"Nonsense. You don't get to call limitations on any scientific discovery. There are always applications that the discoverer never thinks of."

"You love building spaceships," he said, his tone just shy of malicious. He desperately wanted her to say yes, but he wanted her to be *sure*. "You've planned on doing it since you used to follow your grandfather to work when you were just a kid."

"That was before anyone told me the big family secret." Her hands dropped to fists at her sides. "Back when I thought my choices were to build those grand ships I saw growing at the Yard, or sit at a desk like Uncle Jamie, fiddling with equations all day." She raised her hands, palms up, fingers outstretched—delicate hands that belied the strength in them. "I wanted to *build*, to feel the shape and texture of things under my fingers, to see real results from my work." She stared at him, her eyes wide. "But then you told me what you were doing. You let me see the journals. And my whole world changed, Sam."

The tears in her voice brought an ache to his own throat. He'd been so caught up in her after they made love the first—the only—time, he had lost all perspective. Perhaps it was sweet talk when he said how glad he was her grandfather hadn't died before her father was born. He certainly had not thought it through, and when she began asking questions, in that teasing, gentle way of new lovers, he could not lie to her.

Even now, over a year later, he closed his eyes in pain at the memory. Sarah was devastated at the story, and had gone straight to her grandmother and Uncle Jamie, demanding they tell her the truth. She took off for Galway two days later without another word to Sam. Casey had been furious. More than furious. It was the one term she'd set for Sam. He must never involve her family. Jamie alone knew of it, because he'd grown up with the original Sam as his surrogate grandfather. From the time he could walk and talk, Jamie had followed the elderly scientist around, soaked up every word the old man uttered, and brought to pass every plan the old man made. Jamie had stepped up to carry the work forward until Sam himself was born and grew up to become a physicist.

Sarah was suddenly in front of him, pulling him out of the memory, her hands holding his head as she bent to kiss him. Her tears were just under the sweet, familiar taste of her, her lips passionate and warm. His hands covered her back, pulling her tight against him, the counter keeping them both upright. He lost track of time, of everything except the overwhelming feel of her, but eventually she pulled back, turned sideways, and sat gingerly on his lap.

She rested her cheek on the top of his head, her arms around his shoulders, as he held her. "I've never stopped loving you, Sam," she whispered. "I hated you for a while, 'tis true. But I never stopped loving you."

He tightened his hold on her, more aware than he had ever been, just how precious she was to him. He tried to speak, but his voice wouldn't work, even after he cleared his throat. And surely, she was waiting to hear him say he loved her, too. What would she think if he said nothing? Panic rose, he couldn't breathe. She sat up, peering into his face, her expression closed and guarded. Then she smiled and he felt like the sun came out. "You're a sentimental slob Sam," she said, just as she had earlier, and he found his voice.

"Do you have any idea what I've been through this last year? Thinking you hated me forever, and wasn't it just what I deserved? Seeing you today ... ah love," he pressed his forehead to hers. "Tell me you forgive me, Sarah. That you'll let me make it up to you, if I can ever do that. Tell me I can love you again, and you won't turn away from me."

She kissed him again, slowly. He'd never really been kissed before, he realized. All others had just been teasers, leading up to this one.

"There's nothing to forgive, my love," she said, her lips moving lightly on his. "You meant no malice by telling me. And in the end, my family means more to me than ever, because I know these things."

Sometime later, she spoke again, her voice content and languid. "So do I have the job?"

Chapter 2

1980
Three years later

Sarah stared with blank disinterest at the morning news on the lab's wall screen. In truth, it was the digital clock in the upper right corner that had her attention. Three years of experimentation and scrapped prototypes had just culminated with one brilliant insight that woke her up at two-dark-o'clock this morning. She'd left Sam slumbering while she threw on jeans and sweatshirt, to pad her way to the laboratory. Four hours of tinkering brought the insight to physical reality, and wonder of wonders, the bloody thing *worked*.

Her fingernails tapped a dull rhythm on the countertop, keeping time with the ticking of the grandfather clock in the hallway. She'd long since given up trying to keep busy as she waited for Sam and her uncle to wake up and respond to her urgent message telling them to hurry. The TV clock flipped to seven-oh-six.

Men seemed to wake up quickly for just one thing.

Although, she perhaps should not be having such thoughts about her uncle.

Sam, though ...

The sound of footsteps drew her thoughts back to safer territory. She turned with narrowed eyes and pouting lip to regard the men as they at last entered the lab.

"I thought you'd never get here. I sent you a memo an hour ago."

"At six in the morning, lass," Jamie said. "Normal people were still in bed."

Sam carried a large, steaming mug in each hand, and he held one out to her, in the apparent hope he could use it as a peace offering. "I brought you tea."

The fragrance reached her, and she decided not to fight it. As she took the mug from him, he said, "I noticed you were gone around three o'clock. What drove you from your sleep this time?"

She sipped the tea and offered a smile to both men before she turned away, crooking her finger to get them to follow. "The solution to our problem."

"Which one?" her uncle asked. She didn't look back, just rounded a counter and reached for the petri dish in the center. She slid it toward them, then took another sip of tea as she watched their expressions.

Perhaps it was still too early. They stared at the dish, and at the two-centimeter-wide silver cylinder that glinted in its center. They exchanged a glance with each other, before bringing their gazes back to her for enlightenment. She sighed and began to explain.

"Our bridge-builder, which I've started calling CERBO, by the way ... "

"CERBO?" Jamie asked.

"Confined Einstein Rosen Bridge Originator," Sarah said. "CERBO."

He frowned, but did not comment. As a rule, Jamie didn't like acronyms, although he admitted that he'd never find a universe without them.

"So far, we've only been able to build wormholes that stay in this universe." Sarah continued. "This wee chip alters the neutrinos to allow for travel to another universe. One that already exists, anyway."

A strange shadow crossed Sam's face, but her uncle's face lit up with a huge grin. He pointed. "This? You've done it with this?"

She nodded, returning Jamie's grin. But she watched Sam.

He was staring at the cylinder, the steam from his forgotten tea rising to dissipate against his chin. Her uncle turned to face Sam as well. They waited.

At last Sam blinked, put his mug on the counter, and picked up the cylinder, holding it on the tip of finger. "How does it work?"

Sarah shrugged. "It's plug-and-play. You use CERBO to collect your neutrinos and build the bridge that you design. But if we want to return to the first universe ... and we do want to, don't we Sam?" His slight nod did nothing to relieve her anxiety, but she went on. "To travel to the first universe, we insert this wee chip, and input the parameters for the shape of the neutrinos in that universe. That way, the bridge we build will start *here*, and end up *there*."

Jamie whistled and bounced on his toes.

Sam handed the chip to Sarah. She gripped it between thumb and forefinger, and shook it at him.

"It does more than that, though," she said.

He looked a little pale. "What?"

"It also controls the time travel. It's a safety feature, Sam. Used alone, CERBO will only build wormholes within our own universe. Or," she shrugged, "whichever universe we happen to be in. But we cannot travel to another universe, or through time, unless this wee chip is inserted first."

"So no more accidents, eh?" Jamie said.

"No more accidents," Sarah said. She was relieved to see a bit of color return to Sam's face.

His lips twitched. "We better not lose it."

Sarah shivered as a cold hand gripped her heart. She put the chip back in the petri dish. "I'll make more than one."

"Good idea."

"No." Jamie shook his head, and Sarah looked up at him, surprised.

"No?"

"Oh, make more than one," he said. "Indeed, indeed. But take just one with you. It would be disastrous if it fell into the wrong hands." He reached out to touch the chip. "No, I'm afraid we'll have to ask you to design one more miracle before we attempt this."

She sighed, and Jamie showed her a brief grin before turning serious again.

"Program a fail-safe into each CERBO. I want a program that will find you in whatever universe or time you are in, and that will automatically transport you home after a set time. In case you do lose your wee chip. Or if ... something else ... should happen."

Sarah thought about it, noticing Sam's slight nod of agreement. "I can probably do that," she said. "We'll need to wear something that the fail-safe can lock onto. A marker of some kind."

"It should be internal," Sam said. "If we're really going to do this insane thing, we should have a biomarker, perhaps in our bloodstream. Something that carries the shape of the neutrinos in this universe."

"We all carry that already," Sarah said. "Everything in this universe does. But I think I can come up with something that will work." She looked heavenward. "Another sleepless night or two."

"Then we'll be ready," Jamie said, gazing at the chip.

"We'll be ready to run a test," Sam said, his tone firm. "A probe. Build the fail-safe, and we'll send a probe to the first universe. They're a hundred years ahead of us, and we have no idea what's happened in the last seventy-four years. We need data."

"Certainly," Jamie said, as if puzzled that Sam even suggested it.

Sarah just nodded, aware that the cold grip on her heart had not lessened.

Chapter 3

When the probe vanished from the floor of Cave Hill's biggest cave, Sam decided his shaky legs would not hold him upright much longer. He sank to his knees, flicking an anxious glance toward CERBO. The digital timer counted down the mission time.

Four minutes, 55 seconds ... 54 ... 53 ...

CERBO was by far the most promising of Sarah's bridge machines. The tablet-sized prototype did not look as impressive as its name, but Sam considered that a positive feature. They needed something light and unobtrusive.

A ray of sun shone through the cave entrance, as if to spotlight the probe's empty space. A few lanterns lit the rest of the cave, scattered on rocks around the room. They cast enough light to reveal the volcanic walls, and the dusty ground littered with rocks and equipment.

Sam heard a nervous swallow behind him, and his lips twitched in empathy. Sarah was just as anxious as he was. Jamie stood on the other side of Sam, keeping as still as the rocks around them. Jamie was a Nobel laureate, and one of the topmost physicists in the world, but even he was apprehensive about this experiment. That was understandable. All of Jamie's career, all his life, had led to this point: returning to the original timeline from which their world had sprung.

The first Sam Altair had worked for years in this new world, and had trained Jamie to continue his work. He wanted to understand what had happened when he and Casey traveled back through time.

Sam—he refused to think of himself as "the second Sam"—squinted his eyes against the headache he always got when he thought about it. Casey Andrews had brought him into their work eight years ago, just after he'd earned his PhD in physics in 1972. The time travel work had been kept secret, restricted to a handful of researchers and technicians, all of them employed by the Freedom Technological Consortium, which the first Sam Altair, along with Albert Einstein, had started in 1912.

Now in 1980, only five people in the world, Sam, Sarah, Jamie, and their two assistants back at the lab, knew that their world was a divergence from the original history of the universe. In the original universe, the shipbuilder, Thomas Andrews, had died in 1912, drowning when his famous ship, *RMS Titanic*, sank after hitting an iceberg. In this world, Casey and Sam had met Tom, and set out to prevent the accident. Casey had married Tom, one of many changes they made to history. They were successful in saving his life, and the lives of many others, although they had not been able to keep the ship from sinking.

Tom Andrews was one of two people in the early 20th century who knew about the time travel. The other was Albert Einstein, who spent many years working with the original Sam. He helped teach Jamie, who learned of the secret when he was twenty years old. It was Casey's request that they find a way back to the original universe, a debt she felt Sam Altair—it didn't matter which Sam Altair—owed her. The debt was not to go back and prevent their travel through time, but to go back and let her parents know what happened to her.

One minute and 14 seconds ...

Sam chewed on his lip as he watched CERBO's timer. He thought it was a mistake to try this. But Casey had worried all her life, knowing how her parents must have suffered when she disappeared. It was the only way to give her peace, Jamie said. They had to try.

Sam remembered how fascinated he had been at the beginning, as he read through the secret journals kept by all of them. The journals had explained much about the astonishing scientific advances of the 20th century. Sam's Consortium was a mix of business and science, where the brightest and best competed to develop the infrastructure Sam needed to continue his own work. He was not careless about this. He built his consortium into a world-wide powerhouse, introducing the technology of the 21st century into this early time, and turning the world toward what he called "sustainable" methods of power and agriculture.

This was all good, as far as the young Sam was concerned. It was the history of his world, and he was content with it. But he was not comfortable with Casey's request. There were so many ways it could go wrong. At the very least, the political climate of the first universe could be volatile. But that wasn't what bothered him the most.

He didn't want to create another alternate universe. Returning to the first timeline would not do that. But once there, Casey wanted Sam to travel back to 2006 and pay a visit to her parents in Berkeley. It was this backward travel through time that created new universes. The neutrinos had to alter their shape to compensate for the stress. It was all very simple and elegant, once you understood what was happening.

Sam had no desire to play God.

But he couldn't deny Casey, either. He'd read her journals. Her writing was permeated with memories of her parents, her father's dry humor and wisdom, her mother's stubborn liberalism and community work as a physician for women. Casey brought them into her life in as many ways as possible, from the names of her children, to her own work in the suffragette and peace movements. Her journals were filled with frequent references to "Dad would say ..." She once told Sam that she still had the habit of stopping to think about how her father or mother would handle a situation, using that as her cue.

It occurred to him that it would be an honor to meet them.

It all hinged on this experiment. Sam blinked, noticing the timer was down to forty-five seconds. Had the probe crossed into the alternate universe? Would it reappear, as Sarah's programming directed? Or had they made an error somewhere, and the probe had disintegrated?

Thirty seconds.

What if there had been people in the area as the probe appeared? It looked just like the other rocks scattered around the cave, but if someone saw it appear out of nowhere ...

Twenty seconds.

What if the probe appeared in the same spot someone was standing? What if the GPS algorithms were buggered, and the probe ended up in the cave wall?

Ten seconds.

Sam held his breath, unable to look away. He felt Sarah's hand tremble on his shoulder. Jamie stood still, a dignified statue.

If Sam had blinked, he would have missed the moment of return, so quiet was the probe's sudden appearance. It took Sarah's gasp to make him realize the probe was not a figment of his anxiety. He stood, then jumped in surprise when Jamie thrust a fist into the air and yelled, "Whoo! It worked!"

Sarah laughed, holding onto Sam's arm and swinging past him to hug her uncle. Sam's cautious malaise vanished, leaving him giddy as he joined the others, slapping Jamie's back, kissing Sarah, all of them laughing with a timorous trace of hysteria that proved their anxiety.

They turned to the probe as their celebration slowed. It rested on the ground, a rock of the same basaltic material as the rest of the cave. Only the closest examination would reveal its electronic center. They gathered around, staring at it with some apprehension. Sam glanced over at the computer, to see that it was merrily flipping through the data streaming from the probe. He let it work, accessing just the basic probe parameters. Temperature and radiation were normal. The collected neutrinos had all vanished, converted into the energy used to bridge universes.

"Can we take it back to the lab?" Sarah asked.

Sam shrugged. "Sure. Everything looks normal."

"Did it go ... there?" she asked. "Did it really work?"

Jamie shook his head, his brows lowered as he stared at the probe. "We'll have to run tests, Sarah. Look at the video, at least."

"I know." She was staring at the probe, her face a pale light in the cave's gloom. When she glanced up, Sam thought she looked afraid. "Let's get it back to the lab."

∞

"Blimey."

"That's all you have to say, Uncle Jamie?"

The old man shook his head. He started to speak again, but stopped. Then he said, "Blimey."

Sarah gave in to a tight smile. She stood between Sam and her uncle, staring at the monitor. She couldn't blame Uncle Jamie for his shock. The video proved beyond doubt that the probe had been somewhere different. The hills and valleys showed that it was Belfast. Yet the geography also revealed the biggest difference. The shoreline was much further inland, with water reaching as far as Ormeau Park. Most shocking to the three of them was the absence of Queen's Island. Harland & Wolff Shipyard was completely gone. Nearby, there was a huge crater near the first cave, as if a meteor had fallen.

"Or a bomb," Jamie said.

It was impossible to see details of the city from their hideaway on Cave Hill, but the familiar layout was intersected by tall walls that divided the city into separate sections. There was no spaceport.

There seemed a general air of desolation about the place. Houses and other buildings spread out as far as they could see, but they looked deserted and broken. In some places, roads appeared overgrown, as grass and bushes reclaimed them. Sam whistled.

"Why would they desert the suburbs? Where did everyone go?"

"Why is the city divided like that?" Sarah stared at the walls, disturbed.

Jamie touched her shoulder. "Mum and Sam told us about the Troubles, remember? Sam said there were times when Belfast was a war zone."

"But," Sarah waved a hand at the screen, "the Troubles happened a hundred years ago for them. I mean, the Belfast we're looking at is a hundred years ahead of us, right? It's 2080 over there."

"We're assuming that," Sam said.

She shook her head. "I expect cities of the future to look clean and fancy, with flying cars and big, shining buildings. This place looks ... old. Grungy."

They were silent for a troubled minute as the video finished and started over. The camera had been filming throughout the experiment, but it showed nothing of its actual trip through time. There was only the countdown to show them anything had happened, plus the fact they knew the probe had vanished before their eyes. But the cave on the video remained the same as the camera scanned 360 degrees, before the probe rose from its spot and floated toward the cavern entrance. Cave Hill itself seemed the same, except for that crater. But as the camera panned across the valley, bringing into view the closer shoreline and the walls, Jamie sighed and sat down.

"Sam left sketches of the Belfast he remembered. He did mention the city was divided, but not to this extent. You know that reconciliation was the project that he and Mum and Dad spent most of their lives on. Perhaps in the other timeline, without their intervention, things just got worse and worse. Maybe the two sides never stopped fighting."

Sarah glanced at her uncle. "He said they'd made progress in the original timeline. But it doesn't look like it lasted."

"There could be other reasons for it," Sam said. "We can't speculate from one five-minute video."

Jamie nodded. "We have other data. Let's see what they tell us."

The news wasn't good. Sarah grew more disturbed as atmospheric data revealed high levels of pollutants, and soil data showed prodigious amounts of lead, mercury, and even too-high traces of radioactive particles.

"Did they have a nuclear war?" she asked, her dismay evident.

Sam squeezed her hand. "No, lass. The city would probably not be there, in that case. It could be industrial pollution. There's only a trace amount, and your grandmother said they were careless with their waste."

The probe recorded a temperature of minus six degrees Celsius, cold even for Northern Ireland in March. "Doesn't look like global warming," Sarah muttered, but Jamie shook his head.

"There are any number of scenarios possible with global warming. A better term is climate change. Sam and I talked about it a lot before he died. One very possible problem is that with the melting of the glaciers, salinity levels in the ocean plummet. This could cause the Gulf Stream to slow or even stop. Without its influence, Great Britain and Europe could freeze over, at least in the early years of warming. I'm disturbed to see it's as cold as it is."

"Sam ..." Sarah started to say, then tightened her lips.

"What, love?" Sam reached for her hand, rubbing her fingers.

She didn't look at him, not really wanting to make this suggestion.

"Grandma wouldn't want us to go if it's too dangerous in that timeline. Maybe we should not do it." She said it in a rush, hoping Sam would veto her. Hoping that he had reassurances about the possible dangers.

He didn't say anything for a minute, and she still didn't look at him, although she felt the glance he shared with her uncle over her head. Then he nodded, and she held her breath.

"I'll keep it in mind, Sarah. I'd need evidence of more danger than just some pollution and cold weather, though."

"There's the coastline."

"Aye, the water's risen, as we feared it might. But you need to remember that the plan is not to stay long in 2080. We'll be going right on to 2006, to find Casey's parents."

Sarah raised her eyebrows. "Right. To 2006, which we know was filled with terrorist attacks and wars everywhere."

He pulled her into a hug. "Let's send another probe, sweetheart. We need more data."

FIRST UNIVERSE

Chapter 4

2080
Sun Consortium
Belfast, Northern Ireland

Dinnie Warner slid her bike to a stop next to a pole and tapped the answer button on the buzzing interface in her ear. "What?" she demanded, fumbling with the bike's lock.

"Where are you?" Mike Ontrera, sounding frantic.

"Parking my bike. I'll be up in a minute."

"Hurry. You won't believe this."

"Hell, Mike, we're not even on duty yet." She hurried anyway, trotting to the side entrance as she removed her helmet, with her backpack flung over her shoulder.

"Bollocks the time, Dinnie. *Get up here.*"

The line went dead and she raced for the stairs, long legs taking them two at a time, rubber skaters silent on the metal. Mike was young and excitable, far too impressed with his position as a data technician at the Sun Consortium. "Flunky," she often reminded him. "You're a data *flunky.*"

Still, he knew better than to call her without good reason. She kept up a steady trot as she emerged on to the third floor, free hand fluffing her short blonde hair before she reached the door to the monitoring room. She flashed her wrist at the door lock and entered, turning toward her office. Mike's head popped up from the crowd around the Neutrino Detection Device at the back of the room.

"Over here."

"Did you break something?" She joined them, moving forward as the crowd parted to let her see the display. When she realized her mouth was hanging open, she snapped it shut. "What the feck is that?"

"Neutrinos." Mike pointed at the screen, as if she couldn't see for herself.

She glared at him. "I know they're neutrinos, ye feckless eejit." Her eyes snapped around at the rest of the group. "What have ye got? What's the count? Where is this? What else is going on in the area?"

"It's here," Carolyn Max swung a monitor around to face Dinnie. "Up at Cave Hill."

Feck. She could look out a window and see it, if there were any windows in the room. Dinnie glanced reflexively toward the door, as if she could see through it, then forced herself to turn toward the monitor. "Looks like two episodes."

"In and out," Carolyn said. "Five minutes apart."

"Exactly five minutes?"

"To the second."

Dinnie stared at her. "Man-made."

Mike stuttered out a laugh. "What, you're saying it's aliens?"

"More likely rebels."

"Oh." Mike flushed, turning away from Dinnie's gaze. "Shit."

Dinnie sighed, meeting Carolyn's disturbed eyes. "Send me all the data. I'll make the call."

She turned toward her office, ignoring the nervous glances from her staff. Throwing her backpack into the corner, she sank into her chair and stared at the pattern Carolyn had transferred to her screen. "Feck," she muttered, then tapped her ear. "Randy Carmichael, please. Code alpha three-five."

A pause of two beats, then her boss's voice sounded softly in her ear. "Carmichael. What have you got?"

"Neutrino spike, coordinates fifty-four degrees, thirty-eight minutes, forty-nine-point-two seconds north, five degrees, fifty-seven minutes, three-point-six seconds west. Two episodes, five-point-oh minutes apart."

The pause went on longer this time, before his voice came back, pitched high in disbelief. "Cave Hill?"

"Yeah."

"Bloody bollocks. I'll be right there."

Dinnie tapped the connection closed, eyes scanning the data that were now flowing across the display as her team fed instrument readings to her computer. Her stomach clenched with both dismay and excitement. It was happening in her lifetime. On her shift.

Cave Hill.

Sam Altair was coming back.

∞

Dinnie took a chair next to Randy in the small conference room. Her team was on alert, but nothing else was forthcoming, so she'd ordered them back to their regular duties. She was the only one of her team to attend this meeting, which was far too high-level for her comfort. She squirmed as Albert Feldman himself entered the room. Rumor said he was second in command at Sun, but the actual hierarchy was classified. Still, this was the big time, no doubt about it.

Feldman was tall, with thick, white hair. He looked about fifty, but Dinnie knew he was much older, one of the earliest recipients of anti-aging treatments. She'd had only glimpses of him before, but she'd heard a lot about him. Formal, stiff, and closed-mouthed, he never got close to anyone he worked with. Rumors said he knew more about Sam Altair than anyone. That he never talked because he didn't want to talk about *that*.

As he stood near the head of the table, he looked controlled and angry. Dinnie bit her lip, wishing she was on the other side of Randy.

"This meeting is classified," Feldman began, his eyes flicking to each person around the table. "Your presence has been noted by the AI. Your cooperation is mandatory."

Dinnie glanced around the table without moving her head. Five other people, only two she knew by name, all much farther up the hierarchy than she. Her lip twitched. Maybe she'd get a promotion out of this. She wasn't certain she wanted it.

Feldman continued. "In 2006, Dr. Samuel Altair was close to achieving the ability to travel backwards through time. In January of that year, he ran an unauthorized experiment in Belfast Botanic Garden. He worked alone, but his supervisor was concerned, so I was sent as a silent partner to record his actions."

Dinnie swallowed, making a stern effort to not move. "Silent partner" was euphemism for "spy." Feldman had secretly followed Sam Altair that night and recorded him while he ran the experiment. As near as Dinnie could figure out, this never bode well for the person being followed.

Feldman sat. "Here is the recording of that experiment." He looked toward the ceiling to address the building's Artificial Intelligence. "Ari, run film C2-J242006-Altair."

The AI turned off the lights and the recording began, an old-fashioned 2-D video shown against the wall. Dinnie tilted back to give Randy a clear view.

The park was dark and foggy, but the camera adjusted for conditions, and the visual was clear. The time in the corner of the film showed it was 0015. Sam Altair, dressed in jeans and a jacket with a hood over his head, was tucked behind some rocks and bushes, fiddling with a couple of laptop computers. Dinnie felt a chill when she realized one of those computers was the time machine. How in bloody hell did it work? She clenched her hands under the table. She knew that Altair was not supposed to have time traveled that night, and the consortium leaders had assumed he meant to change something. Perhaps gather an army and return to take over the future. Who knew, really? The rumors had been rampant ever since.

She'd never heard of a recording. It didn't surprise her that they hadn't revealed its existence. Did it show clues to Altair's plans? Would they be able to figure out what they were up against?

In the film, Altair suddenly stood, turning abruptly to stare through the bushes behind him. A look of horror came over his face. "Hey!" he shouted, crashing through the bushes and stopping just on the other side. "Get out of there! Hurry!"

Feldman acted fast in his role of silent partner, moving to the side to get a shot of whatever Altair saw. The film showed a small clearing and a girl sitting on the ground, next to a foot-high sapling, her arms behind her as if she had fallen. She was staring at Altair, clearly startled. Her expression changed to fear as Altair raced toward her and she stood, encumbered by a backpack, assuming a self-defense stance. But as soon as he got to her, they both ...

... disappeared.

Dinnie blinked, heard shifting and gasps from the others around the table. Her heart was racing. It was an accident! Someone had fumbled into the time field, and when Altair tried to get her out, they both went back in time. *Fecking Christ* ... Dinnie struggled to get a good breath, fighting off her shock. Randy touched her arm in a discreet brush. Comfort or warning? She didn't dare look at him.

At the head of the table, Feldman didn't move a muscle, just continued to watch the film. The camera moved around the clearing and his voice on the film was heard for the first time. "I don't know what just happened here. I'm going to look around. I'll collect the equipment and return to headquarters as soon as possible."

The film went dark, and the lights came on in the room. Feldman stood and faced the table, his expression grim. "The time machine had turned itself off. I looked around, but there was nothing to see."

He turned to the wall, pressing the remote he held in his hand. A full-size picture appeared, of a girl with long, curly red hair, and bright green eyes, wearing blue jeans and a Queen's University sweatshirt. A cricket game was in progress behind her, and she was laughing at the camera. Feldman kept his eyes on her as he spoke. "The girl was Casey Wilson, twenty years old. She was an American from Berkeley, California, attending Queen's University. According to the police report her roommates filed the next day, she had been studying with a friend at one of the dorms, and left for her flat about midnight. She never arrived." His gaze returned to the shocked people around the table. "The case was never solved. There was no reason for anyone to suspect the consortium was involved, of course. We eventually reported Altair as missing while on a business trip. The police never connected his case with Wilson's. There would be no reason to."

He tossed the remote on the table. Dinnie jumped at the clatter. Everyone looked spooked, but Feldman ignored their reactions. "The time machine was set to send a sapling back in time one hundred years, to 1906. We went through every document we could find from that year. There was never a hint about either one of them. Nor did the adult tree appear in the garden, as Altair had hoped would happen." He looked around the table at them. "They did not end up in 1906."

"Where did they go?" The question came from Nory Johnson at the far end of the table. His voice was shaking. "Were they ... disintegrated, or something?"

"We don't know." Feldman leaned forward, his hands pressing into the table in front of him. "Sam Altair was my friend. I know about the rumors, the guesses of what he was doing that night. But as you can see, what happened was an accident. A terrible accident, and we still are not sure what happened." He straightened, shrugging his jacket back into place. "If Altair had ended up in 1906, he would have figured out a way to leave us a message. There would be a trail. But there's nothing. Did history change? If it did, the change affected every person on earth, altering our memories, and somehow altering our documents, as well." He shook his head.

"I just don't buy that theory. And neither do our top scientists." He blinked, gazing around at all of them. "If they didn't die, then they went somewhere. Our studies point to the possibility that Altair's experiment opened a new timeline. A new universe, if you will, that started as a perfect duplicate of our universe, but diverged from that point. From January 24, 1906."

Dinnie shivered at the chill his words sent through her. "Would ..." she hesitated as Feldman's gaze landed on her, but continued. "Would he know that? Or would he think they were in our past?"

Feldman sighed. "I don't imagine it would be obvious from the viewpoint of 1906. But Sam was too good a scientist not to have considered the possibility."

"And you think he figured out a way to return to our universe?" This from a dark woman, across from Dinnie. "Do you think that's what the increased neutrinos are?"

After a moment, Feldman nodded. "Yes, I do. But it's not Sam."

They all looked at each other, their confusion evident. Feldman tapped a finger on the table, to draw their attention back to him. "Think about it. Sam was sixty years old when he went back to 1906. Most homes didn't even have electricity. Decades before they split the atom. Before space travel and satellites and computers. He would not have had the tools to continue his research." He raised the finger, as if making a point. "I'm sure he worked on it. If he figured out he was in a new timeline, he would have found help. Einstein. Bohr. Plank. He would have increased the state of knowledge and gotten them working on this problem. But he could not have lived long enough to see it completed. And it's not him breaking through on Cave Hill, seventy-four years later."

The obviousness of this silenced them. Feldman sat, leaning back in his chair and pressing the tips of his fingers together. "We are assuming it is Sam's project. But we know nothing about the people from that universe, about their goals. If it were Sam, I wouldn't be concerned. But we cannot assume they are benevolent. We must be ready."

"Can't we stop them?" Nory asked.

Feldman deflected the question to Randy with a raised eyebrow.

Randy straightened in his chair. "We have nothing that will stop neutrinos. If they can open a bridge to our universe, they can come through."

"So we're left with containing the invasion," Feldman said. He pointed at Dinnie. "Your team will be our front line defense. Our lives will be easy if they decide to come through Cave Hill. We're watching it, it's nearby, it's isolated. But we have no way of knowing if they'll do that. They could come through anywhere in the world. They could be planning on many simultaneous invasions. I need you on top of it, Dr. Warner. Double your staff, triple it if you need to. But I want to know the moment neutrinos start building up, anywhere in the world."

He leaned back in his chair, his glance sweeping the faces at the table. "We're coordinating with governments everywhere. But I can't stress enough how important it is that this stay quiet. If people panic because they think invaders are coming through from another universe, we'll never be able to act in time. We'll put out a cover story for the media to disseminate. We're doing an atmospheric study or something. This is Need-to-Know-Only. Just do your jobs and make your reports."

He stood. "Good luck, all of you.

Chapter 5

Strickert Girls Academy
Oxford, England

Moira Sherman peeled off her t-shirt as she entered the locker room, too hot to leave it on another minute. She continued to strip on her way to the showers, carting the sweat-soaked clothing with her just long enough to toss it all into the hamper in the corner. The laundry bots would take care of it from there. She could have left it strung out on the floor and they still would have taken care of it, but Moira had principles. Besides, she didn't need the demerits the bots would have recorded against her.

She reached the shower just as a group of girls entered the locker room, breathing hard as she was, but full of jeering energy, anyway.

"Did you have a date, Moira?" The call came from Leslie Dick-Read, casually removing her clothes in ways that showed off her admittedly nice body. The taunt was taken up by several other girls, all of them unhappy that Moira had out-run them to the extent she had.

She turned on the water, drowning out their voices, soaping up quickly. This late in the school year, she didn't have bruises to hide from them, but she'd found it was better if they assumed she was shy. It was the reason she ran so fast, so she could get to the locker room ahead of everyone else. But that wasn't her only reason today.

It wasn't often the track coach made them run the perimeter, and she wanted to take the chance to plan a possible escape route. Getting away from school unseen was a high priority, and essential to every escape plan she had. Yet she had few choices in that regard. Headmistress Lioness (okay, Amanda Spencer-Lionel, but one couldn't blame the girls for the nickname) was just too firm in her hold over her school. Girls did not *escape*.

Not that Moira wanted to. In all her life, there had never been a better place than Strickert Academy for Girls. She wanted nothing more than to finish out the year and return for her final year next fall.

With a diploma in her hand and an eighteenth birthday on the heels of it, she would truly be free.

Fifteen months. She just needed fifteen more months.

She wouldn't get them. Moira knew that with every nerve in her body.

∞

The late afternoon sun was a novelty, but it filled the classroom with glare. Moira paused in the doorway. "Mr. Green?" Silence responded to her query and she moved over to the teacher's desk at the front. A computer chip on the right had a note attached: *M, please grade.* She carried it to the table along the windows, tossing it down in minor irritation before closing the blinds. Better.

Loading the chip into her Pad, she settled down for the hour or so it would take her to grade the younger students' lab reports. The sun had warmed the room, bringing the usually chilly temperature of the old building to something almost comfortable. As she worked, the peacefulness of the classroom relaxed her. The clock ticking on the wall, the occasional sound of footsteps as a teacher or student hurried by, were all comforting sounds. The vague smell of chalk teased her nose. It wasn't used much anymore of course, but centuries of use had left it ground into every fiber of the building.

She sat on a stool at the high table, her feet hooked around the bottom rungs. Moira considered everything about herself to be average: she was neither short nor tall, her hair was medium-brown and medium-length, pulled into its ponytail with a plain brown band. Her eyes were medium-brown as well, the lashes not overly long, her brows thin and straight. Her build was medium, too, although after a year at school, her weight was up to normal. The school-girl uniform hid any hint of femaleness, a pleated skirt to just below the knees, white button-down blouse, blue blazer. She wore tights against the cold days, and her shoes were brown and clunky.

If pressed, she would have admitted that her intelligence was not average. Her teachers would have laughed at the understatement.

Approaching footsteps did not pass, and Moira glanced over her shoulder as Mr. Green entered, his backpack slung over a shoulder, and arms full of old-fashioned paper books from the library at Oxford. He'd just returned from the university, as was usual for Thursday, and also as usual, he smiled broadly when he saw her.

"Miss Sherman! Busy already, I see."

She raised a brow in acknowledgement, sharing her smile between him and the screen in front of her. "I have about fifteen reports still to grade. How was your class?"

"Fine, fine," he answered absently, searching intently through the backpack. "I have something to show you."

"Okay." She watched him a moment, always happy for a chance to observe the rather plain features of his youthful face. His expression was intent, but he whistled softly as he rummaged around. Ignoring the warmth his presence evoked within her, Moira shook her head in fond amusement, and turned her attention back to the reports. "Did you collect more data?" she asked.

"That's what I want to show you." He appeared at her side, tossing a data stick up and down in his hand. He loaded it onto his Pad and brought up a screen. "What do you think of this?"

The screen held a splash of dots scattered randomly across it, the heading indicating it was a graph from the Neutrino Detection Device at Oxford. This didn't surprise her. Mr. Green's thesis work was in neutrinos and she had been thrilled when he asked her to assist him, for college credit, with his data analysis. This work allowed Moira to participate in physics at a level she'd never imagined. Mr. Green did not give her make-work, and their debates over the data sometimes went on for days.

Moira's brows went up as she took it from his hand. "Wow. Noisy."

Her first impression of the dots was of left-to-right, and after scrutinizing it for another minute, she thought she detected a bottom-to-top tendency, as well. Mr. Green propped himself on the stool next to her, and she was aware that he watched her closely. She ignored him. He had told her once, in jest she thought, that he was afraid to take his eyes off her when she looked at data. That he couldn't stand the thought of missing the moment when she saw what the data were saying.

She always saw it. It was part of her brilliance, he said.

Now, as she stared at the page, the pattern emerged, but it made no sense. A longer moment, as she closed her eyes to banish the silly impression. It couldn't be *that*, but she was afraid that now she'd thought of it, she wouldn't see anything else. This proved true when she opened her eyes and saw the same pattern in stark contrast to the background. She sighed and held the Pad up for Mr. Green to see, pointing at the splash of dots.

"There's a pattern, here."

He studied the screen, and the smile he'd worn while watching her widened. "There is?"

She nodded, looking at him with mock exasperation. "Yes, there is." Her finger traced a space then stopped. "It's very noisy, but it's there."

He leaned down a bit to look her in the eye, arms folded across his chest. "Can you isolate it?"

"Probably." She looked thoughtful, then glanced up at him. "It will take a while."

He picked up her Pad. "I'll grade. You isolate."

∞

Andy Green settled at the table, took over Moira's Pad and applied himself to the reports. At twenty-two, he did not fit the usual profile of a teacher at Strickert Academy. It was not unheard of for the school to have a male teacher, but never had they had one as young as he, or unmarried. His appointment was through the welfare office, and on the order of a favor: Andy's thesis advisor was on the Strickert board, and two years ago had requested they hire his star pupil, who was orphaned, poor, and working his way toward a masters in physics. Headmistress Spencer-Lionel had been uncertain about hiring a precocious twenty-year-old boy to teach her girls, even if that boy was not particularly handsome. But Andy had proven honorable for the two years of his term, and he knew the Lioness was aware of this. She kept a close watch on him.

So he was careful that no one noticed how often he looked at Moira. In discrete moments, he admired the gold highlights in her hair, the delicate line of her high cheekbones, and he harbored many secret thoughts about her lips. But he kept all this to himself, and concentrated on teaching her physics. He mentioned her often to his advisor. Andy was convinced his beautiful pupil was on a par with Einstein and Hawking. He was both humbled and terrified to be her mentor. There was no doubt the physical attraction complicated things, even beyond the fact that she was a minor and his student. He never mentioned *that* problem to his advisor.

Thirty minutes later, she moved next to him at the table and placed the Pad in front of him. The scatter graph now contained a pattern, which Moira had indicated with a red line, as if connecting stars in a constellation. He blinked in shock.

"I've never seen neutrinos do that."

"Was this all of it?" She continued to stand, making them almost the same height.

Andy squelched a desire to put an arm around her waist. "It looks like a worm hole."

"*Looks* like one?" She sounded amused and he hiked a shoulder in answer. Peeking over his shoulder, she murmured, "Well, it does look like a bridge." At his quizzical look, she explained, "An Einstein Rosen bridge."

He spread his hands. "That's what I said."

She laughed. "Okay. Where is it located?"

"Belfast." He laughed at her shocked stare. "I'm sorry, but that's where the signal came from."

"Then it's not a wormhole."

He chewed his lip, not quite as certain as she was. "I know a wormhole would not meet our current understanding of how they work. But what else could it be?"

She hesitated.

He held up a finger. "The first step is always the same, remember."

"Define the problem."

He nodded. "Neutrinos are doing strange things in Belfast. It looks like a wormhole. What's the second step?"

"Figure out what questions to ask."

He just raised an eyebrow, fielding the ball back to her court, seeing her amused annoyance. She'd learned not to just blurt things out in his presence. Taking a cue from his own advisor, he always demanded she explain the logic behind her thinking. He waited with satisfaction as she gave it some thought, his own mind still struggling to make sense of it. A few possibilities occurred to him, but he waited to see what she would say. At least her questions didn't have to appear in syllogistic order.

Finally, she spoke. "How can a wormhole exist on Earth?"

"What would be the result if one did?"

"The planet would explode."

"Would it?"

"Wouldn't it?" She was honestly confused.

He shrugged again. "I would think so. But it hasn't. So this line of questioning brings us in a circle."

He loved how her lips tightened and danced from side to side when she was faced with an annoying problem. She was deep in thought, staring at the screen. He waited ... and watched.

"An opening." Her finger traced the right side of the screen, before she lifted her head to look at him. His lips twitched to one side. He always got chills when she pulled an answer out of the air like that. She'd never been wrong, yet.

But he glanced skeptically at the spot where her finger rested, toggling between her isolated pattern and the original graph. Without her red outline, it still looked like a splotch of random dots to him. He sighed. "I'll take your word for it. But an opening in what? To what? The gates of Hell? Are we going to start chasing demons?"

A flash of anger tightened her face. What had he said to anger her? Then it was gone and he couldn't be sure he'd seen it.

"I doubt it," she said, her gaze back on the Pad. "There's not enough data here to figure out what opened. These data show us the neutrinos. Do you have equipment that will measure other things? Did the atmosphere change in that spot? Pressure, temperature? Was there an earthquake? Any unusual activity at all?"

"Good points." He turned to the room interface, entering a search for Belfast weather. But before he sent it, his fingers went still on the keyboard, while he stared at the 3D holographic display. When he turned to Moira, she was watching him, puzzled. "I'd rather do this from uni," he said. "In case the Sun Consortium has picked up on it and wants it classified."

"Classify the weather in Belfast?"

He shrugged. "No. But we'll be looking for specific patterns and other data, too. I'd feel safer on Oxford's equipment. It's authorized."

She looked unhappy and he didn't blame her. There was something ominous and exciting about the busy dots on the screen. She was smart enough to know she'd be missing out on a possible major discovery. He touched her arm. "I'll bring you everything I find. You'll have access to all of it. I promise."

"When will you look for it? We have that field trip tomorrow."

To the Kielder Observatory in Northumberland. An overnight trip with the advanced science students. Andy had been looking forward to the informal time with Moira. He closed off the interface. "I'll do it now. You can review it on the trip."

She nodded. "Sure. There'll be plenty of spare time."

He grinned. "I'll try to keep the slower students out of your hair." He waved the Pad. "This is great stuff, but let's not forget we have data to verify with that telescope. At least, I do. And you," he leaned down, daring to tease her, "have sworn your considerable talents to helping me do it."

"Which I will do. Assuming I've got these reports graded, so that you can go, tomorrow."

Her retort kept him chuckling as he went back to his car.

∞

In his lab at Oxford for the second time that night, Andy set the computer to search for anomalies of various kinds in Belfast. He had not been entirely truthful when he told Moira why he wanted to use his equipment at Oxford. It was true that the university had authorization for many types of research. The government would not question his search, or even notice it. But the Consortium might. Andy walked a fine line in regards to Sun Consortium. On one hand, they offered the best opportunities for research in faster-than-light travel. He hoped to be hired on once his master's degree was in hand. They had several programs for doctoral students to work part time while earning their degrees. He wanted one of those positions.

But on the other hand, he didn't trust them for a single minute. Their surveillance systems were everywhere, purchased by governments and warlords, alike. Their public persona was a thin veneer covering a wide array of classified projects that put rulers in their debt. As an advanced physics student, Andy was aware of a few of their past projects, since completed or otherwise phased out. There was too much secretiveness. Too many data blackouts, too many rumors of people blacklisted or disappeared. Too much history rewritten.

He had no doubt they knew of the strange signals in Belfast. And would be alert to anyone in the world looking for information about them.

This wouldn't be the first time he'd had to be careful. So his equipment was not just authorized. It was protected.

Illegally, of course.

He'd done it himself and he wasn't the only student to do so. It was considered a rite of passage to figure out how to circumvent the Consortium's extensive spying protocols. Andy suspected that many who thought they had done it, were really not successful. He would never be certain that he was. But he was pretty sure.

The signals could be from a Consortium experiment. If that was the case, he wanted in on it. This was *his* field. He expected to own it one day. Especially now that he knew Moira Sherman. If he could get her to keep working with him, there was nothing they couldn't accomplish.

Chapter 6

"Kielder telescope first opened in 2008 with a goal of public outreach and education. Its location here in the Kielder Forest was one quite free of light pollution." Dr. Hansen, the astronomer assigned to the Strickert group, was bald and stick-thin. He was also quite old, and in desperate need of a dentist. Moira had watched their chaperone, Ms. Beagle, shake his hand from as far away as her arm allowed her to stand. Mr. Green had lifted a hand in casual greeting to the man when they first entered the visitors' gallery, but he had remained near the door, as if already aware of the problem.

Waves of halitosis buffeted the girls as they listened to Dr. Hansen's lecture, and the group had gradually shifted backwards into a defensive huddle against the wall. Moira was sadly certain that one or two of the girls had just given up on pursuing science as a career. She told herself quite firmly that Mr. Green would *not* smell like that when he was old. Or look like that, either.

"By 2060," the lecture continued, "the government was insolvent, bankrupted in the wake of climate change, famines, and pestilence. The Sun Consortium, as part of its New Earth Program, took control of Britain's neglected telescopes, repairing them and setting them back to work in conjunction with the New International Space Station they were building in orbit. The people you see working here," Dr. Hansen waved a hand over his shoulder at the workers sitting at the horseshoe-shaped bank of computers below them, "are processing data from the thousands of images taken by our 'scope. Items of interest are flagged for further study by the new Carter Telescope on the space station."

Moira raised a hand. "What constitutes an item of interest, sir?" It was a mistake to draw his attention, for he approached the group to answer. The other girls shifted back, nudging Moira toward the front. She accepted the consequence and tried to breathe shallow as she gave him her attention.

"Our primary purpose is to find metals and carbon to supplement Earth's dwindling or extinct resources. Thus, suitable asteroids are searched out and marked for mining. In addition, Sun is devoted to finding habitable bodies for human colonization."

"Isn't that what NISS is for?" Ms. Beagle asked, mercifully drawing his attention to her side of the room. Moira breathed out a soft gasp, then stifled a giggle as Janice Brewton waved a discreet hand in front of her face.

"The *New International Space Station*," Dr. Hansen said it as if he'd thought of the name himself, "is indeed an experiment in human colonization, as well as a base for asteroid mining. But one space station will never be sufficient. Humans need sunlight and a planetary atmosphere to flourish."

Moira acknowledged the truth of that, noting that Mr. Green was nodding his head in agreement, as well. She also knew that any colony would have to quickly become self-sufficient. Earth's resources would not recover for millennia.

Dr. Hansen held an arm toward the door. "Now I know you're all anxious to see the wondrous images of our universe for yourselves. If you'll follow me, we'll head down to the control center and let each of you have a turn directing the telescope."

This brought excited chatter from the girls, not least because it meant his back was to them. Moira hung back, pausing in front of Mr. Green. "It won't matter if other planets are suitable for colonization," she said, "if someone does not figure out how to get us there in prompt fashion."

It was an old debate of theirs, given the possible directions of his thesis work. A corner of his mouth twitched and he raised one shoulder in a shrug. "I shall continue to work on it. Call it job security."

She laughed, and they followed the girls to the control room.

∞

The forest had long fallen to darkness by the time the girls began settling into the observatory's guest dorm. Lights Out would be in one hour, until then they had free time. Moira chatted with a small group of friends, but their attention was soon caught by the sound of a guitar chord, as a few of the girls prepared to sing campfire songs. Moira supposed this was in honor of the forest itself, since they were not outside, and did not have a campfire. She took advantage of the distraction to slip unnoticed out the door. She paused in the dim foyer to get her bearings before continuing across the room to the coat closet at the other end. Just before the closet was a nook, where she would be out of sight of anyone coming out to use the loo, but not so far away that she could be accused of leaving the supervised group. Not that there would be a problem. Ms. Beagle was aware of Moira's daily assignment from home, and always allowed her quiet time to get it done.

Moira sank to the floor, with her back against the nook's wall, and adjusted the ear buds of her Pad. The assignment was from her stepfather, and she'd been obliged to do it every evening of her time at Strickert. He was determined that she not forget her place. So she logged on to his website and called up his latest lesson for her. As usual, her body jerked in response to his voice in her ear, a reaction she'd never been able to stop. The voice itself did more to remind her of her hopelessness than any lesson it might be teaching.

The voice that made her forget physics. That denied her any right to dream of a future education. That filled her with terror in case he should realize the thoughts she harbored about a certain physics teacher.

It was her stepfather's fancy that the lesson would last an hour, including time to answer his questions and send them off for his approval. He didn't realize that Moira had long ago discerned the pattern of his teaching, and needed only a few minutes at the beginning to know everything he would say. The range of expected responses was so small she could dash them off in less than five minutes. In fact, she had to be careful to not make her responses too complex. He would not have appreciated it coming from a girl.

For the first minute or so, the voice made her heart race and her throat tighten with fear and disgust. Then her mind took over, falling into its habit of closing off the voice and turning away to other things. While a small part gave the lesson cursory attention and guided her fingers as she typed her responses, the rest of her mind turned to the wondrous day just past.

As Dr. Hansen had said, the Sun Consortium had taken over the country's telescopes as the decimated population struggled to survive. *For their own secret projects,* Moira thought, although she had no evidence for it. Everyone knew it was true.

But today, she didn't care. Today, the telescope was hers, and she had stood transfixed at its base, watching its incremental movements, listening to the quiet clicks and hums as it searched the universe. Her heart had pounded then, as well, only it was with excitement. This was Real Life, living here, spending hours each day in research, applying that research to help solve Earth's myriad problems, interacting with intelligent people who liked and respected her.

Sitting in the nook, with her stepfather's voice quoting scripture to remind her of her evil female nature, Moira closed her eyes and imagined the life of her dreams. She could taste it, she wanted it so much. She saw them again—the galaxies and nebulae, the detailed planets of their own solar system. But she shifted restlessly in her corner. The demonstration had been just that: a demonstration. A show put on for school girls, with old data and faraway sights they'd known about for years. Moira wanted to know what they were doing *now*.

The lesson finished at last, she submitted her responses, then murmured the prayer he expected to hear, as she thanked God for her stepfather's concern for her soul, and her pledge of obedience to his teachings. The prayer must be fresh every night, but she usually recorded it whenever she had a private moment during the day. She could never have faced the humiliation if the other girls heard those words.

She sighed when the website closed down, resting her head against the wall. It took a few deep breaths for the burning nausea to pass, but once it did, she opened her eyes and thought about the telescope. She knew Mr. Green was still over there, and planned to be for most of the night. He was using the telescope to verify the last of the data for his thesis. He'd been good to her over the last year, doing as much of his research as he could at Strickert, so she could participate. But there was still so much she couldn't see, couldn't do, because Strickert didn't have the equipment or the authorization. He did most of his work at Oxford and brought the results to show her.

It wasn't the same. She wanted to see what he was doing.

∞

It was quiet at last, as midnight crept past. The girls had settled into their cots and drifted off to sleep. Moira lay awake, staring into the darkness as she listened to the soft breathing around her.

She sat up, holding her breath. The sounds around her stayed the same, and she eased from the cot. Shivering in the cold air, she pulled her bag from under the cot and slipped out to the loo in the hallway. She didn't bother to dress, just slipped her sweat suit over her long johns and added warm socks and shoes. The coats were hanging in the foyer, and she grabbed hers as she tiptoed by, tucking her bag behind the other coats. She didn't want to leave it in the loo in case someone got up while she was gone.

She didn't have a flashlight, and she waited just outside for the shapes to resolve themselves. It was startling to see all the stars above her. She couldn't take her eyes off of them. Millions, *trillions*, there were, spread across the sky in a blanket of glimmer. Why had the early humans wanted light to drown this out? *We don't even know what we're missing.*

I'll be out there someday. It was something she and Mr. Green talked about all the time. Neither of them was satisfied to just make the discoveries that others would use in space travel. They wanted to be out there too, using their work.

Taking a deep breath, she set out across the compound, sticking to the path. The darkness was deep, and there were wild animals in the forest. The campus was protected by electronic fences, but still ...

She paused at the short staircase leading to the domed building. She'd be so embarrassed if Mr. Green sent her back to bed. Would he do that? Would the other workers laugh at her? She raised a nervous hand to push her hair behind an ear, not sure if she dared continue. Somehow, humiliation from Mr. Green would be far worse than any beating her stepfather gave her.

But her uncertain legs carried her up the stairs and the door slid open before her. She stepped inside quickly, not wanting cold air to make anyone mad before they even saw her. The base of the telescope spread in front of her, obscuring any people from her view. She heard no voices. Where was everyone? A locker clanged shut somewhere above her and she heard a single set of footsteps. But Dr. Hansen had said that most of the work was done in the room around the base. There was no need for anyone to look through the eyepiece of the telescope. The view was scanned and sent to the monitors below, where the programming and analysis were done.

The monitors near her showed screensavers or data processing screens. She hurried around the struts of the telescope to the other side. Mr. Green sat at a desk in front of a monitor, writing something. He turned at the sound of her footsteps.

"Miss Sherman!"

She slipped her hands into her pockets and hugged the coat tighter to her, biting her lip. "Hi," she said. He looked surprised, but not angry, so she continued. "I couldn't sleep. I wanted to see more."

He laughed. She relaxed and returned a small smile, until he asked, "Does Miss Beagle know you're here?"

She considered lying. "Nooooo," she said instead, feeling her way. "She was asleep."

He rubbed his mouth, watching her uncertainly. *Please don't send me back.* At least no one else was around to see her humiliation.

He sighed. "All right. I do have some data to show you. But you shouldn't stay long. We could both get into trouble." He gestured to the side as he turned back to the desk. "You can put your coat over there. And grab a chair."

She did as he said, then rolled a chair next to his. "Where is everybody? I thought astronomers worked at night."

"Not so much, anymore," he said. "They program the telescope and do their analysis during the day. There's just a skeleton crew at night to make sure the program is implementing properly." He glanced at her. "Dr. Kebbie went to get some food. He'll be back shortly."

She nodded, fighting against the distraction of her wild heartbeat. They were alone. She hadn't considered that possibility. Adding to the strangeness was their dress, she in her sweat suit, he in jeans and sweater. She'd never seen him in anything other than a suit and tie. His hair was mussed, as if he had slept for a while and hadn't bothered to comb it before reporting to the telescope.

The other girls considered him ugly, with his horsey face, too long nose and chin, and too large teeth, but she knew he was funny and kind, and his features had long since resolved themselves to comfortable goodness in her eyes. An almost overwhelming desire to touch him made her grip the arms of her chair.

Thank God he had turned back to his paper. "Have you got the data you need?" she asked.

"Not all of it," he said. He handed her a printout. "We'll have pictures in about an hour, but here are the numbers we've gotten so far. Would you like to do the calculations for me?"

"Sure, I'd love to."

And just that simply, they began working, side by side, she conversing with the computer about the calculations, he pulling off the data as they came in, as if he was too anxious to wait for the computer to report. They were discussing the trend the data were showing when Dr. Kebbie returned on a blast of cold air. He still had his coat on when he peeked in, stopping in surprise to see Moira.

"Hullo," he said.

Moira fought down panic. Would he march her back to the dorm and wake Miss Beagle? But Mr. Green reacted with no hint of concern.

"Dr. Kebbie, good! I was hoping you'd get to meet Moira Sherman. I urge you to keep an eye on her. She'll have your job, someday."

"That so?" Dr. Kebbie laughed and lifted an arm in greeting. "I might be ready to hand it over. Love to chat, but I've got to check on the gyros. I'll be upstairs."

As his clattering footsteps disappeared up the winding staircase, Moira let out a sigh and an embarrassed laugh at Mr. Green's amused expression. "I was afraid he'd send me back. That I'd be in trouble."

Her teacher shrugged. "He probably assumes Miss Beagle knows you're here. Honestly, half the people in the world wouldn't think anything of it. Still," he held up a finger, "we must follow the rules."

She sighed again. "Yes, I know. I suppose I should be going."

"I always appreciate your help. And your company. You help me see things I might otherwise have missed."

"I doubt that," she said, standing. He held up a hand.

"Hold on, I just remembered. I noticed your name was missing from the list for Oxford's High School Day. Surely an oversight; you should check into it."

A tight dread pushed deep in her stomach as she tried to think of an answer. His brows lowered in confusion.

"Are you not considering attending Oxford? I just assumed you would want to. I was rather hoping we could work together once you were there. But if your heart is set on another university, I understand."

Moira rubbed her forehead, trying to think. The list of colleges a student wanted to visit was always sent home to her parents. She didn't dare let that happen, so had not signed up for any visits.

"No, it's not that. I'd be thrilled to attend Oxford. It's just ... I wasn't going to ... sign up ... yet." She closed her mouth firmly on her stammering. Really, she should have been prepared for this.

He still didn't understand. "Can't attend the school day? But why not? You realize it gives you an edge on admission. You're able to tour your chosen college, meet the professors, sign up for early admission and such. I was hoping to introduce you to my advisor. I've told him all about you and he's anxious to meet you."

She stared at him in misery. She'd have to tell him the truth. But she wouldn't tell him all of it. "I can't sign up for college yet, you see. I'll have to wait until I'm eighteen."

"What?" He sprang to his feet, face astonished. She fell back, the familiar terror of facing an angry male filling her. He would strike her. He would strike her and her heart would be broken, forever. Nothing would ever matter again, if he hit her. She turned to run, gasping when he grabbed her wrist.

"Moira, wait." He dropped her arm at once, his voice soft. He'd never used her first name before. She waited as he commanded, still facing away from him. "I'm sorry, I didn't mean to scare you," he said. He truly sounded sorry. And bewildered, as if he didn't understand what had happened.

She found she couldn't speak, so she just nodded, holding her hands tightly in front of her and trying not to shake. She heard him sit back down. "Will you tell me why?" he asked. "Why must you wait until you're eighteen?"

She shook her head, still unable to speak. He sighed. "Is it money? I know all about having to work one's way through college. But you know there are scholarships and grants. Good Lord, Moira, if anyone qualifies for a full scholarship, it would be you."

Perhaps she could use that. She cleared her throat, but didn't turn to look at him. "Money will be one problem," she said. "But not the only one."

"Moira, please. Let me help you. You are too brilliant to let this opportunity go by. Whatever is holding you back, I can speak to my advisor about it. He'll know what to do."

"No." She stood straighter and took a step away from him, speaking over her shoulder. "Thank you, but I have my own plans. I'll take care of it. May I go now?"

"Yes, of course." He sounded resigned and hurt, and she felt a stab of guilt. No matter. She didn't dare tell him the truth.

She ran.

∞

Moira squatted off the path halfway between the telescope and the dorm, arms wrapped around her knees as she stared into the darkness. *Bloody eejit. Why didn't I think of this? They'll all be asking, eventually. They all expect me to apply to universities. I've got to figure out how to explain without telling them the truth.*

She felt tears on her cheeks. Mr. Green had been startled, that's all. He wasn't going to hit her. Normal men did not hit women. She knew this now. But she felt a trickle of despair. She had reacted with fear and automatic submission. Would she ever learn to stand up for herself? To not be afraid? She'd spent two years at Strickert studying martial arts, learning self-defense, how to fight. She was not very advanced yet, but she knew enough to protect herself a little. She was certain she didn't need that with Mr. Green. But if she reacted to *him* with fear, how could she ever stand up to her stepfather?

Was there no hope for her?

She sighed and stood, moving quietly through the night. The dorm was warm, bringing her chill up through clammy skin to dissipate against the coats along the wall. She stripped down to her long johns and tiptoed to her cot, laying down with another sigh. As she turned to her side, her imagination placed Mr. Green behind her, his arms pulling her close. Comforting. Loving.

But she tightened her jaw and banished the dream. There was no help from outside. Her best option was to stick it out until her eighteenth birthday. The law in England still held eighteen as the age of emancipation, even for girls. She knew that in many countries, it was older. In the United States, they had to be twenty-one. In Eastern Europe it was twenty-five, and in the Middle East and Africa, women weren't allowed emancipation at all. So she counted herself lucky. At eighteen, she could walk out, and the police and judges who belonged to her stepfather's enclave could not force her back. She would have no money and no place to go. But she'd get through that. She had her mind.

Her greatest fear was that her stepfather would decide she'd had enough education, and he would pull her out to marry her off. She would soon be pregnant and stuck for life. If that's what he did ... that's what the self-defense classes were for. That's why she learned to run fast. Why she had a plan of escape from school.

They might easily find her, using the ID chip everyone had to have in their arm. But she had to try. She would not have her degree. She would be underage, but she had heard that people could disappear into the underside of London. She heard horrible things about the life there, but even that would be easier to escape, if she stayed off drugs.

Perhaps she could find a rebel cell. Those shadow groups, spoken of in whispers, such that one could not be certain if they were truth or fiction. But Moira thought they existed. With the world's population held prisoner to restrictive theocracies, and the power of the Sun Consortium, she was certain there were brave people doing whatever they could to fight against it. There had to be, because she wanted to fight with them, as a scientist, from a ship in space.

Chapter 7

Andy stood as Moira left, frantic confusion driving all other thoughts from his mind. What on Earth had that been about? What did she mean, "her own plans"? Why did she have to wait for college? He turned at the sound of Kebbie's staccato steps.

The older man raised a brow at Andy's expression, then glanced around the room. "Where'd she go? Is something wrong?"

"I don't know." Andy brushed a hand through his hair in frustration. "I just asked a simple question and she went into fits. Dashed out of here like demons were on her tail."

Kebbie sank into a chair, lips pursed as if he were trying not to laugh. He held up a finger. "Now Andrew, you've been around those girls long enough to know that sort of behavior is not unusual. Teenage girls are silly animals."

"Moira's not." Andy flung himself into his chair, crashing the back of it into the console. He stared at the floor. "She's bloody brilliant, Kebbie. She's assisted me for two years and she knows almost as much as I do. But now she tells me she's not going to college." He held up a hand. "Worse, she acted terrified. Almost like ..." He let his voice fade away as he stared at the floor, trapped in a memory.

"Like what?" Kebbie was leaning forward in his chair, a finger not quite touching Andy's knee.

Andy blinked and glanced up. "Like the day I met her. My first day teaching at Strickert, at the start of term two years ago. I was bloody nervous ... intimidated by everyone I met there. Especially the girls."

Kebbie winced. "I can imagine. All those tits and you couldn't even *look* interested."

Andy shook his head. "I was too nervous for that to even be a problem. Teenage girls can be vicious. My early class was with primaries. They were bad enough, but at least they were only ten years old. Then I got the older girls." He narrowed his eyes at Kebbie, certain the man wasn't seeing his point. "I wasn't much older than them, you know. They'd never had a male teacher as young as me. You're a handsome man, Kebbie. You don't realize how cruel girls can be if you don't meet their criteria for good looks."

"Oh, I'm familiar with the phenomenon." Kebbie brushed a finger over his lips. Andy still saw his smile. "But after all, you weren't there to date them. What matter if they didn't swoon over you?"

Andy's brows flicked upwards. "They broadcast contempt and boredom quite well, and they had it turned up full blast that first day. I had an introductory lecture prepared, on the history of physics. It was like talking to ice cubes. I tried to get them involved, asking questions, but no one answered. Then one girl finally raised her hand."

"Moira?"

Andy nodded. "I called on her and she mumbled something, looking at her desk. A school rule is that students have to stand when addressing the teacher or class, so I reminded her of that and asked her to repeat her answer." He paused, remembering. "The girls weren't nice to her, either. I learned later that it was her first day at Strickert, too. They were all snickering at her. She started to repeat her answer, but she was still looking at the floor and no one could hear her."

He saw her again in his mind: small, shapeless in the uniform, unremarkable. "She looked so scared and shy. I felt like a bully, but I had to tell her to look at me or the class when she answered, and to speak up." He shook his head. "She looked at me as if I were mad. As if it never occurred to her to look at a person when speaking. But she came through it, started in about Richard Feynman's *Letters*, and how the natural log underlies all that we see."

He glanced at Kebbie. "You know what it's like, when you get a student who *belongs* in your field, who understands it in a way that the average student doesn't. Even on that first day, I knew she could see the reality of the universe, that it wasn't some abstract thing "up there," that she had to learn about for a grade. By the time she finished speaking, her face was bright and she sounded confident and happy."

He bit his lip. "But tonight, she looked like she did when I first called on her to speak. Terrified." He tapped a fist against his knee, "Why?"

Kebbie shrugged. "You'll have to ask her, I'm afraid." He jerked his chin at the monitor behind Andy. "How's the research coming?"

"Good," Andy said, glancing back at it. "Bloody good, in fact."

Kebbie snapped his fingers. "That reminds me. I need a favor. You have Hubble access, don't you?"

Andy nodded, watching as Kebbie searched through a couple of pockets and finally pulled out a datastick.

"I can't get to it for a few weeks, yet," Kebbie said, holding the stick out. "I need a spot of data from the January search. The Read Me file will explain it. Do you mind?"

Andy reached for it. Whatever instructions the Read Me file contained, it wouldn't have anything to do with Hubble. This wasn't the first time he'd done "favors" for Kebbie, who passed the information on to a rebel cell. Andy approved, in principle, of the rebels' work. He didn't mind helping them, but he refused to risk his career by actually joining them.

His hand shook as he slipped the stick into his own pocket. No doubt it was just a simple hacking job. But the consequences if he was caught …

His thoughts returned to Moira and her fear. She faced consequences, too, that much was obvious. But from what source? He couldn't allow her to miss out on college. He would ask her again, perhaps ask her other teachers. He was not the only one enamored of Moira's genius.

But he would be careful how he asked.

He understood about avoiding consequences.

∞

Just after breakfast the next morning, Andy realized he hadn't given Moira the data on Belfast. He saw the datastick in its pocket as he threw clothes into his backpack, and hesitated. *What's the point? If she's not serious about a career in physics, why am I bothering?*

He drew the datastick out of the pack and stood staring at it. *She's brilliant. I need to know what she thinks of this.* He didn't believe that she wasn't interested. Whatever was keeping her from college was something beyond her control. And anyway, he had a contract with her. She would assist him with his work, and he would see that she got college credit for it. He'd already completed the paperwork for that with the Headmistress. The fact that these data were above and beyond the scope of his thesis work was irrelevant. He'd give it to her to look over on the trip back to Strickert.

Still, he wavered when he saw her waiting to board the bus. She was standing with her friend Grace, staring at the ground and making no attempt to talk. Her hair was loose, which hid her face from him, but when she reached to push it back after a breeze blew it in her eyes, he sighed. Her mouth was tight, her eyes half closed. He suspected she hadn't slept much. But damn it, what had he done that was wrong? He'd been perfectly correct to ask about the college day. How was he to know there was a problem when she'd never mentioned one?

He waited to board until all the girls were on, this thought disturbing him most of all. Moira had let him think she was going to college. All the months they'd worked together, she'd never once suggested otherwise. Why?

She looked up in surprise when he stopped by her seat, holding the datastick out. He tried to keep his voice matter-of-fact. "I forgot to give you the data I collected the other night. Can you look it over on the way back?"

Her face reddened, but she took the stick without meeting his eyes. "Yes, of course." The words were a whisper, and she looked down at the stick in her hand. He blinked, seeing again the terrified little girl from early in their acquaintance. What was wrong with her?

He tapped the top of the seat in front of her. "Right, then," he said, falsely enthusiastic. "I'm anxious to hear what you think." He left her to it, sliding into a seat at the front of the bus. Too disturbed to engage in conversation, he took out his Pad and lost himself in working on his thesis.

An hour went by before his seat shook with the weight of another body. Moira sat next to him, holding her Pad for him to see. She made no effort to look at him, instead pointing to the screen. "I double-checked," she said, sounding slightly breathless, "and Belfast has not blown up. Since that is true, I added a fudge factor to the equation, so we'd come up with that result." Andy choked back a laugh, relieved to see a brief, answering grin touch Moira's lips. "I realize the fudge factor is totally bogus," she continued, "but I want to use it as a starting point. What do you think?"

Just as if their talk last night had never occurred. He perused her work for a few minutes, scrolling back to the beginning of the equation, nodding slowly as he followed her logic. He tapped a spot and handed the Pad back. "It's unconventional." His voice held a warning.

She tilted her head, her eyes meeting his for a moment before glancing back down at the Pad. "But we've admitted that this occurrence has not ever been seen before. Moreover, it's impossible by every physical law we know. This was the only thing I could think of to try. Although," she held the Pad against her as a shield, "there could be any number of functions that I'm not yet aware of. If so, can you give me an idea of where to look?"

"If there are, I'm not aware of them, either," he said. "And you're right. This is something new. Still, it's always wise to apply what we know before looking elsewhere."

She nodded. "But everything I know says that there should have been a release of energy big enough to rip the UK off the planet. That didn't happen, so there's something going on that we don't know about."

She looked at him then, worry and excitement warring in her eyes. "Hasn't anybody else said anything about it? There was nothing on the news sites."

He shook his head. "Complete silence. And you should know that some of the data I found the other night are no longer available. Or they've been changed." He raised a finger and spoke very low. No one was paying attention to them, but he didn't want anyone to hear.

"That means this event has been classified. I don't know who classified it, or why. But you need to understand they may not be happy we have this much information."

She stared at him, her face pale. "But ..." she stopped, thinking about it as she continued to watch him. Then she glanced back at her Pad. "Are we supposed to just forget about it?"

He smiled. "If I wanted to forget it, I wouldn't have asked you to look at it. But we'll have to do this under the radar. No web searches that might hint what we're looking for. Electronic work can be traced too easily, although I think I can use some of the Oxford equipment. The thing is," and he raised an arm to rub his neck, "something about this makes me itch. It's close to ideas I've been thinking about myself. You might not have noticed the overlap with my work. It's rather subtle. But some of this would have come into play during my doctoral work, if this year's study proves a dual nature in neutrinos. And I think it will. In fact, after this weekend, I'm certain it will."

A small thrill lanced him at Moira's quiet gasp, and he smiled. "I've just got to write it up. And I'll need your help with the last bit of data mining. But you saw where the data were trending last night."

He was afraid that mention of last night would return her to her funk, but her eyes were shining. "Yes," she said. "It did look good for you. But," she tapped the Pad, "you're saying that the neutrinos in the Belfast occurrence have something to do with your duality hypothesis?"

He almost laughed out loud. He could see her mind zooming off into all the possibilities. "Yes, I do. But it's my idea, Miss Sherman. You'll have to find something else for your PhD thesis."

She rolled her eyes. "I'll have to, I guess. You'll have it all sewn up by the time I get there." She laughed, and he laughed with her, their sudden cheerfulness mingling with the chatter and laughter surrounding them in the bus.

He was relieved at the apparent return of normalcy to their relationship. But he couldn't ignore the confusion he felt. If she wasn't going to college, why did she say things like this?

Chapter 8

Feldman's office was bigger than Dinnie's flat. She paused just inside the doorway, letting Randy cross the carpeted expanse to Feldman's desk by himself. It disturbed her that he seemed to shrink as he moved farther from her.

The office wasn't *that* big.

Feldman stayed in his chair as Randy approached, the bank of windows behind him providing enough glare to force a visitor's eyes downward. Perhaps he didn't like people looking him in the eye.

Dinnie took in the gold-lined, plush furniture, the Rembrandts lining the walls—she'd heard rumors they were originals—elegant vases and statues placed strategically around the room. As she took her first step toward the desk, she noted that the only exit was behind her, although it wouldn't surprise her if there was a secret hallway behind the bookcase. Or the private loo, which appeared to be off to the left.

Feldman didn't give them time for pleasantries. "There have been two more detections in the last twenty-four hours in the Belfast area alone. I need to know what's happening in the rest of the world. What's our status?" Randy had reached the desk, but Feldman spoke to both of them. Dinnie hastened her steps.

"Detectors have been deployed around the world, sir," Randy said as she arrived at his side. "We'll be operational by morning."

"Where have you placed them?"

Randy raised an eyebrow in Dinnie's direction.

She took half a breath. "We started with locations that already have modern neutrino detectors in place, so they could get on it immediately. Super-K, Sudbury, CERN, Oxford, all the others, are all alert and ready to measure any increase in neutrinos. So far, no one has reported any unusual activity."

She paused to take another breath, managing a complete one this time. Feldman's expression had not changed. Unsure if that boded good or ill, she continued with her report. "Detectors are on their way to other areas. We're concentrating on places similar to Cave Hill: remote, but near a population source. I've sent the list to your Pad, with asterisks indicating those areas already working. The others will start going online by about five p.m. GMT. All should be operational by ten this evening."

She stopped talking, but there was still no change in Feldman's expression. Desperate, she let words tumble out. "I've increased staff to triple numbers. Remote detectors are reporting to us in real time, with our own analysts looking them over. Any increase over zero-point-five percent is flagged for duplicate analysis. If they come through, we'll know before they get here."

She was sure about that, but she couldn't imagine what good it would do them. They couldn't have troops available at all those locations, could they?

If they could, she didn't want to know.

Feldman nodded, as if in eerie answer to her unasked question, and finally spoke.

"Stay on top of it. This increased activity means they're coming through soon. I want to know if it's an invasion or just a scouting mission. Mr. Carmichael, I'm placing Ms. Warner in charge of this one. She can report directly to me."

Dinnie's body jerked in surprise at his words. She started to ask for clarification, or to protest that she wasn't qualified, but he waved a hand toward the door.

"Dismissed."

Feldman turned back to his work and Dinnie followed Randy out with her panic caught in her throat. When they passed into the corridor, she grabbed Randy's arm.

"I can't do this." She spoke low, her face near his ear. "You know I'm not qualified to lead this mission." *The most important mission in Sun's history.*

Randy guided her to the lift, a bead of sweat appearing on his forehead. "He knows what he's doing." His eyes were troubled.

A chill raced down Dinnie's spine. "I'm the fall guy. If something goes wrong."

He stared at the floor numbers on the lift display, blinking. Then he straightened, and patted her hand. "Don't be silly." His voice was normal, and loud enough for the sensors to easily pick it up. "You're a smart woman, Dinnie. You're better at things than you think you are, and you're good at holding a team together. Feldman can see these things about a person. It's an opportunity for you. Hell, I'm jealous. In a few months, you'll be *my* boss."

She swallowed hard and turned her gaze to the lift doors. She nodded. "Sure. I'll wow everybody." She couldn't quite sound confident, but she came close. Randy nodded.

They said nothing else.

∞

As soon as his office door closed behind them, Feldman stabbed a button on his desk, and spoke to the air. "You heard all that? We're ready for them."

"As ready as we can be." The air answered in a low, grating voice, as if it had laryngitis. "What about the other?"

It was an effort to remain still, but Feldman managed it. "Plans are proceeding as directed, for now. I won't make any changes there unless forced to by Altair's people."

"The timing couldn't be worse." The voice gave the impression of a knife on rough steel.

"True," Feldman said in a soothing tone. "But even a delay of our plans is not insurmountable. The pieces remain in place until we pull the string."

"Send your beta team up to the station on schedule, Feldman," the voice ordered. "They won't be needed down here, no matter what Altair is up to."

Feldman forced himself to fold his hands on top of his desk. "I'll see to it, sir."

The voice went away. But Feldman knew there was never any certainty that the ears were gone, as well.

SECOND UNIVERSE

Chapter 9

1980
Dunallon
Belfast, Ireland

Sam rested his head against the back of the bench, squinting to track the path of the moon through the rustling leaves above him. The Dunallon garden was cool, but the breeze remained high in the trees, so he didn't feel chilled. His finger tapped the electronic tablet on his lap as he considered the words he'd been skimming. His other hand had firm hold of a glass of scotch, which was half as full as it had started out not too long ago.

Footsteps crunched toward him and he raised his head. Sarah approached his hiding place, a glass in one hand, a larger object in the other. She had freed her hair from the ponytail she'd worn all day, and the freshly-brushed curls gleamed in the muted light from a garden lamp. She paused in front of him.

He grinned at what he saw in her other hand. "Brought the bottle, I see. Smart woman."

Her lips twitched as she placed the bottle on the little table to his side, then slid onto the seat beside him. "Aye, well," she sighed, and took a sip from her glass. "Anyone can see you're morose and pining, and you came out here to mope. I wasn't sure ye'd brought enough alcohol to do it proper."

He laughed. "That bad, eh?"

She smiled in response and gave his leg a pat as she nodded at the tablet. "What are you reading, love?"

"One of your grandmother's journals."

"Och, it's worse than I thought." Sarah lifted her glass. "To Gran, then. May her restless soul find peace."

Sam did not raise his own glass. "I don't know if I can do it, Sarah."

"'Course you can."

He groaned and glared up at the moon. "Just like that? Press a button and create another bloody grand universe like there's nothing to it? Drop in, then walk away and leave them like they mean nothing?"

Sarah reached across him for the bottle and splashed more scotch in her glass, ignoring Sam's. He lifted his head and watched her in wary concern.

Her lips tightened. "Which argument do you want, Sam? The one that says you're only human and can't be responsible for a feckin' universe in the first place? The one that reminds you the people in that universe will enjoy life as much as we do, and can bloody well make their own way through it? Or maybe the one about us just dropping in long enough to tell two people a story about their daughter, then we leave with no other interference? That it's possible the new timeline will just jog off from ours for that brief bit, then it will drift right back in line with ours, and no real change?"

"Bloody nonsense," Sam said to his scotch.

"Uncle Jamie thinks it's likely." He didn't answer, and she held out a hand. "Which journal is it?"

He shrugged and handed her the tablet. "1928. When your Aunt Terry was leaving for college."

Sarah stared at the tablet without saying anything. He couldn't tell if she was reading it. After a moment, she said, "Oh."

Very quiet was that "oh."

He took the bottle from her and brought his glass back up to the halfway point. Casey's words echoed in his mind, as if she were reading them from deep in a cavern. Worse than that, the journal had been scanned into the tablet, and the photocopied pages revealed the wrinkled splotches of paper and ink that had resulted from Casey's tears as she wrote. She had wept a lot while writing that entry.

Tomorrow, we take Terry to school in England. All I can see is the past. The future past, when my own parents put me on the plane to Belfast the first time. And all the times after that, for three years. Every year, after every holiday, they sent me back, with half-serious/half-joking reminders to behave myself and to stay safe.

How could I bear it, to receive a phone call from someone, telling me that my daughter was missing? To rush there, to search and wait and beg ... to never find her. To never know.

Sam is so old now. He knows he won't figure out time travel in his lifetime. Albert (Einstein) tells me that he doesn't think they'll figure it out even within his lifetime. It will have to be Jamie, and the next Sam Altair, if we can get him to help us. Decades from now.

I don't care if it's a hundred years from now. Someone must go back and tell them. I will not let my parents live a lifetime of never knowing.

"It won't be them," Sam said. The old, exhausted argument burned in futile flame down his throat, along with the scotch. "Every time we go back, we just create a new universe, with new, grieving parents. The original Jim and Terry Wilson lived and died without ever knowing what happened to their daughter. We can't change that."

"I know." Sarah's fingers curled around his, her thumb stirring his knuckles. "She knew that, too. But it doesn't matter."

He couldn't stop the repetitive words of their script. "She's dead now. It no longer matters to her ..."

Sarah stood. "Come to bed, Sam." Her weary voice told him that she would not finish the script, and he knew this would be his last attempt to stop the experiment. He could not say the words one more time. Sarah's hand pulled at his, strong and needy at the same time, and he rose to stand beside her. The light glinted off her eyes as she gazed at him. "We have our own lives to live, you and I. Let's finish Gran's work, and get on with it, aye?"

FIRST UNIVERSE

Chapter 10

Strickert Girls Academy
Oxford, England

"What do you mean, you're not going to School Day?" Grace stopped dead in the path as she and Moira made their way to class on Wednesday. Moira continued a few steps before realizing Grace wasn't with her. She turned as a tangle of girls split around them with annoyed cries of "look out!" and one "ow!" when a second termer stubbed her toe trying to avoid Grace's violin case.

Moira raised a brow at Grace, but jerked her head toward the Languages Hall and turned to continue on her way. After the confrontation with Mr. Green last weekend, she'd taken some time to figure out her response to this question, knowing quite well it would be coming from many people over the next week. Already, she'd had a go 'round with her poly sci teacher. Good practice, that was, since there had never been any hope of Moira majoring in political science. That particular teacher didn't have years of support and encouragement invested in Moira, and was willing to accept a plausible cover story without argument.

Unlike Mr. Green.

Grace's staccato step sounded behind her as she caught up, and Moira sighed. "I mean I'm not going to Secondary School Day. That's not hard to understand."

"It's impossible to understand," Grace said. "You can't tell me you're not planning on going to college. I won't believe you. So why aren't you going to Oxford on Saturday?"

"Because my parents don't want me to." The words tasted like wood on her tongue. It felt so strange to say something this close to the truth.

"What do you mean, they don't want you to?"

Moira laughed, but it rang hollow to her ears. "Grace, you're sounding like a broken Pad."

"Don't change the subject." They had reached the Languages Hall, and Grace set her feet on the path, stubbornness visible in her tight jaw. "This has something to do with all that religion crap, doesn't it?"

"Probably." Moira had used a humble and pious expression on the poly sci teacher, but that wouldn't work with Grace. So she just shrugged. "You know I don't like it. But they've made it clear I can't argue with them." This was a version of the truth. She'd always known she couldn't argue, but she had never allowed even a hint of her desire for college to reach her parents. Grace knew about the daily "lessons" Moira had to complete, but not about their content. "College will have to wait, Grace. I'll get there one day. When I don't need my parents' permission."

Anger drew the corners of Grace's lips down, nearly to her jawbone. "But it's harder to get in if you don't come straight from secondary school. Especially for a girl."

Moira shrugged again. "I'll have a diploma from Stickert. That's good for a lot. They'll let me take the tests, anyway. I'll blow them away, and they'll have to let me in. Assuming," she punched Grace lightly in the shoulder, "I get to class on time and don't have a record full of demerits."

Grace stepped around her to start up the stairs. "We're not through with this," she said. "There's got to be a way to fix it."

Moira kept silent. A watered-down version of the truth had seemed the best hope for deflecting questions. But it left the nagging problem of those who would not be satisfied until they'd tried everything they could to change the situation.

Grace could not do much harm.

But a teacher's meddling could get her killed.

∞

Moira took a deep breath before entering Mr. Green's classroom that evening. He had not brought up the topic of School Day since their confrontation on Saturday. There had been the usual gang of students around all the time, and no chance for conversation. He could have called her into his office to discuss it, but that would not have been like him. She knew he respected her wish to not talk about it. But this evening, it would be just the two of them, working on his thesis. His respect for her wishes might only go so far.

He was intent on his typing as she stepped inside, but he spared her a quick grin. "I just sent chapter three to your Pad," he said, eyes already back on his own Pad, fingers tapping the virtual keyboard shimmering on his desk. "It needs your impeccable editing skills in a desperate way."

Relief made her laugh louder than his remark called for, but he didn't seem to notice. She slipped into her own seat and called up his file. She'd finish and leave before he got done with his current writing.

Unfortunately, chapter three had a lot of equations, and she had to verify each step. She was halfway through when he turned off his v-board and stood to stretch. She glanced at the time in the corner of her Pad. An hour had passed. Her vision was fuzzy and she blinked a few times, setting her stylus down to massage her fingers.

"I'm for some tea," he said, and she glanced up, nerves jangling a warning. He was already heading into his office. "Want some chamomile?"

Darn it all, she did. "Sure," she said, raising her voice so he'd hear, although she knew his question was rhetorical. For Christmas, he'd presented her with her own mug, to be kept in his office for their evening sessions. The mug boasted a hologram of Deep Space Field #12, taken a few years ago by the new orbiting telescope. The field was popular in cosmological circles, and Moira had been hard put not to cry when she opened the present. It was her first real gift, given to her by a friend, something not under her stepfather's control. In all her dreams of the future, she carried that mug.

But tea time opened the danger of chatting. Tightening her lips, she picked up the stylus and bent over her Pad, starting on the next equation. He would know the chapter required careful attention. Perhaps he'd just place the mug on her desk and return to his own work.

She didn't look up when the mug appeared in front of her, but the fragrant steam flooded her sinuses with a sense of renewal. She put the stylus down and reached for the tea, to bury her face in the steam. "Thank you," she said, sounding perhaps too grateful. She took a sip, closing her eyes to savor it. "This should clear my brain enough to understand your equations." She picked up the stylus and held her breath.

He didn't answer, but didn't move away, either. Seeking a distraction, she pointed at the equation on her screen, and opened her mouth to say ... something.

"Miss Sherman." He sat in the chair before her desk, turning it to face her. She at last looked up at him, wondering what in heaven her face revealed. She felt paralyzed.

His own face was pale and tight, and it occurred to her that he didn't want this confrontation anymore than she did. Maybe he had to do it. Maybe his job demanded it.

He held his mug on his knee, both hands wrapped around it. His eyes were steady on her face, and despite the fear clenching her stomach, she couldn't look away.

"It was clear the other night," he said, "that you don't want to discuss your college plans. I don't understand that, but I respect it.

Nevertheless." He lifted his mug, his cheek twitching as he sipped the tea. Moira felt an irrational longing to touch that cheek, and at last found the power to look down, her own cheeks flaming in sudden heat.

"Nevertheless," he said again, "I must speak of it. Your other teachers have noticed the absence of your name on Saturday's list. They know I'm mentoring you, and have left me the task of finding a satisfactory answer. You must help me know what to tell them."

Sneaky bastard. She was surprised at the thought, but as she glanced up, a glint in his eye verified the trace of trickery she'd heard in his voice. His excuse was plausible, but she suspected he was glad the other teachers had asked this of him.

Oddly, this gave her courage. She sat back in her chair and tilted her head, curious. "What would you do?" she asked. "To help? What would *they* do?"

He placed his mug on her desk and leaned forward, eagerness in his eyes. "It's hard to say without knowing the problem. But there are countless programs in place, for financial assistance, housing, jobs, whatever you might need. If you start now, and with the influence of this school behind you, not to mention your own excellent grades, you'll find you qualify for more help than you can imagine. The thing is, it takes time to apply for these. If you wait until you're eighteen, why it could be four years or more before you finish all the paperwork. As well, you won't qualify for as many programs. So many of them are geared toward the secondary student who plans on starting college as soon as she graduates."

He ran a hand through his hair and shook his head, as if to throw off the bewilderment that crossed his face. "I don't understand what keeps you from applying now. Waiting until you're eighteen is practically a death sentence."

She sat still, her mouth tight, staring at him. He returned her look, his face hopeful, and she felt the hinges of her jaw loosen, her chin drop as if to prepare her mouth for speaking. But it wouldn't go any further. How could she say the words? Shame flooded her at the thought of him hearing the truth. At the thought of the consequences if his effort to help failed.

Her mouth stayed closed.

She leaned forward, hiding from him as her fingers traced wetness from her cheeks.

"You can't know how much I want to go to college." She could only whisper, and sensed him leaning closer. "You've shown me a future I never imagined was possible, and I want that future." Her hands clenched in front of her, but she didn't see them. Didn't even see the desk as she stared at it. "But as a minor, I need my parents' approval to pursue it. And they won't give it." She finished the words on a rushed breath and waited, not looking at him.

He didn't move or speak, as if expecting her to say more. After a moment, he shifted.

"Mrs. Burke mentioned that you'd said something about that. But I don't understand. Surely they know how brilliant you are. Perhaps if I, or perhaps Headmistress Lionel, talked to them ..."

"No!" Moira brought her fists down to the desk hard enough to make her Pad bounce and the tea slosh in her cup. She looked up to glare into his eyes. "That must not happen. Not you, not anyone. Whatever you think, whatever ideas you come up with, *no one* from this school must ever contact my parents in any way about this." He started to speak, and she plunged on, over-ruling his attempt. "It's more than not giving their approval. They are against the idea of college, for me or for any girl. No, they don't *know* I'm brilliant, and they wouldn't care if they did. My only hope, and I mean this, Mr. Green, is to wait until I'm considered an adult, and can make my own choices. If you interfere before that, while I'm still in their control," her voice shook and she was powerless to stop it, "I will never get away. Do you understand? *Never.*"

"Why?" he asked. "What is behind this? Help me understand, Moira."

She blew a breath out in frustration and stood, pacing away a few steps before whirling to face him. Wincing inwardly at the confusion on his face, she shook her head. "I can't tell you. I can't tell anyone. If you don't understand, then we must leave it at that. You may tell the other teachers, if you feel you must. But I am counting on you to make sure no one interferes. You must promise me."

He opened his mouth, but when no sound came out, he closed it again. He cleared his throat. "All right." His voice was rough. "If it must be, then I promise no one will interfere. But Moira," and there, he'd used her name again, making what he said even stronger, "You must accept that I am concerned about you. Perhaps more than is proper for a teacher or mentor. I am concerned for you *as a friend.* We all have responsibilities to our friends, Moira. Yours is to always remember I am here to help you, if the time comes that I can."

His words brought a swell of desire and love rising through her, and she swayed, off-balance from the onslaught. She forced herself to look him in the eye as she answered. "I will remember. That is my promise. Now," she stepped forward and reached for her Pad, "you really must give me some time with this chapter, or you'll turn it in with all kinds of typos."

Chapter 11

The next evening, with classes over, Andy headed to his room before leaving for Oxford. The Lioness, trim in her Frombeau designer suit, her hair neat in its chignon, waylaid him as he passed her den.

"A moment of your time, Mr. Green."

He sidetracked into her office, placing himself in the sage-and-pink upholstered chair she indicated. He watched as she glided around her desk and sank into the soft leather of her own seat. An unobtrusive inhalation helped him regain the equilibrium her office always scattered when he entered. He was certain not even Buckingham Palace could compare with the elegance the Headmistress of Strickert Academy established around herself.

Her expression was not unfriendly, but neither did she seem pleased, as she folded her hands on her desk and regarded him across its gleaming cherry expanse. "Two of your colleagues have informed me that your mentee, Miss Sherman, is not expecting to attend college. They said you were quite firm that they must not interfere with this decision. That is, of course, your prerogative, and hers, as well. However, you must realize this will not look well on your record."

She held up a hand, although he'd made no attempt to speak. "I understand that teaching is not your career of choice. Nevertheless, the reference you receive from this academy will reflect on your university record."

This was true, but he could not forget Moira's fear. He tilted his head. "I assure you, I haven't given up on her, Headmistress. But she was quite adamant about no interference."

"Did she give you a reason?"

He held his breath, thinking, then let it out in a rush. "No, ma'am, except to say that her parents will not give their permission." He decided to take a risk. "Would you have any information about the family that might shed light on that?"

She hesitated, which surprised him. But she sat back in her chair, jaw tight with decision. "You understand this is sensitive information.

You must not speak of it to anyone. If you feel it will help with Miss Sherman, by all means speak to her about it. But she must not know this came from me."

He nodded, thoroughly alarmed. "Of course."

"I have nothing specific, you understand. But my years at this school have given me a sixth sense, if you will, about the girls in my care."

He nodded again.

Her gaze seemed to shift inward, as if searching for the right words. "I suspect Miss Sherman's family lives in a Fundamentalist Protectorate. If so, this may be what is holding her back from college."

Andy realized he was holding his breath, and he sighed as he shook his head. "She's never mentioned anything of the sort."

"Has she mentioned *anything*, Mr. Green, about her life or family?"

"Of c ..." but a dawning uneasiness rose in his chest. He stared at the desktop, ransacking his last two years in Moira's company. He shook his head in shameful disbelief. "No, she hasn't," he said. "I can't think of a single instance." He gazed at the Lioness, mentally kicking himself for missing this. "But I can assure you, Headmistress, that Miss Sherman does not subscribe to a fundamentalist belief. If her family belongs to one, she is there unwillingly."

For the first time in his experience, Headmistress Lionel-Spencer looked disturbed. She caressed her desk, her hand gliding a feather's width above the sheen, her eyes following the movement. Her cheek twitched. "Hence, her hope to wait until she is eighteen, and can legally leave." She met Andy's gaze. "It is the scenario which makes the most sense, given what little I know of her family, and of my observations of her over the years. It would be helpful if you could find out what the situation is. Encourage her to speak to me, please. I have tried a few times, but she never opens up. She may feel more comfortable with you. Assure her that there are steps I can take, including holding a slot for her application to university. This is allowed in special circumstances, and I would make sure she qualifies. But she must declare herself in need of asylum."

"She's afraid," Andy said, his voice soft.

"I know," the Headmistress said. "It's the one consistent emotion I've seen in her during her years at Strickert."

∞

Later, in his lab at Oxford, Andy inserted Kebbie's datastick into his computer and called up the Read Me file. *Cargo manifests for NISS? What in bloody hell do they want with that information?*

He chewed his bottom lip while he thought about it. The data stream for The New International Space Station lay under an extra layer of security in Sun's servers. He could get into them, of course. He even had a low level clearance for some of it, as he sometimes worked with scientists stationed on NISS. But shipping did not fall under his certificate.

Best to go in through an unrelated back door, he decided. Don't leave crumbs for them to chase. He set it up, taking his time to triple-code the worm before he slipped it into the system. The worm went to work, restoring his computer to its proper functioning. The stick lit up as data began streaming onto it.

Andy nodded once, then flipped his screen to a concealed search engine, and called up the archives for the British parliament. Headmistress Lionel had mentioned protectorates, and he wanted to look over the actual law which had first established them. This took longer than his usual searches as the government had never learned how to store data efficiently. But in about ten minutes, he had it up and began to read.

Fundamentalist Protectorates

Be it enacted by the King's most Excellent Majesty, by and with the advice and consent of the Lords Spiritual and Temporal, and Commons, in this present Parliament assembled, and by the authority of the same, as follows:

A declared Fundamentalist Protectorate holds clear and inviolate protection under the law, to function solely according to the established and recorded creed of its members ...

Andy swallowed in distaste, lifting his hand from the keyboard in an effort to put some distance between himself and the abhorrent law. He'd never agreed with this ruling. But parliament had passed it fifty years ago, in response to the famines and religious wars of the 2020's, amid the public's clamoring for safety and food. His reading of history showed the work of tyrants and war lords, in the guise of priests, imams, and ministers, convincing the starving survivors of their need to repent, to live in enclaves of strict discipline, to obey in all things.

That the enclaves had worked, was more a sign of how bad things were, in Andy's opinion, than of any truth or reason to the creed.

You don't know that Moira's family belongs to one, he chided himself. But he couldn't shake the feeling the Lioness was right in her assessment of Moira. And that he, with all his vaunted admiration of the girl, with all his secret, hopeful love for her, had never even suspected.

Do I truly care for her? Or just for the idea of such a brilliant girl being with me?

He turned to the computer behind him, protected against traces with the best fail-safes he could write. His fingers hesitated over the virtual keys, his jaw working as he thought, before he typed, <Search: fundamentalist enclaves, Sherman>, and stared in shocked awe at the twenty-page response to his query. *Bloody hell ...*

Was it that easy?

Fool. Foolish, eejit bastard, so lost in the turn-on of getting a genius like her to notice you.

"I never saw her pain." He spoke out loud, unable to move his eyes from the screen.

And opened the first web page.

∞

Andy could not stop trembling the next evening, as he entered his class room, which was empty of all except Moira, who was perched on a stool near the windows. Her back was to him, her attention on the lab reports turned in by the fifth-year students. He let the door close, clutching his Pad in both hands, biting his lip so hard he winced. He would do anything in the world to not hurt or frighten her. Yet he was certain that tonight, he would do both.

He walked to her side, silent. She glanced up, her smile of greeting fading as she saw his face. He held the Pad to his chest, a shield.

"I've done some investigating," he said. Her face went pale, but she didn't look away. "You may hate me, you have every right to hate me. But you must talk to me about this."

He set the Pad in front of her, its screen displaying the home page of the Chelmsford enclave, the leader's visage staring at them from an upper corner.

Her hands flashed in a violent slash, sending the Pad clattering off the table to slide along the floor. She moved faster than he thought possible for anyone to move, dashing past him to the door. But he caught her before she could open it, holding it closed and touching her shoulder with all the tenderness he could muster. Her hand slapped the handle, her mouth open in a silent scream.

"Moira, please." He knew he should remove his hand, but he couldn't let her go. "All this time, I never knew this. I considered myself your friend, yet I never guessed. You may never forgive me, but please, *please*, let me help you. If not me, then the Headmistress. Or another teacher. *Someone.*"

She stiffened, facing the door, her head bowed, eyes squeezed shut. He controlled himself enough to remove his hand from her arm. He took her hand in both of his. "I understand that you never wanted anyone to know. That you don't trust anyone to help you. You may have very good reasons for feeling that way. But I am your friend. It would be improper for me to say how much I care for you, but you must at least know that I am your friend. That I will never rest until you are safe, and until you have the future that you deserve."

69

There was the slightest release of tension in the hand he held. She still did not move, but she bit her lip. She was listening.

"You have plans for your future. Plans for attaining it. I am in awe of the strength and courage that must take. You may feel you can't share your plans with me, and that's fine. I won't press. But talk to me, Moira. Please."

The hand in his pulled away, and he let it go. She stared at the door handle. "I'd like to go, please."

It was a test. And he knew as sure as he knew anything that the rest of his life depended on passing it.

He opened the door. "Certainly. You know where to find me."

She disappeared down the hall without a word. He turned and sank to the floor, resting his head against the wall, swiping tears from his face. He didn't know how to help her. Should he go to the Lioness? He was certain the Headmistress knew all of it. She was as capable of research as he. But would Moira consider it a breach of trust? Did it matter, if in the end she was safe?

Footsteps stopped at his door and he looked up, uncaring of whatever explanation would be demanded for his state.

Moira stood in the doorway, her face washed, tissues clenched in her hands. She looked at him with trepidation, then shook her head a little and slipped into a chair.

"Where do I start?"

Relief warred with his nerves. *Don't scare her again.* Questions crowded his mind, but he started with safest topic he could think of.

"I read the creed. Some of his articles, some of the debates. He holds one of the most misogynist viewpoints I've ever seen published. Why did he send you here, to a school famous for turning out strong, independent women?"

She twisted the tissues, not looking at him. "He has a couple of reasons for that. One is that he can be sure I'm kept from boys. The other is that I'm an embarrassment to him. Girls in the enclave are not educated past the seventh year. If I were home, and attending the local school, I'd be a constant affront to the other parishioners. This way, I'm sort of out-of-sight, out-of-mind." She shrugged. "I can't tell you exactly why he chose Strickert, but I can tell you he couldn't care less about its reputation for a strong education."

"Okay." Andy steepled his fingers, tapping his lips. "But why is he continuing your education? Why didn't he pull you out after the seventh year?"

She stared at the shreds in her hand. "I think it has something to do with my father."

"Your father? I don't understand."

"Cyrus Sherman is my stepfather. My mother ... left my father, and brought my brothers and me to the enclave when I was eight. My father didn't want us to go, but he was sick, and couldn't stop her. In fact, he was dying, although I didn't know it at the time. Evidently, he made Cyrus promise to educate me. Cyrus told me he was honoring my father's death-bed request."

She glanced up to meet Andy's gaze. "He teaches that honor between men is sacred, something about the agreement between the Father, Son, and Holy Spirit." Her lips twitched, possibly at the doubtful astonishment Andy couldn't keep from his face. "My father was not a Christian, at least not how Cyrus defines one, and his request was improper, Cyrus said. Nevertheless, Cyrus felt it was his duty to carry it out."

"He's looney, isn't he?"

She nodded. "Although in this case, it's worked to my advantage. Cyrus is so entrenched in running the enclave, and in his own teachings, that he truly never considered I would learn about the real world. About history, and the reasons for our current government. He never considered I would learn I could be free."

She ended on a whisper, and Andy had to look down, breathing deep to hold back tears. He had to know more.

When he could speak again, he raised his head. He had to be careful how he phrased this. "I read his teachings that women are the cause of evil in the world. That they gain their salvation through a man." He stopped to swallow, to quell the nausea his words caused him. He could hardly speak such hateful nonsense. How did other people live and die by it?

Moira shrugged into his pause. "I decided a long time ago I'd rather not have salvation on those terms. I no longer believe any of it is true, anyway."

"That's good," Andy said. "I didn't think you believed it, but I'm glad to hear you say so. But Moira," he leaned forward, elbows on his knees, "his teachings are so extreme. He doesn't describe methodology on the website, but I am concerned. Moira, does he use ... that is to say ... does he teach that it's acceptable ... to use violence against women?"

Her gaze dropped back to the tissues, her face flushed with color. Seconds passed. When she nodded, his heart seemed to split in two.

He stood and lifted a small chair, to place it quietly next to her. He sank into the chair, near enough to touch her, but taking care not to do so. "Has he hurt you?"

Her feet slid forward, as if to carry her away, but she brought them back against her chair. The tissues were dust in her hands.

"Yes. Nearly every day I'm home."

"God *dammit*." He whispered the curse, overcome with agony. He touched the back of her head, her hair soft against his fingers. He murmured her name, then other things, not quite aware of what he was saying. He could not see past the rage and shame her words had roused in him, and he felt helpless to control himself. He kept his hand on her head, his forehead pressed to her crown as he whispered.

"Don't." She stood in one swift move and stepped away, before turning to face him. "You're shocked because you've just learned this," she said, her words spilling out as tears fell down her cheeks. "But I've lived with it for years. I don't want your comfort. I want what you've always given me. Do you have any idea how much you've helped me? Your respect for me and your friendship. All the talks we've had, how you spoke of your studies, all the things you were discovering. You shared that with me, all of it, as if ... as if I were your equal, as if my thoughts and opinion mattered. It seemed to make you happy, helping me to learn, and I never want that to end. I always wanted to be free, but you showed me a life to be free *for*. Please, don't ever stop showing me that."

"I never will." He stood, reaching for his own tissues and turning to his desk. By the time he got there he'd pulled himself together, at least as much as possible. He faced her, propping himself against the desk.

"You're quite right, pity won't help you. Although, in my defense, pity is far from what I'm feeling. Still," he paused, studying her for a moment as she wiped her face. When she glanced at him, he continued. "Miss Sherman, it has been the highest honor of my life to be your teacher. To be your friend is my greatest delight. I am horrified at what I've learned today. On some level, I feel that I've failed you." He held up a hand against her protest. "I do, and you must allow me this. I've worked with you for two years and never saw this. All the holidays, when I simply said good-bye, never knowing what you went home to." His voice shook, and he stopped to bring it back under control. He tapped the desk near his leg. "It ends," he said. "I don't know how, but I will see to it, that it ends, now."

She sighed. "Are you thinking of police? Of social services and courts?"

"It's a place to start."

"No, Mr. Green." She came up the aisle between desks, to toss the shreds of tissues into the wastebasket and stand in front of him. Her cheeks were splotchy from crying, but her eyes were dry and determined. "It's been done, you see. Four years ago, some new people moved next door to us, and saw my stepfather beating me. They called the police. Who came promptly, to stand guard while he finished the beating. The neighbors filed reports with social services, even went before a judge. But the law is quite clear in these cases, Mr. Green. And in Chelmsford, most of the townspeople belong to my stepfather's enclave. All of the police do. All of the elected officials, including the judges. The neighbors moved away quite soon, with reason to fear for their lives."

He couldn't make himself speak. A sad smile curved a corner of her lips, and she turned to stand next to him, leaning against the desk. Her shoulder brushed his arm. "I've made plans for getting away. They are far from perfect, but I must work within the reality I have. I don't intend to go home this summer." She glanced up, as if to gauge his reaction, before continuing. "Most enclave girls are married off by fourteen, for convoluted reasons having to do with husbands and salvation. My stepfather takes my salvation quite seriously. Enough, I'm afraid, to overcome his sense of *duty* to my father. I'm almost seventeen, and I don't believe he'll allow me to return to school next year. His recent lessons have taken a turn toward this, and I'm sure he plans to marry me off this summer." She shook her head. "I cannot be there for that to happen."

He felt himself coming undone again, but he managed to stop his hand before it touched her. He let it drop back to the desk. "Most assuredly not," he said, his voice shaking. "I'm relieved to hear you say that. You must understand that I would not be able to stand by and watch you go back there."

She turned her head to regard him. Her voice was gentle, but her words were firm. "I do not want you to get involved, Mr. Green. I do not want you to help me."

She may as well have stabbed him. "Why? Do I frighten you, that I care for you as much as I do? That I haven't always acted properly? Because I swear I'll never put you in an awkward ..." She was shaking her head, and he stopped. "Do you just want to handle it yourself? I can understand that, but this is far too big a problem for one person. No one can escape from these things, alone."

Her eyes were full of affection, enough to make him hold his breath in wonder, but she remained serious. She placed a hand on his arm, its warmth making him shiver.

"I need you, Mr. Green. I need you to do what you do, and be what you are. So that when I'm free, when later I begin to build my life again, you'll be there. I'll need your references, your contacts, anything you can do for me, to help me get back into school. If you try to help me now ... the penalties are too severe. If it doesn't work, I could be trapped for life, and so could you. You could spend your entire life in prison. If you'll take no other arguments, take this one: if I do get away, you won't be able to help me from prison."

He couldn't breathe. "That ... That's dreadfully unfair," he gasped at last.

She removed her hand and he felt empty without it. "If you can find one thing about this situation that's fair," she said, her voice bleak, "you be sure and tell me about it."

"You should know," he said, "that Headmistress Lionel-Spencer is aware of your situation. She at least suspects it. She's the one who advised me to look at fundamentalist enclaves." Moira's lips moved as they did when she was deep in thought, but she said nothing. Andy tried to squeeze a breath past the tightness in his chest. "Keep in mind that she does have resources. Far more than I do. Her reference will mean more than mine, although of course, you have mine, always. But consider letting me tell her about this. Or you could go to her, yourself. She is willing to help."

Moira rubbed her face, covering a small groan with her hands. "I don't dare. One wrong move, one *hint* to my stepfather, and he'll take me out so fast, we'll never know it's happening. He has so many spies, so much surveillance in place." She stood to face him, balancing on her toes as if she were preparing to run. "I've researched this. Asking for asylum sets in motion dozens of proceedings, all of them available to the abuser. Do you know that last year six hundred and eighty-seven cases of asylum for women were filed in Great Britain? Do you know how many were granted?" She didn't wait for his response. "Fifteen. *Fifteen,* Mr. Green. My odds are better on the streets of London. Don't let her get involved. If I disappear and he comes to question her, when he sends the authorities, she must be able to say that she knows nothing. Please, Mr. Green."

Her words were like a slammed door. No wonder she was so desperate.

"All right. I'll take care of the Lioness. I'll assure her you have the situation under control. But I need you to promise me something, too."

He could not take the chance she would refuse him. Friendship and respect would not get it for him. He took her hand in both of his and held it tenderly against his chest. She had to step closer to keep her balance, leaning against his legs. He looked into her eyes with all the frustrated love he harbored for her. Her pulse pounded against his hands, and a flush rose in her cheeks. But he didn't let go of her and she made no effort to move.

"If your plan does not work, if you find yourself in danger, you must promise to contact me. You have my Pad number. If you don't have it memorized, do so. I can do things, Moira. With computers, with security programs. My computers at Oxford are secure. They are that way because I circumvented the protocols." He pressed her hand, pushing it against his chest. "You have my heart, Moira. Promise me. If you end up trapped, you will call me. Promise."

"Yes," she said, breathing hard. "All right. I promise."

He wanted to lose himself in her eyes, to hold her and know she was safe. But he had sworn, so with the lightest caress of her arm, he let her go, and folded his arms across his chest. He nodded. "Thank you."

He had sworn, and he would keep his word. But he memorized every movement as she left.

Chapter 12

The scotch was single malt and old, laid down at the turn of the century, and kept cozy in an underground vault for eighty years. Feldman took a minute to just breathe it in, letting the warm vapors tease his senses with dark perfume. The first sip was a caress, and he set the glass down with quiet regard.

The pub was old as well, having a storied history hosting many of Northern Ireland's famous authors over three centuries. The wooden bar was filled with the after-work crowd, but Feldman sat well back in a quiet corner booth. He preferred his club, but came here often enough to be considered unsuspicious. It was a convenient place to meet various contacts. This was his business tonight, and he glanced up when a body slid into the seat across from him.

He nudged his glass a bit to the side, preferring to savor the sensuous scotch in private. "Is everyone in place?"

"Aye." A ring glittered on the man's hand as he drank from his pint. "Last team went up this morning. They'll need a few days to set up the equipment."

Feldman nodded. "They'll have time. What is happening with O'Malley's cell?"

"Business as usual far as I can see. Recruitment's at about the same level and they've got a few combat training sessions going. We haven't tried to interfere with them."

"Don't leave them alone completely," Feldman said. "Harass them a bit, otherwise they'll wonder why you're ignoring them."

"Yeah, all right. We have agents around where they can see them, so they know we're still paying attention." The man took another drink. "We've located a couple more splinter groups in the area. They don't seem to be affiliated with the main rebel alliances, at least not officially. But if we know about 'em, there's no doubt the rebels know about 'em, too. Fact is, I'm bloody sure they're already hooking up with each other. O'Malley's been especially eager to build up the ranks within Orion. He's got his eye on a big prize, I'm thinkin'."

Feldman leaned back in his chair, the picture of calm. "Not a problem. Once our current mission is completed, the rebel groups will be knocked out of existence. Let them play their games, for now."

The man nodded, and soon went on his way. Feldman addressed his scotch and thought about Sam Altair. In some ways, the threat of an invasion from another timeline was an annoying distraction, interfering with the plans and actions of this world. But Feldman saw another way. Whoever came through from Sam's timeline would be handled promptly.

And could possibly be quite useful.

∞

Dinnie sat at her desk, scanning the pingback report that shimmered on her virtual terminal. The back of her neck itched with discomfort. So far, no other detectors had reported activity. There'd been eight probes around Belfast over the last two months, but that was it. If this was an invasion, they were sure going about it in a weird way.

Why Belfast? Why not London, Washington D.C., and all the other major cities, if a world invasion was their plan? Dinnie rubbed her neck, unable to relieve the itching. The only reason she could think of was that Belfast was where the Sun Consortium's headquarters were.

I'm just a cog in the wheel around here. But I know enough to know who pulls the strings connected to world leaders.

If people from the second timeline wanted to dominate this world, taking down the consortium was the first step. Sam Altair would have known that. He would have warned his own leaders about it, and thus, their first target was Belfast. Perhaps they were hoping for a clandestine attack, to infiltrate Sun and bring it down quietly.

Memories surged. Dinnie closed her eyes, fingers shaking on the virtual keyboard.

The man in front of her was taller than her da'. The sun was behind him, blurring his face, but the smaller, duller sun-on-blue patch on his uniform jacket was clear. Almost, she turned to run, but indignation locked her knees and gave boldness to her thin voice. "My brother said he hacked into Sun's 'puters. Said he told the rebels about it and that he was gonna do it again."

The man was nice. He gave her an apple and took her home, and told her to go play in her room. She obeyed, but after a minute slipped back down the hallway and peeked into the living room where the man talked to her ma and brother. Ma always defended Dinnie's brother, and Dinnie wanted to make sure he got what was coming to him. But the scene in the room froze her in sudden fear.

Ma was on her knees, tears covering her face. She made no sound, hands clasping her throat as if she couldn't breathe. The man stood by the sofa, holding onto her brother's arm. Billy was still, his face so pale every freckle seemed to glow.

The man was talking. " ... lockdown until we get to the bottom of this. If he's found guilty, it will mean a prison sentence. If he's innocent, he'll be sent to infantry training to help him understand where his loyalties should lie. He'll be assured of a job and a good future that way, ma'am."

Thirty years later, in front of her computer at the Sun Consortium, Dinnie covered her face with her hands as she heard once again the wordless, echoing moan her mother had made as the man walked away with Billy. The hearing did not prove his guilt, but it was five years before they saw him again, tall and brooding in his own Sun uniform.

I was only four years old, Dinnie thought. He broke my only doll on purpose. I just wanted to get him into trouble.

"I didn't know." She whispered the words to the data on her terminal, her whole body shaking with guilt. How could a four-year-old understand the ways of power and control?

Billy had been just thirteen at the time.

Whoever these people were who were trying to cross here from another universe, they couldn't be any worse than the monsters who ran her own world.

Could they? Did she dare take the chance?

Did she dare do nothing?

She locked her computer and stood, reaching for her jacket. It was time to set things right. Her bosses played their positions like a game, trading the lives of innocent people for power and riches. Sam Altair was bringing in new players, but right now, only Sun's leaders knew that.

She'd never tried contacting the rebels before, but she had to now.

It was time to alert the other side.

SECOND UNIVERSE

Chapter 13

1980
Cave Hill
Belfast, Ireland

Jamie bounced on his toes, unable to keep still as the last bit of preparations for the journey were completed. After three months of analyzing probe data, they were actually doing this crazy thing.

His mind flitted to a loose end and he turned to his niece. "Are you wearing your thermals, Sarah?"

She didn't answer right away, instead rolling her eyes toward Sam, as if for assistance. But Sam was kneeling in front of the main CERBO unit, busy with inputs, and Jamie didn't think he was listening.

"Yes, Uncle Jamie," she said. "The latest temperature reading in the other Belfast was minus eight in the middle of the afternoon. Do you think I'm daft, to go without warm clothing?"

"I don't think you're daft," he said. "But you might have forgotten. And I'd prefer you took extra air, too."

"The atmosphere is perfectly breathable," Sam said, rising from his knees and staring at the time machine. He'd been listening, after all.

"For a loose interpretations of either of those words," Jamie said. "I do wish we had taken readings in other places on the planet."

"We're not going to spend enough time in 2080 to make it necessary," Sam said.

Jamie continued to bounce with his last-minute jitters. He always had them before a big experiment."I know you've built fail-safes into the machine. It's shielded ..."

"And there's that automatic return built in, too, and the chemical tracker we put in our bloodstreams ..." Sarah said.

" ... so you'll be returned to our own universe after seven days, even if you're unconscious. Or dead." Jamie finished. "That makes me feel so much better." He squelched an upsurge of annoyance as Sam and Sarah exchanged a glance. "Do not attempt to humor the old man. My concerns are more than valid."

Sam leaned against the wall of the cave. "Sure you don't want to come with us? You've worked on this your entire life."

On the verge of spouting off his usual answer, Jamie paused and gave it some thought. This would be his last chance. Then he shook his head, turning a troubled look on Sam. "I don't. I remember, you see."

Sam's head jerked sideways. "Remember what, sir?"

"Grandpa Sam." Jamie found himself speaking softly as he thought of the old man. "He was happy enough, I think. But I always sensed that he was ... disturbed. That he never quite fit."

He glanced at Sarah, smiling reassurance. "My mum was just my mum, always there, and somehow always a part of my father. An extension of him, I guess. Or he was of her, more likely. Either way, they were nearly one being in my mind. I never noticed that she was different from everyone around her. But Grandpa Sam was like a splinter in your hand. It was easy to see he didn't belong. That he pushed constantly at the boundaries of our world, not because he was curious, but because he was desperate."

Sarah touched his hand. "I don't understand," she said, her eyes concerned. Those eyes were so much like his mother's.

"He felt responsible, you see," Jamie said. "He wanted to get back to his own world, sure enough. But even that would not have satisfied him, for he felt almost as if he had created us. Our world. He had to understand, because it was his fault this timeline existed."

He looked from Sarah to Sam, and shook his head again. "Crossing to the first timeline won't hurt anything. But going *back* again, to 2006, will create still *another* universe. Quite honestly, I do not want that responsibility. And I don't envy you taking it on."

Interesting how the two kids avoided looking at each other. No doubt they had already discussed this very thing. Sam had always been unhappy about that part of the project.

A beep broke the silence and they all turned to look at CERBO, to find its green ready light staring at them. The next move was theirs.

His niece took a deep breath that she did not quite let out, scooped her jacket from its perch on a nearby rock, and pulled her gloves from a pocket. Jamie watched her in slight shock, knowing she was really going through with it. Sam reached for his own jacket, his movements not quite as confident as Sarah's.

Jamie waited until she lifted her eyes to his. He held out a hand, and with a small smile, she put herself in his arms, squeezing him gently. Her hair smelled like summer.

"We'll be careful, Uncle Jamie," she said against his chest. She didn't promise to be all right.

He nodded. "That's all I can ask." He found he couldn't say more around the tightness of his throat. She moved away and Jamie turned to Sam, grasping his arm in both his hands. "I know you'll take care of her."

"Of course I will." Sam's voice was confident, but his eyes betrayed his uncertainty. He huffed, "She'll probably be the one taking care of me, you know."

"Aye, well, we all expect that, lad," Jamie said. Placing an arm about each of their shoulders, he walked with them to the middle of the cave. With a final squeeze, he left them there, moving to his place behind CERBO.

Sam tapped his gloves against his leg. "No time change. Just a straight shot across the chasm to the other universe. Over there, the year is 2080."

Jamie nodded. This wasn't new information. It was more like Sam's final pep talk. Sarah was pale, as if she was just now realizing what they were doing.

Sam glanced at Sarah, then back at Jamie. "We'll look around the cave area, and take our own samples, just to get our bearings and do a check of the portable CERBO." He gestured toward the backpack at his feet. The portable time machine was packed into it, along with the chip that directed the neutrinos back in time. "We'll send you a message no later than," he glanced at his watch, "sixteen-hundred hours." Jamie glanced at his own watch. That was thirty-five minutes from now. "Once we get your acknowledgment, we'll light up our CERBO and go back in time to 2006."

Sam looked as if he was going to say more, but no words came. He stared at Jamie, then nodded, as if to himself. Jamie nodded back, feeling his features sink into a frown. His eyes moved from Sam to Sarah and back again. He watched as they helped each other zip jackets, and put on hats and backpacks, touching each other in timorous, loving ways. Jamie flinched, as if his body wanted to jump up and pull them out of the isolation field. He forced himself to stillness.

Then they were all staring at each other. Sam turned to Jamie, lifting his wrist to tap his watch. "Ready," he said.

Jamie reached forward and flipped a switch. "Ten seconds." He couldn't look away from them.

Sarah suddenly smiled, a big, happy smile that lit up her face, and she lifted a hand. "We're doing it, Uncle Jamie. I love you."

He lifted his own hand, watching as the two of them took each other's hands, and vanished.

"I love you, too," he said.

FIRST UNIVERSE

Chapter 14
Cave Hill
Belfast, Northern Ireland

Sam didn't feel any different, but he knew without doubt that something had happened. He noticed the cave looked different, and on the heels of that, so close it was nearly the same observation, he noticed Sarah stood next to him, whole and well.

They stared at each other in stunned silence. Sarah was pale, her eyes like green beacons against a white sea. He squeezed her hand.

"Are you all right?" His voice was reedy and he suspected he was experiencing some shock.

Her fingers tightened against his palm. "We did it," she whispered. He grinned, and her face lit up. "We did it!" she shouted, and threw her arms around him. He held her firmly and laughed into her neck.

"Let's look around," he said. "We've got to report to your uncle soon."

"Right ..." she began, but paused as the sound of running feet crunching on dirt floated into the cave. Sam stepped in front of Sarah just as a wall of white-suited soldiers burst through the entrance.

The soldiers wore helmets with opaque facemasks, white coveralls belted with black utility packs, black boots on their feet, and black gloves on their hands. Their menacing black rifles pointed straight at him.

He held up his hands. "Please, we mean no harm ..."but there was a sound of air singing through a tube, and his body exploded in agony. The blank darkness that followed was a welcome relief.

∞

Pain brought him back, but it was a distant ache, and he could bear it. Sam moaned and realized he was cold. He reached for Sarah.

His hand wouldn't move.

He choked out her name, forcing his eyelids to rise against the bricks laid against them. Fuzzy shapes moved above him in the sparkling light, and he focused on them. "Sarah?"

"She's safe," a voice said, and memory washed over him, clearing his vision faster than any drug could have done. The face staring down into his was handsome and stern, a white male about sixty years old. Sam realized that he was strapped to a table, and his reflexive lunge of alarm only earned him more pain.

"Where is she? What have you done to her?"

"She's in another room. A doctor is looking after her. I don't believe she has regained consciousness yet, but I've been assured she's had no adverse reactions to the taser."

"Oh, God ..." Sam moved his head against the panic rising in him. Tears trickled from his eyes. "Why have you done this? Who are you?"

The man looked beyond Sam and lifted a finger. A soldier appeared at the man's side, pistol trained on Sam. He wore the same white coverall as the soldiers in the cave, but no gloves and no helmet, revealing a freckled young man with red hair and a no-nonsense expression. At the same time, another figure stepped to Sam's other side. Sam glanced that way in fear, but the lab-coated man just reached to release the straps, beginning with Sam's legs.

"Now that you're awake, Dr. Anderson will remove the restraints," the first man said. "They were there for your protection. But I trust you understand not to make any threatening moves." His head tilted ever-so-slightly to the soldier.

After a moment, Sam nodded. Doctor Anderson slipped an arm under his shoulders and helped him to sit. Residual weakness made him tremble, and his nerve endings still sent poignant protests along his extremities. He gripped the edge of the exam table and concentrated on a deep breath. A drinking glass appeared in his vision, with a straw sticking out a hole in its cover.

"It's water," the doctor said. "Sip slowly, but drink it all, please."

The first swallow restored Sam's equilibrium, and he gratefully took another long swig. His stomach immediately let him know he should follow the doctor's advice and drink it slowly. He lowered the glass and fixed his gaze on the man waiting against the wall.

"Why did you shoot us?" Sam asked. "Where are we?"

The man's eyes narrowed. "My name is Albert Feldman," he said. He waited, his eyes never straying from Sam's face.

A moment passed as Sam squelched the polite "how do you do?" that rose up in his throat. Hardly appropriate for the situation, but what was the man waiting for?

After a few seconds, Feldman sighed. "The name means nothing to you, I take it?"

Was Albert Feldman someone important on this world? Sam tried to decide what to do, but there was nothing for it. He didn't know who this person was.

He kept his voice hesitant. "No. I'm sorry, it doesn't."

Feldman turned to a table, on which lay Sam's suit and packs. He picked up a card, reading it before turning back to Sam. "You are Samuel John Altair, of Belfast." Sam flinched at his dark gaze. The man looked haunted.

He was holding Sam's ID card, a replica of the original Sam's driver's license. But that ID stated it was issued in the year 2004, and that it expired in 2012. It showed his birthday of 2 July, 1946. Since they had planned on traveling immediately to 2006, Sam had not brought ID for 2080.

Sarah's identification would be similar. Sam stayed silent, certain that anything he said would only make things worse.

Unexpectedly, Feldman laughed, a bitter, cynical rasp. He threw the card on the table and in three quick steps, stood in front of Sam. "Let's not play around. I know who you are. I know, at least in theory, where you're from." He paused, but Sam remained silent, his eyes locked in terror on Feldman's face.

Feldman's voice was cold and hard. "You see, I knew Sam Altair. I worked with him for years. We were friends."

Sam gasped, his head jerking in one shake of denial. "That's impossible. You'd be well over a hundred years old."

"One hundred and thirty-five," Feldman said. "Just a couple of years older than you, yourself, at least according to your driver's license." He folded his arms across his chest, amusement warring with the anger in his eyes. "You make me think that I should have done more extensive rejuvenation, so I could be thirty-five again, and not sixty."

He moved away, to pace a few steps back and forth. The soldier's gun remained steady on Sam as Feldman paced and talked. "Sam Altair was researching time travel. Which, of course, you know." His fingers flicked in Sam's direction, but he didn't cease pacing. "The idiot managed to get himself transported back in time to 1906. At first we thought he was in our past. We looked for signs, for messages from him. But there was nothing. Eventually, we deduced that time travel creates a new universe. Sam was lost to us as surely as if he'd died. But in the new universe, he had free reign. With his knowledge, there's no telling what he could have accomplished in the early twentieth century."

Feldman stopped in front of Sam. "He surely died at some point in the early decades of the twentieth. But he left his work for you to carry on. Didn't he, Sam?"

Sam tightened his lips, staring into those black eyes.

Feldman leaned closer, his breath brushing Sam's cheek. "You figured out how to bridge the universes, didn't you?" he whispered. He straightened, the cold amusement back in his eyes. "Good of you to bring us the information, Sam. I can assure you, we'll make appropriate use of it."

"No," Sam said. "That was never our intention."

"Oh, I'm quite curious as to your intentions," Feldman said, as he turned back to Sam's things on the table. "We'll find out all about that, soon. But first ..."

He lifted the black case from the table, gazing at it with rapt pleasure before glancing up at Sam. "This is the time machine, isn't it? It's the same basic design that our Sam Altair developed eighty years ago." He lifted the lid, but didn't touch anything, one finger idly tapping the edge of the case. Then he turned to Sam.

"You're going to show us how this works, and you're going to build one for us."

Sam let his confusion show. "After all this time, you haven't figured it out yourselves? Did no one work on it after Sam disappeared?"

Feldman pursed his lips, displeased. "We've had other concerns. You will help us catch up."

"I can't do that, sir. We never expected to stay in this time. We have no intention of getting involved."

Feldman frowned and glanced at the machine. "We can always reverse-engineer it, I suppose. That might damage it, you realize. Possibly irreparably."

There was no doubt it would. "You must let us go," Sam said. "Return the machine and let us go. I promise, we won't return."

Feldman laughed at that. Sam found himself wondering how the original Sam could ever have been friends with this man.

"No, you're going to help us Sam," he said. "You'll be quite busy for a while. But rest assured, we'll explain everything to Miss Andrews and provide her with comfortable accommodations until you are done. You do understand, do you not?"

Clearly. What kind of world is this?

"I want to see her," he said. "I'll help you, but I must know she's all right."

Feldman nodded as if he had expected this. "I'll arrange it. You'll see her later this evening, and in the morning, someone will escort you to your lab. Be sure to let your handler know if you need anything we haven't provided."

Sam watched under the gaze of the soldier as Feldman rolled the table with his equipment out the door. When everyone else had gone, the soldier stepped to the door. "I'm Private Cunningham. I'll be standing guard," he said. "There's an intercom here," he pointed. "Buzz me if you need anything. Facilities are behind you, and a meal will be provided shortly. Be aware the room is monitored. You'll be under observation at all times."

"Wonderful," Sam said, not hiding his bitterness. Private Cunningham stepped outside and the door slid closed.

Chapter 15

Moira sat at her desk in Mr. Green's empty classroom, working on edits to her last term paper for English Lit. That is, the report was displayed on her screen, and occasionally, a phrase penetrated her brain, but her thoughts were a few miles away at Oxford University where Mr. Green was defending his thesis.

It was silly to be worried, she chided herself. The thesis was solid, and Mr. Green knew the material from every direction. He would not fail. Her fingers tapped the screen, bringing up his message from yesterday for the tenth time in the last hour.

Got the job. I start on Thursday.

A job with the Sun Consortium had been Mr. Green's immediate goal for both this summer and for graduate school. She stared at the message, picking at a ragged fingernail. Would the new job allow him to work on his doctorate? Surely, it would. He wouldn't give up on that.

She glanced at the time in the corner of her screen. What was taking so long? He knew she'd be on tenterhooks waiting to hear. If he wasn't coming straight to Strickert, wouldn't he send her a message? Her lips twitched in amusement. If he was out celebrating with friends, she'd kill him. He could celebrate *after* letting her know the results.

She'd made it through an entire page of her report when footsteps hurried down the hall. She froze in her seat and stared at the door, rewarded when Mr. Green appeared with a huge grin, and flung his backpack from his shoulders.

"Success!" he said, arms spread wide. Moira couldn't stop herself—she rose and threw her arms around his neck with a happy squeal. He gave her a brief squeeze, but let her go at once, holding her away with his hands on her shoulders before turning to retreat behind his desk.

"I can't stay long," he said as he sat. He propped his chin on folded hands to gaze at her. The grin had not left his face. "Some friends are holding a table at the *Pots and Pans*. We're all buying each other dinner in honor of our new degrees."

She sat at her desk again. Since their discussion two months ago, they had taken to holding conversations with the length of the classroom between them. If they stayed any closer, they always found excuses to touch each other.

"I'm glad you came by to tell me first," she said. "You would have been in terrible trouble if you'd made me wait much longer."

He laughed. "I would never have done that. This is your degree too, you know. You've been the best assistant anyone could hope for. And I have a surprise for you." His face held a quiet, pleased look as he watched her, as if he didn't want to miss the moment when she saw his gift.

"Me?" Moira flushed with embarrassment. "You're the one graduating. I have something for you." Afraid to look at him because she might start crying, or worse, giggling with excitement, she reached into her desk and pulled out a box, wrapped in silver mesh paper. She'd bartered with Grace for everything.

She placed the box in front of him, not daring to look at him until she saw his hands reach for it. His smile had turned soft as he gazed at it, and she trembled when he looked up at her.

He touched her hand. "Thank you."

She forced herself to be casual as she turned and retreated back to her desk. "You have to open it before you thank me." Her voice faltered, but she went on, "I wanted to get you something really nice, but I'm afraid I couldn't manage that. I do hope you like it."

"How could I not?" he said as he pulled the ribbon. "I'm already touched beyond words." The wrapping lay on the desk with the box waiting in the middle. Moira held her breath as he lifted the lid and rustled aside the paper, but his expression filled her with relief. His eyes were large and round with astonishment, the pleasure obvious in his gaze as he lifted the book from the box.

"A printed book!" he said in wonder. "*The Eddies of Time in Multiple Dimensions* by Samuel Altair. This is amazing." He opened it and read the inscription she'd agonized over for thirty minutes. *To Mr. Green, Congratulations and Good Luck with the next step!* It was a phrase which came nowhere near expressing the pride and love simmering within her. He would understand it wasn't safe for her to write anything more personal. He looked up at her. "I've never heard of this author. However did you find it?"

She leaned back in her chair, trying to appear relaxed. "Grace mentioned she saw it in a re-use shop in town. I asked her to pick it up for me." This was the truth, although Grace thought the book was for Moira. She was afraid he wouldn't accept it if he knew it was supposed to be hers.

His eyes returned to the book as he flipped pages. "This is marvelous. A true collectible. I'll treasure it always. Thank you, Miss Sherman. Truly."

Moira hugged herself to keep her giddiness in check. She owed him so much. His pleasure in the gift went a long way toward fulfilling her desire.

He set the book down, fixing her with a teasing smile. "As it happens, I got you something to read, too. It's on your Pad. I sent you a link."

She felt her face heat up, and she ducked her head as she called up his message. When the link opened, she stared at it without comprehension for a moment, then read the title in a voice gone dull with shock. "The *State of Neutrinos in Five Dimensions* by Andrew Green and Moira Sherman, under the advisement of Frederick Colson, Department of Physics, Oxford University, England."

She looked up at him, finding it difficult to make any more sound come out of her stiff lips. "You can't ... you can't ... ."

"Fred can." Mr. Green leaned back in his seat. Moira blinked once before remembering that "Fred" was Dr. Colson, Mr. Green's thesis advisor. Mr. Green pointed a finger at her, his whole face alight with joy. "It's to be published in Science, the August issue. I tweaked it a bit, but it's essentially the same paper you wrote for the science fair last year. I promise you, that's the first of many scientific papers to be written by the team of Green and Sherman."

It took two tries before she got air into her lungs. "A paper," she murmured, touching the screen in wonder. "A real scientific paper."

He laughed. "You'll get tired of them soon enough."

She laughed too, but the desire to kiss him instead made it sound rather forced. She wasn't thinking of just a friendly peck, either. Her face got even hotter. She covered it with her hands, hoping he'd put it down to happiness, then made herself stand. "I've got to meet my study group," she said, using all her bravery to face him. "Your friends are waiting for you. Will I see you tomorrow?"

"Yes." He stood as well, packing his gift into its box. His voice was hesitant, and she knew he wanted to ask about her plans, a topic she refused to discuss. "I've got to file the final grades in the morning," he said. "I'm to report to Sun in the afternoon, for orientation and to meet my supervisor. How many tests do you have left?"

"Two. Somehow I managed to get into the last roster, so I won't finish until about four tomorrow."

"Bad luck," he said with a small laugh. She laughed too, but when their eyes met, his laughter disappeared. "At least tell me you've got everything prepared. Tell me you'll be all right."

Her chest rose with the effort it took to breathe as she stared at him. Her nod was slight. "As much as I know to do, I've done," she said.

He nodded, shifting his gaze to the gift she'd given him, crumpling the ribbon in his hand. "I've been working on something ..." he glanced up at her, his face filled with hope and doubt all at once. "I understand your reasons for not wanting me involved. But I've been working on a way to alter your chip, hopefully to give you a false ID. It's just surface of course. They can still check your DNA. But it will get you past a cursory checkpoint. I'll have it here by about seven tomorrow night. Will you wait to get it?"

She smiled to cover her raging emotions. "Is there any nefarious thing you don't know how to do?"

He shrugged, laughing a little, but his gaze remained on her, the strangled ribbon in his hand betraying his tension. "Will you wait?"

"Yes, of course," she said. Then before he said anything else, and before she gave in and threw herself at him, begging him to run away with her, she slung her backpack on her shoulder, hugged her Pad to her chest, and fled the room.

Chapter 16

Sarah watched through narrowed eyes as a woman in blue scrubs rolled a cart into the room. Her guard, who had introduced herself as Private Mary Murphy, stood in the doorway but made no attempt to touch the gun belted to her hip. A gentle odor promised that the cart held food, and Sarah's stomach growled. Did she dare eat anything here?

The woman waved a hand at the covered dishes on the cart. "Dinner is an amaranth and mushroom casserole that was served in the cafeteria tonight. Will you need anything else?"

Sarah made no move toward the cart, instead repeating the statement she'd been making since waking up. "I want to see Sam."

She was surprised when Private Murphy nodded. "Dr. Feldman has arranged that. I'll escort you to a meeting room at nineteen hundred."

Sarah's mouth fell open, and she closed it with a snap, glaring at the guard. "When were you going to tell me that?"

Private Murphy returned the glare with a poker face. "When we brought your dinner." She waved the server out the door and tipped her head to Sarah. "Enjoy your food, miss."

∞

"Just hold me." Sarah pressed herself against Sam as tightly as she could, arms around him, face, chest, and hips pressed into him. Real. He was real. Which meant this situation was real too, but she'd deal with that later. "What's happening to us? What do they want?"

"Tell me first, are you all right?" His voice was low, cracking on the last word. Sarah tried to look up into his face, but his arms tightened even more around her, one hand holding her head to his chest. His heart was racing.

She nodded. "They took some blood for tests and put some kind of blasted chip in my arm. Otherwise, I'm not hurt. But they won't answer my questions." She swallowed a lump in her throat, but couldn't keep the tears from her voice. "I didn't know where they'd taken you."

"Just a little room. They did the same to me with the chip, and taking blood. They asked me questions. Did they ask you anything? Did a man called Albert Feldman talk to you?"

He still hadn't let go of her, and Sarah finally realized they were under surveillance. He was trying to keep their conversation from being heard. But his voice was so low, she was having trouble hearing him, especially with his hand over her ear. She shook her head hard to loosen his hold, lifted her face to his, and raised herself on tiptoe. She parted her lips.

In the way of lovers, he obeyed the signals she sent, lowering his head to meet her lips. She gave herself to the kiss for a moment, savoring the overwhelming realness of him.

Her Sam.

Moving a hand to his neck, she kept his head bent to her as she broke the kiss enough to whisper into his mouth. "A woman talked to me. She didn't ask for anything beyond personal information."

Sam deepened the kiss before answering, his lips moving against hers as he spoke. "They know about the time travel. Feldman knew Sam from before. He understands who I am. He has CERBO."

Sarah jerked in alarm, almost pulling away from him. His hold tightened and he traced her jugular vein with his lips, mumbling into her neck. "He wants me to show him how we travel between universes. You're his bargaining tool."

She moaned, both in pleasure and despair, and his lips met hers again. When she could pull away, she cradled his head in her hands, her face against his. "Stall for time. I think I can hack their system. I'll figure out a way to escape."

"We can't leave CERBO in their hands."

"One step at a time, Sam."

Chapter 17

When her last exam was finished the next day, Moira spent a few minutes in the library, returning her books and chatting with Grace and a few other girls. Giddiness warred with nervousness in her stomach, but she laughed with them, caught up in their easy excitement for the coming term break. Her preparations for getting away were complete. She had only to wait for Mr. Green's new chip, then she would go for a run. The track would be empty this late in the school year. No one would pay attention to her. She'd hidden a few things underground, near the school's border. A change of clothes, food, water. A little money. Her Pad. It would be safer to wipe its memory and leave it here, but the thought left her feeling lost. So she'd wiped its memory of personal information and tucked it among her clothes. Then she'd memorized her path to London, where she hoped to lose herself among the street population.

She passed through the main hall after her exam, her thoughts jumbled with fantasies of her meeting with Mr. Green. Her body tingled with the thought that from this point on their relationship would be different. True, she was still underage, but he was no longer her teacher. She was going into danger to escape a greater danger, and could not say when she would see him again. More than anything, she wanted to kiss him tonight, to feel his arms around her, his lips on hers. Would he allow it? Was it too dangerous to try? She had no doubt he would want to do it, but would he remain sensible and stay on the opposite end of the room?

Passing out of the main hall, Moira committed the cardinal sin: she wasn't paying attention.

So she didn't see him until he was in front of her, blocking her way. She knew who it was. Even without looking up, her heart skipped a beat, and she knew.

"Get in the car." His voice. She took a step back and dared a glance up that did not quite meet his eyes before she averted it. In a way, the rule about not looking a man in the eyes was convenient. If she had to look at him, she might throw up.

The proper response would have been a simple, "Yes, sir" but shock mangled her thoughts. "I'm not packed."

He took the step between them. "A few months away and you forget your place. Must I repeat myself?"

Her vision narrowed. His pants were gray, the shoes black, with a small scuff on the toe of the right one. "No sir," she said. She stepped past him and went outside. He was not following and she dared a glance back to see him talking to the office clerk. She turned toward the car and saw Missy Trotts coming toward her. Moira had often tutored the eight-year-old in math. Moira stopped her.

"Missy, please give Mr. Green a message the minute he gets back. You must watch for him; he'll be back around seven o'clock. Tell him my stepfather came. I had to go home early. Tell him exactly that, please? I ... I was supposed to grade some papers for him, but I won't be able to."

The little girl looked frightened, and Moira could only guess at what her own expression was like. She couldn't wait for Missy's response, but she tried to smile as she turned away. She heard Missy's whispered, "Okay. 'Bye, Moira,'" over his footsteps as he came out the door. If he suspected she'd talked to the little girl, he didn't seem to think anything of it. He waited next to the car to make sure she entered the backseat, then went around front and they drove away.

∞

He did not speak a word to her on the one-hour journey, but that was normal. He put a chip in the player, a recording of last Sunday's service. She sat still as she was expected to, her head bowed, which was also expected, while her mind raced a million miles an hour. Her breath was shallow, her skin clammy. Terror had never felt so close.

Why did he come early? Her mind refused to consider the possible reason, only the question raised itself. *What do I do? How do I get away? He came early! He'll never let me go back.*

She closed her eyes. *Don't cry. Tears will make it all worse. But what is going to happen?*

When the car pulled into the garage and stopped, she got out, watching herself as if from a distance. With her head bowed and her shoulders hunched, her school uniform hung limp on her frame. Her traitor mind gave her no instruction.

No one greeted her as they entered the house, although her mother stopped slicing carrots and turned to face her husband, waiting for his instructions. Moira hardly noticed her.

He said, "Moira, Ruth, my office," before heading that way. Moira tried to think, to come up with some idea of what to do, but she couldn't find her mind. She followed her mother's bare feet through the house, to his office.

He sat in the chair behind the desk. They stood, Moira beside and a step behind her mother, both with bowed heads. She noticed the desk was clear of papers, with his computer in its spot in the center, and his old paper Bible in its spot on the lower right-hand corner. He began to speak.

"The role of wife is the most blessed role God has given a woman. Her position as helpmeet to her husband is sacred, and is her full joy and completeness. The accomplishment of her wifely duties shall fill her days and nights, her humble work shall never cease in her quest for salvation. Her salvation is through her husband. His pleasure or displeasure in her is the judgment of God.

The wife shall submit to her husband, who is her Lord. She shall come hither when he calls, and go forth when he sends. Her spirit is his and he shall teach and prepare her spirit for its heavenly home. His word to her is as God's word, and she shall listen with all diligence and humility...."

He said more. He spoke for some time in his stern preaching voice that echoed righteousness. Moira listened, but could not hear the words. Her mind was locked away, watching them all from a distance, the man at the desk, the women standing before it with their heads bowed.

It was when he stood that she was able to again hear his words. "My wife, prepare your daughter for her holy marriage. She is to bathe to remove the stench of the world from her flesh. Dress her in the wedding garment and veil. Then, Moira, you will wait in this office, kneeling in prayer and holy supplication. When the bridegroom arrives, you will be taken to the Holy Church. The elders assemble now in prayer. You will submit to examination of your knowledge of wifely scripture. You will submit to the minister in humble examination to prove your virginity. If you have remained godly, you will be given in marriage. If examination proves you have sinned against God, and against your father, by taking a man, you will be taken out and stoned, according to holy scripture. Go. Prepare.

"Thy bridegroom cometh."

∞

The bath was just a bath, although she was told to wash her hair, as well. Her mind was still away, but getting closer. She could think a bit, although her thoughts were slow and jumbled.

Examination by the minister? The minister was her stepfather. Was he going to check to see if her hymen was intact, in front of all the other men? Well, better that than in private, where the bastard could do whatever he wanted. In fact, there would have to be other men. It would take several to hold her down. She'd never heard of such a thing being done, but of course the women would never talk about it.

She was a fast runner. If she ran, faster than she had ever run, she might escape all of them. If she didn't, the consequences... well, the consequences would be just one more beating in a lifetime of beatings. She would be injured though, and unable to escape. The marriage would take place. Running would only work if she got away.

Her mother slipped the "wedding garment" over her head, a brown sack-shaped dress, made from actual sackcloth. Then a veil, made of the same material, that covered her head and face, so that both breath and vision were curtailed. No shoes, of course. All females went without shoes, although they were permitted stockings.

Her mother led her to the office, and to the corner where she was to kneel. Her brother entered and sat on the sofa. "The bride," he taunted. "You don't deserve heaven. You'll never please your husband. You'll never make it."

As if that mattered to her. But she knew that wasn't the point. Humiliation was the point. Convincing her she was nothing.

That was the point.

∞

Andy stood in his dim cubicle at Sun Consortium's Oxford facility, and stretched his arms out to both sides. Nope. Not big enough. At Strickert, he'd had a classroom, a laboratory and an office containing a desk, sofa and table, a wall of bookshelves, and another wall of windows. But this cramped cubicle offered him a future bright with promise. The promise of the stars.

He sat before the monitor and allowed it to scan the chip in his arm. Andy *Green reporting for duty.* The monitor beeped a welcome and resolved into his first set of instructions, the familiar blue background and yellow sun of The Sun Consortium hovering over the text forming on the screen. A voice spoke in his ear, giving him the verbal version in case he was too busy to look at the monitor. "Welcome, Andrew Green. We are happy to have you on board. Your personnel file reveals we need an updated address for you, as your current address expires tomorrow at 5:00 p.m., GMT." *Well, yes but I need an address, first. Haven't found a place to live, yet.* "This requirement will be waived for the duration of your first assignment, listed below."

That was strange. Andy watched the screen scroll down to the "Current Assignments" section. The Voice continued, "Report to Headquarters, Belfast by close of business tomorrow afternoon. Accommodations are provided at Fitzgerald's Hotel. Your travel voucher has been uploaded to your Chip. See your supervisor for details."

101

Belfast! The neutrinos. It could be nothing else.

Peeking down the hallway, he saw that his supervisor, Joe Beauchamp, was in his office and the door was open. He wandered down and presented himself in the doorway. Joe was talking to someone on his Pad, with a privacy screen shimmering off of his black, bald pate, but he waved Andy in with a cheerful hand. Andy took a seat and waited, thinking through the schedule. He had to be in Belfast at close of business, say no later than six p.m. It was only an hour's flight. He'd just have to make sure he took care of things early. His classes were done with their exams. He had only to file the final grades to finish his contract with Strickert. This also signaled the end of his living arrangements with them. Tomorrow had been slated as a moving day.

Worry for Moira was making him anxious, though. He'd hoped to keep a discreet eye on her as she made her way to London. His modified chip would allow him, and no one else, to track her, although he had no intention of letting her know that. He could track her from Belfast, but if she needed help, he wouldn't be immediately available.

Joe finished a few minutes later and shut off the privacy screen, turning his chair to eye his newest recruit with something approaching pity.

"Some folks are just luckier than others, Andy, and it seems like your luck is the worst of all. Most people get to at least settle in for a day before the powers-that-be start sending them around the globe."

Andy shrugged. "It's just Belfast. Not quite around the globe, yet." He remembered he wasn't supposed to know anything about the neutrinos. "What's it about?"

Joe shook his head. "Not the details, I'm afraid. Just that they've found something and it's up your alley. Neutrinos acting strangely, that sort of thing. They want you to check it out."

"I'll find out more when I get there?"

"Something like that. Did you download the travel voucher?" At Andy's nod, Joe waved him on. "They don't need you to report until tomorrow afternoon. You'll have most of the day to take care of whatever. Try to be there by four o'clock or so."

Back in his cubicle, Andy stared at his monitor a few moments, biting the inside of his cheek thoughtfully. *Belfast may be the best answer. If Moira's going to run off, anyway, maybe I can use this chance to get her out of town, so she won't be on her own.*

The more he thought about it, the more plausible it seemed. Logging out, Andy left to make some arrangements.

∞

As she knelt in her corner, Moira's mind began to come back to her, bringing with it a rage against herself. She should have run away.

She'd made all those plans and didn't try any of it. Mr. Green said he would help and she never gave him a chance.

She made an effort to put this line of thought aside. It was as useless as the catatonia had been. She had to deal with the situation as it was. Right now, it was pretty bad, but as long as she was alive, she owed it to herself to keep trying. Her stupor had made it far too easy for her stepfather. She needed to start making it difficult. But she needed to be smart about it.

In general, she would not be touched unless they felt physical coercion was necessary. So there would be chances. Brief chances, true, but if she kept close watch, there would be a chance to run. It had to come down to that.

She clamped down on sudden hysterical laughter. *Close watch? With this veil covering my head? Run with no shoes?* Despair began to eat at her again, until another thought came to her. She let it come and watched it grow, as calmness settled around her. It was risky. It was probably suicidal, but it might work.

During every church service, there was a fire burning at the altar. It would be the work of a few seconds to knock the brazier over, perhaps get one of the burning sticks to use as a weapon or defense. The turmoil should buy her time. The shoe problem would not be solved, but she'd have to use what was at hand.

The office door opened and she heard footsteps, then his voice.

"Thy bridegroom has desired to see thy face, as is his right. Stand and remove thy veil."

Shaking, she stood and turned to face them, lifting the veil over her head, keeping her gaze on the floor.

"Art thou satisfied, Wayland?" her stepfather asked, and Moira felt a surge of fear so powerful it nearly knocked her over. *Wayland? Wayland Connor?* A man so vicious, his wife and daughters were never seen without a broken bone or burns. They wept constantly, either from pain or from despair. He had once, at some imagined slight, dragged his wife into a side room of the church and raped her, hitting her all the while with a ruler, until it broke. He had not bothered to even close the door and the other women had stood stunned, covering their eyes or ears, until her stepfather came over and told them to leave, that "it is not our place to interfere between a man and his wife." Dear God, had his wife died?

Moira's head shot up, startling the men and her brother, who was still in the room. All she saw was the terrifying man who stared at her in surprise.

"No!" The word burst from her and she tensed to run. "Not him!"

He moved. She saw him coming, saw his arm draw back, saw the fist, but had no time to register any of it, before the fist struck her stomach, driving all thought, all fear, all emotion, from her mind in a storm of pain. She sensed she was falling, flying through the air until she slammed against the wall, and crashed to the floor, her head hitting hard.

No breath came. She couldn't move, even to touch her stomach, or force air into her lungs. He was beside her. She had no strength to even contemplate what was coming next. He grabbed her hair, his knuckles tight against her skull, pulling her head back with a jerk that she had no breath to gasp against.

He bent down and whispered in her ear. "You'll learn. It doesn't matter to me what's broken, as long as the cunt works." Another stab of pain then, as he bit her ear, hard. A shudder passed through her as he licked her ear, his tongue probing sickeningly inside. He laughed, a low and menacing sound.

She fainted.

Chapter 18

Missy Trotts took her duty seriously, seating herself on the small wall outside the Admin building at exactly six-forty-five. Moira had said Mr. Green would be back around seven. She didn't want to miss him.

Missy was only eight, but she knew what fear looked like. She'd seen that look on her mother's face, the night the security people came to question her father about something. That's what Moira looked like when she got in the car with her stepfather. Maybe he worked for Security.

It was good Missy came out early, because she only waited five minutes before Mr. Green's old red Toyota came rattling up the drive. The girls always laughed at his car. It was at least twenty years old and had to be plugged in to charge it up. Missy didn't care, though. Mr. Green was nice.

He looked surprised when she came up to him after he parked, staring down at her as she blocked his path. He looked like he wanted to hurry. "Hi, Missy. Did your exams go okay?"

She nodded. "Yes sir. But I'm s'posed to tell you that Moira had to go home early and can't grade your papers."

He seemed to stiffen, like one of the columns behind them. Then he squatted down to look at her and his face was very serious.

"When? When did she leave? Who picked her up?"

Missy blinked. That was the rest of the message that she forgot to give him. "Her stepfather came. It was about two o'clock."

The fear showed on Mr. Green's face, too. But he just patted her shoulder and stood. "Thank you, Missy. I'll take care of it."

She watched him as he left, running over to the teacher's dormitories, and breathed a sigh of relief. Somehow, she thought he really would take care of it.

Damn. Damn, damn, damn, damn! His mind a whirl, that was the only word Andy could think of as he raced to his rooms. Once there, he did the essentials, as if his subconscious already knew the plan and guided his steps. He changed into dark clothes—blue jeans and a black sweatshirt and his dark running shoes. With no idea what to expect, he threw an overnight kit into his backpack: a change of clothes, toothbrush and paste, his comb. He had a flashlight in the car. He had spent the last two hours in his lab at Oxford, creating Moira's false ID chip. That was also in the car, already in its syringe, along with a set of tools for microscopic work. As an afterthought, he grabbed his raincoat and two extra sweatshirts. One never knew.

Back to the car. Missy had gone in. Good. There were a few girls around, but most were either in their dorms packing, or in town celebrating the end of term. He drove off nonchalantly, as if all was normal, but once clear of the gates, he floored it, causing the computer to scream in protest. He kept the speed just below the limit where the onboard monitor would insist on taking over the driving, judging him under the influence of one thing or another. He couldn't block the tracking device, but he did keep the navigator ignorant of his destination. He knew how to get to Chelmsford. Once there, he'd have to program in the address, and hope the system would not automatically alert the residents that a visitor was coming.

He thought of Moira, afraid, and perhaps hurt. The unbidden picture of someone hitting her caused him to increase speed and swerve to pass a car in front. The monitor pinged. "Do you need assistance to reach your destination?" The voice was calm and friendly, but he didn't let that fool him. He eased off the speed, and took a few deep breaths.

"No, there's no problem."

He mustn't think of her. He mustn't think of someone hurting her. He had to concentrate on something that would keep him calm, and driving normally. At the second warning, his Chip had begun sending his vital signs to the onboard monitor; another small increase in tension and he would lose control to the auto pilot.

So instead, he thought about his steps to save her, deciding that assuming victory was his best bet. A plan began to form.

∞

Full darkness had fallen by the time he approached the house indicted by his nav. He parked on the street a few houses down, and stared at his destination. Lights shone in two windows, one downstairs, one upstairs. The neighborhood was quiet. Street lights cast pools of light every thirty feet or so. Somewhere a door closed, somewhere else a spate of music, occasionally, he heard a distant voice.

What were his choices? Ring the bell and ask for her? Ring the bell and ask for her stepfather? Try to talk him into handing her over? No, no, and no.

How would a home like this be secured? The neighborhood was not wealthy, but neither was it poor. The people who lived on this street would all have jobs with sufficient income. Security systems would be good, but not top-of-the-line. Could he talk their system into believing he belonged there? A guest, perhaps?

Reaching into the back, he pulled forward the small box tucked under his raincoat. He slipped his penlight and the syringe into his pocket and pulled out his Pad. Moving quietly, he eased out of the car, into a biting wind. He didn't try to remain hidden. Surreptitious behavior would call him to the attention of the street monitor. But someone walking down the street, engrossed in a game on his Pad— the monitor would not be interested in that.

This game would get him arrested, if he were caught playing it. A couple of years ago, he and a few of his classmates at Oxford had challenged each other to develop a search program on their Pads. Such a program was illegal without proper authorization, but they kept it a friendly competition to see who could do it fastest. Extra points were awarded for efficiency and elegance. In the end, Serena Torbeny had beat them all, with a program able to search an entire two-story building for vital signs, requiring just a few seconds of scanning time. He'd charmed her into showing him some of her tricks, resulting in an interesting week of electronic and sexual manipulation. The sex hadn't lasted, as she started dating a TA in O-Chem. But he'd kept the program on his Pad.

Aiming the search signals toward the house, he located eight people in various rooms. The program wasn't fine-tuned enough to differentiate between male and female, child or adult. How could he discover which of those bodies was Moira?

Wait. Two more bodies came into focus as he neared the house. They were around back and were moving. Underneath the house? It made no sense. Stopping just before a street light and remaining in the dark, near a hedge, he watched the Pad in confusion before it dawned on him ... they must be in a cellar. Leaving that screen, he went into the programming and called up a signal to let him talk to the house's security system. He felt himself sweating at the danger. If the system were too sensitive, it would scream bloody murder at the attempt.

The system was nervous: *who was that?* He tickled it a bit, reassuring, his fingers flying on the keys: I am on your list of acceptable persons. The system resisted: parameters do not match. He repeated his input, fingers slipping with sweat, offering more reassurances. The system seemed to sigh: *what do you want?* He assured it he just wanted in the yard, to go around back. It took a minute, but the system acquiesced, stretching to include him in its perimeter. Good. With the house pacified, the street system would ignore his movement into the yard.

Sticking to the shadows near the hedges, he crept around the house until he saw cellar doors waiting open in the ground next to the building. He squatted and watched his Pad. And damn if the screen didn't now register a third body in there. Cooler than the others, with weaker life signs. His Pad had not detected it through the bulk of the house. He felt his heart pounding. Was that Moira? Was she hurt? Fuck them! They'd only had her for a few hours and already she was hurt?

Shadows moved in the open doorway and two figures stepped leisurely into view, coming up the stairs. Two men, about his age, talking and laughing. They shut the doors and threw a bolt across, plunging the cellar into darkness. He held his breath and heard them as they crossed to the back door:

"She got out of it, tonight."

"Won't work again tomorrow, I guarantee it."

Their voices ended as the door slammed shut. Andy realized he was shaking, his eyes darting back to the Pad and the weak vitals it displayed. He watched, biding his time. The light downstairs went out. He counted to one hundred, checked the vital signs, then dashed for the cellar.

His shaking added to the difficulty of moving quietly, but he hoped the wind would cover any noise he made. It seemed to take forever to remove the bolt and open the right side. As he did so, the cellar light came on, but he heard no movement. Afraid the light would alert someone in the house, he frantically tapped at his Pad, instructing the house to turn it off. Easing the second door to the ground, he took out his penlight and descended the stairway. It was a root cellar, cold, dirt floor and walls, with shelves along the sides, stocked with jars of food and piles of vegetables.

At the end, next to a basket of potatoes, lay Moira. She wore a brown dress, her feet and legs bare, with no blanket to cover her. She was on her side, curled into a fetal position. If she knew he was there, she was not showing it. Her eyes were closed and she wasn't moving. Was she asleep? Surely the light would have awakened her. He touched her face, gently.

"Moira?"

No response. Shit! What was wrong? He didn't have a medical monitor. Making a quick decision, he took the syringe out and lifted her left arm. No time for finesse: he inserted the modified ID chip quickly, trying to be gentle. She stirred as he plunged the stopper home.

"Moira?" His voice shook. "It's Andy. Wake up, Moira."

She came to abruptly, turning her head to him, terror stark on her face, then freezing as she stared at him. He put the syringe away and reached for her. "We have to go. Can you walk?"

She touched his arm. "It's you." Her voice was weak, soft.

"Yes." He slipped his arm under her shoulders. "We have to go *now*. Quietly."

Her hand clenched his shoulder and she started to rise, stopping halfway with a quickly swallowed yelp of pain, collapsing back to the ground.

"Moira!" Desperate, he picked her up and hurried to the stairs. Somehow, he got up them and raced across the yard to the hedges, unable to run as silently as he needed to. He didn't wait, just kept going to the street, afraid to even listen for sounds behind him. She moaned, stifling the sound as she buried her face in his shoulder and held on.

He arrived at the car, whispered desperately to it, instructed it to open the passenger door. His voice was too soft and didn't register at first, but after a second try, the door popped open. He placed her inside and fastened the restraint, miserably aware of the tears streaking her face, the teeth clamped over her bottom lip as she tried to stay quiet. Christ almighty, what had they *done* to her?

A glance at the house revealed it was still dark, but he wasn't taking any chances. Keeping the car lights off, which really pissed off the on-board monitor, he backed down the street to the intersection. Once there, he turned the lights on, and drove away with sedate care.

He glanced at her. She had turned a bit in the restraint to stare at him, clutching her stomach. In the half-dark, half-light of passing street lamps, her eyes looked glazed, and she was crying in shuddering breaths. He touched the top of her head.

"It will be all right. I'll take care of you."

"You came." The words sounded strangled around her sobs. "You got me out. It's really you."

He fought back tears. "It should never have come to this. I should have been there."

He felt her touch him, a brief caress on his arm, before the hand fell to the seat next to him. He glanced over to see her tear-stained face relaxed, eyes closed, head rolling against the seat back. Had she fainted? His lips tightened and he stared at the road. He didn't dare use the auto-pilot, too afraid of being tracked. Just drive. Get her to safety.

Just drive.

Chapter 19

"Dr. Warner, you are asking us to believe an unbelievable story." The spokesman for the rebels, a misplaced Dubliner who said his name was Phil, had downed half his pint in two long swallows before greeting Dinnie when she first approached him. Now he drained his glass and shoved it toward his partner, who was manning the pitcher while ignoring Dinnie.

She didn't think the partner was really ignoring her, but she made an effort to play their game, and directed her comments only to Phil. "I know it's hard to accept," she said, needing to shout to be heard over the live band howling on the stage of the busy pub. "That's why I went through the danger of smuggling the data out." She tapped the storage chip with an angry forefinger and glared at the arrogant fellow across the table from her. It had taken weeks to get this meeting set up. The situation had morphed into the biggest event the human race had yet seen, and the rebels sent this joker? She was risking her life and they weren't even taking her seriously.

"I swear it's all true," she went on, "and Feldman is planning on ways to use the travelers and their technology for Sun's, and his own, benefit. I suggest that you take these data to one of your physicists. I'm sure you have one or two working for you. It needs to be someone with the knowledge and experience to understand what these data are saying."

"Oh, aye, that's true enough." Phil sat back, with one arm resting on the back of his booth, and regarded Dinnie from under greasy brown bangs. It annoyed her that he didn't have to shout to be heard. "It might help your case if you could produce a piece of this equipment you've been talking about. A probe, the time machine, the wee green men ... ?" The hand on the booth waved in a nonchalant circle, and Pitcher Bloke snickered.

"They're as human as you and I." Dinnie sighed and sat back into the booth. She'd done her best, and what she'd done was enough to get her executed. She shivered, her hands twitching toward the chip.

Phil reached it before her, tossing it into the air and catching it. Dinnie watched him, her heart pounding with booming pain.

Pitcher Bloke surprised her when he spoke, his accent marking him as British. "We'll examine the data thoroughly, Dr. Warner. What you're saying happened is not probable, but I will admit that it's possible." He held out his hand and Phil gave him the chip. He slipped into a pocket without a glance.

Phil grinned at Dinnie, salacious and dangerous all at once. "If you get more information, let us know. Otherwise, it's best you forget this conversation happened."

Dinnie nodded, holding her hands closed in tight fists to hide her shaking. *In over my head, and there's no way out but through.*

Angels and saints protect me.

∞

Somehow, Moira knew the rocking had stopped, but dizziness kept her floating even as she tried to open her eyes. *Mr. Green.* Memory came flooding back, and she came to with a gasp and shock of pain. But the pain didn't matter, because her eyes showed her it was true. Mr. Green was next to her, kneeling outside the passenger door, reaching to loosen the restraint that held her in place.

The pain kept her still. "You came." That seemed to be the only thing her mind could process.

He moved the restraint, slipped an arm around her shoulders. "Yes. Can you walk, Moira? It's just a few feet. I can help, but the monitors will be suspicious if I carry you."

She gripped his arm and sat up, but stopped as pain lanced through her stomach. She wanted to scream, but that would have hurt more. Instead, she moaned, a sound forced out beyond her control.

He gasped. "Jesus! How do I help you?"

"I can do it," she said. "Just slowly. Please, just slowly."

He helped her turn and slide her legs outside the car. She sat a moment on the edge of the seat, her hands on his chest, head bowed, waiting for the pain to recede back to a deep ache. When she thought she could move again, she nodded at him. "Help me up. Slow."

It felt like a chain was hooked to opposite sides of her stomach and was pulling, stretching her past endurance. Her whole body shook, her legs nearly collapsing. It was impossible to stand straight and Mr. Green stepped close to her, his arms around her, holding her upright. She wrapped her arms around his waist, moaning.

"One step, Moira. This way."

She scuffed her foot forward and he continued to talk her through it, one step at a time. She focused on his voice and her feet, on each step forward at his command. He walked backwards, guiding her, holding her up. He stopped and issued a "door open" command, but the mechanical voice of the monitor stopped them.

"Do you need assistance?"

"Nah." Mr. Green sounded incongruously nonchalant. "She just had too much to drink. Right, love?"

"Yeah," Moira managed to gasp. "Too much ..."

The door opened, and they continued a few slow feet to a lift. "Second floor," Mr. Green said, holding her closer, taking her weight, keeping her upright. "Just a little further," he whispered.

It hurt too much to nod, but she shuffled with him into the lift. As they rose to the next floor, she took a careful, deep breath, relieved to have lungs full of air. Too soon, the lift stopped and she had to move again, aware only of a thin, blue carpet under her feet as she moved with Mr. Green into the hall. An odor of cheap antiseptic and pesticide made her breathe shallow through her mouth. He kept an arm around her waist, half carrying her to a door two down from the lift. She leaned against him, feeling his rustling movements as he fumbled a cardkey from his pocket and swiped it in the lock. She closed her eyes, concentrating on that movement, on the soft fabric of his sweatshirt, and the touch of his body against hers. He was really here.

Once inside, he picked her up. She bit back a moan, clinging to his neck. His walk caused dizzy nausea to grip her, but at last he stopped and lowered her onto a bed. She curled around her stomach, gasping into the pillow. He lay a blanket over her and she felt his fingers, gentle on her head.

"I'm going to get a med kit," he said. "I'll be right back."

She nodded, but he was already gone. She could hear his movements, opening and closing cabinets in another room. It hurt to raise her head, but she studied what she could see of the room. She lay on a red blanket, and over the edge of the bed was more of the thin, blue carpet. A dresser stood against the opposite wall, its top cluttered with socks, a docking station and a Pad. A bong lay on its side in the corner between the dresser and the door to a bathroom. Mr. Green came through that door with quick strides, placing the soft med container on the floor as he sat with gentle care on the bed.

She glanced up at him, struck by the quiet, haunted look on his face as he gazed at her. His mouth was tight as he reached to move her hair back from her ear. She flushed from head to toe as she remembered how it was injured, and her hand lifted to cover the ear in automatic protest. "Don't look at it," she said, closing her eyes so she wouldn't have to see his face.

"I need to treat it," he said. He was whispering, his fingers stroking her head, but not going near the ear. "It needs to be cleaned, you've got an infection starting."

She flushed hot with humiliation. "Please ..." But she moved her hand to cover her eyes, wiping away the tears that welled up.

"It's all right, Moira," she heard him murmur, along with the tearing sound of a sterile packet being opened. "I'll be careful."

He was, too, although she hissed at the stinging medicine. She kept her eyes covered, his gentle touch a sharp contrast to the memory of Wayland's bite and probing tongue. That contrast made her cry harder, tears escaping the hand that covered her face.

Mr. Green's distraught voice broke through. "I'm sorry, dear. I'll be done soon, and it won't hurt anymore."

"No," she gasped. "It's okay. You're not hurting me." That wasn't quite true, of course, but the pain was not his fault, and it wasn't why she was crying, either. But she couldn't force herself to tell him how it happened.

At last, he stopped and fumbled around in the kit. She sensed he'd bent down near her face, his fingers tickling her head. He spoke quietly. "This wasn't your fault, Moira. Whoever did this is a monster. Don't let yourself feel ashamed about it." His fingers continued to stroke her head. "I won't ask you what happened, but you know you can tell me, if you want to. You know how I feel about you, Moira. Something like this makes no difference at all."

His words caused more tears to come, but she stayed silent.

He sat up. "I want to put some Nu-skin on it, but I'm not an expert at this. Do you want me to try?"

She nodded. "If you think it needs it."

"I think it does. You'll have to be as still as you can." A teasing lilt entered his voice. "It would be best if your ears match, as much as possible."

She nodded again and tried to relax, taking a deep breath, but wincing at the pain this brought to her stomach. Mr. Green hesitated and she waved a few fingers at him. "I'll be still."

He took his time, his touch light. She felt the tickle of the Nu-skin as it adhered to her ear, and the nano-cells embedded in its polymers sought out the ends of her damaged tissue. Mr. Green's concern was primarily cosmetic. The Nu-skin would heal the injured tissue, but a careless placement could leave noticeable wrinkles or creases. At this point, Moira didn't much care about that, but she knew she might care later.

What did 'later' mean for her, now? For Mr. Green? If they were caught, he could go to prison. He'd risked everything to help her.

At last, he sighed and sat back, hands resting in his lap. Moira glanced out of the side of her eye. "Done?"

He shrugged, then took a penlight out of his pocket and examined his work. "I think it's okay." He stroked her head.

Moira kept her eyes on the floor. "When he showed up at school, I was trapped." She whispered the words to the air in front of her. On her head, Mr. Green's fingers stilled. He didn't say anything, but after a moment, he started stroking her again. She continued. "I don't know what was wrong with me. I just couldn't think. I could hardly move. I did what he said. I had a chance to leave a message with Missy, but that was all."

"She told me," Mr. Green said. "The minute I drove up."

Moira squeezed her eyes tight. "He was going to marry me off. To this awful, awful man. That's who hurt me. Because I protested. He punched me in the stomach and he ... he ..." her hand jerked toward her ear as a flood of humiliation washed over her again, at the thought of his tongue licking her. That was almost worse than the bite. *I own you,* that lick had said. *You are mine to use as I wish.* She shuddered with the strength of the fury and shame battling within her. She'd been so damn helpless.

"He hit you in the stomach? Does it still hurt?" Mr. Green asked.

She nodded. "It hurts a lot. I can hardly move."

He pulled something else out of the medkit. "Let me run a Feinberger over it."

Her hand jerked and she grabbed her dress, holding it down. "No." Feinbergers could read internal injuries by just scanning, but they had to work against bare skin. She wasn't about to lift her dress up.

Mr. Green didn't seem to get it. "We need to see if you're injured, if there's any internal bleeding."

"No." She felt her face flame and she couldn't look at him, but she reached for the probe. "I'll do it. I have to use the loo, anyway."

He released his grip on it, but his jaw was tight with uncertainty.

She reached for his arm, to pull herself to a sitting position. Clenching pain made her stop and he grabbed her shoulders to hold her up. She forced herself to sit. "I want to take a bath."

"Moira, you can't even sit up ..."

"I want to take a bath." It seemed important, and she refused to budge. "I'll manage it."

He blew a breath out, but nodded. "Let me start the water for you. Then I'll go dig up some clothes. I'm sure there's some spare jeans and shirts lying around." He stood, watching her. "You practice sitting there. See if you're up to it."

She nodded, her hands gripping the sheets as she leaned against the headboard. She heard him rummaging in another room, drawers opening and closing. What was this place?

He returned in a few minutes, a pile of clothes in hand. "I think these will fit," he said, heading into the bathroom. "I'll leave them on the shelf in here."

"Okay." She heard water start in the tub, so she didn't try to say more. Tightening her lips, she forced her legs to move around so they hung off the bed. Stabbing pain shot through her stomach, and she sat still, breathing in shallow gasps. Mr. Green's hand under her arm made her look up.

"Maybe you should just rest." His eyes betrayed his worry and sadness, and she managed a small smile.

"Just help me up."

It took all her effort to not cry or gasp, but she stayed silent as he helped her stand and walked with her to the lavatory. At the door, she gripped the doorjamb and lifted her chin to look him in the eyes. "Ignore any groaning you hear." She tried to sound light-hearted, knowing she only sounded grotesque. "If I really need help, I'll say so."

His sad expression didn't budge, but he nodded. She moved inside and closed the door, pausing to lean against it and just breathe. She wanted to sink to the floor and rest, but she knew if she did, she'd just stay there. With great care, she lifted the horrid gunnysack up and over her head, quite unsuccessful at holding back a moan. Shaking, she managed to sit on the toilet, and fumbled with the Feinberger. When the ON light turned green, she moved it toward her stomach, gasping in shock at the solid mass of blue and black that covered her entire abdomen. No wonder it hurt.

She sat straight, running the boxy probe up and down, over and across, trying to get every inch. It was hard to go slow enough since she was shaking like a sonic cleaner. Twice, the probe slipped and tapped her skin, making her jump with pain.

At last, the light began blinking to indicate it was finished. Still shaking, Moira squinted at the display. Mr. Green had set it for layman mode, so in plain English, the probe informed her she had massive bruising and was still bleeding internally. Under "Treatment", she learned that the best course was to seek immediate medical care. However the bleeding was slow, and she had the option of resting, while performing Feinburger checks every two hours, to track the rate of hemorrhage, and monitor her temperature. Injuries of this kind often healed on their own in a few days, although she could expect to be sore for a few weeks or more. The display continued with advice about diet and general care, including the cryptic note that bathing, especially in warm water, was not recommended, as this might increase the bleeding.

So much for her bath. She was dusty from the cellar, though, so she climbed into the tub and washed off as well as she could without immersing herself. Then she examined the clothes Mr. Green had given her. The pants were too long, but the real problem was the pain in her stomach when she tried to button them. It would be impossible. Fortunately, the sweatshirt was long and loose. It would have to cover the open pants.

She had no shoes. As it turned out, Mr. Green had a plan for that.

"I have to clear out my room at the academy," he told her when she asked about it after sinking wearily onto the bed. "I'll do that early tomorrow. If you tell me where you've hidden your supplies, I'll sneak out there and get them."

The idea made her nervous, but she had so many necessary items buried out there: toiletries, warm clothing, extra socks, shoes ... So she told him where to find her cache. "If you stay to the right, the loganberry bushes will hide you from the buildings. Make sure no one sees you."

He smiled and covered her with another blanket. "Cross my heart. Now what did the Feinburger say?"

She gave him an abbreviated version, hoping he wouldn't demand to see the injury. But he just nodded, his face thoughtful. Then he patted her shoulder. "Get some sleep. We'll see how you are in the morning. I will be right outside your door all night. If you need anything at all, just call."

"All right." She touched his arm. "What is this place? Whose clothes did you give me?"

His face flushed pink. She could swear he was embarrassed. "Just student apartments. Some friends of mine rent this place, and several of us have a key. Um ... the clothes were somebody's ... girlfriend's."

Moira tried to cover her own embarrassment. "Oh," was all she managed to say.

"Sleep," he commanded, heading for the door. "We'll discuss our next step in the morning."

Chapter 20

By noon the next day, they were ready to go. Mr. Green had given her some warm cereal for breakfast, but she ate just half of it. She did force herself to drink some tea, and then a glass of water. The Feinberger showed that she was still hemorrhaging, but the rate had not increased, so she told him she wasn't worse. She could hardly move from the pain.

Now, however, she had to move, and she had to look as normal as possible. Mr. Green's instructions were explicit. "The chip I injected into you last night holds your new identity. It's rather hasty. It won't get you out of the UK. But it should be fine for travel to Northern Ireland. They'll just do a cursory scan."

He helped her walk to the car. "The new chip only covers over your old ID. It doesn't eliminate it. So a deeper scan will show a discrepancy, which means you have to not give them a reason to *do* a deeper scan. Your new name is Sandra Williams. You were born in Brighton on April 14, 2061 so you are nineteen years old. You're a student at Oxford, and you're on your way to Belfast to visit your aunt and uncle, Peter and Blythe O'Connor. All of that is programmed into your travel documents."

She nodded, hardly able to think over the pounding of her heart. "What if they ask where my parents are?"

"You shrug and say they're at home in Brighton. Act casual. I know you've never done any traveling, but they don't usually ask questions. They don't care basically, as long as your chip and papers are in order. Just keep that in mind, and act accordingly. One other thing ..."

They had reached the car and he paused before opening the door for her. "You and I are both college students. I'm travelling for business, you're on your way to see relatives. It's not a problem that we know each other—we're both physics students, after all." He grinned at her, and she managed a weak smile in return. "So," he went on, "we need to be on a first name basis. Call me Andy. I," he sighed, "will try to remember to call you Sandy." He shrugged. "We can act like it's a running joke, in fact. Andy and Sandy, friends from Oxford."

Moira nodded and settled into the car. She caught Andy's worried expression as he watched her cautious movements. "Can I continue the charade of drinking too much?" she asked. "Now I have a hangover?"

He helped her buckle her seatbelt, as he shook his head. "Hangovers are too easy to treat. But if you tell them you're sick, they won't let you travel." He knelt by the car, and touched her face. "Can you do this, Moira? Can you stand straight and walk without the pain showing? Everything depends on not arousing the guards' suspicions."

She stared at him, taking in the bit of dark hair that always curled over his forehead, the deep brown eyes, serious and worried, the too-big nose, and the too-long chin over those so-tempting lips ... and she nodded. "I will, Mist ... Andy." Her nerves tingled when she said his name, but she forced herself to concentrate on his concern. "I'm sure I can manage for a few minutes at a time. While we're driving, you need to tell me every detail about getting past the guards and onto the train. Everything you can think of."

∞

Moira was relieved to see that Andy was right about the guards. The bored girl at the checkpoint just waved a detector over Moira's arm, glanced deliberately from Moira's picture ID (with the name, Sandra Williams, on it) to Moira's face, and handed everything back, gesturing for the next person in line. "Have a good trip Miss Williams."

She would not have called it a good trip, but Moira was at least able to rest as the aerotrain made its silent way across England. The jump over the Irish Sea was nerve-racking, as she had never done it before, and late spring storms ripped the atmosphere around them. Andy sat beside her and read the book she had given him, apparently unconcerned at the buffeting, so she assumed the conditions were not any worse than usual. It did take all her concentration to not wince against the sharp pains some of the bumps caused her.

Once past the guards at the Belfast station, she let herself bend over against the pain, holding her coat tight against the gale tearing through the port. Andy carried her pack. "I'll hire a car," he said, his face creased with worry. "At the hotel, we'll continue to act as college friends on holiday. Just stay with me and try to act normal. We're almost there."

∞

Moira wondered how Andy would get her past hotel security, but when at last she was able to sink onto the bed in his room, she no longer cared what he'd done. She moaned in relief at giving in to the pain, lying curled up on her side, with her arms wrapped around her stomach. She trembled under the force of the spasms.

Andy covered her with a blanket, then knelt next to the bed, and placed a light hand on her forehead. "I've got to report over at headquarters," he said. "I don't know how long they'll keep me today. Will you be all right?"

She managed a nod. "I just want to stay still. Sleep, if I can."

"The med kit is right here on the table," he told her. "There's one dose of painkiller left. I'll try to get more while I'm out. And I'll look for a doctor, too."

Her eyes flew open. "No. A doctor will report me."

"I'll find one that won't. But you need treatment."

"No. I'll be fine. Just don't chance it." She stared into his eyes, just inches from hers. Saw him hesitate, and wondered if he would lie.

He didn't. "Listen. One of the things we need to do is find a rebel cell. That's essential to getting you to safety. I'm expecting they'll have a doctor among them. But I have to look, and there is some danger in that. I promise I'll be careful."

He stood and she closed her eyes again. "Sleep," he said. "I'll bring dinner back. If I'm going to be later than six, I'll call you."

∞

The guard at Sun's reception office was bored, and made no effort at small talk while Andy waited for his guide. He used the time to thumb his Pad. He knew one person in Belfast who might help Moira, and who wouldn't talk. He sent a short text requesting a meeting.

He turned when the door slid open. A thin woman with spiky blonde hair, and dressed all in black—sweater, jeans, and skaters—thrust a hand toward him. "Andy Green? I'm Dinnie Warner. Come with me and I'll catch you up on your assignment as we walk."

He shook her hand, then she was off through the door. He scrambled after her before it closed and left him trapped with the guard again.

She talked in rapid-fire counter-point to her steps as they hurried down the hall. "I run the neutrino detection lab. I've seen your work, and I think you can jump in without a lot of background, but if you need clarification of anything, shout it out." She flashed her wrist at a security point, not stopping her forward rush, clearing the barrier just seconds after the laser beam flashed off. "You'll have a few hours today to examine the data. First thing tomorrow, we'll put you to work with our subject matter expert. He's ... visiting ... as well, but we're prepping the third-floor lab for the two of you to use."

Another wrist flash, this one before a steel door that slid open with alacrity. Andy suspected nothing around here dared refuse to work in a timely fashion when Dinnie Warner expected something. She waved him into a chair that faced a green screen, and stood beside him, speaking to the air. "Ari, run ID scan for Andrew Green."

A female-robo voice answered. "Scan running. Hold still, please."

Andy froze as a red laser beam surged over him, from head to toe. In three seconds, the voice spoke again. "State your name, please."

"Andrew Green." His voice was raspy.

It didn't seem to bother the AI. "ID scan complete," she stated. "Subject entered into security parameters." Andy thought he detected a note of satisfaction.

Dinnie handed him VR goggles and gloves. "I'll leave you to it. You'll have access to all we know at this point. Look it over and we'll talk when you're ready. Do you have any questions before you start?"

Andy slipped on the gloves. "No ma'am. Let me see what you've got."

Her eyes flickered to the ceiling. "Ari, run data file X3-2080NT6, set to Mr. Green's control."

He caught her sharp nod just before the goggles covered his eyes. Then he was lost in patterns of neutrinos.

∞

Sarah took her dinner tray to the little table tucked into the corner of her room. She placed her tablet on the table, directly above her plate. A cup of tea went in the spot just to its right. With everything in place, she sat with her back to the corner, facing the room and the solid steel door that kept her locked in.

This corner was the closest she could find to a blind spot for the room's sensors. It wasn't perfect, but with the tablet providing both cover and excuse, she had a few minutes to fiddle with the remote she had palmed after they'd let her exercise in a workout room down the hall. The room's camera would show her back, but as long as she took a bite or sip once in a while, and read occasionally, the guard wouldn't bother to check on her.

Her cursory inspection of the medical equipment which they had used to examine her, and of the machines in the gym, convinced her their energy substrate functioned on solar or fusion power. Their hardware used a similar encoding technology to what was used in her own timeline. Since there were only a limited number of ways to talk to a computer, she was fairly confident that she could get on friendly terms with the AI running this feckin' nightmare. She just needed to reach the heart of the bloody thing using a simple machine that could do little more than talk to a virtual hydro-planer.

A wire she had wiggled out of the bed frame became a low-tech sensor used to probe the guts of the remote. Fifteen minutes into her surreptitious dinner, she'd managed to hack into the security system far enough to display a list on her computer's screen, showing the names of anyone in the hallway. So far, the only name on the list belonged to her guard. Well and good.

Opening a separate window, she urged the remote to expand its range and let her code-bunny search where it wanted, then display the information in map form. Her bunny was blocked by the system's firewall, showing on her screen as a gremlin holding a shield. She instructed the bunny to give the gremlin a candy code, one her systems at home found irresistible. The gremlin, having never been exposed to it, instantly became the bunny's best mate, stepping aside to let it move further into the system. She left it a trickle of code to play with in reward.

Her map grew, showing her the entire wing which housed her, then growing to show the floors above and below. She saw the narrow shaft for the lifts, then blinked in shock when the name "A. Feldman" appeared in the lift, moving downward. Her fingers froze as the name stopped moving at her floor, then proceeded through the hallway toward her room.

Her mind refused to think, but her body moved with automatic urgency, reverting her computer back to dumb terminal status, and stowing the remote and wire inside her bra. They'd find it easily if they looked, but Sarah knew they'd find it no matter where in the room she hid it, if they had a reason to look for it. Had the system reported her?

She leaned on an upraised arm, staring at her computer while her other hand lazily twirled her fork in the spaghetti strands on her plate. A deep breath helped her school her features to boredom, but slowed her pounding heart only a little. Still, she managed to glance up in wary nonchalance when her door opened. She even registered the right amount of surprise and dismay as Feldman entered with the guard. She stood, sending the guard a questioning glance. Good acting, Andrews, she told herself. Just remember to breathe.

Feldman gestured toward her food. "I apologize for interrupting your dinner. Please, continue eating while we talk."

"Wouldn't be good for my digestion," Sarah said. As if he cared that he'd interrupted her dinner! She slid around the table and sat on the edge of her bed, leaving the chair for Feldman if he decided to sit.

He did, bringing the chair to the front of the table in an unhurried manner. This put him just a few feet away from her. He seemed perfectly at ease, one foot resting on the opposite knee. He reached into his jacket pocket and pulled out a computer chip, turning it in lazy circles between his fingers. He had blue eyes, and despite his polite demeanor, they regarded her with a cold inner light. Sarah suppressed a shiver, but could not look away from the chip he held. It looked like CERBO's neutrino alteration chip.

"Dr. Altair tells me," he said, "that your CERBO will not work in this universe, due to a difference in neutrinos. I'm curious as to what this chip does. I found it tucked away in a separate compartment of CERBO's case."

He stopped talking, his gaze on her as if it were her turn to talk. She tightened her lips and looked away. Sam's statement was not true, of course. CERBO would work just fine in the universe, but she trusted that Sam had a reason he wanted Feldman to think otherwise. Had Feldman already asked Sam about the chip? If so, what had Sam told him about it? What was her part?

When she remained silent, Feldman continued. "In the morning, Dr. Altair will begin working with some of our staff, to build a new machine that will work in this universe. Its application for instantaneous travel is remarkable. I'm sure you understand how helpful the device could be if applied to movement around the globe."

"I do, of course," she said, trying to avoid saying anything that would contradict Sam's story. She nodded to the chip in his hand. "We can't do anything without that chip, though. You'll have to give it back."

He smiled, and she could tell he didn't believe her. *Bollocks. What had Sam told him?*

"I'll hold onto it for now," he said. "We'll see how far you can progress without it."

She decided to bring up what was basically a meaningless topic. "You must realize that we didn't build CERBO for travel within a single universe. When we direct neutrino action, there's a counter-reaction somewhere, and you have to compensate for that if you stay in the same universe."

Feldman tilted his head in acknowledgement. "It's one of the things Altair is going to help us with." He leaned forward. "What I want to know, is what part you play in all this. Altair tries to pass you off as a tourist. A granddaughter dutifully fulfilling her grandmother's last wish. But you're more than that, aren't you?"

"What do you mean?"

"Come now, Miss Andrews. We have all the equipment and belongings you brought with you. That includes a fascinating photo album showcasing your grandmother's life in the second timeline. It also shows you working alongside Altair and others, as they build these machines. In fact, it's obvious that you are the genius behind the hardware. I would be remiss if I did not request your assistance with our project."

Sarah fought the urge to put more distance between them by sliding further back on the bed. To appear weak would put her even more in his power. "Request, is it? Are you suggesting I have a choice?"

There was no humor in his smile. "Of course you have a choice." He turned his head, eyes taking in details of the tiny, windowless room, before settling once more on her. "Has it occurred to you that no one knows you are here? As far as anyone in this world knows, you and Sam Altair do not exist. No one will question your disappearance or ever ask about you. Your stay in this room can last as long as you do, Miss Andrews."

"That's my choice?"

He lifted a shoulder in casual acknowledgment.

Sarah glared at him. "Why? What is it you want us to do for you? Surely, if you put your resources into it, your own people can figure this out in time."

"That is not your concern," he said. "All you need to know is that if you cooperate, you and Altair can return home. Obviously, I can't give you a timeframe, but when we have what we need, you'll be free to go."

"You want us to help you do a bloody immoral thing, with our freedom as the price? You're a monster."

He laughed. "Immoral? Your very presence here is an abomination to the natural order of the universe, and a specific attack on our sovereign rights to our world. You are lucky we don't simply have you executed with due diligence." He leaned forward, eyes burning with intense feeling. "But we are merciful. Come, Miss Andrews. Do you really want to spend your life in this room? Or do you want to return home to hearth and loved ones?"

He stood and Sarah blinked up at him, confused and wary. "I will instruct your guard to escort you to your laboratory tomorrow," he said. "Your cooperation, or lack of it, is up to you."

He stepped toward the door and Sarah cringed as a desperate longing pierced her. "Dr. Feldman ..."

He paused at the door and turned to face her. "Yes?"

"My grandmother's journal. I want it back."

His eyebrows rose. "I have use for it, at the moment."

"Please." She stood, but made no other move as the guard came to tense attention. She kept her eyes on Feldman's face. "It's all I have left of her. Did you not have a grandmother? Can you understand? Promise you'll return it to me."

He watched her through narrowed eyes, giving no hint of his thoughts. Sarah held her breath and waited.

He nodded to the guard, who pressed a button on his belt. Behind Feldman, the door slid open but he continued to watch Sarah. Finally he spoke. "Naturally, I had a grandmother." There was no emotion in his voice, but he dipped his head. "Once I have no other use for the journal, it will be returned to you."

Sarah waited until he and the guard walked out, and the door slid closed behind them. She let her breath out in an explosive *whoosh,* then stepped to the little table, picked up her dinner plate, and hurled it with all her strength at the door.

Chapter 21

Andy took a grateful sip of Guinness, his brain whirling from the demo at Sun. With an effort, he dismissed its wonders, and tried to concentrate on the large man who sat across the table from him. The man he hoped would put him in touch with the rebels. He grinned.

"It's great to see you, Pete. How are you and Karen liking it here?"

"We're keeping busy." Pete tossed back a gulp of his own brew and lounged back on the small, fragile pub chair. It squeaked in protest, and his blue eyes danced with amusement as he returned Andy's grin. "Karen's job seems all right, and I'm getting on with my profs well enough. It's a good program at Queen's. Too bad you decided to stay at Oxford."

Andy shrugged. "Also a good program." He leaned forward, too distracted to stick with small talk. "Listen, I'm afraid I don't have much time. I'll have to grab dinner to take with me. I hope I can spend more time with you later, but I'm wondering if you can help me with something."

"Sure. What's up?"

"I have a friend who needs treatment for an injury." Andy kept his hands on the table, and lifted one finger in caution. "I need a doctor who is willing to go off the grid."

Pete's eyes flickered in momentary seriousness, then his relaxed public expression was back, and he raised his glass for another sip. "It's harder here, than in Oxford," he said, his voice soft, but still loud enough so that it didn't look like they were talking in whispers. "Security's tighter. The risks are greater."

"Please, Pete." Andy covered his anxiety in his lifted glass. "This is important. Can you point me to someone?"

"I'll have to ask," Pete said. "Ask around, that is. How urgent is this? Life-threatening? Minor?"

"I don't know for certain." Andy stared into the dark depths of Guinness. "It's not minor, I'll say that. It doesn't seem to be life-threatening yet. But I'm worried it could be."

"If I get back to you tomorrow, is that all right?"

Andy nodded.

Pete's forehead creased. "I assume it's someone in Belfast. Do I know him?"

Andy hesitated. "It might be best if I don't say."

"To me? Come on, Andy."

"For your sake. And Karen's."

Pete stared at him. Andy met his gaze with a twitch of his brows and another swallow of Guinness. Then he shook his head and raised his hand to signal the waitress to bring Pete another glass. "Wait," he told Pete, "there's more. I'm just not sure how to phrase this."

Pete shrugged. "Any way you want. I can take it."

Andy smiled at that. "The doctor needs to treat her off the grid, as I said. But she needs a safe place to stay. She can't go back to Oxford."

Pete shook his head, but said nothing as the waitress dropped off his new glass, took the empty, and brushed a cloth over the still-clean tabletop.

When she left, Andy jumped in before Pete could speak. "She'll more than make up for the trouble, I promise. She can run circles around any physicist you pit her against, and she wants to help. This is essential, Pete. She needs to be someplace safe. You know what I'm asking."

"Christ's balls, Andy."

"You have to help me, mate." Andy allowed his desperation to show. "I'll muck around by myself on the streets trying to find a contact, if you don't. I can't just do nothing, and I won't rest until she's safe. You're my best bet."

Pete rubbed at a scratch on the table, his mouth pursed in thought. When he looked up, he was smiling again. Andy couldn't tell if it was the public act, or if Pete was really amused about something.

"You've always dabbled," Pete said. The smile remained in place, but his voice was serious. "You're on our side, and you've helped when you could. But you've always put your career first, refusing to go too far or do too much for us. Now you're even working for Sun, when you know they're behind every miserable mess in the world."

He lifted his glass and tilted it in Andy's direction. "If you ask for this, mate, you'll have to pay for it. The girl too, whoever she is, especially if she's as smart as you say. But *you*," he paused for a drink, "you will have to make a choice. Once and for all."

Andy had no doubt about his answer. "I'm in, Pete." He met Pete's gaze with a firm expression. "My life for hers. Whatever it takes."

"That's good, Andy. Because there are things happening at Sun, and they're right up your alley." Pete leaned over the table. "Start by telling me what you've been hired to do."

∞

Moira moved the hairbrush in slow strokes, her movements timed to keep the pain in her stomach to a minimum. It felt best when she did not move at all, but she was determined to look decent when Andy returned. She had shuffled to the loo, managing a careful shower while avoiding the glaring bruise that covered her midsection. Now, freshly clothed in her own sweat shirt and pants, she sat tailor-fashion on the bed and attempted to bring order to hair tangled by wind, and sleeping on trains and hotel pillows.

When the brush at last flowed unimpeded through her hair, she set it on the bed next to her, and with slow, ginger movements, shifted until she was leaning against the headboard, with a pillow held over her stomach by upraised knees. She didn't dare check the Feinberger to see if her activity had increased the rate of bleeding. More pain medication would be nice, but Andy had said there was just one dose left. Best wait to see if he was able to get more. She might have to ration out what they had.

Distraction, that's what she needed. Her Pad was within reach, so after taking a slow breath, she pulled it to her, letting it lay on the upraised pillow. She brought up Andy's Belfast data and put herself to work.

She'd only been at it a few minutes when the beep of the door lock sounded. Her pulse sped up despite her pain as Andy entered, a bag of food in his hand. Whatever happened, she was here with him. She would never have dared dreamed of such a possibility.

He smiled, not quite hiding his anxious expression. "Are you feeling better?" He placed the bag on the nightstand, but remained standing, watching her with suppressed tension. She couldn't tell if he was excited or anxious. Perhaps both.

"A little," she said, not quite sure if that were true. "I could use more pain meds, but wanted to make sure you found more."

He nodded, his fingers brushing a soft flutter on her forehead. He searched her face with concern evident in his eyes."I picked up a few doses, but try to eat something first. I brought you some soup and crackers." He pulled containers from the bag, removing the paper lid from a cup and handing her the soup and a spoon. The comforting aroma of thyme-scented broth told her that she was hungry, and she ignored her sore muscles to hold the cup and take a sip. Her stomach protested, so she waited before trying any more. Best take her time.

Andy took his own cup to the little desk by the door, turning the chair so that he faced Moira. He stirred the soup with moody thoughtfulness, not eating. Moira watched him.

"Is something wrong?" she asked.

He glanced up as if he'd forgotten she was there, then shook his head. "Not wrong, exactly," he said. "I'm just worried about you." He finally lifted the spoon to his mouth, and Moira took another cautious sip of hers.

"At Oxford," he said, "I knew people with connections to the rebels. I had one or two dealings with them myself, but nothing very big. I thought I'd be able to connect with someone here, but their security is tighter than at Oxford." His jaw tensed as he gazed at her, his face creased with worry.

"That makes sense," Moira said. "Oxford is a peaceful hamlet of learning. Belfast has been a hotbed of rebellion for centuries. They take it seriously here, and they know what they're doing."

"That's true," Andy said. "And with Sun headquartered here, they have to be even more careful. But we've got to get you over to them before we're caught." He tapped his spoon against the cup rim. "I have two good friends who moved to Belfast a couple of years ago. They did some work with the rebels in Oxford, and I'm sure they're doing the same thing here. I was hoping to not get them involved, but they're the best ones to help us. So I contacted Pete."

"I don't want to get more people in trouble," Moira said, but her heart wasn't in it. Her stomach was a constant dull ache, and she felt weak and tired no matter how much she slept. The Feinberger's advice was right. She needed medical treatment.

Andy was ready to take advantage of her ambivalence. "I'll do whatever I need to, Moira. You need help. I thought I could take care of you, but I can't. Not alone. It won't take long for hotel security to realize you're here. Another day, perhaps two." He gave a decisive nod. "I've already talked with Pete. That won't look suspicious, in fact, it would look odd if I didn't contact him. We grew up in the same village, we've been friends all our lives. I stood up with him when he married Karen."

"Don't tell them about me." Moira blinked back sudden tears. She was so bloody tired. "You can try to hint about the rebels, but don't let on anything about me. Please."

"I agree. I told him nothing about you other than that you needed a doctor and a safe place to stay." He moved to her side and patted her shoulder. "They don't need details about anything. Pete will talk to his leaders and get back to me tomorrow."

Relief warred with Moira's worry, but she managed a small smile. "That's good. If you trust him, then I'm sure he'll be careful." She handed him her cup. "I'll eat more in a little while. I think I'll take some meds now."

He traded her soup for a patch from the medkit. "Do you feel up to some more work?"

"Yes. What did you learn?"

He sat on the bed and reached for her Pad. "May I? I'll have to recreate it from memory."

She nodded and he took the Pad, calling up a blank screen. "I had to sign several confidentiality statements, and I couldn't bring anything out with me. So if you're ever questioned, you don't know anything about this, right?"

"Ignorance is my middle name."

He chuckled. "You wish. As it turns out, Sun has been tracking neutrino behavior world-wide. The only unusual activity has been right here, but there's been more of it than you and I saw. They've been suppressing it, just as we suspected."

"You mean there have been more wormholes?"

"Yes." He worked while he talked, writing with urgent strokes. "Several, in fact, over the last three months. The origin seems to be outside our own universe." He stopped and glanced up at her, his face solemn. "I know how farfetched that sounds. But the woman I worked with today, Dr. Warner, assures me it's true. They aren't giving me all the details, of course. But starting tomorrow, I'm going to work with someone who knows all about it. I'm supposed to assist him with part of the project."

Moira realized she was holding her breath. "To do what?"

"Don't know." He flipped the Pad, holding it out to her. "Have a look at it. While you're doing that, I'll work on recreating the rest of what I saw today. It's amazing stuff."

It was amazing, and Moira lost herself as she analyzed it, forgetting about her pain, and even the combined awkwardness and forbidden thrill of being in a hotel room with Andy Green. He described more of what he'd seen, and all that Dr. Warner had told him. Moira stroked the data further with each new piece of information, watching the patterns.

After two hours, Andy stopped her. "You need to try and eat more, then rest. You can look at this tomorrow, while I'm at work."

She nodded, but didn't relinquish the Pad. "I will. But this is really weird, Andy."

"You mean, besides the obvious weird?"

She heard the teasing lilt, but didn't respond to it. She could hardly get enough breath to say what she thought the data revealed. "There's no doubt it's an Einstein Bridge. But ... I think something came through it."

Andy stared at her in silent astonishment. She shook her head. "No, wait. I don't mean something came through. I mean, *someone.* Two human beings crossed between universes. And they are here in Belfast. Somewhere."

∞

After leaving Andy, Pete drove a lazy route to a warehouse on a dark street. The warehouse was the home of a legitimate delivery business, which Pete was not interested in. In the cavernous central room, he settled in front of an isolated computer and scanned the chip Dinnie Warner had given him the night before.

Hours later, he was joined by a skinny Irish-Chinese fellow, who took one look at the holographic data, raised both eyebrows, and began pacing behind Pete's chair.

A short time later, Pete sighed, and turned to face him. "Hell of a thing."

"Is it legit?"

"I suspect so."

"Can your friend help us?"

"This is his bloody field, Ned." Pete rubbed the bridge of his nose. "He told me as much as he knew about what he would be doing at Sun. It's definitely this project, but he didn't seem to know anything about travelers."

"What did you tell him to do?" Ned pulled a chair over to Pete's desk and straddled it.

"His job, but to keep his eyes and ears open. To tell me everything he learns and anything he suspects."

Ned nodded. "Good."

"Should I tell him about Warner? They can work together."

"No feckin' way." Ned pounded a fist on the table. "They're both amateurs. They'd just get each other killed." He stood to leave. "Make arrangements to pick up your friend's girl tomorrow. You're sure he'll cooperate?"

"Andy keeps his word. You'll see."

"He'd better. That girl's his collateral."

∞

Dinnie Warner slouched in her favorite chair, shivering in the cold air of her flat. It was possible that some of the shivering was a result of the computer chip she held. Another fecking chip. She turned the thing over and over with her fingers, as if keeping it in motion absolved her of any crime of possession.

It was from her brother, delivered all unwittingly by their mum, who was waiting with tea and sandwiches when Dinnie got home. "He stopped by for just twenty minutes," her mum said in answer to Dinnie's surprised questions. Dinnie stood by her tiny fridge in quiet resignation, as her mother finished scrubbing the cutting board with bicarbonate of soda. Her mum always cleaned the cutting board, no matter how often Dinnie insisted she never used it. "Said one of his unit mates was killed in a training accident, and he'd been assigned to pay the army's respects to the lad's family. He's already left to go back."

Mrs. Warner gave the cutting board a violent shove with the scrubbing wool, gouging a strip of wood off as she muttered something about "the almighty Sun army couldn't even let a boy have dinner with his mum once they'd sent him to town." Dinnie thought it wise to stay silent, and after a frustrated "pfft!" her mum continued. "He said to give you that wee box." She jerked her chin at an old Tupperware container on the kitchen table. "Said you'd know what to do with it."

An interminable hour later, her mum had finally gone home, and Dinnie sat with the box's contents on her lap. A deck of cards, three old American coins, and a wee plastic decoder ring like they used to play with when they were kids. The chip had been in the ring's secret compartment.

Dinnie turned it over and over, and tried to understand. To her knowledge, Billy Warner was a loyal minion in Sun's occupational army, deployed to assist in operations at the Galway spaceport. The chip hinted at subterfuge. Dinnie admitted the thought frightened her.

No, she wasn't shivering from the cold.

Moving quickly in case she might change her mind, she grabbed her Pad and shoved the chip into the port. For two slow seconds, nothing happened, then the screen lit up to display a document. Brows knitting together in confusion, Dinnie thumbed through the file. Cargo manifests. Page after page of them. *What the hell?*

But soon she began to see the pattern. The cargo was for the space station, delivered over a period of several months. This kind of thing conceivably fell within Billy's job description. But each manifest was altered, and the original work order was displayed alongside it.

Dinnie no longer shivered, having passed into terrified numbness. Each manifest showed a small amount of explosive material, hidden among innocuous cargo, and deleted from the official record. Each original order carried the approval signature of Albert Feldman. The official record was revised to show the signature of *Ned O'M ...,* something that ended in a scribble.

Ned O'Malley, the infamous rebel leader? Why would Mr. Feldman smuggle explosives up to NISS using O'Malley's name? It looked like a setup.

Did it have anything to do with Sam Altair?

Don't be daft, she told herself. Why would it?

Perhaps the explosives were part of Sun's planned defense in case of interdimensional invasion. But in that case, why smuggle them aboard? Albert Feldman did not need to explain himself. If he wanted explosives stored on the station, he had only to say so.

Yet here he was, smuggling, and framing someone else for the deed. And her own dear brother had evidently not been recruited heart and soul into Sun's paradigm. He wanted her to do what he had no opportunity to do: give the information to the rebels.

Bloody hell.

She wasn't excited about another conversation with Phil and Pitcher Bloke. She couldn't tell them what the explosives meant, only that it was happening. Billy didn't know about the complication of time travelers, of course, but she couldn't shake the idea that the two things were related.

Dinnie's neck itched with her jumpy nerves. She ejected the chip and hid it back in its ring, her mind chewing on the clues and questions she had. She would wait. Keep her eyes and ears open for a hint of whatever Feldman was up to. Tomorrow, Andy Green was supposed to start working with Sam Altair. She'd read up on Andy Green and was impressed. After meeting him, she was even more so. He could make neutrinos dance and sing if he wanted to.

Although she was sure that whatever Albert Feldman wanted from Sam Altair and Andy Green, dancing neutrinos were not part of it.

Chapter 22

During the night, a late storm off the Atlantic met up with a high-pressure area moving down from Scotland, drenching Northern Ireland in a powerful rainfall. Andy, wrapped in a blanket on the floor, woke to darkness punctuated by near-constant flashes of lightening, and howling winds throwing rain against the window above him. A distant moaning alarm told him that the Irish Sea had once again breached the levees built inland against it. The sound was low in the register, indicating that for now, it was just a leak.

A fainter signal brought his attention into the room, and he scooped his Pad from the floor where he'd dropped it when he fell asleep. The message alert showed a text from Pete, and he tapped it open, hopeful and anxious about what it would say. Whatever it was, it would be in a code of some sort. Pete would never send real information over the web.

Good to see you again, mate. Congrats on the job at Sun. You'll have to tell me everything you're learning. You know I'm jealous. Karen says she'd be happy to show your friend around uni. She'll meet her at two in front of the Lanyon Building.

Andy had been holding his breath, but now he let it out in quiet relief. The rebels would take Moira. The fact that Pete expected to hear everything Andy learned at Sun was a small price to pay.

He glanced over at Moira, still asleep on the bed. She was little more than a dark shape on the bed, but he could see that she faced him, curled on her side, the blankets pulled to her chin. Her hair fell over her face, and he had to resist the urge to go over and smooth it back.

They had talked long into the night, after her discovery that humans had entered their world from another universe, trying to fathom the meaning of it. He still felt a thread of disbelief. How could such a thing be true? Moira was inexperienced. Surely, she was misinterpreting the data. True, her explanation seemed fool-proof, and he could see the logic of her path. But he was inexperienced, as well. They had to be wrong.

He shivered, thinking about the neutrinos. They were altered from their usual state, proving a multi-state ability. He didn't know if that was a result of the bridge-building, or if they had somehow been altered first, to make them useable for the bridge.

He shook his head. Questions. He had nothing but questions. After a glance out the window into the darkness of the storm, he turned and quietly slipped into the loo to dress. He'd wake Moira before he left to make sure she understood how and where to meet Karen. Then he would go to work. If the answers existed at all, he'd find them at Sun.

∞

Sam woke to a dark room. As had happened every morning since his capture, his hand searched the empty spot beside him, looking for Sarah. Like every other morning, he drew his hand back, afraid.

A low, continuous moaning forced itself into his awareness. It sounded like a fog horn. He wondered if the building was close to the harbor, and realized that here was a clue to where he was. He didn't know how it would help, but knowing anything was better than knowing nothing.

He was finishing his breakfast tea later, when his door opened and a guard came in, followed by a blonde woman. Her short, spiked hair and black leathers reminded him of biker chicks back home. She bounced on her toes with nervous energy, but dark circles under her eyes made him think she wasn't sleeping much.

She held out a stiff hand and spoke in a quick staccato. "Good morning. I'm Dinnie Warner. If you'll come with me, I'll escort you to your lab."

He took his time reaching to shake her hand, looking her over with cold disdain. "You don't seem to see anything odd about my need for an escort?" he asked. "Do you people always keep your scientists locked up and under guard?"

"You'd be surprised, Dr. Altair," she said, turning to the door. He had to admit, he was surprised. He'd expected her to prevaricate.

He followed her out, the guard a few steps behind him. "What is that moaning sound?" he asked as he caught up with her. "It's been going on for an hour or more."

"Levee breech." She walked as fast as she talked, her black boots tapping a refrain on the hallway floor. "Happens once in a while, but all the people have moved inland, so it's just a matter of repair."

"Inland? Do you mean levees against the sea?"

"Of course." She glanced at him, puzzled, then her face cleared. "Your world is a hundred years behind ours, isn't it? Climate change isn't as advanced there."

He remembered the vids brought back by his probes. "We'd noticed the sea was further inland than in our time. I didn't realize it was still rising."

"It is." Warner ushered him into a lift, stepping in after the guard, who ignored their chatter. "The North Pole is completely thawed, but there's still some ice at the South Pole that's melting. The Gulf Stream has been effectively shut off for twenty-five years, which is why it's so cold here. That cold reacts with hotter atmosphere flowing from the west and south, creating massive storms. The sea continues to rise, and all the storms drive it inland, too."

Sam shuddered. "The original Altair suggested this was possible. I'm sorry to see it's come to pass."

She shrugged. "We're living with it."

Sam looked away, struck by a sudden thought. *Are they hoping to take over our world if their own becomes uninhabitable? Is that what's behind Feldman's actions?*

Not that Sam felt he could attribute any altruism to Feldman. His plan was probably to send over the elite of their population, and let everyone else die off.

Warner seemed willing to let the conversation lag. When the lift stopped, she dashed out, leaving the guard to make sure Sam followed. They caught up with her outside double doors with a sign that declared this was "Lab 3B." The sign was partially blocked by another guard, who seemed appropriately burly. At Dinnie's gesture, he opened the door and stood aside to let them pass. Dinnie held out an arm, indicating that Sam should enter.

The first thing he saw was his own portable CERBO, still in its case, on a nearby counter. He forced himself not to rush over to grab it. He'd never get anywhere with it, not with two guards behind him. So he directed his gaze around the room, a typical laboratory with a hood, sink, and cabinets on the far end, and long tables creating rows down the middle. The room boasted two scanning tunneling microscopes, one each on tables to his left and right.

He turned to Warner, raising his eyebrows in question.

She mirrored his look. "Mr. Feldman says that you already know your assignment. Everything you need should be here. If not, just let your guard know and I'll take care of it."

"What I need," Sam said, "is to be allowed to return home. With Miss Andrews, and with my equipment."

Warner sighed, and Sam thought he detected a flicker of sympathy in her downturned mouth. "Just follow your instructions, Dr. Altair. You'll have an assistant, who should be here soon. He doesn't know who you are, by the way. He's only seen a little of what happened when you came through. I'm sure you'll appreciate the need to limit knowledge of your work."

Sam nodded. "I do, but if I'm going to accomplish anything, I'll need an assistant who knows what we're doing."

"It's up to you, of course," she said, turning to the door. "I'll collect him shortly and let you have time to find your way around the lab."

∞

The levee-breech sirens had shut off by the time Andy waved his new security badge at the entrance to Sun Consortium HQ. Dinnie Warner was waiting for him on the third floor. She made no effort to chat, and he glanced at her profile as he followed her down the hallway. Her tight jaw, and shadows under her eyes indicated a rough night. He wondered if it had anything to do with people from another universe, but he hadn't figured out a way of broaching his suspicions.

Dinnie stopped in front of a sealed door, an alert guard standing next to it. She turned to Andy, her expression empty of emotion. "You'll be working in here. There's a guard inside as well. Remember all those nondisclosure forms you signed?"

He raised an eyebrow and nodded, more uneasy than ever.

"The presence and identity of your coworker is top secret information. Once you enter this lab, there's no turning back."

She had to see how nervous he was. This was one reason he never wanted to get too involved with the rebels. He didn't have the stomach for it. But Moira was counting on him. He gestured to the door, inviting Dinnie to open it. She did, and he followed her in.

∞

Sarah stood in the laboratory the guard had brought her to, and glared at the computer screen that displayed her instructions in indifferent black and white. Feldman had been thorough, as if leaving nothing to chance. She was to design a new time machine, based on CERBO, that was useable within this universe, as well as for interdimensional travel. Further, she was to design shielded containers that would allow them to transport people within the Sol system, including the earth-moon-NISS system, whatever NISS was, and around the planet itself.

Her glare turned into a confused scowl. *Shielded containers? Shielded from what?* This must be Sam's doing, throwing red herrings around to keep Feldman unaware of CERBO's true versatility.

"If so, that's good," she muttered. "I just wish I knew what the red herrings *are*."

She also wished Sam had told Feldman that they couldn't transport within a universe. They could, of course, but it had not been a priority. Well, she could use that to stall. Tell Feldman she wasn't sure of what she was doing.

Turning her back on the monitor, she saw her own computer on a table near a wall of cabinets. She switched it on, then gasped at the obscene blue-and-gold sun logo that appeared on her screen. *What had that bastard done to her computer?*

Then she realized that he'd done nothing to it. It was just that Sun's was the only network available to its signal. Sure enough, the logo went away, replaced with an innocuous home page chronicling the best of Sun's public projects. Sarah doubted the public would ever know about the bridge.

Lips tight, she accessed the virtual keyboard and sent the home page to computer purgatory. Then she opened her own program for neutrino alteration, shaking her head in understated despair. *I'm just an engineer. I need Sam or Uncle Jamie to give me the numbers.*

She could do it, though. Uncle Jamie would never approve, unless he'd personally checked each equation, but there was no denying that she could do it. She typed furiously, overwhelmed with the thought that this world had no Uncle Jamie, or Dad, or Mum. Well, maybe a woman the same as Mum, except she wouldn't be *Sarah's* mum. This world had no Sarah, for that matter.

Home was suddenly very dear.

∞

Inside the lab, clicking sounds led Andy and Dinnie around a hulking STM at the end of a long table. A man fiddling with its innards turned at their approach, giving Andy an appraising glance before turning his attention to Dinnie. As she introduced them, Andy tried to figure out why Sam Altair looked, and his name sounded, familiar.

Before he could give it much thought, his new co-worker issued a challenge. "Your file says you've just earned your masters. You realize this is pretty advanced stuff we'll be doing?"

The implied "are you up to it?" rankled a bit, but Andy supposed he shouldn't let it show. Instead, he shrugged. "At the moment, I'm rather in the dark about what we'll be doing. But if it involves the neutrino bridge I saw last night, I assure you I can keep up."

Sam looked skeptical, but Dinnie put a hand out. "Mr. Green is as knowledgeable as anyone else in the world about this subject. If he doesn't know it, no one else does either."

"Why?" Sam raised his shoulders in obvious confusion. "You had the basics of it a hundred years ago, yet you don't seem to be any further along in the study of it."

Dinnie flushed, but her chin jutted out in defiance. "We've had other priorities, Dr. Altair. Such as survival. A good deal of the knowledge gained during the twentieth century was lost as climate change accelerated. We're catching up now."

"And surpassing it," Andy said, now certain that this man came from another universe. His hands trembled with the knowledge, and he stuffed them into his pockets. "My next step is to study the deliberate manipulation of neutrinos."

Sam pressed a button, bringing the STM to humming life. "Prepare yourself for a crash course in that subject, Mr. Green. Just the Cliff Notes version. I don't have time for details."

Andy watched through narrowed eyes. "Did you build that bridge, Dr. Altair?"

"I did." Sam was peering into the tunnel, making minute adjustments to several knobs. "Our job here is to make another one, and teach Albert Feldman how to use it."

"Feldman?" Andy jerked at the name of Sun's notorious executive. "Is he involved in this?"

Dinnie handed him a file. "Not your concern, Mr. Green. I believe Dr. Altair will need these data input into the STM's computer. Why don't you have a seat, and have at it? I'll be back in a couple of hours."

Chapter 23

Dinnie hurried down the hall and up a flight to the lab where Sarah Andrews was working. *I wish Feldman would let them work together. Keeping them apart is only a hindrance. Damn elitist paranoia.*

The hallway guard nodded as Dinnie passed him. Working alone meant that Sarah did not need a guard inside the lab at all times, but Feldman was still keeping a constant eye on her.

Sarah glanced up from her Pad when Dinnie entered her lab, but made no other effort to acknowledge her presence. On the monitor, a 3D image of a probe was taking shape. Dinnie studied it, then moved her glance to Sarah, who sat with a jaw clenched tight on a pale face. Her eyes, the same green as in the picture of Casey Wilson, reflected a weary sadness. Sarah Andrews was not a happy prisoner.

Dinnie tried to be friendly. "I haven't had a chance to meet you yet, Miss Andrews. I'm Dinnie Warner, in Neutrino Tracking. I want to make sure you have everything you need. Is there any equipment or assistance I can get you?"

Sarah turned back to her keyboard. "I could use a physicist," she said. "I told Feldman I was just the engineer. Sam is the one who understands the phase change."

Dinnie sighed. "Yes, I know. But Mr. Feldman knows far better than I what is needed for this project. I can assure you that Dr. Altair is working on the problem and I'll see to it you get any data you need."

Sarah's fingers stilled on the keyboard at that information, but she started typing again without turning around. "Please make sure he knows that we need the neutrinos to stay in this universe, and within this system. It's delicate work, and we'll need to allow for the counter-reaction. Also, Mr. Feldman needs to understand that I must know the mass of whatever he is transporting. He didn't seem prepared to give me that information."

Dinnie moved closer, watching as the image rotated. It wasn't a probe, she realized. It was a container, meant to hold something. Her brows wrinkled. "Inside the system? Are you sure about that?"

Sarah shrugged, and tapped a key, bringing up Feldman's instructions. "These are the coordinates he gave me for the destination. Something called NISS, just a couple hundred thousand kilometers from Earth. In this universe."

Dinnie stared at the numbers, then cleared her throat. "NISS," she said, but had to clear her throat again. "The space station. Mr. Feldman probably just wants to do a test run."

Sarah shrugged again, tapping keys to bring her half-designed container back to the screen. Dinnie watched for another minute, then turned to the door.

∞

Because a guard stayed in the laboratory with them, Andy didn't feel safe enough to ask Sam Altair any of the fifty or so questions whirling around his brain. Sam seemed intimidated too. Their conversation was limited to necessary information, given in stilted, uncomfortable tones. But when Sam described the method for isolating and altering neutrinos, Andy forgot his fear.

"How do you know this?" he asked. "I've searched the data extensively and never found anything about it." He scrubbed the top of his head in frustration, pushing the hair in all directions. "Surely my advisor would know about it, yet why would he let me waste my time on a duplicative effort?"

Sam shook his head. "I don't know. I'm certain most of this was known in the early part of the century. There should have been papers written. What happened to them?"

"A great deal of information was lost during the famines and wars," Andy said. "I suppose that's what happened." He longed to confront Sam Altair with a question about the neutrino bridge. About the other universe, and his conviction that Sam came from that universe. But he didn't want the guard to hear that conversation.

Sam didn't seem interested in pursuing it, either. He tapped the STM. "You do know how to manipulate atoms, don't you?"

"Of course."

"Good. That's the first step. You can get started on building a framework for the bridge. We're building wormholes, but we must control the shape in order to control the destination. I've found it best to model it on a regular bowstring style. While you're doing that, I'll work on finding us some neutrinos."

Bowstring? Like a physical bridge? What the hell? But Andy set up his field within the microscope and started shifting atoms around, nudging them into the shape he wanted. After a few minutes though, he found himself staring at the atoms, the delicate sensor lying still in his hand. Did he dare? He resisted an urge to see if the guard was watching him. *Act normal.* It would be bad for him if he was caught. But it was worth the risk.

He touched his stylus to the slide. The nearest atom quivered. Jaw tight, Andy settled onto his stool and began rearranging atoms into a different shape.

After twenty minutes, he stood, blinked several times, and looked again into his viewer. Words, the start of a conversation, he hoped, shimmered up at him from the slide. *Come over ER Bridge? Prisoner?*

He straightened, twisting his neck to loosen the tight muscles. Sam was still at the other table, making miniscule adjustments to the isolation unit.

Andy cleared his throat. "Sam, could you take a look at this? I need another pair of eyes, here."

"Sure thing." Sam pushed back from the table, rubbing his eyes before coming over to Andy's table. Andy stepped aside, keeping his expression nonchalant, as Sam peered into the scope.

Sam did not react, but Andy sensed a deep stillness grip his co-worker. Sam straightened and met Andy's eyes. "Yes," he said. A thrill went through Andy at the simple word. Sam continued, "You're on the right track."

Andy tapped the table. "Good to know. Let me tweak it a bit more, and see what the next step is."

Sam glanced around the room, pausing on the bored guard before his gaze came back to Andy. He nodded and went back to his table. Andy bent over the microscope.

An hour later, they had the framework of a plan. Andy took a deep breath, trying to still his shaking hands. He couldn't believe he was going to do something so risky. But his choices were all risky from the moment he first found out about Moira. Life was not going to follow the careful plan he'd set for himself.

Chapter 24

Moira rested her head against the window and breathed through her nose until the pain in her stomach eased. Bending over to put on her socks and shoes had turned into the most difficult part of her day. At least it was over with, and she could rest for a while before going to meet Andy's friend.

She remained on the window seat, not moving being less painful than standing up. Despite her reassurances to Andy, she was relieved to know a doctor would see her. Her stomach felt as if it had ripped in half when Wayland hit her.

She still felt nervous about going alone to meet a stranger. Andy had insisted she could trust Karen Jones, but she didn't know if she could quite trust his interpretation of Pete's message. "I've known Karen and Pete all my life," he'd told her. "Our parents were friends before any of us were born. If she's promised to meet you, that means the rebels have agreed to take you in."

They would take her, in exchange for Andy providing them information. He had not said that, but she knew that was the price. This was so dangerous for him. If he got caught, she'd never forgive herself.

Her mind wandered into the odd behavior of neutrinos and people from another universe. What kind of people manipulated neutrinos for interdimensional travel? They had to be far more advanced than humans in her world.

The chill from the window forced her to move to the bed, where she wrapped herself in a quilt and called up the bridge on her Pad. She traced paths through the pattern, trying to discern where it started and where it ended. The equations describing the paths were complicated, and she lost track of time as she double-checked her work. A whining buzz was her only warning before the room's door clicked open, and a cleaning bot trundled in.

It stopped just inside the room, a bullet-shaped cylinder two feet tall, with sensors blinking red and blue on its pointed top. Three arms, two on one side, and one on the other, extended from their storage space and waved up and down. The fourth arm remained in its retracted position. The top of the cylinder rotated so that the sensors faced Moira, who sat frozen on the bed.

"This unit regrets the interruption." Its mechanical voice was high and annoying, indicative of its cheap industrial provenance, but Moira was too fearful to let it bother her. She remained silent and the bot spoke again. "Room 432 is registered to Andrew Green, an employee of Sun Consortium. The house reports that he left the premises at 0723 hours. Please state your name and authorization."

Moira's lips moved twice before she got any sound out, remembering at the very last second, who she was supposed to be. "I am Sandy Williams of Oxford. I am here ..." she floundered and continued weakly, "to meet Mr. Green for dinner. I was early, so I'm working until he arrives."

She held her breath as the lights blinked in silence for a small eternity. Her eyes flicked to the door, measuring the distance she'd have to jump if she needed to escape. The bot spoke again.

"Acceptable. Do you approve if this unit cleans the room?"

"No, thank you." Moira sat straighter and tried to sound official. "I require no interruptions so that I may concentrate on my work."

"As you wish." The arms retracted in silent motion, disappearing into the body. The unit reversed without turning, backing out of the room. The door closed.

"Holy Jesus," Moira breathed. Then she found herself standing, gasping as the sudden motion pulled at her stomach. Her glance darted about the room, taking in the two backpacks, her hairbrush on the nightstand, and the pile of extra blankets which had served as Andy's bed. The bathroom contained two sets of damp towels and two toothbrushes. *Shit.*

The bot would report her presence, and her story, to the House AI. Security would investigate. Her heart banged against her ribs as she shuddered into movement. It took her a few minutes to clear her things into her pack, thrusting her Pad into its outer pocket at the last moment. She paused, willing her stomach to behave, as she scanned the room a final time. Only Andy's things were left. Security could pick up any cells she left behind of course, but after all, they already knew she'd been here. But if they did a DNA analysis, they'd know who she was. They'd know that Andy had helped her escape.

She hesitated. Andy had said that her new chip would pass a cursory examination. If she stayed and continued her bluff, would Security be satisfied with a superficial scan of her chip? The story was plausible. It was even plausible that Andy might have had a girlfriend stay the night. It was against the law, but Belfast was an industrial hub. Security might not care.

Indecision tore at her. If she left, would it force a deeper investigation? But if she didn't leave, they might investigate anyway, and she'd end up back in Chelmsford.

Her feet made the choice for her, transporting her out the door before she'd made a conscious decision. At the end of the hall, she pressed the button for the lift. A room door opened further down the hall and she jerked with fear. But it was only another woman, reading the Pad she held in one hand, while rolling a briefcase behind her with the other. Moira kept her eyes on the lift door, hoping to avoid any conversation.

The door slid open. Next to Moira, the woman stepped forward without lifting her eyes from her Pad, still pulling her briefcase. Two men trying to exit collided with her, one tripping over the case and ripping the handle from her grip as he fell. The case slammed into the opposite wall, and the sound of breaking glass could be heard inside it. Amid the racket, Moira saw security badges swinging from the men's lapels, and she slipped into the lift before any of the three could recover, slamming her hand on the first floor button. No one bothered to look at her as the door slid closed.

Chapter 25

As soon as Dinnie Warner left the lab, Sarah flipped her screen back to the diagram of a tracking chip she had been studying. She paused, thinking over what Warner had said.

Sam was building a bridge. That meant he had CERBO, and that meant that he could track her location using her blood marker. It also meant that Sam could build a bridge from and to anywhere he wanted, although she had the impression that Feldman didn't know that. Sarah did not consider for a moment that Sam was doing what Feldman wanted.

So Sam would soon be able to get them out. Unfortunately, they would be leaving without her grandmother's journal, and Sarah was not giving it up. They'd have to hide until she could figure out a way to get it. And if they stayed in this universe, even for a short time, they'd need to do something about those bloody chips the creeps had put in their arms.

Nice to know she was on the right track. Her hand moved in self-conscious protection to rub the spot on her arm where they'd inserted the fecking thing. Feldman had explained that tampering with it set off an alarm, so even if she were to dig it out, it would not do any good. She wasn't anxious to try that, anyway.

Her lips hardened into a pout as she thought about the problem. She knew nothing about the biological aspects of the chip. But biological or not, it was still a machine, and she did understand machines. It had to send out a signal that was picked up by a sensor. Blocking the signal was the obvious thing to try.

And yet ...

Surely there were many people in this timeline who objected to constant tracking. Sarah was certain those people had already tried everything to block or cancel the signals, or otherwise skew the readings. She itched to know what had been done, what worked, and what didn't. She only had one chance, and not much time.

She could build an EMP emitter, but if they hadn't shielded their chip against EMP disruption, then they weren't smart enough to be dangerous.

Of course, blocking the signal probably wasn't a great idea, anyway. If the signal stopped, they would check at once to see why.

So. She wanted a duplicate signal that would remain in the lab, while she blocked the signal coming from her arm.

Yes. *That* made it easier.

Wait. It does make it easier. Sarah sat up straight with the relief that flooded her. *All I need is the frequency.*

She leaned over her keyboard, and with quick taps, began to build a search program.

∞

Dinnie's hands were shaking as she walked away from Sarah's lab. *The space station. My God. The space station.*

She could never tell what made her leap to that conclusion, but she knew. As soon as she'd seen the coordinates on Sarah Andrews' computer screen, she knew. Feldman was using Sam and Sarah to build a transporter. He'd said that much. But not to place equipment and soldiers in strategic places around the planet, as guards against an interdimensional invasion. Not even to send an invasion force to the other timeline.

He was sending those explosives to NISS. He was going to blow up the space station, and she was pretty sure he would make it look like the rebels had done it. Failing that, he could pin the blame on the other timeline. Either way, Sun would be given unlimited resources and authority to wage an all-out war. Against everyone.

∞

Andy peered into the microscope, watching each movement as he constructed a scrambler for Sam's tracking chip. He remained aware of the guard, but had relaxed as he realized the man did not know what Andy and Sam were supposed to be doing. While Andy knew he couldn't talk freely, he felt sure that he could *do* just about anything with the equipment, and the guard would just assume he was working.

So he'd scrounged up bits and pieces, and set about making the scrambler. Sam continued his work with the STM. He had not tried to explain what he was doing. His atom-message just said, "trust me." Andy supposed that he would have to.

He added a drop of neodymium and stepped aside to let it settle. He took the time to stretch, rotating his shoulders and shaking his arms to throw off the effects of fine-motor work. The guard watched him, as if glad for something to look at. Had to be a boring job, sitting there with no one to talk to, nothing to read or watch, just a couple of people peering into microscopes.

By now, he knew that the guards rotated every two hours, to keep them alert. He thought he'd wait until the next guard, O'Brien, was back on duty. He was a kid, more likely to do what he was told during an emergency, rather than stick to the rules. Andy needed someone malleable.

Sam was not going to like Andy's plan, but Andy had not bothered to explain it. Sam was going to have to trust him.

Chapter 26

Moira felt her mind shutting down again, just as it had done when her stepfather showed up at school. She seemed to be looking down on herself, as if she'd flown up to the security camera. Then her hand closed in a fist and she scolded herself. *Not again. Come right back here and deal with this.*

Her mind cleared with an abruptness that made her body jerk. Her hand shot out and snapped the button for the second floor. When the lift stopped, she slid through the door before it finished opening, dashing for the stairway across the hall. Once inside, she hunched over against the pain in her stomach, but did not slow down until she reached the basement. Vast laundry machines filled the space, two of them spinning water and fabric. Pipes lined the ceiling. She heard voices to her left, so turned right, her soft shoes soundless on the concrete.

She turned right again at a corridor, then left. At the far end was a short flight of steps rising to meet a door. The words "Way Out" glowed red at the top. Fear masked her pain as she raced past stacks of boxes and shelves of linen. The lights were dim, and dark shadows on the floor seemed to shimmer with a water-like glint, making her skip past them to avoid slipping. At the door, she hesitated, hands resting on the metal bar that would release the catch. Was a guard waiting outside in case she tried this very thing?

She drew a quick, angry breath and slapped against the handle, hurling out the door, into cold rain. Blinking the water out of her eyes, she saw she was in an alley at the back of the hotel. Good. To her right, the alley stretched for a few hundred meters, with several large dumpsters against the hotel wall, overflowing with boxes and broken dishes. To her left, the alley ended a scant ten meters away. She turned right, just far enough to reach the dumpsters, where she stopped, ducking between two of them. Holding her nose against the smell, she caught her breath, and thought.

Did they know who she was? *No,* her mind said. *Ask that later. Right now, ask how you get to safety.* There were cameras in the alley.

She needed to get by them. For that matter, there'd been cameras in the stairwell and the basement of the hotel. But she couldn't do anything about that, now. It was the alley she needed to worry about.

Andy had told her about his trick to get into her yard in Chelmsford. She didn't know how to hack into the security system, but there was some sense to just acting normal. The rain had stopped, so she pulled her Pad from its pocket and called up a game. Better to actually play one, than just pretend to play one. Once the game was going, she ducked her head and focused on the screen as she started a distracted ramble down the alley. Her walk was slow as she maneuvered her character through an obstacle course. She even stopped once, heart banging against her ribs, to get over a difficult spot. *Nothing going on here,* she thought to the cameras. *No one's in a hurry in this alley.*

At the street she turned left, away from the hotel. Two blocks down, she stopped amid a crowd of pedestrians and glanced back. The men from the lift appeared, running around the corner from the hotel entrance. They stopped. One was reading a Pad, the other looking up and down the street, as if searching. She saw him spot her just as a bus stopped to disgorge a passenger. He tagged his partner and they headed for her at a run. She stepped through the crowd and onto the bus, waved her chip over the payment sensor, and forced herself through the standing passengers to the middle of the bus.

She sighed in relief as the bus moved forward, but it stopped again before it reached the next corner. Mutters of complaint worked their way down from the front of the bus, but people quickly fell silent. Moira peered past bodies and backpacks, and caught a glimpse of one of the hotel men talking to the driver. Stifling a moan, she turned and began pushing her way farther back.

Her movement was oddly easy. Purses and briefcases were held closer to bodies, feet shifted and hips swung back as she squeezed by, then everything surged back into place after she passed. Shouting reached her from the front of the bus, she felt the tension of the crowd as everyone reacted to what was said. The sense of it had not yet reached the back of the bus when she stopped at the back door, closed and guarded by a uniformed porter. He blocked her hand as she reached for the handle, and she dared to look at him, trying to judge if she could sneak past him.

He met her eyes. In her peripheral vision, she saw that everyone else was staring ahead, refusing to see whatever transpired. She understood. They had done what they could to help her, but it was all she could expect. Behind her, she felt the shifting of bodies as the men forced their way back. The porter stared at her for the space of a breath, then his eyes shifted forward as he declined to see her. The door slid open a few inches. She turned sideways, squeezing through just as the muffled shouting became a clear command to "lock down all exits by order of Security." Then she was through, her pack catching as the door slammed closed. It tore free at the last nanosecond. Desperately hoping the men could not see out the bus windows, she ducked into the nearest store.

Her stomach screamed in pain, and tears streaked her face despite her best efforts to stop them. Her behavior did not pass unnoticed. Several people glanced at her, then looked away, maintaining their ignorance. But she knew the cameras remained focused, so she looked down, swiping her cheeks with the end of her scarf. This was a store for cheap clothing, sparsely furnished with shelves of sweaters and pants. Hoping there was a door to the alleyway, she moved further in, as if looking for something specific.

Halfway back, an open corridor connected this store with the one next door. She turned into it, seeing crowded tables that held a conglomeration of tools and metals stacked in haphazard piles. Fighting her anxious stomach, she weaved in and around the tables and spied a door at the back. She hurried toward it, but an annoyed clerk blocked her path, smirking at her past his nose. "This store is not a throughway," he said. "If you are not purchasing, you can't go that way."

"Okay," she said, her voice high. "I'll just look over here." She stepped past him to the third table a row closer to the door. Her hands shook as she rummaged through what looked like lug nuts. He watched her, his lips pursed in disapproval. She slipped behind the pile, hoping to keep an eye on him without having to turn around. As soon as she did, she saw her pursuers hurry through the corridor, looking in all directions. She gasped and the snotty clerk turned in her direction, not quite out of the way of the men. More alert this time, they avoided him, heading for Moira unimpeded. Frozen in place, she commanded her muscles to run, jump, dive ... do something.

Abruptly, her muscles obeyed. Both arms shot out, shoving the pile of lug nuts onto the floor in front of the men. She didn't stay to watch, although she did catch a glimpse of one man grabbing for a shelf filled with fishing tackle as he fell. The crash behind her was very satisfying.

Chapter 27

Dinnie hurried toward Sarah's lab, her attention on the numbers her Pad displayed. A door opened just in front of her and she stopped with an inch to spare for her nose. "Bollocks!" She couldn't stop the startled exclamation, but she swallowed any further retort as Albert Feldman stepped through the doorway. She backed away, hands and Pad raised in apology.

He glanced up. "Dr. Warner, good. How is our special team proceeding?"

She wondered if he'd even noticed that he'd almost brained her. But then, when was the last time she'd noticed stepping on a bug?

"Altair and Green are making good progress on the neutrino manipulation," she said. "Mr. Green is working on the substrate, and Dr. Altair estimates he'll have enough neutrinos within the next few hours. Miss Andrews has a completed diagram for a container, but she did say she needs to know the mass before she can finalize it."

"We won't have exact numbers until we're ready to transmit," Feldman said. "I don't believe we need to know until then. The container just needs to hold about two thousand pounds. Say enough for ten men with light equipment."

Feldman's army. Dinnie's fingers shook as they skimmed over her Pad. "I'm on my way to her lab now. I'll give her the message."

"I want to meet with all of them at two o'clock. I'll come to the lab in 3B. Bring Miss Andrews there at that time." He turned toward the lifts without waiting for an acknowledgement. Dinnie kept walking, thinking of bugs.

∞

Andy turned from the microscope, with a chip held in tweezers. He slid a Petri dish toward him, letting it stop just at the top corner of his Pad, on the side facing away from O'Brien, the young guard who had just come on duty. He dropped the chip into the dish, adjusting it with delicate pokes of the tweezers. It fell into two pieces, and without changing his rhythm, he picked up one and brushed the edge of his Pad just enough to send the chip into the assimilation slot.

It disappeared into his Pad.

He gave the chip in the Petri dish a last poke and a satisfied nod, then moved the dish back to the center of the table. Noting that Sam was engrossed in a pattern on his computer screen, Andy turned to peer once again in the microscope, silently counting the seconds.

Three minutes later, a strangled cry from Sam made him look up. Sam had stiffened on his stool, his left arm jerking in rapid spasms. The blood had drained from his face, leaving a mask of agony as he grabbed at the arm. He fell from the stool just as Andy reached him.

O'Brien was two steps behind, his gun drawn and shifting from Sam to Andy, and back again. "Get away from him,"

"He's got chip shock." Andy eased the jerking body onto the ground and backed away with his hands up. "I've seen it before."

"I know what it is," O' Brien said. "I've alerted Medical that we have an emergency, they'll be here in a minute."

"He could die in a minute!" Andy stepped forward, but stopped as O'Brien 's gun snapped back to him. "Turn it off. I know you have the control for it."

"It's not allowed."

"He's not going anywhere, damn it!" Andy had to shout over Sam's sudden screech. He sank to his knees, oblivious of the gun, and put a hand under Sam's head to cushion its repeated bangs against the floor. Sam's eyes rolled up into his head.

"Shit!" O'Brien grabbed his Pad and pressed a short series of buttons. An alarm began to ring at the security desk. Sam's body stopped jerking, except for a slight tremor in his left arm.

"It's off," O'Brien said. "Check him. Is he breathing?"

Andy could hardly hear over the alarm and the panicked roaring in his ears, but he could feel Sam's heart pounding under his hand, and as he bent over Sam's head, he felt the brush of air past his cheek. He nodded. "Yeah, he's breathing."

"All right, get away from him." The gun gestured. "Over there."

Andy slid away until he reached the table behind him, watching Sam for any more signs of distress. O'Brien silenced the alarm and over the silence they heard steps running down the hall. A few seconds later, the door burst open to admit another guard and two women wearing medical scrubs, one of them pushing a crash cart.

"I shut the chip down," O'Brien said as the women knelt on either side of Sam.

Andy stood and sank onto a stool, relieved to see O'Brien holster his gun. He rubbed his hand where it had hit the floor under Sam's head, certain there would be a bruise starting. He glanced up as another man entered the room, and both guards came to stiff attention. Andy started to stand, but he noticed the nervous fear in

O'Brien's face, and decided it would be best if he didn't move at all. The women ignored everyone, one of them giving Sam an injection, the other one watching a blood pressure monitor.

Rage reddened the man's face as his gaze touched everyone in the room. "What happened here?"

Andy blinked in surprise. Whoever he was, the man sounded truly upset.

O'Brien answered without moving, his gaze steadfastly forward, looking at nothing. "He went into chip shock, sir. I made the decision to turn his chip off, based on his apparent condition."

Andy shifted his gaze back to the man, who was regarding Sam with an odd expression of regret and amusement. "No doubt that was the correct decision, Mr. O'Brien. He wasn't going to escape during chip shock."

O'Brien remained stiff, but his eyes flickered once in Andy's direction as he nodded. "Thank you, sir."

Sam stirred, lifting his right arm to touch his left. "Bloody hell." His voice was just a whisper.

One of the doctors tucked a pillow under his head. "Stay still for a few minutes. You had a bad shock, but you should recover in a bit."

Sam gazed at her, his expression bewildered. Then his face cleared and his glare turned to the man. "What the hell was that, Feldman?"

Andy watched with increased wariness as Feldman knelt next to the doctor. So this was Sun's mysterious executive. One of the most powerful men on the planet, if you believed the rumors. Andy suspected there was a lot of truth to rumors.

"We call it chip shock," Feldman said. "It's not very common, but it happens often enough that we can treat it quickly. Essentially, the host has an incompatibility with the security chip, which degrades and delivers a shock. O'Brien disconnected your chip to stop the shock, and Dr. Russell has given you a shot of adrenaline. How is he, doctor?"

The woman next to Feldman sat back on her heels, regarding Sam with tight lips. She kept watching him as she answered Feldman. "He's fine. No burns beyond the local injury surrounding the chip. His heartbeat was erratic, but has settled into a normal rate. He has a bump on the back of his head, from his fall."

"He was banging his head pretty hard on the floor," O'Brien said. "Mr. Green used his hand to cushion it best he could."

Feldman's glance flickered to Andy, then back to Dr. Russell, who turned toward Feldman.

"I need to remove his chip," she said. "It's fried, for one thing. But I don't recommend implanting another one, sir. We don't know enough about his universe. There could be differences at an elementary level that we haven't seen yet. The next chip might kill him."

"All right." Feldman stood, gazing at Sam before turning to Russell. "Take it out. I want a full analysis on it, and your report this evening. Make it your priority. Can he return to work?"

"I want him to rest for at least fifteen minutes, but after that, yes." Russell was already pulling supplies from her kit while her assistant swabbed Sam's arm with alcohol and an anesthetic.

"Fine." Feldman turned to go, but Sam reached out his free hand. "Wait. What about Sarah?"

Feldman turned back. "What about her?"

"Take her chip out too. I don't want this to happen to her."

"We don't know what caused ...."

"You're damn right." Sam said. "You don't know, and you have no right to take chances with her life. Take it out."

Feldman's eyes narrowed, but he said, "See to it, Dr. Russell. Miss Andrews is in Lab 4D. I'll tell her guard to expect you."

He walked out, and Andy felt as if the tension in the room went with him. He was pretty sure everyone else felt it, too.

Russell made a tiny incision in Sam's arm and plucked the chip out with tweezers. Andy could see a blackened edge of it before she dropped it into a vial and snapped the lid closed. Her assistant wiped away a small dot of blood and placed a bandage over the incision. They were finished in thirty seconds.

"The anesthetic will wear off in about five minutes," Dr. Russell told Sam as she helped him into a chair. "Drink some hot tea and rest for fifteen minutes, longer if you feel the need. Have your guard call me if you feel any nausea, dizziness, or pain. All right?"

Sam nodded. "Will you let me know once Sarah's chip is removed?"

Russell hesitated, then nodded. "I'll notify your guard."

"Thank you."

Russell turned to Andy and held out her hand. "Is your hand all right? Let me see it."

Andy lifted it, then shrugged. "I'm fine. Bit of a bruise is all."

She prodded it with gentle fingers. "I'll leave you a cold pack. Hold it for a few minutes. That should reduce the bruising."

Andy took the pack the assistant offered and sat next to Sam. O'Brien went to fetch Sam's tea, leaving his partner to guard them.

Sam leaned back, letting his head rest against the wall behind him. "What a nightmare."

"I'm sorry about that," Andy said in a soft voice. He stared ahead, toward the floor, but kept an eye on the guard at the other end of the room. "But your chip is out and Sarah's is coming out. And we now know where she is."

Sam didn't answer right away and Andy dared a glance, to find his colleague staring at him in suspicion. Under cover of O'Brien's return with four cups of tea, he said, "Get your bridge ready. Move Sarah out first, then us. I'll get you the coordinates for Lab 4D."

He stood, not waiting for Sam's response. Thanking O'Brien for the tea, he went back to his Pad to set a search for a map of the building.

∞

Sarah held a finger to the small bandage that Dr. Russell had just applied to her arm. Relief at having the hateful spy out of her arm made her dizzy. As Dr. Russell left, Sarah turned to Dinnie, who had watched the procedure without comment. Dinnie met her gaze with a serious face. *No,* Sarah thought. *She's sad.*

Or regretful. Did that mean that Dinnie Warner might tell her the truth?

"Can I trust Dr. Russell?" Sarah asked. "Is Sam really all right?"

Dinnie raised both eyebrows, as if surprised at the question. "I don't think she has a private agenda. Yes, I think you can trust her." Sarah nodded, but Dinnie continued, "If you'd like, I can run down there and chat with him a minute. See for myself what's happening there."

"Yes, could you? It would make me feel better." Sarah hesitated, but decided to speak further. She didn't know why, but she felt more comfortable with Dinnie than anyone else she'd met here. "You have such a frightening world. Such tight control."

Dinnie tilted her head, as if to regard Sarah from a different perspective. "I guess it looks that way to an outsider," she said. "You may be right. But we're fighting for survival, Miss Andrews. Species survival. The Earth has become a hostile environment for humans. In many places, it's almost like living on another planet. You wouldn't put people on Mars without tight control, would you?"

"No, but … is it really that bad?"

"Do you know how many people have died in the last forty years?"

"No."

"Over three billion. Two hundred thousand continue to die every day."

"Because of climate change?" Sarah's voice rose with her shock.

Dinnie shrugged. "It was a perfect storm. Climate change was the trigger. Overpopulation and world-wide travel contributed. Once the famines and diseases got started, we were like apples in a barrel. There are places where the dead never got buried at all." She shrugged again, as if acknowledging there was no other outcome possible. "Our society may look totalitarian. I suppose it is. But martial law is the only reason there are still people in the UK at all."

"I'm sorry," Sarah said.

"Just wait," Dinnie crossed her arms. "Your world is a hundred years behind ours. In 1980, there was barely a ripple of this kind of thing. It was easy to ignore the warning signs, even though many people tried to sound an alarm. No one believed it back then."

Sarah nodded, not sure if she should mention the changes made by the first Sam Altair. Besides, she didn't know the future. Just because they thought they were safe, it didn't mean they were. "I understand what you mean about the control. But how can you trust anybody?"

"You can't." Dinnie leaned forward, her face just inches from Sarah's. "Keeps things simple, don't you think?"

"Why is Feldman using our bridge to send men to the space station?" Sarah asked the question in a rush.

Dinnie jerked back. Her mouth opened as if to speak, but then she snapped it closed, her eyes blinking rapidly, as if to hide from Sarah's gaze. It seemed to take some effort for her to morph her expression to amusement. "Surely you realize that Mr. Feldman's decisions are several ranks above my pay grade," she said at last. "I have no idea what he wants to send to the space station. Why do you think it's men?"

"When you asked him about mass for the container, his answer was to build it strong enough for ten men." Sarah shrugged. "Ergo, he plans on sending men."

"I doubt he would be so obvious. Nor," Dinnie straightened, as if she wanted to try for arrogance, "is he in any way obligated to explain himself to you."

"I don't agree with that at all." Sarah leaned against the table, arms crossed in casual pose. "Maybe in your totalitarian society no one ever questions him, but I didn't grow up like that. In my world, I'm responsible for the things I do, and I cannot do something immoral just because someone higher up orders me to."

"You're not in your world, are you, Miss Andrews?" Dinnie asked the question softly, bringing her face close to look steadily into Sarah's eyes. As Sarah watched, Dinnie moved her eyes to stare at something behind and to the left of Sarah. When her gaze returned, Sarah shivered at the warning displayed there. She'd known there was a camera in the room. Of course there would be a microphone, as well.

Dinnie arched an eyebrow, as if in question. *Understand?* Sarah nodded once and Dinnie moved away. "Perhaps you'd like to read a brief history of the Sun Consortium," she said. "You'll see how much Sun has done over the years to help people all over the world. I think it's safe to say that far more than three billion would have died, if not for their expertise."

"That would be interesting, yes."

"I'll go check on Dr. Altair," Dinnie said. "And let you get back to work."

"Thank you," Sarah said. She glanced once at the camera, and went back to her prototype.

Chapter 28

Boarding another bus, Moira sat next to an old woman who was curled up against the window, sleeping soundly through the jerks of the bus. Once seated, Moira had to double over, gasping as her tortured stomach took revenge on all her running. She huddled over her backpack, breathing through her open mouth as she tried to hide her tears. *Stay quiet. Don't call attention to yourself.*

The pain began to recede in slow increments. Soon she could prop herself on her elbows, but she couldn't force herself to sit up straight. Her stomach wouldn't let her go any farther.

This was the first bus she had seen after running from the shop. Its destination, Falls Park, was unknown to her. It was still a couple of hours before her meeting with Andy's friend, but Moira had no idea where the university was, either. She had planned to look up a map from the room, but her sudden flight had prevented it.

However, route maps adorned the backs of every seat, and as her pain receded to a manageable level, Moira focused on the one in front of her. *Drat.* Her bus was heading north and west of the university, which as it turned out, had not been very far from their hotel. Well, she'd simply have to exit, and catch ... yes, the bus for the Queens/Botanic Garden route. The map was live, and she saw the dot representing this bus would soon intercept the route she needed. Dreading the movement, she pressed the button for a stop, and rose from her seat.

On the street again, she sank onto a public bench, shaking with pain. Her eyes burned and she let tears come, unable to fight them. Whatever was wrong with her, all the running had not helped it.

It helped to be still, and soon she was able to wipe her face. She sat back, pulled her feet up to rest on the bench, and desperately hoped no one else would show up to chase her. She didn't think she could run anymore.

Why had the men chased her? True, her presence in Andy's room violated at least a couple of laws, even if she were the nineteen-year-old college student that her fake ID claimed she was. But this was not such a serious crime that Security would feel it necessary to pursue her on and off buses, and through stores. Did they know who she was? Andy had said that his plan was not foolproof, but she found it hard to believe that her stepfather had figured out the subterfuge so quickly. He did have many resources, though. If he was determined to find her, he could have called someone well-trained in finding people.

Her lips trembled. If they'd traced her to the hotel, then they knew about Andy. In fact, he may already have been arrested. Her hand jerked at the thought, as if her nervous system wanted to wipe the possibility away. What should she do? Was it safe to call him? If he'd been arrested, then the guards would have his Pad. If she called, they'd be able to trace her location.

In fact ... Moira stared at her arm, which she'd blithely waved at the payment sensor on the bus. Damn. Anytime she used her chip, it would log her location. If Security was tracing her, she was leading them like a light bulb.

But there was no other way to pay for a bus. She closed her eyes, picturing the route map, trying to estimate the distance to Queen's. It would hurt like hell, but she had little choice. She'd have to walk it.

She decided that it wasn't safe to contact Andy. Once she was with the rebels, his friends would be able to find him. If he'd been arrested, they would find out. She'd deal with it then. Once this decision was made, she became aware of another problem caused by her abrupt flight from the hotel room: she was thirsty, and she had no water.

If it were raining, she could drink the rain, despite the pollution it carried. But although it had been raining hard all night and most of the morning, all the time of her race from the hotel, the rain had held off. She glared at the clouds racing overhead. It was cold and windy, and rain would complicate things for her. Hyperthermia was a possibility if she got wet. But she did need a drink.

And a bathroom. It was possible some of the pain would lessen if she could just pee. There would be public loos at Queen's. With this final thought as motivation, Moira stood, and began a slow walk back the way she'd come.

∞

"There she is."

Andy looked up at Sam's mutter, hearing the triumphant tone in his voice. Sam's fingers danced over his keyboard, his eyes flicking back and forth across the screen of his computer. Andy slid into place beside him, leaning on the table as he peered at the screen. A yellow dot blinked in the lower right corner, the electronic signature of the blood marker Sam had told him about.

Andy suppressed a grin, glad to see there was no chip frequency displayed. "Ah, she's clean." His voice barely registered above the hum of their machines, but Sam nodded. The rest of the screen displayed a 3D model of the bridge Sam had built, presided over by an hourglass counting seconds.

Sam's fingers ran arpeggios up and down the screen edge, and when he glanced at Andy, his eyes were bright. "Destination?"

"Queen's. I think." Andy bit his lip as he wondered again where they should go. Theoretically, Sam could program his bridge to drop them off anywhere on the planet. Remaining in Belfast was probably a mistake for many reasons. Forcing Karen to deal with two interdimensional travelers would be one of the crueler things he'd ever done. But he had to make sure Moira was safe. And in the long run, Sam and Sarah would need the help of the rebels. He tried not to think much about what use the rebels might have for Sam and Sarah, as well.

Sam tapped a finger on the table and opened his mouth, but closed it without speaking as their guard began another stroll down the aisle in their direction. He did this whenever they got together to discuss something. Sam just nodded and Andy went back to his fake neutrino search. He'd just reached the monitor when the lab door opened and Dinnie Warner came through. The guard tipped a finger at her, keeping his slow pace back to his starting point.

Dinnie whipped past him without a glance, stopping next to Sam and looking him up and down, lips pursed. Sam returned her regard with puzzled brow raised. She smiled suddenly, managing to look abashed. "I promised Miss Andrews that I would personally verify your good health. She isn't disposed to trust anything Mr. Feldman has to say."

Andy decided that Sarah Andrews was a smart woman. He smiled to himself, but kept his eyes on his work, not wanting to draw Warner's attention.

"I think I've recovered well," Sam said. "No harm, I guess, but I hope you people keep your technology out of my body from now on. I take it her chip is also out?" He managed to project the right amount of concern and distrust, as if he didn't already know the answer.

"It is." Dinnie turned to Sam's screen. "How is the model going?"

Sam launched into lecture mode, half of which Andy knew was pure BS. Sam had not explained everything to him, but based on what he'd seen so far, Andy was sure that Sam could build a bridge in a matter of minutes. But he wanted Feldman to think it took hours of intricate work, and so he had created a labyrinth of smoke and mirrors.

Andy was impressed.

But when Dinnie turned to the TSM, he jerked upright in alarm. He'd left Sam's last message in there: *escape bridge.* If Warner saw that, what conclusion would she draw? He had to stop her ... but she was already peering into the lenses. Andy sent one desperate glance at Sam, who continued to watch Warner.

She was frozen to the TSM, head bent, eyes intent on the lenses. None of them moved until the guard gave an uncomfortable cough from his station near the door. Dinnie lifted her head, staring at the wall behind the TSM. Then she straightened and met Andy's eyes, before turning to Sam. "I'll see to it that Miss Andrews has this information. She'll be ready for it before we meet with Feldman at two. I'll be bringing her down here for that meeting, by the way."

She walked down the aisle to the door and Andy swung around to peer into the scope. Warner had already scrambled the letters, leaving a scatter-shot of elementary particles.

∞

Moira did not stop walking until she reached campus. Even as the streets grew more crowded, she did not waver from her course, did not even look right or left. She couldn't. Every step required intense concentration. She had settled into a reverie of pain, her mind once again moving a set distance away from her body. A small segment remained alert for security badges on any of the people around her, but she never noticed one.

Her path took her through a garden. The Botanic Garden, she remembered from the map. It may have been beautiful once, but now it was a shamble of dead grass and weeds. She sank onto a bench across from a broken glass building, and breathed through her mouth, trying to reduce her pain. It didn't work, and she didn't think the pain would go away this time. Wherever the Lanyon Building was, she'd have to find it through her haze.

She stared ahead, until her sight cleared enough to reveal an electronic directory on the corner of the grass. Since the pain was not going to get better, she stood and made her slow way to the directory, letting it hurt as much as it would. She called up a map and asked for directions. The yellow line was blurry, but she stared at it until her mind had the pattern. Then she walked, concentrating on putting one foot in front the other, and left the rest to her tired mind.

∞

Dinnie threw a brief nod at the hallway guard near Sarah's lab, but did not slow her rush into the room. Sarah looked up from her work on a container model, her eyes wide in startled fear at the slam of her door. Her face relaxed when she saw who it was.

Dinnie crossed the room in a few steps and placed her Pad on the table in front of Sarah. She stood so that her back was to the camera, blocking the Pad. "Dr. Altair tells me that you need to see the bridge configuration before you can finalize your design. We don't want to connect your computers yet, so I told him I'd bring this down to show you."

Sarah started to say something, her confusion evident. Dinnie chanced a quick shake of her head and pointed firmly at the Pad, her lips tight in warning. Sarah snapped her mouth closed and glanced down at the message it contained. *Building esc. bridge. Will get you b4 1400. B ready.*

Sarah nodded, squinting slightly as if trying to figure something out. Dinnie let herself breathe easier. Sarah Andrews was a quick study.

Even better, she added to the deception. "If he's using this configuration, I'll need to make some adjustments." She turned to her computer, sitting and pulling it into her lap, as if determined to take it with her.

Dinnie took a moment to observe the model while she wiped the message from her Pad. The model was just a frame, and she could see that Sarah had been working on shoring up the corners. Once the paper was secure, she rounded the table and pulled up a chair next to Sarah. "Will the changes put you behind schedule? Dr. Feldman wants a meeting at two to check everyone's progress. I'm to take you down to the lab."

Sarah was tapping her keyboard, spinning the 3D image on her screen. "I'll need about an hour," she said.

"Make it fifty minutes," Dinnie suggested. She pointed at the screen with her left hand, drawing Sarah's attention to the image. "Is this the part that's problematic with the configuration?" As she spoke, her fingers brushed Sarah's cardigan, dropping her brother's chip into the pocket. Sarah did not notice, and continued to play along, with an easy torrent of techno-babble. For a wild moment, Dinnie wished she could stay near and be transported out of Sun's hold with Sarah. She could see the chip safely into rebel hands and help them stop the attack.

But she saw her mother, bringing a gift from brother to sister, hopeful that her children might at last be getting along. If Dinnie disappeared, Albert Feldman would be on her mother's doorstep in no time, adding interrogation and torture to a lifetime of suffering. He would no doubt trace Dinnie's connection to Billy, as well. There would be no peace for either of them.

No, she had to stay and see the thing through on this end. When Sarah reached the end of her explanation, Dinnie stood, her manner once again distant. "Thank you, Miss Andrews. I'll be back a few minutes before two, to escort you to the meeting. Get done what you can. I'm sure Mr. Feldman understands your time constraints."

She held Sarah's gaze for a moment, trying to say everything in a glance, that could not be said at all. Then she left, her steps on the tile ringing in her ears.

∞

Bent over with pain, Moira entered the first building she came to and found the loo. She spent a minute catching water to drink from the faucet in her cupped hands. Wiping her mouth, she stared in the mirror, shocked at her appearance. No wonder people she passed were looking at her strangely. Her cap hung precariously to the side of her head, and her hair sprang from it in all directions. Her face was white and drawn, but her eyes glittered, as if she had a fever. Her lips were pale, shading toward blue. She closed her eyes, lifting her hands to flatten her hair, then straighten the cap. Better. Not worse anyway.

She stood straighter, but gave it up as pain ripped through her. Fine. She'd crawl to the Lanyon Building if she had to. She walked without attention to her surroundings, her vision restricted to the sidewalk in front of her, and the foot she placed there with each step forward. Time went away, but somewhere, her mind kept track of distance and location. Finally, she turned a corner and after several more steps along the wall of a great building, she came to a bench. Glancing up, she met the gaze of a young woman in a blue raincoat who stood near the building's front door. Moira broke the contact, turned, and sank onto the bench.

A few seconds later, she heard the clatter of boot heels behind her, and the blue raincoat sank onto the bench next to her. "Are you Andy's friend?" the woman asked.

Desperate fear stole Moira's voice, and she didn't dare look up, but she forced her head to nod. *Please be Karen Jones.*

"I'm Karen," the woman said. "Andy says you need medical help. My car is just there. Can you make it?"

Moira looked across the lawn, toward the street, where several cars resided along the curb. She nodded again. "Slowly," she said. Croaked, actually. She seemed to have forgotten how to talk.

"I'll help you." Karen placed a hand around Moira's waist. "Take whatever time you need."

Moira gripped the offered arm, and pushed herself up, allowing no more than a grunt to escape her. "No time," she said. "Security ..."

The arm on her waist tightened. "How far back?"

"I don't know. Lost them downtown."

"We'll go, then." Karen's arm pushed her forward, and Moira's feet obeyed. Once again, she narrowed her vision to each footstep, letting Karen guide her.

∞

Sam added the last bit of code into CERBO, and glanced at the clock. Ten before two. It was now or never. He noted the dot that represented Sarah. Good, she was not moving. Easier to pick her up. He felt Andy step next to him, holding onto his Pad. He shifted his gaze to the younger man, who nodded once. Holding his breath, Sam pressed the final button and watched Sarah's dot disappear. A moment later, an alarm pierced through the building. Sarah's guard must have been watching her. Angry at that thought, Sam picked up CERBO, met Andy's eyes, and pressed the button again.

He released his held breath as cold air and the buildings of the university appeared around him. He heard Andy's startled exclamation, but forgot about it as a cannonball barreled into him, wrapping her arms around his neck and yelling in his ear.

"You did it! You got us out!"

He caught Sarah around her waist, holding her fast against him, so he could kiss her thoroughly. He applied himself to that until he felt a heavy hand on his shoulder.

"Belay that, okay?" Andy said and Sarah leaped away in alarm, her hands coming up in fists.

Sam grabbed one clenched hand. "Sarah, this is Andy Green. He's helping us." With a quick glance around him, Sam noticed they were next to the Administration building near the quad. Thankfully, there were no other people around. He glanced at Andy, whose pale face indicated shock.

Andy pointed a shaking finger to his right, his eyes on Sam. "You're going to tell me, in detail, how you do that, as soon as we have a chance. But we're not safe yet, and we've got just a few minutes to meet Karen."

"Wait." Sam kept hold of Sarah's hand, but he spoke to Andy. "I appreciate your help, but I can't just blindly follow you around. Who is Karen and where are we going?"

Andy's lips tightened and he half turned away, one foot out in the direction he wanted to go. "The rebels are the only people who can keep you safe," he said. "Karen is meeting a friend of mine at two o'clock, in front of Lanyon. She can get us to safety, but she's not expecting us, so she won't wait." He started walking, and yelled over his shoulder, "I'll explain what I can on the way, but we need to move."

Sam hesitated, but Sarah flipped around, picked up her computer from its resting place on a wall, and with a jerk of her head to Andy's back, indicated that she expected Sam to follow. If he had a good reason not to, he'd best let her know.

He could think of no good reason beyond his own fear, so he went with her, catching up to Andy. He held CERBO in front of him as he trotted with them, glad that it blocked some of the wind. Too bad they couldn't have brought their coats.

"This place is a mess," Sarah said, glancing around at the broken walls, cracked sidewalks, and unkempt lawn, without losing her stride. "What the feck happened to it?"

Andy shrugged. "Storms. Bombs. Fires. General fighting and a lack of maintenance."

Sarah's lips twitched, but she didn't say anything. Sam was dismayed. Their probes had not shown them this much detail. As they rushed around a corner, he heard Sarah gasp, and for a brief moment, his step faltered. Across the street, the medicine building was a pile of rubble, guarded by walls on two sides. He wondered if the few people he saw walking around were indicative of a nearly non-existent study body.

Andy pointed. "There they are." His stopped walking, staring hard. "Moira ..." He began to run towards two women walking across the grass. One had an arm around the other, as if she were hurt. Sam exchanged a troubled glance with Sarah and they trotted after Andy.

The women stopped, their expressions alarmed. They weren't expecting Andy, so Sam understood their confusion. He saw two men on the other side of the quad, and some internal warning buzzed through him. He yelled just as both men raised their arms to point weapons at Andy and the women. Two electric bolts passed so close, Sam heard the sizzle. Andy grabbed the injured girl, swung her up in his arms, and made a wild run toward a blue car. The other woman kept up with him, while the two men ran toward them. Sam and Sarah raced for the car, clutching their equipment to their chests.

One of the men shouted at them. Sam thought he heard something about "security action," and put speed to his feet. Whatever else happened, he was pretty sure he didn't want to be detained by this world's version of the garda.

Andy threw the girl into the back of the car, as the woman slid into the driver's seat. Sam saw the car lurch but Andy stood by the door, waving his arm in wild swings to urge Sam and Sarah to hurry. Sam shoved Sarah ahead of him into the car, and he shot in on top of her. The girl screamed. Had she been shot? But he couldn't think because then Andy was on top of him, and the car jerked away, throwing all of them against the front seat.

"Fecking Christ!" That was Sarah, who forced her way to the top of the pile, then dove into the front seat as the car took a corner on two wheels. She didn't say anything else though, since the driver was providing an even more colorful stream of invective as she glared at the road, shifted, and turned the wheel in great circles. Sam didn't dare look out the window.

Andy pushed past him, lifting the girl from where she'd fallen on the floor. She was unconscious, and Andy's face twisted in panic. Was she his sister? Sam wondered. Or sweetheart?

Sam braced his legs against the front seat and the door. He held onto Andy's shoulders, holding him still whenever the car lurched, doing his best to help Andy keep the girl from further injury.

Did they not have seatbelts in this world?

After another wild turn, the car stopped so fast, that Sam lost his grip and joined Andy and the girl halfway on the floor. He caught a glimpse of Sarah heading toward the windscreen, arms out in a useless attempt to stop herself. As he began the process of disentangling himself, he was grateful to hear a belligerent tone to Sarah's cursing. More mad than hurt, at least. He reached forward to grip her shoulders. "All right, love?"

The driver opened her door and jumped out, yelling, "Andy, get her into the truck." Sam lost track of her as he helped Andy lift the girl out. Sarah dipped into the back seat for their computers and CERBO. Andy was already running ahead, where a windowless van waited with its motor running. They were in an alley, amid broken furniture and boxes, surrounded by dark buildings. This wasn't any part of Belfast Sam recognized.

Andy disappeared into the van, but before Sam and Sarah got there, the driver of their rescue car stepped back into sight. Spreading her feet to maintain balance, she raised both arms and very professionally pointed a serious-looking bullet gun directly at them. They stopped short, tripping a bit as they fought to stay upright and not drop their equipment.

"What the hell?" Sam stepped in front of Sarah. "We're the good guys."

"Are ye now?" The woman said. She jerked her chin toward the van. "Him, I know, even if he's not supposed to be here. But you, I know nothing about. That means this is as far as you go."

"What the hell are you doing, Karen?" Andy, voice high with startled shock, appeared in the doorway of the van. "They're with me. I promise, Ned's gonna want them."

That wasn't exactly reassuring, but if it kept them from getting shot, Sam could live with it. He remembered his earlier impression of the men who were chasing them. No, he did not want to be in their clutches. Which meant they'd have to take their chances with this "Ned."

"Dammit, Andy." Karen didn't lower the gun, or look away from Sam and Sarah. "You're not part of this. You can't just show up and start making demands."

"When you see what these people have, you'll realize I can do exactly that," Andy said. "Karen, Moira's still unconscious. We need to get her help. And we're not safe here."

It would take a hard person to ignore the fear in Andy's voice, and evidently Karen was not a hard person. Her scowl might have killed them, but she put the gun away and motioned them into the van, slamming the doors harder than was needed. Once inside, Sam noticed the shadow of a fellow in the driver's seat. A moment later, Karen jumped in on the passenger side, and the van drove off, well within the speed limit.

The back of the van was equipped with benches down each side. Sam and Sarah sat with shoulders touching, across from Andy, who still held the girl in his arms. Sam could feel the anger buzzing through Sarah.

Sam addressed Andy with his voice low. "I never agreed to be used as a pawn in your political games. You have no right to make promises on our behalf."

Andy shook his head. "It wasn't me. The rebels already knew about the neutrinos. Hell, I knew about them back in March. Moira and I were working on it, but it was obvious that Sun had suppressed the information. They just hired me two days ago, and yesterday was the first time I found out about your probes. I didn't find out about you until this morning."

"Who are the rebels?" Sarah asked the question through clenched teeth. "And what are they rebelling against?"

"Laws that let the powerful hold innocent people captive without due process, for one thing," Andy said. "Martial law, army conscription, universal tracking ... Want me to go on?"

Sarah leaned her head against the wall behind her, and shook her head as she stared at the ceiling. "What a miserable world," she whispered.

"It's happened before," Sam said, as if reminding them both. "We have the same history up until 1906. There are plenty of examples." Sarah squeezed his fingers, and when he glanced at her, she nodded towards Andy.

He was holding the girl close, watching her face as his fingers rested against her carotid artery. Sam held his breath until Andy moved his hand, stroking the girl's hair in a comforting gesture. "You'll be okay," he whispered. "We're almost safe."

Feeling oddly voyeuristic, Sam looked away, returning Sarah's squeeze. He'd save his questions for Ned.

Chapter 29

Pandemonium engulfed Dinnie's lab. First the neutrino alarm had gone off, drawing everyone's attention to the detector, but before any of them could move, another alarm, this one a floor or two away, shrieked over the first one. Seconds later, another alarm, closer to their lab, joined the first two. Dinnie didn't have to act startled. The alarms scared her witless, and her reaction was no more or less real than anyone else's. She raced out of her office, pointing at the detector alarm and yelling, "Turn that off!" as she ran past it. Someone silenced it, while two of her team stared at the detector, at least trying to do their job. The others stared at each other in uncertain fear. Part of the problem was that no one was sure what the other alarms were for. A fire or hazard alarm was a deep buzz at one-second intervals, along with flashing exit lights. This alarm was a nonstop ringing bell, first one, then the other. They sounded the same note, but came from different directions, as if each alarm was focused on a particular area. The first came from above them, the second seemed to come from the south wing. *Where the labs are.* Before Dinnie could speak, they all heard the ominous *click* of doors locking.

"What the hell?" That came from Dinnie's secretary Cass, who ran to the door, jerking at its handle. When it didn't budge, she kicked the door, then slapped her hand against it. Dinnie reached her, grabbing her hand before it hit a second time.

"Take it easy, Cass." Dinnie tried to sound reassuring.

"We're locked in!" Cass' eyes were wild as she gripped Dinnie's shoulders with both hands. "They're going to keep us here. They won't let us go home, and I've got kids to take care of. What will happen to them?"

Dinnie looked around in frustration and saw her data technician Mike, approaching at a quick trot.

"Mike, take her," she said through clenched teeth. Cass's fingernails were digging into her arms. "I've got to make some calls and find out what's happening."

Mike put an arm around Cass, pulling her away from Dinnie. Holding Cass firmly to his side, he turned to Dinnie. "Wait," he said. "You need to know that just before the first alarm, we had a sharp peak in neutrinos. Right here."

Dinnie stared at him, then glanced around the room. "Here?" She hardly got the word out.

"Not this room," Mike said. "But this building. It was almost simultaneous with the first alarm."

"Get her settled." Dinnie pointed to Cass's desk. "Then get on the detector. Check Labs 4D and 3B. I want to know if the neutrinos originated in one of those."

She turned to her office, but turned back before moving. "Mike."

"Yeah?"

"Find out where they went."

∞

Feldman cased Lab 3B in quick steps, his eyes darting everywhere, not missing anything. There just wasn't anything to see. O'Brien stood at attention, staring straight ahead, with his lips squeezed tight, as if to keep any more words from falling out. O'Brien's supervisor was at the guard station, running the room's security video of the event. Feldman had already seen it once. The fact that it corroborated O'Brien's rambling story only made him madder.

"Th-th-they were both standing at Altair's station," the guard had stammered. "Just talking, sir. They were just talking, not loud, but not whispering either. Then the alarm went off, and I came right around to tell 'em to back off and put their hands on their heads. But before I could say anything, Altair just picked up his computer and they both vanished." He shook his head and ran a hand over his buzz cut. "Just vanished," he repeated.

Feldman stared at Altair's work station, then turned to Green's. "Did Mr. Green have his Pad?" he asked.

O'Brien's eyes darted to his supervisor, and the security feed. "I believe he did, sir."

"Mr. Feldman." The supervisor glanced up from the screen. "Dr. Warner is calling you sir. It's marked urgent."

Feldman tapped his Pad to put her on the speaker. "Where are you, doctor?"

"In my office, sir," Her voice was crisp and professional, with no hint of fear. Good. Feldman liked that in an underling. "Sir, you should know that we picked up two spikes in neutrinos, just before the alarms went off. We've traced the bridges. They have a different signature than the interdimensional one. These are local."

"Excellent work! Where did they go?"

"Queen's University. Just off the old quad."

167

Feldman turned and snapped a finger at the supervisor, who was staring at him, open-mouthed. "We have a team on campus. Get them over there, now! I want those people returned. Alive."

He brought his attention back to his Pad. "Dr. Warner, did you know our guests have slipped the cage?"

There was a pause before she spoke. "No sir, I didn't know it. But I knew it was a possibility, unless you'd given them the go-ahead to run an experiment."

"You would have been told if I had," Feldman said. "Now, I want to know everything you've got on Andrew Green. I want his complete record, but send me whatever you've got available as soon you as have it."

"Mr. Green?" Her voice climbed a register. "Isn't he there?"

"He vanished with Altair. Get me that data."

"Yes, sir."

Feldman closed the connection, pressed another button to call Dr. Russell, and turned to the supervisor, who barked, "The Queen's team is looking for them, sir."

"Keep me informed immediately, whatever happens," Feldman said. "Also, I want a complete sweep of this room, and Lab 4D. I want it yesterday." He turned his attention to the woman waiting on his Pad. "Dr. Russell, what have you got on those tracking chips?"

"Full-spectrum tests aren't done yet, sir. So far, I'm not seeing any anomalies."

"I want you to check through all your tests on Altair and Andrews. See if there's something in their tissues that can be used as a tracker. Altair had to have some way of finding where she was, before he could transport her."

"Sir?" Dr. Russell was clearly bewildered.

"Just do it doctor. I need that information now."

"Yes, sir."

Feldman closed the call, grinding his teeth in fury. It took all his control to not hurl the Pad against a wall. Eyes closed, he counted to four, then turned to the guards. "Get a team to go over today's feed. I want to know what they did and what they said. Do the same with the Andrews feed. You've got an hour." He swung around on a heel and covered the steps to the door in four strides. "I'll be in the neutrino lab with Dr. Warner."

∞

Moving with gentle slowness, Andy lay Moira's head in his lap. Her hair was wet and tangled, and he ran his fingers through it, starting at her scalp, brushing down until he hit a snag. He continued the movement, watching her face for any sign of consciousness. His mind raced in a hundred circles, fleeing from worry over Moira to the presence of Sam and Sarah, to life in the Allied Rebels. He had always had a plan for his life, with clear short-term goals to achieve on the way to long-term goals. Now he was racing into a supernova. He had no idea what would happen next.

He felt a pressure on his hand and looked down to see Moira's eyes open, fixed on his face. Her hand covered his, hindering his massage of her head. He was keeping her balanced with the other hand against her waist, so he just smiled down at her. "Are you all right? How do you feel?"

"It hurts," she whispered. Then louder, "What are you doing here?"

"It's a long story. But Karen's taking us to meet the rebels. There'll be a doctor for you. For now, don't try to move. You're safe."

"They caught me at the hotel," she said, her eyes closing. "I had to run, and I think it made the injury worse." Her eyes popped open. "Someone was shooting at us. Are you all right? Where's Karen?"

"Shhh." He patted her head. "Everyone's fine, don't worry."

"Who were those people with you?"

He gestured toward the other side of the van and she turned her head. "Sam Altair and Sarah Andrews. Your interdimensional people."

Sam nodded, and Sarah lifted a hand in a brief wave.

Moira started to sit up, but jerked to a stop, gasping. Andy gripped her around the shoulders. "Moira, stay still."

Sarah rose with swift grace and knelt by Moira, adding her hands to Andy's. "Please don't try to get up. We're not going anywhere."

Moira stared at her. "You ... you're real." She moved a hand to stroke Sarah's arm. "You really came over that neutrino bridge?"

"Yes, we really did." Sarah smiled, but Andy thought it was a bitter one. "That's the last thing that went the way it was supposed to."

Moira returned the smile, but the pain behind it was obvious. "Our plans seem to be coming out the same way. But you must tell me how the bridge works. I did some equations, but I have so many questions, starting with how you found our universe. How are the universes placed relative to each other? What sort of ..."

"Moira." Andy touched a finger to her lips, as Sarah and Sam exchanged an amused glance. Andy was dizzy with relief that Moira felt well enough, and alert enough, to jump right into questions.

The lips under his fingers moved sideways and she glared at him. "You," she said from behind his hand, which he finally moved, "have been working with them all day. You've had all your questions answered."

He shook his head. "It hasn't been that way, I'm afraid. Sam and Sarah were taken prisoner as soon as they got here, and we've been working on Albert Feldman's ominous projects. It's been pretty tense all day."

Sarah stood, and bent down to pat Moira's shoulder. "We all have questions. Sam and I did not know what to expect here, and I don't mind telling you that I'm terrified. But I hope we do have a chance to talk about the science. It really is amazing."

The van eased to a stop as she was speaking, then began a backup turn. Sarah sat close to Sam, taking his hand. When the van stopped again, Karen and the driver got out. Andy slipped a hand under Moira's knees, hoping they had reached their destination.

"I can walk," Moira said in faint protest.

Andy glanced with some concern at the van door, while sparing a tiny smile for Moira. "No, you can't." He could hear voices out there. What was Karen playing at?

At last, the back doors opened. Andy was relieved to see Karen holding onto a wheelchair, but not the people behind her. Two women and two men, all pointing pistols at the van's occupants.

No one moved.

"Is this necessary? Andy asked.

Karen shrugged. "You wanted safety. They don't stay safe without precautions."

Moira turned her head to look. "She has a point, Andy."

Karen held out an arm. "They won't shoot unless you give them a reason to. Come on. Everyone's waiting for you, including the doctor."

Andy glanced at Sam, who tilted his head and swept an arm toward the door. So he stood, striding forward with what he hoped looked like confidence. He had nothing to hide from these people. They're the good guys.

He tried to project his confidence as he placed Moira in the chair. She was biting her lip, but managed to smile at him. He stroked her hair one more time, then Karen turned the chair around and entered the building. Sam and Sarah waited with Andy until one of the guns indicated they should follow.

Chapter 30

Dinnie's team hunched in their chairs in the main room while they sifted through data, all of them gathered in a loose group in the farthest corner of the room. Dinnie knew they were trying to stay away from Feldman, who paced behind her in her office, alternately yelling at people in his earpiece, or watching as she flipped through the information on her display. She didn't blame her team. She wished she could join them.

He had been yelling at someone on a call as he dashed into the bullpen, and the workers had scattered like cockroaches. He paid no attention to them, just turned into Dinnie's office with a list of rapid-fire demands, most of them instructions she was to give to various department heads. She passed all the messages along with shaking hands. Now she was back to going over Andy Green's personnel file, but nothing in it satisfied Feldman. None of this was in her job description, but she wasn't about to tell Feldman that.

One of the messages she'd sent had been to one of Sun's Intel teams, ordering up-to-the-minute information on Green. When her computer *pinged* with a message from them, she pulled it up just as Feldman leaned over her shoulder to glare at the man on her display and demand, "What have you got?"

"We've got a man who's too busy to get into mischief," the Intel officer said. Everything about the officer was crisp, from his black suit jacket buttoned just so, to the clean lay of the black tie against his white shirt. Light in his office bounced off the steel-rimmed glasses he wore, and he didn't seem the slightest bit intimidated by Feldman, which impressed Dinnie no end.

"Besides his full course load at Oxford," Intel continued, "he taught part-time at Strickert Academy, a boarding school for girls. Lived in the teacher's dorm at Strickert, had a few friends he'd play pool with on weekends, but he didn't even do that very often. The odd date now and then, but no serious girlfriend."

He paused to flip through data displayed at his side, then turned back. "You already know he grew up in Shelton Village. He was friends with a few people that we suspect are rebels, but there's no indication he's done anything for them. Hold on, here's an odd thing ..." he scanned something, then flashed it over to Dinnie's display. A photograph appeared beside him, of a girl with brown hair pulled tightly behind her head. She stared into the camera with solemn attention, while over her head, the words "Declared Dead," attracted the viewer's eye. Dinnie sensed Feldman shifting impatiently behind her.

"Moira Sherman," the officer said. "A student at Strickert. She was reported a runaway from her enclave two days ago. They declared her dead a few hours after that."

Dinnie shuddered. While it was possible Ms. Sherman was not yet dead, she would be, as soon as someone recognized her.

"Why do I care?" Feldman asked.

"Mr. Green is on the list of people to question," the officer said, unconcerned about Feldman's bluster. "All her teachers are, so ... no wait, he's just been updated to Person of Interest." His eyebrows rose. "Evidently she was TA for Mr. Green, and also worked as his research assistant." He looked up from the news ticker he was reading. "No doubt they'll be contacting his supervisor at our Oxford office. However, local security tends to let these cases slide, so they may not be in a hurry."

Feldman crossed his arms. "So he likes young girls. It's not our concern, unless we need to pull strings to keep him out of jail. Personnel can deal with it."

Intel tapped another part of his display. "He's only twenty-two. But sir," he looked up, "this might have bearing on your search beyond handling the enclave government. Green is not stupid. If he did help the girl escape, say, for instance, he brought her to Belfast, he would know they'd be found out. It might jeopardize his position with Sun, and I don't get the impression he would want that." Feldman nodded and Intel continued. "If he's helping her, his best plan would be to turn her over to someone who could hide her. Sir." Intel went quiet to let Feldman reach his own conclusion.

"The rebels," Feldman said. "But it's a stretch to think he brought her to Belfast. He'd be smarter to turn her over to someone in Oxford. Check on both possibilities and get back to me."

Intel acknowledged and closed the connection. Dinnie was sorry to see him go.

"Dr. Warner," Feldman said, and Dinnie jerked in surprise, "given his background, is it possible that Mr. Green knew of the neutrinos before we hired him?"

"He never reported anything, sir," she said. *Document and report at once* was the requirement for anyone working in the field. In Andy Green's case, he should have reported it to his advisor.

"That isn't what I asked." He moved to her side and leaned against the wall, watching her face. "He's ambitious. Perhaps he noticed and kept quiet because he wanted credit for a breakthrough."

"Oh." Dinnie ran through a mental image of his personnel file and gave a reluctant nod. "He's a tenacious researcher, and he had clearance for detectors at Oxford, Belfast, and CERN. In addition, he received regular updates electronically from ten other detectors, as well as NISS." Her throat closed when she mentioned the space station and she had to cough before she could go on. "It is possible that he saw the original detection in March, before we suppressed it."

"Do you have access to the work he was doing this year?"

"Yes, of course."

"Look it over. While you're at it, call Intel back and have them send you access to the girl's work at Strickert. Let's see if any dots connect."

∞

Once inside the warehouse, Andy, Sam, and Sarah found their way blocked by more guards. Panicked, Andy glanced around for Moira, but she was already gone. He did see Karen, standing to the side with Pete and a few other people.

Karen caught his eye and jerked her head toward a hallway. "There's a small infirmary up a few floors. Doc has her. He'll be in touch." She held up both hands. "I'm sorry, but a search is necessary. Just stay where you are."

The guards first ran a scanner over all their equipment, but they showed no particular interest in any of it. At a guard's request, Andy stepped forward and stood with legs straddled, as another guard first ran a scanner over him, then did a pat down. Sam went next, staring straight ahead with a stoic expression. When the guard approached Sarah, she jerked back, arms tight at her sides. All the guns came to attention, two trained on Sarah, the others on Andy and Sam.

"Sarah, easy ..." Sam said. His voice was soft. He glanced at Karen, but watched Sarah as he said, "We don't do this kind of thing on our world. She's just nervous."

Karen nodded. "I understand. But you're not on your world, and here, we search people."

Sarah bit her lip, her face red. "If this is really necessary, I'd prefer it if a woman searched me."

Karen glanced at the man standing next to Pete, an Asian whose mixed-Irish blood showed in his red hair and a line of freckles across his nose. He lifted a finger and nodded once, watching Sarah with lively interest. Most of the guns returned to a guarded rest, but one stayed on Sarah, and another one stayed on Sam and Andy. The guard who had approached Sarah stepped back and one of the women came forward with the scanner.

"All right?" she asked. Sarah nodded, and spread her arms and legs. Her lips trembled, but she made no sound as the guard skimmed the scanner along her right side, then her left. When it reached her left hip, a beep sounded. Sarah jerked, as if preparing to run, and more guns came to bear on her. She went still, arms and legs still straddled. Her hands shook with violent tremors, as she stared at Sam with wild eyes.

Andy placed a warning hand on Sam's arm, keeping him in place.

The guard handed the scanner off. "Empty your pockets, Miss. Slowly."

Sarah sniffed, wiping a tear on her shoulder, before moving her hands to the pockets of her cardigan. "I don't have anything in there," she said, just before her hand slid inside. Her face went white. Andy was afraid she'd faint, but she stayed upright, bringing her hand back in sight, a tiny computer chip pinched between finger and thumb.

"That's not mine," she whispered, her eyes on the guard, begging to be believed.

"How did it get in your pocket?"

"I don't know. Please believe me, I didn't know it was there." She looked at Sam. "I really don't know."

The Asian stepped in front of Sarah and held out his hand. She stared at him, but dropped the chip without any other comment. He turned it over a couple times, lips pursed in thought. Then he gestured to the guard to finish searching Sarah. She did it efficiently, and stepped back, shaking her head.

He held Sarah's gaze. "Name and sector?"

She blinked. "Excuse me?"

"What is your name? Where are you from?"

"I'm Sarah Andrews. From ... Belfast." Her chin went up. "And you are?"

He bowed slightly. "I am Ned O'Malley. I lead this cell. Now tell me, you are from Belfast, you say. But not from ... this ... Belfast, I understand?"

"No."

"Why don't you elaborate, Miss Andrews." It wasn't a question.

Sarah licked her lips. "I don't know how much you know or understand about it. We're from ... a different universe. One that is an offshoot of this one, but there it is 1980."

Behind Andy, someone snickered. A few of the guards looked amused. Ned just nodded. "I have been told some of this. We have much to talk about. But first," he held the chip up. "If this isn't yours, then someone put it in your pocket. Who?"

She stared at him. Andy held his breath and kept his hand on Sam. They all watched Sarah.

Her face relaxed suddenly. "The only person I've been around today was Dr. Warner. Well, and Dr. Russell when she came to take out my chip. But I think it was Warner. She came to the lab and showed me a note, telling me that Sam was working on an escape bridge. I don't know why she was helping us, but she was. When I was on the computer after that, she sat down next to me. She must have done it then."

Ned tilted his head. "Dinnie Warner?"

"Yes. Is she one of your people?"

He exchanged a glance with Pete, who shrugged. Andy spoke up. "She did help us. She saw what we were doing. She could have turned us in, but instead she told us Feldman's schedule, and she said she'd make sure that Sarah was ready."

"Okay." Ned gave the chip to Pete. "Check it."

Pete moved to a computer near the door. At Ned's gesture, the guards released Sarah who ran to Sam.

Andy followed Pete. "Should you insert it in there? What if it carries a virus?"

"This computer's isolated from any network. We use it for this kind of thing," Pete said.

Ned and Karen approached, shepherding Sam and Sarah ahead of them. Ned looked from one to the other, his appraising glance taking in each of them. The guards lounged back into casual poses, but Andy had no doubt they could pull those guns in lightning time.

"I expected the girl," Ned said. "Karen and Pete have vouched for you," he nodded at Andy, "and Karen tells me that you insist I want to meet these two. If they are who they claim to be ..." His inclined head and raised brows made it a question.

Andy nodded, shooting a nervous glance at Pete, who flipped a hand without looking up from his computer. It was up to Andy. "It's quite complex," he said. "The short explanation is that these two people come from an alternate universe, using a quite advanced form of physics. They were prisoners of Albert Feldman."

"Which begs a question." Ned held up a finger and fixed a sharp gaze on Sam and Sarah. "That's an incredible bit of technology you've got there. How did Feldman manage to imprison you? Can't you just use your time machine, or whatever it is, and go back where you came from?"

"We were stunned unconscious." Sam shrugged. "Feldman filched our equipment. When he returned it, he kept the chip that facilitates travel between the universes. We can go anywhere in this universe, but we can't go home without that part."

"That's Feldman, all right." Ned's finger twirled in a "please continue" gesture. "What is it he wanted you to do?"

"Build him a bridge machine of his own," Sam said. "He wants to use bridges as transport corridors around the planet, and out to the space station."

"Is that possible?"

Sam rubbed his forehead and sighed. "Look, I'm not unsympathetic to the problems in this world. But can you understand that we did not come here to be used as pawns in your war? Feldman wants to use our technology, and now, so do you. How can we truly understand what's going on here, even assuming we wanted to get involved?

"Well of course, I understand," Ned said. "But you must understand that there's not a bloody thing I can do about it. Leaving aside the question of why you came here, you must have known that you were taking a wee chance. You didn't know what you'd find, but you came anyway."

He smiled, but Andy saw very little amusement in it. "I could just let you wander out of here. Let you take your chances with Feldman and his security forces. I can guarantee you'd be back in his clutches in a few hours."

"We could build a bridge," Sarah said. "We can go anywhere. He won't find us."

Ned laughed, and this time Andy heard real amusement. The guards thought it was funny, too. "How much do you know about this planet? Even if you were lucky, and picked a place that wasn't toxic, you'd just be picked up by that sector's security. Assuming they didn't kill you outright."

Pete chimed in, turning his chair to face the group. "Feldman's got forces deployed all over the world, too. He's the closest we have to a world-wide despot."

"And he's got neutrino detectors everywhere," Andy said. "He wanted to be ready for you no matter where in the world you came through. You remember the men who found us at the university? He could find you that quickly no matter where you go."

Sarah took a breath, as if preparing to argue, but Ned jerked his chin at Pete. "What'd you find?"

"That you've been busier than any of us thought." Pete swung the monitor around so it faced the group. Andy could see that the screen displayed a manifest of some kind, but he wasn't near enough to see detail.

Pete tapped a button, flipped through documents. Ned peered over his shoulder, and after three quick pages, his finger started tapping on the back of Pete's chair. "What the feck is he after?"

Pete shook his head, intent on his screen. "Framing you, for whatever it is."

"Is he trying to blow up NISS?"

"With this many explosives, there's no "try" about it."

"NISS is your space station, isn't it?" Sarah asked.

When no one responded, Andy answered. "Yeah. It's in a LaGrange orbit ..."

"I know its orbit," Sarah said. "And its coordinates. Feldman had me designing containers to transport over the bridge to it."

Everyone turned to look at her. "Containers for what?" Ned asked.

"Didn't say. But he wanted the containers to be weapons-proof."

"Maybe he's trying to take it over?" Sam asked.

The crowd was silent, exchanging glances. Pete held up a hand. "Sun already controls security on NISS, and they're de facto managers of the place. But it really is international, and there is strong favor for the rebels among the people who live there full time. They can't act overtly, but they still manage to cause headaches. So Feldman blows up the station, or at least part of it, making it look like we did it. Then he gets his army on site, using new technology. The army declares martial law and restores order, with Sun firmly in control and Allied Rebels thoroughly discredited."

"But people will die." Sarah's face revealed her shock.

"That's never stopped Feldman before," Ned said.

"I would think," Sam said, looking to Ned, "that with your extensive drop in population, human life would be considered precious. That your governments would be engaged in protecting lives to increase your numbers."

"Oh, they are." Karen hoisted herself onto a table and let her legs swing loose as she answered. "Governments all over the world have been sure to protect girls and women of childbearing age. Vast numbers of them are restricted to the enclaves and spend their lives having babies."

"Babies whose only purpose in life is to have more babies if they are girls, or to work in Sun or government labor camps if they are boys," Andy said.

"But you're not doing that." Sam looked around, then turned back to Andy. "You're in school, doing ground-breaking work in science. Why aren't you in a labor camp? Was your mother in one of those enclaves?"

"No, she wasn't." Andy shrugged. "The majority of the population went into enclaves after the first famines, and their descendants are rarely allowed to leave. But some people refused to enter them at the start, preferring to take their chances on their own. In my village, several families stayed behind and helped each other survive. Karen's and Pete's families were among them, as well as mine."

Sam's brow was still wrinkled and Sarah stared at him with her mouth open, obviously disturbed. So he tried to explain further. "Our *leaders* have molded it all into a system beneficial to them. The enclaves provide slaves, and the rest of us toe the line to stay free.

Troublemakers, or those people who flunk out of school, are assigned to an enclave. They get a choice as to where, but not whether, to go."

"At least half the rebels in the world are people who've escaped from enclaves," Karen said.

"Moira is one of them." Andy looked troubled. "That's her story to tell, though."

"I'll talk to her later," Ned said. "For now, I need an answer." He pointed at Pete's screen where a damaging document was displayed. "If Feldman's working on blowing up NISS, how do we stop him?"

"What are the dates on the documents?" Karen asked.

"The oldest is dated six months ago," Pete said. "The most recent was two weeks ago." No indication if that's all of them or not."

Ned paced, his fingers drumming with restless energy against his leg. "I can't contact the station until Arkady comes on duty in four hours. He can start searching for the explosives, but we need more information." He stopped and turned to Pete. "Warner rides a neutrino detector. Her job has nothing to do with shipments to NISS. How'd she get this chip?"

"Ah, I believe I can answer that." Pete spun his chair so he faced another computer, waving his fingers over the virtual display with furious speed. "I remember seeing something when we checked her out ... yes. Right here." He jabbed the air and a photo appeared: a sharp man in the white and black uniform of a Sun soldier, the bill of his formal cap shading a freckled face and stern mouth. No personality dared shine through.

"William Warner, Captain." Pete said. "Her big brother. Currently assigned to the Western Brigade in Galway."

"Where shipments for NISS are loaded." Ned paced behind Pete's chair, his eyes on the photo.

Pete waved the photo away and flipped up a flow chart. "He's in our files. A couple of our Galway operatives are acquainted with him. He's provided Intel before, but he's cautious about it."

"Has he ever used his sister before?" Ned asked.

"Nope."

"Uh ..." Andy half-raised a hand, not sure what the protocol was. Everyone turned to him, but it was Ned's narrowed eyes that told him to finish what he started. He cleared his throat and tried to speak with more confidence than he felt. "Feldman's had neutrino detectors on alert all over the world since March. It stands to reason that defense units would also be on alert. If Captain Warner knew about the neutrinos, he probably knew his sister was involved. Maybe he just wanted her to know that Feldman had another agenda."

Everyone was silent as they thought about it. Ned nodded slowly. "Could be." He slapped his hands together and swung on his heel to pin a challenging stare on Sam and Sarah. "As you said, people will die. This isn't your world, but you're here, and you have the means to save lives. Will you help us?"

The travelers exchanged a look. All Andy could see in their glance was worry, and maybe fear. But Sam nodded as they faced Ned. "Yes, we'll help. But I'd like your promise for something when it's over."

Ned took a deep breath, as if holding back a shout of triumph. He spread his hands. "If it's in my power."

"Help us get the rest of our equipment from Feldman. And let us go home."

"Mate," Ned said, his voice deep with feeling, "we want a society where people are free to come and go, and live in peace. We'd never stop you from going home. But yes, I'll do what I can about your equipment."

Chapter 31

Feldman stepped from the lift onto the silent 28th floor. The stark lines and gleaming metal and glass were designed to intimidate. The artwork, sculptures and fountains were perhaps of a higher magnitude than he could afford, but it was just a matter of time.

There was no reception desk, but he turned left, walking with unhurried steps. He stopped when the wall on his right morphed from a marble surface into a floor-to-ceiling screen showing the city beneath them, and the restless Irish Sea in the distance.

He waited.

A few seconds later, the city disappeared and was replaced by the ten-foot image of Sun's AI, in the form of a beautiful woman in impeccable business dress. Her dark brown hair flowed in casual waves around her shoulders as she turned to face him.

"Good afternoon, Mr. Feldman," she said. "He is expecting you in the Greeting Room."

"Thank you, Ari." He nodded before continuing forward. At the end of the hall, two oak doors clicked open as he approached. He entered, aware that his jaw was tighter than he wished. He permitted himself to attribute the tension to his anger. It wouldn't do to appear nervous.

Green leather sofas and chairs littered the large room, in between tables for magazines and drinks. The bar at the far right end was quiet, the mirror reflecting the room and the clouds visible through the wall of windows across from him.

No one else was here.

His cheek twitched once, before he forced himself to be still. He took one, slow breath and let it out while he stared at the window.

Before he drew another breath, a voice broke the silence. "You let Altair walk away with the most advanced technology we've seen."

"It's a temporary situation, sir. He can't go anywhere that we won't find him."

"I'd feel better about that statement if we had a better track record of rounding up rebel commanders. But some of them manage to elude us, don't they, Feldman?"

"Some," he admitted. "But Altair will be back, sir. Soon, I suspect."

"Why is that, Mr. Feldman?"

"I have his chip, sir. The one that allows them to return home."

"Ah." The voice was silent. Feldman felt some of his tension lighten, until it spoke again. "Surely, he can build another chip?"

Knowing he could be seen, Feldman propped himself on the arm of a sofa, the picture of nonchalance. "I'm certain he could. Eventually. But he would have to test it, and we'd have him in seconds. In addition, some of the components he would need are tightly controlled. It's possible we could find him before he ever got another built. And by then, we might be able to use the chip I have to transport into his universe." Feldman shrugged. "His cooperation is guaranteed."

"What about Green? How the hell did he get by us?"

"There's no evidence that he's working with the rebels. Despite his brilliance, it looks like he has the morals of a gutter-rat, and the sorry connections that go with it. In fact, I can use this situation to our favor. I just need to make a couple of calls."

"Get on it, then. Your ass has never been so close to the fire, Feldman. I don't like it."

"Can't say that I like it either, sir." Good, that was said with just the right amount of humble aplomb. Feldman stood up, his confidence returning. "I'll keep you appraised, sir."

The connection closed without another word from the voice. So. He was still in hot water. The best he could hope, was that the water had cooled a few degrees. He walked to the bar and poured a Scotch. "Ari," he said, watching amber lights shift within the liquid, "place a call to Cyrus Sherman in Chelmsford. I'd like a word with him."

∞

Moira didn't open her eyes immediately upon waking. As consciousness returned, she listened, searching for voices, footsteps, the beeping of equipment ... anything to give her a sense of place and time.

She heard only silence at first, but soon made out the Doppler sound of someone approaching, then receding. She opened her eyes to find a ragged, plaster ceiling above her. She lay on a bed, with a pillow under her head and a blanket covering her. The air of the room touched her face with warmth. Such comforts assured her that she had not been turned over to Security preparatory to being sent back to her stepfather.

That worry had crossed her mind just as they were administering the anesthetic for the surgery, probably a last-second firing of nervous neurons. Thank goodness it had not haunted her drugged sleep.

A glance around the room completed her quick inventory. Beside her bed, there was a white, metal cabinet with a small pitcher, and an empty glass with a bent straw in it. An open door to her left revealed a loo. The closed door to her right must by the way out.

She sat up, only then realizing that her stomach did not hurt, although there was a pulling sensation in her skin. Pushing the blanket aside, she lifted the hospital gown to see a small white bandage taped below and to the right of her belly button. Her abdomen was still a spectacular montage of yellow and black, but there was no pain. She decided she was probably still heavily drugged.

The door opened and Moira dropped the gown as she glanced up. Her visitor was not one of the nurses she'd met last night, if it had been last night and not any longer. Like them, this woman wore scrubs, with a medical Feinberger sticking up from the large front pouch of her shirt. She was about the age of Moira's mother, and her skin had the splotchy brown-and-white characteristic of people from the ozone-free west coast. Her smile as she approached Moira seemed friendly and heart-felt.

"Mornin' love," she said. "I'm Sheila, and imagine my surprise to come to work and find a wee, beaten girl to be in my care. Escaped from an enclave, did you? That's bravery, that is, and such good luck you had with it, too. You're safe now, though, so you just breathe easy and let us take care of keeping your presence a secret. It's what we do, ye know." While she was talking, she smoothed Moira's gown, fluffed the pillow, and produced a hairbrush from the cabinet drawer. She stroked it through Moira's hair with gentle pulls.

"They tell me your name is Moira, is that right?" Moira started to say yes, but the avalanche of words swept over her voice. "That's a pretty name, one of my favorites. Now, you need to tell me how you feel. You've been on a monitor, o' course, which shows you're healing nicely, but I like to hear it from the patient's own mouth. I've got a nice warm breakfast waiting for you, nothing too hard to digest, you understand. Want to give your poor sore muscles a chance to recover, but Dr. Mullweather has a deft hand with the lasers, and he did a right job sealing up your wounds. Still, no need to overdo, is there?"

Whereupon she stood straight, hairbrush held in folded hands as she beamed at Moira, and waited for a reply. Moira cleared her throat and ventured to speak, surprising herself when her first words were, "I'm starving."

Sheila did not quite clap her hands, as the brush was a hindrance, but she tapped it once before returning it to the drawer. "Splendid. That's what I like to hear. I'll bring your tray right in, dearie. The loo's behind you if you want to freshen up. I'll just stand close for a minute, in case you've any dizziness, there's a good girl."

Her left hand stood guard a few inches from Moira's shoulder as her right hand pushed aside the blanket and helped Moira swing her legs off the bed. Realizing that she did need to use the loo, Moira planted her stockinged feet on the floor and stood, with a deep breath to banish the vertigo that swept over her. As it receded, she met Sheila's sharp gaze and smiled. "I think I can manage now. Thanks."

"In with you, then," Sheila said, making shooing motions with her hands. "Take your time, dearie, don't move too fast."

Moira took a step in obedience to the shooing motions, but paused, suddenly anxious about what had been happening while she was unconscious. "Can you tell me," she asked, "if Andy Green is still here? Do you know where he is?"

Sheila lifted her eyes to the ceiling. "That young man has been a thorn in my side since I came on this morning, pesterin' me about when you'd wake up and be sure to let him know the second you'd come around." She fixed her gaze on Moira with a confidential wink. "I'll be doin' that, Miss, unless you'd rather I didn't?"

"Oh, no," Moira hurried to answer, embarrassed at the heat that flushed through her body. "Do, please. I want to see him."

"Well then, you get yourself washed and dressed, and eat a good breakfast, then we'll see about taking you to join them. They're all workin' on the Project, and Mister Ned has left instructions you're to assist as soon as you're able. Will that suffice?"

Moira's heart seemed to soar, and she provided Sheila with a giddy smile. "Yes, it will. I feel fine, truly. I'll dress right away."

She turned to the loo and found she could indeed walk without pain. When she reached the door, Sheila gave a satisfied nod and turned on her heel, with a promise to be right back with breakfast.

Dr. Mullweather stopped in as Moira finished eating. He checked the surgical site, and pronounced himself pleased at the condition of the tiny holes. As Sheila covered them with a fresh bandage, Dr. Mullweather gave Moira final instructions.

"Ned wants you helping on the project, and I think you're good to go. I want you in a comfortable chair, with your feet up most of the time. Every hour or so, you should walk around for ten minutes. Continue eating soft foods for today. I think tomorrow you can start on a regular diet. No running or active exercises for a week or so." He dropped his Pad in the pocket of his lab coat, then leaned down to peer at her ear. "That's healing nicely. I can't replace the Nu-skin, but it's not a bad job. This ear should match the other one pretty well."

"'Course it will," Sheila said, patting Moira's shoulder. "Your Mr. Green did a fine job of it."

"Speaking of Mr. Green," Dr. Mullweather said as he turned to go, "he's waiting for you at Sheila's desk. He can take you to where they're working, whenever you're ready."

"I'm ready now." Moira tried not to look as if she were scrambling to her feet, even though that's what it felt like. Dr. Mullweather winked at Sheila while he held the door open for Moira.

Sheila's desk was in an open space down the hall to Moira's right. She recognized the double doors on the other side of the desk as the place they'd brought her for the procedure. Andy sat in a chair, frowning at his Pad. When he heard her steps, he glanced up, and the frown turned right-side up as he stood. She stopped a few feet away and held her arms out to her sides.

"All better," she announced, and watched, fascinated, as his expression morphed into an even bigger smile that nevertheless seemed to be holding back tears.

"I should never have left you alone," he said.

"You had no choice in the matter. In the end, we made it." She glanced around, seeing Sheila and Dr. Mullweather talking quietly near her room, the small infirmary, with its one operating theater and a few supplies, wonder building within her. "We really made it," she said, and laughed. "I'm free. Dr. Mullweather said I was supposed to help with some project."

Andy nodded. "I'll take you. It's this way."

She waved to Sheila, who lifted a hand in return, then she caught up with Andy. "Are the ... um ... travelers ... still here?"

"Yes. They're helping us."

"Helping us with what? Why are they here? What happened yesterday? Tell me everything."

"It's a long story, but I'll give you the broad outline while we walk." He turned and she followed, thankful that he matched his pace to hers. "The guards found a chip in Sarah's pocket that contained information about a plan to blow up NISS. We think a woman at Sun slipped the chip in there, knowing we were trying to escape. It turns out she's given information to the rebels before. So she's on our side. Helped us escape, actually."

"That was lucky," Moira said, then shook her head. "But blow up NISS? Why? Are you saying someone at Sun is doing that?"

"Yeah," Andy said. "It looks like a plot to insinuate the rebels. If the world's population thinks the rebels have done that, they would all approve Sun's taking over the station."

Moira closed her eyes. "More control."

"Exactly. Ned plans to stop them, using Sam's machine. That's what we're working on. For now," he finished up, "we're waiting to hear from Wilbur Arkady, who heads civilian operations on NISS. He's really a rebel operative. Sam and Sarah are helping me build a prototype copy of CERBO, so we have the technology even after they leave. You're going to help with that."

He paused next to a closed office door and grinned in self-conscious pride. "Sam says I would have had it figured out in five or ten years anyway. He couldn't understand why we hadn't done it already, because the original Sam Altair had written many papers on his work. They've all been suppressed somehow, probably by Sun, after that first time travel accident in 2006. It turns out that book you gave me for a graduation present is quite the rare find. As it is, I've been making discoveries that Sun knew about a hundred years ago, which is simply maddening."

"But why didn't they build more machines themselves?" Moira asked.

"We don't know." Andy opened the door and waved Moira through. "Sam thinks that at first they were just covering their tracks, but then they got caught up in the global catastrophes same as everyone else. And at the time, they didn't know what else the technology would be good for."

The conference room Moira stepped into was a hive of activity. Its large table was littered with machinery, computers, communication equipment, tea and coffee mugs, and a tray of sandwiches. Moira recognized Sarah at the left end of the table, and she shyly returned her smile. At the other end, Sam Altair was heads-together with a tall blond man Andy said was his friend, Pete. Neither of them looked up as she and Andy entered. A vid screen covered the wall behind them, showing NISS in its orbit.

In the center of the room behind the table, Karen stood by a virtual map of the interior of NISS, which hovered in the air in front of her. She was wearing hologram gear, walking through and around the display as she murmured into the mike attached to her goggles.

Moira followed Andy to Sarah's end of the table and slid into the empty chair, while Andy went to collect another chair from around the table. He surprised Moira by placing it next to hers and lifting her feet to rest on its seat.

"Doctor's orders, remember?" he said. His face was troubled, although he smiled and spoke in a teasing tone.

Moira nodded, determined to not make him feel any worse. "Thank you."

"How are you feeling now?" Sarah asked.

"Much better," Moira told her. "I guess I had a couple of small tears in my stomach, which were bleeding. Dr. Mullweather sealed them, and he's given me a morphine patch. So I feel fine."

Sarah laughed and Andy brought another chair over for his own seat. He also handed Moira her Pad. "We're working in the file labeled Andrews, which I've downloaded for you," he said.

"We don't know how much time we have," Sarah said. "So I want to make sure we leave all the information you will need to build your own machines. If we have time and the proper facilities, we'll begin work on an actual prototype."

"Okay." Moira accessed the file, which displayed several folders. Not knowing which one to open, she glanced up at Sarah, who smiled in an apologetic way.

"There is a discrete difference between the neutrinos in our respective universes. This may have been what was confusing you when you were working on the equations yesterday. The neutrinos change when we attempt time travel, which is what creates a new universe." She gestured to Moira's Pad. "Our equations will work once we've accounted for the difference. Andy says you're a whiz at that kind of thing, so that's your assignment. It's all in the folder labeled Neutrino Delta. Have at it, and shout out if you have any questions."

An hour passed, with nothing more eventful than occasional murmurs. A young boy brought in a new pot of tea, which they all ignored. Moira remembered she needed to walk around, and Sarah wandered out with her.

Moira forced the jumble of equations to the back of her mind, to focus on a different concern. "After you and Sam get back home," she said, as Sarah matched her slow pace down the hall, "will you want to restrict travel between our universes? I wouldn't blame you if you try to do it," she added quickly as Sarah pursed her lips. "To prevent Sun from sending an invasion force."

Sarah lifted a shoulder. "Sam and I talked about it last night. Of course, we have no idea how it could be done, but I … we … think it might be necessary to try." She stared at the floor, her expression disturbed. "It occurred to both of us that Feldman, and others perhaps, may want to use our world as a refuge." She touched Moira's shoulder. "We might be willing to help in that way. But you realize that three billion people cannot all move into our world."

"Of course not," Moira said. "That would destroy your planet as thoroughly as this one. That's one of the things I was worried about. No," she shook her head, "if there's no way to prevent interdimensional travel, then both worlds will need to set up controls. And I'm afraid our politicians will want to do all the controlling."

"Which is another reason Sam and I are helping you here. I don't know if the rebel alliance will do any better governing your world, but it's obvious that the current system cannot stand. If we can assist in … changing … your government, perhaps that can only help us."

Moira blew a breath out in a half laugh. "Saving the space station is about all I can concentrate on, at the moment."

Sarah laughed. "One step at a time, I guess."

Ahead of them, Ned rounded the corner and came toward them with quick steps. He crooked a finger without slowing. "Come with me."

They sent each other bewildered looks, but turned and followed Ned back to the conference room. He slapped his hands together, getting everyone's attention as he continued to the side of the room, snagging the communications remote as he went. Three clicks and the wall screen switched its display from the orbiting space station to a recorded program. Ned stared at it and the others followed his lead, uncertain of what else they were supposed to do.

A news program was in progress, the bespectacled announcer staring with earnest concern into the camera as he talked. "Belfast garda are searching for a young woman who has gone missing from her Chelmsford enclave."

Moira closed her eyes in slow horror when her recent school photograph displayed on the screen. She felt Sarah shift next to her, then place a hand across her shoulders. She opened her eyes, but fixed them on the screen. She didn't dare look at Andy.

"Moira Sherman was reported missing two days ago, by her stepfather, Reverend Cyrus Sherman, who heads the enclave. Investigators have now revealed a shocking development: she may have been kidnapped by a trusted teacher, Mr. Andrew Green, of Oxford."

"Oh no," Moira murmured, as Andy's teacher photo appeared next to hers on the screen.

"As a welfare student at Oxford University, Mr. Green was assigned to teach at Strickert Academy for Girls, also in Oxford. He was recently employed by Sun Corporation, in their student-assistant program. He was sent, two days ago, to the Belfast office of Sun Headquarters. Investigators believe he kidnapped Miss Sherman before leaving for Belfast. Her stepfather reported evidence of a violent altercation in his home, and believes his daughter tried to resist her kidnapper. They are concerned she might be injured, and indeed, in these surveillance photos taken on the air-train, she appears to be drugged and lethargic."

On cue, a video started, showing Moira swaying unsteadily in a train car, as Andy guided her to a seat. Moira had to admit she looked pretty bad, despite the careful preparation she'd given to her appearance that day. She was surprised that Security had even let her through. From the corner of her eye, she saw Andy shaking his head.

"In an ominous twist," the announcer continued, "Sun has just reported that Mr. Green has vanished from his assigned location, absconding with vital, and irreplaceable, Sun property. They now suspect he is working with Ned O'Malley's Rebel Alliance, and Sun has joined in this investigation. Miss Sherman remains missing, and is believed to be a prisoner of the Belfast rebel cell. We are joined now by Reverend Sherman, the missing girl's stepfather."

Moira felt her chin come up in defiance at the sight of her stepfather. She was grateful for Sarah's steady presence beside her, and wondered if she might have to be the first person to request asylum from Sarah's free world.

The reporter asked, "Mr. Sherman, how does your stepdaughter fit into this? It seems strange that Mr. Green would call attention to himself by kidnapping her, just before he steals vital property from his employer."

Moira shuddered as Cyrus' voice filled the room. "I doubt she has anything to do with it, sir. It appears that Andrew Green worships the baser sins of human nature, giving in to the temptation of female flesh. It is possible that his appointed welfare representative made a serious error by placing him at a school for girls. Someone so young, and alone in the world, would have no resistance to such a strong pull of Satan. Women cannot always control their evil natures, as Eve demonstrated so clearly for us. I hoped my daughter would be safe at Strickert, with no unchaperoned exposure to men or boys. I was mistaken."

"So you think the events are unrelated?"

"I think that, with his employment at Sun, Andrew Green knew he would no longer have access to young girls, and perhaps to my daughter, specifically. I think he kidnapped her in a moment of extreme weakness and evil desire. He then continued with his rebel assignment, and my daughter ..." his voice broke, and Moira shook her head as he rubbed an eye, " ... my daughter must be dead to us, now. I believe she tried to resist, but God's law is clear: she must be put to death. I only pray that Mr. Green will be brought to justice, as well."

The announcer responded with an appropriate murmur of sympathy. The image of Moira's stepfather went away, replaced with the front quad at Strickert, and the announcer continued. "Amanda Spencer-Lionel, Headmistress at Strickert, insists that her students are properly chaperoned at all times. However, investigators have received reports that a clandestine relationship may have existed between teacher and student. They allowed our reporter to talk to one student."

A video replaced the announcer, showing a reporter sitting next to a girl in a Strickert uniform. The girl's back was to the camera, but Moira knew beyond any doubt that it was Grace.

"You were close to the kidnapped girl?" the reporter asked.

"Yes. We were friends." The words were garbled, as if Grace were speaking with food in her mouth.

"To your knowledge, was there anything unusual about her relationship with Mr. Green?"

"She ... liked him. All the girls knew it. They called her Teacher's Pet. Not me. But some of the other girls."

"Did she tell you she liked him?"

"Yes, she did."

Moira groped for the chair behind her, and she sank slowly onto it. Grace was lying.

"Did she ever say that Mr. Green returned her feelings? Did he do or say anything inappropriate?"

Grace was silent for a few seconds, her head hanging down. Then she whispered, "Yes."

"I'm sorry, Miss. You'll need to speak up."

"Yes." Stronger, this time. She lifted her head. "He often had her in his office after hours. She was his T.A. He wanted her to ... do things. She was afraid not to." Grace's voice broke and she half-turned to the reporter, as if begging her to understand. Her profile revealed the shading of a bruise and a massively swollen lip. Moira held a hand to her own mouth as she watched, tasting tears and horror.

The reporter was gentle. "What things, Miss? Did she tell you what he wanted?"

Tears tracked the bruised cheek, and Grace shook her head, turning away so they saw only her back again. "Please don't make me say it again."

"Why didn't you report it?"

Grace glanced at the reporter. "What?" A shadow of movement came from the side, away from the camera's sight, and Grace looked that way, uncertain.

"Why didn't you tell the Headmistress what you knew?" The reporter spoke quickly, but her lips tightened as she followed Grace's gaze to the side. She touched Grace's shoulder. "Never mind. You're upset, so I won't bother you any longer. Thank you for speaking with me."

The announcer came back, promising to keep everyone updated. Ned flicked the screen off.

Moira stared at Andy, who returned her gaze, his face pale, and his jaw clenched so tightly, it had to hurt. She could see that he wanted to ask. She knew he wouldn't.

"I never told Grace any of those things," she said. He had to believe her. "Did you see her? They beat her, Andy." Her chest heaved in a great sob. "They hurt her and it's my fault. She's ruined now. And the Lioness ... the school ..."

Andy knelt beside her. She saw her guilt mirrored in his eyes. "Yes, I saw. I know you would never tell her such things."

"Now why," Ned said, his voice softly threatening, "would they go to the trouble of doctoring the story?"

Andy stood, glancing first at Pete, who just raised a brow. He turned to Ned, who held out a hand to stop him.

"Tell me first, what part of the story is true?"

"The part about Grace and me being friends," Moira said. She stood, to add her support to Andy.

Ned regarded Moira for several seconds before turning back to Andy. "Is that what you say, too?"

Andy was silent, as if thinking through the broadcast. Everyone watched him. Moira knew she wouldn't be able to draw a breath until he spoke. At last he nodded.

"Yes. That, and the information about my background. I was a welfare student, I was appointed to teach at Strickert, and I was just hired by Sun two days ago." He glanced at Moira. "I think it's obvious that we have feelings for each other. But it's not the vulgar, ugly thing they are saying it is." He met Ned's gaze with steady eyes. "Everything else is conjecture and outright lies."

Ned's sudden laugh startled them all. "You have to admire them, sometimes," he said to the room at large. "Masters of spin, aren't they?"

Moira burst into tears.

"They beat her." She felt Andy's arm go around her, and she leaned against him, glad when he wrapped both arms around her. She sobbed into his shoulder.

"I'm sorry about that, lass," Ned said. "They will do whatever they think is necessary. They always have."

"Which brings us back," Pete said, "to the question of why? Why do they think it was necessary?"

"Convenience, I think," Andy said, patting Moira's back. "They've connected me to rebel activity, which most of the public would secretly have sympathy for. But if they can paint me as a monster, no one will condone anything I do."

"And everyone will be looking for you," Karen said. "And by extension, *us*."

The screen buzzed. Everyone turned at the sound, as if glad for the distraction. Moira used the moment to step away from Andy and pull out a handkerchief. Ned checked the incoming-call ID and put the call on the screen.

"Arkady, what do you have?"

"I got two bombs, is what I got. One of 'em live."

Moira turned to face the screen, her gasp echoing Sarah's. The screen showed a thin man in the blue NISS uniform, blond hair cut short, his blue eyes creased and fearful in a stern face. Behind him, a window looked out on a hallway, and beneath the window Moira could see part of a console, with screens, buttons, and a holographic display. Someone sat in a chair in front of the console, halfway out of the camera's view.

"Where?" Ned asked. "How much time?"

"Six hours. The second bomb was partially assembled. They must be smuggling the components up and someone here puts 'em together." Arkady leaned closer to the camera, as if to keep his words from being heard. "Rhyder has 'em. He caught my team while they were reporting to me. Took possession of the bombs, and said he'd handle it. I wanted to do an Abandon Station, but he nixed it. Said they had it under control. Thanked my team for doing a good job." Arkady ended with a growl.

"Damn." Ned whispered the word, and Moira saw his dismay. "Do you know where he took them?"

"Aft cargo station, according to Rhyder. Said it was the safest place to defuse the thing. Says he's sure there aren't any more than this, but he'll have his people search. He won't let us assist."

"We're out of time." Ned turned to Sam. "Security on NISS is controlled by Sun. Rhyder is head of security, working directly under

Feldman." He held out a hand, begging. "You've got to get us on that station now. I can send a team of fighters to take on Security while the rest of us search for bombs, and you set up your bridges to transport them off."

"You want us to go to a space station that could blow up at any time?" Sarah clutched Sam's arm, anger lining her face. But her eyes watched the scene on the screen, and Moira followed her gaze, watching as a group of school children wandered past the window behind Arkady.

"You have children up there," Sarah said, as if just realizing it.

"It's a colony," Ned said. "Workers bring their families to live there."

Sam reached for CERBO. "Get everyone in here you want to send. I'll get the bridge programmed."

"Feldman will see the bridge when we activate it," Andy said. "They'll be here in five minutes. Or less."

"Fuck me." Ned grabbed his Pad and his fingers danced a short pattern over the keys. All over the room, personal Pads jingled in a rapid series of repeating rings. People instinctively grabbed their Pads, and Moira heard Ned's voice coming from all over the room as he spoke into his.

"Red alert, folks. I'm initiating self-destruct, Plan 2A. Repeat: Plan 2A. Security, report to the conference room, tasers and hand weapons only." He glanced to Sam. "How long before the first bridge is ready?"

Sam waved a hand. "Five minutes."

Ned went back to his Pad. "Begin self-destruct immediately. You have ten minutes, folks."

Sam spoke up before Ned finished closing his connection. "I need a space large enough to send people into. Coordinates."

Ned turned to the screen, and flipped the microphone to the station. "Arkady, give us a clear space big enough for eight people at once."

On the screen, Arkady motioned to someone off screen. The camera changed to show a woman. She slammed a headset on and tapped a screen to her side, glancing into her camera at Ned. "Theatre's the best bet. The stage is empty."

"Give us the coordinates."

She tapped another set of buttons and nodded. "On your screen."

Sam glanced up. At the same time, three guards rushed into the room, dressed in full riot gear, and bristling with weapons. Sam ignored them. "Sarah, Andy, Moira, work on that equation. I want the same answer from all of you before I send human beings out on this thing."

Moira grabbed her Pad, her fingers trembling as she entered the coordinates into the equation. The tricky part was accounting for the station's rotation. She didn't look up, but she could sense Andy and

Sarah working on either side of her. *It's not a race,* she reminded herself. *You don't have to be first, you just have to be correct.*

She heard Ned briefing the security team as he grouped them together in the center of the room. Her Pad displayed an answer and she stared at it, reviewing the steps in her mind, looking for an error. Andy stopped working, and a few seconds later, Sarah did, too. Not finding any errors, Moira sent her own answer to Sam's Pad, then went back over her equation again. Just in case.

"Got it." Sam said. He looked to Ned, who held up a finger.

"Real quick. Tell them what to expect. No one's ever done this before." Ned flashed a strangely nervous smile at the guards, reminding Moira that these weren't just random soldiers. The people who worked here were all friends. "Lisa, Phil, Trevor," Ned seemed to be naming them as a solemn acknowledgement. "Listen up and don't panic. Do us proud."

They all nodded and turned pale faces to Sam. "You just stand where you are," Sam said, his eyes moving from one to the other. "In one second, you'll find yourself standing on the stage on NISS. No weird feelings, no sounds, no visions." He glanced around the room. "Those of us who remain will hear a clap of thunder, due to atmosphere displacement after the people leave. It's just the molecules slamming together. Perfectly normal phenomenon."

Ned nodded. "The rest of you, get ready. As soon as we send the first team, Sun will know where we are. We leave within a minute."

"Yes," said Sam. "That means you three," he gestured to the guards, "will need to move off the stage posthaste. We don't want two bodies trying to occupy the same space."

With that odd vision in her head, Moira began stuffing Pads and paraphernalia into her backpack. Everyone but Sam was doing the same thing. She felt her heart racing, but didn't know if was fear or excitement.

Ned said, "Go," and Sam positioned his fingers on the keyboard, eyes on the squad, who stared back at him, grim and alert. Two men, one woman. Lisa, Phil, Trevor. Moira wondered if their names would end up in some future history book.

"On three," Sam said. "One. Two. Three."

Moira was watching the squad, so missed when Sam pressed the final button. She couldn't suppress a small scream when the people vanished. The thunder that accompanied it made her jump. Andy's arm went around her shoulders and she realized she was shaking.

Then she realized that he was shaking, too. But he didn't hesitate, just nudged her forward to stand where the squad had been. She remembered that he had done this already, when he and Sam and Sarah escaped from Sun.

It wasn't just the bridge travel that had her rattled. She'd heard all her life about NISS, and in the last few years, she had learned a great deal about it. She knew it was pressurized, and that spin provided artificial gravity. She wasn't afraid of going there. Awed, perhaps. Overwhelmed, and with no time to mentally prepare.

As the others crowded around her, and Andy kept his arm firmly around her shoulders, she glanced upwards, as if she could see the sky, and the star that was NISS. But as her eyes looked up, she found herself staring at a catwalk, lined on two sides with royal blue drapes. Around her, people sighed in relief. Ned said, "Bugger me!" in a reverential tone.

She glanced at Andy, who was looking down at her, his grin tremulous. The arm he held around her tightened in a quick squeeze, then he released her. The guards, who had followed Sam's instructions and jumped off the stage as soon as they arrived, now clambered back up, big grins wreathing their pale faces.

"Ya gotta tell me how you do that!" Lisa declared. Ned shook off his dazed state and waved a hand.

"They'll tell us later. We've got the element of surprise here, people. Let's use it. Guards point and aft. You're going to clear our path to any bombs we find." He tapped his ear. "Arkady, we're in."

"Bloody hell. How'd you get here so fast?" Arkady did not sound convinced.

"Ask me later, mate. Where's the closest bomb from here?"

"I'm sending you the coords of where I *think* both of them are. But remember, the Sunnies have possession of them."

"So we'll convince them to give 'em up. Where're your teams?"

"All over, just like a normal day. They're covering each other to take breaks and search for bombs, but they have to do it in secret, and it's slow. The Sunnies are making it hard. Us finding those bombs tripped 'em up, but they've been planning this for a long time. We're just an annoyance."

"Okay." Ned flipped up the virtual station map on his Pad. Moira could see blue dots moving around as he continued speaking. "I'm sending you a couple of civvies. They have a job to do, but your work takes priority, if you need 'em."

"Got it. Arkady out."

Ned pointed at Karen, his eyes still on the map. "Take Sarah and Moira to the communications center, then join the search for bombs."

"You're splitting us up?" Sarah threw a nervous glance at Sam as she interrupted Ned. Moira understood how she felt.

"Yeah," Ned said. "You two keep working on the prototype. We might need it. Andy can help Sam with the bombs." Sarah opened her mouth and he held up a hand. "I don't need a bunch of noncombatants to babysit. My priority is to protect Sam and the machine." He raised a brow at Andy. "You grew up in a free village. Know how to use a taser?"

"Yep." Andy caught the gun Ned tossed to him.

Moira shook her head. "You have a lot of strange talents, Andy."

He grinned, but Ned wasn't waiting for banter. "Move out, people. We don't have much time."

Karen headed for the door. Moira started after her, but stopped when Sarah held her ground and glared at Sam. "Don't die," she said.

Sam brushed a kiss on her lips. "Same to you."

Sarah gave a sharp nod. Her lips were tight when she turned to catch up with Karen. Moira glanced at Andy, realizing for the first time that they could die up here. *And we've never kissed at all.*

He must have been thinking the same thing, for his gaze dropped to her mouth, but he just winked at her before falling in next to Sam. Shouldering her backpack, Moira left him to his job, and went to do hers.

Chapter 32

"Got another one!"

Dinnie, who was trying not to sleep as she read through Moira Sherman's school work, jerked upward at Mike's yell, and flew from her seat to join him at the detector. She longed to shove him out of the way and type in the calculations herself, but he was doing it faster than she could have, the way her hands were shaking. She sensed the ominous weight of Feldman's presence behind her, watching over her head as the bridge's alpha point appeared in a three dimensional grid over Belfast.

The sweat on Mike's forehead gave away his nervousness as he kept typing. A moment later, the omega point blinked into existence.

In space.

"NISS." Feldman hissed the word behind Dinnie, and deep inside her, she felt something start to scream. Her soul it was, sure of its impending death. She stood frozen, staring ahead at Mike, watching him begin to turn, to nod in verification.

Then relief swept through her, from head to toe. *They did it. They found the chip and went to NISS. They're going to save the station.* By the time Mike completed his turn, she had recovered, and met his eyes with a brisk nod of approval, before turning to face Feldman. Alert and professional, ready for anything.

Except for the desperate shock on Feldman's face as he stared at the display. Behind him, to his right, the security supervisor was on a call, already sending a team to the alpha point. Dinnie's voice was too high when she asked, "Sir? Why would they go to NISS?"

The shock left his face as a slow smile moved his lips. "I don't know, Dr. Warner. But we've got them."

He pointed at Mike. "I want to know how many people were transported. Hurry."

Mike turned back to the display, began typing again.

"It takes a few minutes," Dinnie said, not wanting Feldman to yell at Mike.

"I want it now." Feldman jerked his chin at her as he tapped his ear. "Help him."

It was a one-person job, but Dinnie stepped next to Mike and ran her finger over the bridge, hoping she looked like she was doing something useful. Mike grinned tightly at his racing fingers to acknowledge her."

Behind her, Feldman said, "You have intruders on your station, Rhyder. Don't ask me how I know. Just listen. Put that station on lockdown. Get your guards ..."

"Shit! There's another one!" The shout was out of Dinnie before she even realized it, as a new virtual bridge shot through her hand. She could feel Feldman's eyes boring into her back, but she didn't turn around. "Same alpha and omega, sir."

"How many fucking people?"

"Three on the first one," Mike said, gasping a little. Dinnie thought she could see smoke coming from his fingers. She stared at the display, thought she could see where the numbers were going ... and took a leap.

"More than three in the second one." She stared and counted. "Five ... no, seven. I think."

"Yes," Mike said, breathing hard. "Seven in the second."

"Rhyder, you've got ten intruders," Feldman said. Dinnie listened, but didn't take her eyes off the display, terrified she would see another bridge. "Find them all. You can kill the soldiers, but no one else. Make that clear, Rhyder: no one else gets killed. Confiscate their equipment immediately, but do not let any equipment get broken. They've got some irreplaceable stuff. You make sure your people understand that. Are you on lockdown?"

Dinnie didn't hear the answer, but Feldman said, "Keep them that way until all ten are rounded up. Move."

He turned back to them. "Any more?"

Dinnie shook her head. "Not so far."

Feldman moved closer, to peer at the display. Dinnie watched him without turning her head. "Why," he said, as if asking the display, "would they go to NISS?"

∞

When the lockdown alert came over the PA system, Ned stopped walking and shook his head. "On to us already. Damn."

"Not surprising," Andy said. "They saw our bridges."

"I know they saw the fucking bridges. I was just hoping for more time."

They were in a corridor, a tight circle with Sam in the middle. They had kept their weapons holstered out of deference to the civilians, but at Ned's nod, the guards and Pete armed themselves. Ned pulled his taser out, as well, and after a moment of hesitation, Andy did, too.

"We continue to our objective," Ned said. "When we meet resistance, Sam and Andy get down, try to get to cover. But let us protect you. Andy, you shoot if you have a clear aim, but your first priority is to protect Sam and the machine. Got it?"

He didn't wait for Andy's nod, he just turned and gestured onward. Andy went with them, tapping his taser with nervous fingers, and regretting his lack of rebel involvement up to now. If he'd been with them earlier, maybe he'd feel more confident about his ability to fight.

They'd traversed half the corridor when their luck ran out. Ahead of them, two Sun guards rounded a corner. Andy quickly lost track of the action. The Sunnies ordered them to halt, their own guards were swinging around, the Sunnies were pointing weapons, someone pushed him, and in a blind panic ... he fired. He had time to see that his shot arced wild before he went down under Pete and Phil, and as the corridor filled with sizzling energy and shouts, he knew with sick certainty that he had fired first ... thus giving the Sunnies plenty of excuses to fire back.

In the next few minutes, he and Sam were shoved back a few feet, then into an open door. Their team followed and Pete pointed them to another door opposite them. Andy grabbed Sam's arm and they ran through.

"Hang right!" Pete yelled. Andy turned without seeing, pushing Sam ahead of him, down a flight of stairs. They rounded a corner and crashed against a closed set of double doors. There was nowhere else to go. The sounds of taser shots and pounding feet grew ominously near. Andy exchanged a glance with Sam, who shrugged. "In for a penny ..."

Andy slapped the switch and the doors slid open on soundless tracks. Lisa appeared around the corner behind them, her taser firing back the way she'd come. Swinging around on one leg she saw them and shouted, "Go!" before continuing her spin to shoot in the other direction. Andy grabbed Sam and pushed him through. Inside were row upon row of plants in various stages of growth. They took shelter behind the nearest one and Andy peeked around it, taser ready. He felt more in control, remaining alert for either friend or foe to come through the door, prepared to not shoot if it were the first, or shoot fast and duck back, if it were the second.

Pete dashed through, then Ned and Lisa, neck and neck. Ned and Pete took cover, while Lisa turned to face the door, her taser held ready. A shot came through, but she didn't flinch. The next moment, Trevor fell through the door as if he'd been thrown, then Phil dived in, slamming the switch on the wall as he came. The doors slid closed, and Lisa fired a five second blast at the switch mechanism on the wall. By the time the Sunnies got there, the doors refused to budge.

∞

Out of the frying pan into the fire. Moira remembered her real father saying those words to her mother during an argument about her mother's desire to join Sherman's enclave. Moira had been too young to understand any of it, but her father's words came back to her now.

She'd escaped the enclave, but now people were shooting at her. She suspected the enclave was the real fire, and this was just a minor hitch in her plans. She'd be dead for sure if her stepfather had his way. Here, she at least had a chance to get out of it.

Provided she stuck close to Karen Jones. Andy's friend was a small woman. Moira would have called her delicate, her thin frame causing one to expect fairy wings, and her single, blond braid taking years from her already young features. But when an approaching Sun guard pulled a taser on them, with a demand to "freeze!" Karen did the opposite, whipping her own taser out as one leg flew up to shove Moira and Sarah into a side hallway. Her taser arm remained focused on the guard, sending a steady stream of energy in his direction, as the rest of her body twisted to follow them into the hall. In the space of two minutes, Moira knew she would never think of Karen as delicate again.

They heard the guard call for backup, and Karen popped into the main hall to send another surge toward him. Twisting back into hiding, she sent a blast into the corridor's surveillance camera, and muttered one word to her charges. "Map."

Moira shuffled the backpack off her shoulder and scrabbled for her Pad. Sarah reached around to close the pack and shift it onto Moira's back so she'd be ready to run. Karen rang off another shot. In the background, Moira heard an announcement starting, declaring a lockdown and instructing people to shelter in place. *To make it easier to catch us,* she thought as she brought up the virtual station overlay. It was visible by the time Karen popped back into the hall.

"This hall leads to a roundabout," Sarah muttered, her gaze following Moira's finger through the display. "If we take the second walkway to the right, there's a bank of lifts and a stairway."

"Stairs. Go." Karen flattened against the wall, holding her gun against her chest. "I'm right behind you."

She dashed out once more to shoot. Moira did as she was told, her run clumsy with her Pad and backpack. Ahead of her, Sarah was having the same struggle. But the roundabout brought them a reprieve, as station personnel trying to obey the lockdown raced through in a frenzy. The guard stopped firing, yelling instead for everyone to get down. Then Sarah was through, Moira just a few steps behind. She wasn't sure of her count, but she thought they'd missed the second corridor off the roundabout.

When no lifts or stairs appeared, she knew she was right. Sarah realized it too, and threw a hand against the wall to stop her forward rush. Moira collided into her, but managed to move enough to the side to make it a glancing blow. "Keep going," she said, then on impulse pushed on the first door she came to. It opened and she fell into darkness. Sarah crowded behind her and Moira managed to swallow a scream of pain as her stomach lurched. Damn it, she wasn't supposed to be running.

"Where's Karen?" She managed to whisper the question. Good. Better than screaming.

"Don't know," Sarah whispered back. "Where are we?"

Moira flipped on her Pad's light. Before they could look around, the sound of running feet outside the door made Moira kill it instantly. They waited, not breathing.

The feet slowed to a walk, then stopped. They heard a muttered "Feck," and Sarah pulled at the manual door handle "That's her ..." a seam of light appeared at the door edge, and a moment later the business end of a taser poked through, with Karen's eyeball glaring just above it. Then the taser disappeared and Karen pushed her way in with them.

"You said the *second* path of the roundabout," she said in a loud whisper.

"I was too busy to count," Sarah said. "Where's the guard?"

"Sleeping. But he did get a call out for backup. Where are we?"

"We were just starting to look," Moira said, flipping on her light again.

Karen and Sarah added their lights. Moira moved hers slowly, trying to see everything, but Karen's light danced around to specific points, as if she were looking for something. All Moira could see was that they seemed to be in a supply closet of some kind. The room was small, with wide shelves on two walls and storage canisters stacked on the floor. Karen nodded, as if reaching a decision.

"This'll work for now. Up there." She pointed while pushing on Moira's back. A top shelf was empty. Karen folded her hands together and bent down. "Up with you. Hurry."

Moira swallowed her questions, slipped off her backpack, and put her foot in Karen's hand. She wasn't quite prepared to be thrown toward the ceiling, but she managed to catch the shelf. With the women pushing on her feet, she hauled herself up, biting her lip to keep back a cry of pain. Once on the shelf, she lay on her stomach and let them pass up all the packs. Then Sarah scrambled up and turned to help Karen. But Karen waved her off and moved a few feet to her right, doing a quick run and jump to reach that part of the shelf. This put several large boxes between them. Sarah sent a quizzical glance to Moira, who shrugged.

The boxes moved toward them and Sarah instinctively reached out to balance it. "Put them in front of you." Karen's voice floated to them over the boxes. "Get back against the wall and use them to hide you."

In a few minutes, they had it all arranged, but they both peeked over the boxes when they heard Karen's feet hit the floor.

"What are you doing?" Sarah asked in a frantic whisper. "Get up here."

"Turn your lights off," Karen said.. "Stay quiet and still. They'll be searching. I'm going to draw them away."

"You're what?" Moira asked. "No! Stay with us until they leave."

Karen pointed at her, then went back to packing various weapons in her pockets. "You cannot keep running. I need to buy us some time and space. Just stay put, keep the lights off, and don't make any noise until I'm back."

She leaned against the wall and cracked the door open to listen and look. Then she opened it further, slid through and closed it behind her. Moira heard no sounds other than their own breathing.

Sarah fumbled with her Pad. "She's right. She'll be back. Turn your light off."

Moira had dropped her Pad on the shelf so she could look over the box, and she turned now to pick it up. A glimmer in the dark recesses of the next shelf caught her attention. She had to twist her neck a little to see it clearly, but when she realized what it was, she grabbed Sarah's arm.

"My god. Can you see that?"

Sarah bent nearly in half, and finally sat back, shaking her head. "I don't see anything. What is it?"

"It's sort of a ball, with wires and lights. And numbers. I think it's a bomb."

Sarah swallowed, as if it were a difficult thing to do. "Can you read the numbers? Are they moving? Counting down?"

"Yeah." Moira killed her light, and stared straight ahead in the darkness. "Counting down. Three hours, twelve minutes."

Chapter 33

"Am I correct," Sam asked, "in assuming that the Sunnies outnumber us?"

He remained trapped with Ned, Pete, and the three guards in a hydroponics lab, surrounded by rows of plants growing in pools of water. The room was warm, with a damp, green smell to it. Oddly, the Sunnies had made no attempt to get inside, which made Sam nervous. He supposed they were content just with keeping them in one place.

In the final moments of the shootout, Trevor had been hit, sustaining a deep burn to his arm. In that, hydroponics was fortuitous, for the lab boasted several aloe vera plants. Ned had applied the ointment to Trevor's burn and settled him against a box of hemp bushes.

Andy was scanning his map for the location of a first aid kit, while Ned examined his map for more Sun guards. Pete, Lisa and Phil were searching for another way out.

"About twenty to one," Ned said without looking up. "Not counting civvies."

"Which are ...?"

"Civilians," Andy supplied. "About eighty percent of the station's personnel are civvies. Scientists, of course, but also teachers, medical personnel, cooks ..."

"Accountants," said Ned. "Though God knows why."

"We can't depend on them to help us fight?" Sam asked.

Ned glanced up. "If I had time to take volunteers and organize them, a lot of them would help. A lot of them probably *are* fighting, if I know Arkady. But we're still outnumbered. And for the most part, the civvies are in the way. Sun doesn't care if any of them get hurt, but we do."

Sam tapped an aimless pattern on his Pad. "There has to be a better way to find the bombs. We could search the station for days, and never find them."

"Arkady's assigned areas to search, but I'm open to suggestions," Ned said as he went back his scanning.

"Well, look, we know the bombs were smuggled aboard with other equipment, right?"

"Yep."

"You know which equipment? Perhaps the bombs are buried within."

"It was all kinds of stuff," Ned said. "The bombs Arkady's people found were still in the cargo area, probably the most recent ones sent up. They're sending up components, y'see. One of the bombs was assembled and sitting in a locker for extra space boots. The other one was still in pieces, packed among other standard items."

"So someone up here is meeting the shipments, separating out the bomb materials, assembling them and placing them somewhere else?"

"That about sums it up."

Sam continued to tap his Pad. "Do you have some way to track cargo? Chips, radio frequency ...?"

"Radio frequency," Pete said, joining them on the floor beneath the Aloe vera. He shook his head at Ned's silent question. "We've got two Sunnies guarding the hallway to this section. I guess they feel they've got us trapped, and can handle us when it's convenient."

"Arseholes," Ned said.

Sam stayed on his thought. "Do you disable the frequencies once the shipment is received?"

Ned looked thoughtful. "No. Everything's tracked throughout its lifecycle. We've learned not to throw things away."

"You're thinking we can trace the bombs using the RFI?" Andy asked.

"Do we have that information?"

Ned scratched his head. "For the items on the final manifests, yeah. But the smuggled items aren't going to have an RFI listed."

"Not on the *final* manifest," Sam said, and looked at Pete.

"I'm on it." Pete flipped his Pad on and his fingers began a furious dance.

"They'd be idiots if they didn't disable them," Ned said.

Sam shrugged. "Bureaucracy takes on a life of its own. If some clerk is responsible for maintaining RFI's, he'll do it unless someone tells him not to. Objects-in-motion kind of thing."

Ned grunted.

"Ye-e-esss," Pete ended on a hiss. "We have them. Bloody hell, we have them on the original manifests!"

"Trace, man. Start tracing them." Ned sat up on his knees, face hopeful. Andy grinned.

Pete's brow furrowed as he worked a series of taps, then a pause, another series of taps, another pause. He started to shake his head, eyes dimming with discouragement, but a sudden beeping emanated from his Pad, and he jerked to his feet in startled dismay.

"Holy hell, there's one right here!"

Sam felt his body go still, in the same way an animal freezes at the whiff of a predator. He sensed that everyone in the room did the same. They stared at each other.

"That explains why no guards followed us in here," Andy said, his voice just above a whisper.

"We're trapped, so they can blow us up at leisure." Pete turned his head, staring down a row of spinach leaves. "It's down there somewhere."

Sam stood, moving to the aisle, CERBO at the ready. "Give me the coords."

Pete's fingers moved over his Pad. "You have 'em."

They all watched Sam. Lisa and Phil abandoned their lookout posts, joining their injured comrade on the floor. Trevor's ragged breathing was the only sound. Sam nodded toward the row of spinach plants. "Third plant box from the other end," he said. He started down the aisle.

"Where the hell you going?" Ned asked, soft.

Sam stopped and looked back. "Don't you want visual confirmation that it's actually a bomb?

Ned fidgeted. "Suppose I do. But not you." He gestured with his taser. "Lisa, you're on."

Lisa gave a sharp nod and moved with quick steps to join Sam. A jerk of her head sent him back to the end of the aisle. She holstered her taser and inched her way down the corridor. Once in front of the box, she began an intense examination without touching anything, searching from every angle she could. They saw her shake her head.

She raised her hands, touching each finger to her thumbs in quick succession, then bent into a squat, fingers playing over the frame with a feather-light touch.

Sam could feel his heart pound, setting up a dizzying thumping in his ears. He reminded himself to breathe, and the thumping quieted to a background knock.

Lisa sat, flipping on her wrist light. She stretched out on her back, sliding head and hand beneath the box, light poking into the darkness. When her body went still as death, Sam knew she'd found it.

Using just her heels, she slithered out and stood with care. "Wires," she said. "The bomb is attached to the bottom of the planter."

Sam crooked a finger at her. "Come this way." As she came toward him, he sent the planters coordinates to CERBO and set a destination.

"Go," Ned said.

Lisa had nearly reached Sam when he pressed the final button. At the sudden clap of thunder behind her, she threw herself forward.

Sam let out a yell as she crashed into him, sending them both to the floor in a clatter of weapons and Pads.

"Bloody hell!" Sam yelled, pushing her off of him and sitting to rub his head. "What'd you do that for?"

Nervous laughter from the others brought a flush of embarrassment to Lisa's face, but she laughed, too. "I thought the bomb went off. I forgot about the thunder."

Pete slapped Sam's shoulder. "Be grateful for her quick reflexes. She just saved your life."

Lisa snorted. "Doubtful, if that had really been the bomb."

"It counts," Sam said, and held out a hand to help her up. They all took a moment to stare down the aisle at the now-empty space.

"Find the others, Pete," Ned said. "Lisa, Phil, I want ideas for handling our personal guard team out there." He nodded at Sam. "Good work."

Sam shrugged.

"Where'd you send it?" Ned asked.

"Three hundred kilometers in that direction," Sam said, pointing behind Ned. "Into the big, dark middle of cold space."

"My hero," Ned said, and tapped his Pad. "Arkady, my man," he said when Arkady answered, "I'm reporting our first success." He gave a brief run-down, and they all heard Arkady's whistle.

"Good job," he said. "I've got your original manifest. I'll help with your search on this end. Oh, did you ever send those civvies down here?"

Sam clamped down on the fright those words gave him, but he turned to face Ned. Pete and Andy did the same thing.

Ned stiffened. "I did, thirty minutes ago."

"They haven't made it here. No word from them, either."

The men stared at each other, none of them willing to speculate.

"Shit," Sam said under his breath. "Shit, shit."

∞

Dinnie splashed cold water on her face, then stared at her reflection in the bathroom mirror. Water dripped down as she listened to the hard, frantic pounding of her heart. She fancied she could see it beating through her blouse.

Feldman suspects something. He's watching me. Waiting for me to trip up.

She shuddered, and reached for a towel, certain that she was going to crack. Feldman terrified her, and she was losing the ability to hide it.

Her Pad went off, on a triple-urgent alarm sound that sent her a foot into the air. She was out the door and heading back to the lab before she finished pulling it out of her pocket. Two steps later and she was racing inside, snapping the alarm silent without answering it. Mike and Feldman were in front of the detector. She joined them there, not even needing to ask.

"Bloody things are becoming commonplace," Mike muttered when she reached his side.

"Into space?" Dinnie said, confused by what the display showed her. "They sent someone into space?"

"Or something, Feldman said, his cold eyes lowering her body temperature several degrees when he looked at her.

She shivered, then rubbed her face, as if to wipe his glare away. "It doesn't make sense."

"No people were on that bridge," Mike said. "Whatever it was, it was small and inert."

A bomb. Please, all the saints, let it be one of the bombs. Afraid that Feldman could hear her traitorous thought, Dinnie glared at the display, as if looking for the answer there. Mike sent her a little smile. She wasn't the kind of boss who hovered, but she thought he was grateful for her as a buffer between him and Feldman.

She wondered who would buffer her.

∞

"We have to find them," Sam said. He struggled to contain his fear for Sarah, as well as his bewilderment at the other men. He could understand Ned's attitude: Ned had to command the entire team, and that meant being willing to accept losses. But he didn't understand Pete at all. How could he be willing to ignore the danger his wife might be facing? Even Andy was strangely ambivalent. Moira might be Andy's student, but it was obvious to all of them that he was in love with her. Yet he seemed to be taking his cues from Pete and Ned, and wasn't willing to go after the women.

Ned had already nixed the idea and was ignoring Sam's diatribe, busying himself in a discussion with Phil and Lisa. Pete was likewise ignoring him while he ran a search for more RFIs on bomb components.

Andy placed a hand on his shoulder. "It's not happening, mate," he said. "Ned's right. It won't do any good to find the women but have the station blow up around us because we didn't get the bombs out of here."

"Just like that?" Sam swallowed the bitter bile that rose in his throat, and shrugged off Andy's hand. "Maybe at your age, girlfriends are a dime a dozen. But it's not like that with Sarah and me."

"No, damn you." Andy shoved him, not hard, but seeing the anger on his face made Sam curl his hands into fists.

"I'm scared, too." Andy said. "I've never been this deep into the rebellion, the way Pete and Karen are. I'm not used to this, and

Moira's not prepared for it at all. But I know Pete. And I know Karen. She's never let anyone push her around. If Pete doesn't seem worried, it's because he knows her abilities better than anyone. He trusts her to handle bad situations."

Sam glanced at the door, with the Sunnies still on the other side, keeping them trapped in hydroponics. He tried to think of an argument, but finally just sighed, and rubbed his eyes.

"I won't tell you they're probably fine," Andy said. "Because I don't know if they are. But whatever trouble they ran into, I do know that Karen will do everything she can to get them out. And that's saying something."

"All right." Sam nodded and looked around the room. "I just need to do something. I feel so helpless."

Pete glanced up from his Pad. "I've found another one. That should keep you busy, if we can manage to get to it."

They all turned to Ned, who bounced on his toes and nodded toward Phil. "This bloke's got the right idea. Pete's got the coords for the bomb. Sam can just port us over there, and we don't have to worry about our Sunnie friends out there."

Sam pursed his lips as he thought about it. "All right ..." he said. "But we need to know what we're porting into. There must be enough room. And what if there are Sunnies there?"

Ned called up his holo map. "Where are the coordinates, Pete?"

They all gathered around the display as Pete sent the coords to the map. A red dot appeared, flashing deep within the upper right quadrant of the station.

Ned whistled. "Bloody hell. Those are living quarters."

"Families?" Sam asked.

Everyone nodded as they stared at the dot. Ned flushed red, highlighting the freckles on his face. "Those bastards are framing me for this? Killing children?"

Pete shook his head. "No one would believe them, Ned. You're in the news all the time, and whatever people think of your activities, they all know you don't hurt innocents."

"It's like your wee calling card," Lisa said.

"What is in that room?" Sam asked. "I need specifics."

Ned tightened his lips, as if to suppress his rage, and adjusted the map to zoom in. "Looks like a bedroom."

"Is there furniture? How much space is available?"

"Can't tell that from this map, mate."

"Well, I can't send anyone where I don't know the layout. It has to be a clear space."

"What about the corridor outside the flat?" Andy asked. He thrust his hand into the display and traced the corridor with his finger. "Just outside the flat entrance."

"That will be clear," Ned told Sam. "With the station on lockdown."

"Except for potted plants," Pete said. Sam threw him a puzzled look, and Pete explained, "To help with O_2. You remember seeing potted plants in the corridors while were searching?"

Sam nodded. "Sure. We do the same thing in our universe." He pointed at the corridor Andy had traced. "The pots are always along the walls, right? To keep from blocking the corridors?"

"Yeah," Ned said. "You can port people to the middle of the corridor, can't you?"

"Yes, but the next problem is how do we know there aren't people in the corridor? I don't care if they see us, but I don't want to port someone into a space that's already occupied."

"What would happen?" Ned sounded curious.

"It would probably kill both people."

"Bollocks." That came from Phil, who looked as if he was having second thoughts about using the portal.

Ned raised a brow at Phil. "Station's on lockdown. There shouldn't be anyone in the corridors. Still ..." He tapped his Pad to put it one speaker. After a moment, they heard Arkady answering.

"I need a clear hallway at these coordinates," Ned said. "Can you do anything? And while you're at it, who lives in Flat 62, and is anybody there right now?"

"Hang on." Everyone stared at the 3D display, lost in their own thoughts while they waited for Arkady to come back. Sam counted to twenty-eight before Arkady spoke again. "The hallway is clear. We're on lockdown, so they're all inside. There's no one home in 62, though. It's occupied by Candace Lightfeather and her teenage son, Ryan. Candace is one of our doctors."

Ned and Pete exchanged a glance and Pete shrugged to indicate he couldn't make sense of it, either. Sam went to work inputting the coordinates of the hallway, half listening to the rest of the conversation.

"There's a bomb in one of the bedrooms," Ned said.

"Shit." Arkady's voice was soft. "Is it live?"

Pete shook his head.

"No," Ned said, "but we're on our way to get it. We'll port to the hallway. Can you unlock the flat for us?"

"No can do, mate. Only security can do that, and I don't recommend asking them. Can't you just port inside the flat?"

"It's not safe to do that, evidently. I'll explain later. So we'll just have to break in."

"That'll set off an alarm in security," Arkady said.

Ned grinned over at Phil and Lisa. "Guess we'll have to be ready for them," he told Arkady. "One more thing: we've got an injured mate. Can I port him to your location? Just clear a space for him."

"Oo-kaay." Arkady sounded doubtful, but they heard him instructing people to clear the center of the room. Sam got busy deleting his previous coordinate entry and told his CERBO to access Arkady's location. Arkady's voice came back to them. "I've got a space about two meters in diameter. Will that work?"

"Yeah, hang on." Ned moved over to Trevor, who was laying down where they'd left him, under the aloe vera plants. Andy had found a first-aid kit and put a pain-patch on his shoulder, then covered him with a blanket. Trevor was half asleep, and Ned shook him gently as he knelt next to him.

"Can you sit up, mate? Just for a few minutes, then they can take care of you."

Trevor mumbled something and reached for Ned's arm. Ned propped him up against the planter box, but Sam shook his head. "He'll have to move away from the box or I'll have to send it with him."

"I can do it." Trevor sounded more awake and he scooted forward a couple of feet. He wobbled a bit, but gave Sam a tight nod. "Ready."

They all jumped at the clap of thunder, but grinned at each other to hear the astonished shouts coming through Ned's Pad. Arkady's voice came through over the racket. "You have got to tell me how you do that."

Ned grinned. "I'll buy a round when all this is over and let Sam answer all your questions."

"Sure you will. Stop fooling around and go get that bomb."

"On our way." He snapped the connection closed, and sent Sam a look of regret. "We should have done that with the women. I didn't think of it."

Sam stood very still, his own regret weighing him down.

Next to him, Andy shifted. "New technology," he said, brushing a shoulder against Sam. "Even in your universe, it's new, isn't it? We can't know all the ways it can be used."

Sam nodded, blinking down at his Pad. He flipped the data back to the coordinates for the hallway. "Let's get moving," he said. Even to himself, his voice sounded bleak.

The others stepped closer. Lisa and Phil flanked them, facing outward from their circle, tasers ready.

Ned took a breath. "Go."

Sam closed his eyes for the port, but opened them as soon as he heard exclamations from the people around him. He suppressed a grin. It took a while to get used to. He was relieved to see the corridor was empty. Pete joined with Lisa and Phil to guard them while Ned did something dirty and fast to the door. It slid open and Ned stood, jerking his head to point Sam inside. "There's an alarm going off in Security right now," he said. "You're on the clock."

Andy rushed in. Sam followed, unsettled at the simple normality of the flat. A living room with a kitchen off to one side, and a small dining table in between. Ned pointed to a hall, eyes on his Pad. "Down there. Second door on the left."

As the map had told them, this was a bedroom. Had to belong to a teenage boy, Sam thought, taking in the scattered clothes, oversized shoes, one on a chair, the other half under the bed, and a dart game on the wall.

He glanced at the bridge machine. "Bloody thing is under the bed."

This time it was Andy who lay down to look. He didn't crawl under, just lay on his side and peered into the darkness, then shook his head as he sat up. "Hooked to the mattress. No lights or anything."

"Hurry," Ned said. He was watching the hallway.

Sam handed CERBO to Andy. "You gotta learn how to do it." He grinned at the expression on Andy's face, one of sheer terror and delight. He understood. "Talk it through, but don't waste time. I'll stop you if something's wrong."

Andy stood and took the machine. "Bomb's attached to the bed, so I'll have to send the entire bed out." Sam just nodded, but Andy didn't look up to see his reaction. He fiddled with the coords, then nodded. "Field is locked on the bed." He tapped a few more times. "Omega is the same as you used for the previous bomb." He hesitated, then grinned at Sam and jerked a thumb over his shoulder. "I'm sure we're okay, but let's step back a bit, eh?"

Sam laughed, but followed Andy to the bedroom door.

"Hurry up," Ned growled.

The bed disappeared.

"Wooh!" Andy jabbed a fist to the sky.

"Okay." Ned pulled them into the hallway. "Let's go. I want us back at Hydro."

They joined the others in the living room. Through the open door, they could hear running steps. "Everyone get close, " Ned said. "Go."

Sam grabbed the machine and punched keys in rapid clicks. Before they could get a glimpse of whoever was approaching, the flat disappeared, and hydroponics took its place.

Chapter 34

"Goddamn ..." The word was cold and hard, coming from Feldman as an unbelievable four bridges appeared and disappeared in less than ten minutes. "What just happened there? Where did they go?"

Mike was tapping furiously, alternating with glares at the display. "I don't know, sir. Three of those bridges were too small to measure at this scale. Those all had people in them. The long one went to the same spot in space that the last one did. Another object."

"Are they porting around the station?" Feldman asked.

"Yes, I think so."

"Find out where they're going."

Mike leaned closer to the display, as if it might help him see better. Dinnie broke in. "We don't have access to NISS maps," she told Feldman. "We need them hooked up to the detector, and the scale adjusted."

"Get it," he said. "Get it now." His face was scarlet. Dinnie thought she saw his temple throbbing, and had a faint hope that he might drop dead from stress and save all their lives. But no. He turned from her on stiff legs and ran to her office, slamming the door. In a few seconds they heard his voice raised to a near-bellow.

Dinnie's office was not soundproof. She wondered if Feldman thought it was, or was just too angry to care. Her people stood around the room, eyes on whatever was in front of them, trying to act as if they were working. But they were listening. There was nothing else they could do. She listened with one ear while she placed a call to Technical Support, ordering the upgrade.

"I told you to confiscate their equipment," Feldman shouted. "You haven't done that, and those people are flying around your fucking station like they own it. Where are your people? You've got ten fucking intruders on your station, and you're not doing a goddamn thing about it."

He paused, presumably for Rhyder's excuses. When he spoke again, his voice was louder than before. "They are transporting objects off the station. Do you have any ideas about what those object are? I know you do. Are you trying to pretend you don't know? Your fucked-up people can't even hide bombs properly ..."

Dinnie closed her eyes, frozen in place, numb with horror.

" ... and all the rebels have to do is look for them, and they can get rid of them."

Rhyder's desperate voice could be heard for a moment, though they couldn't make out the words.

Feldman overrode him. "Of course you didn't know people could transport themselves around your station. You didn't have to know. I told you to confiscate their equipment. I made that very clear. It was the first thing you were supposed to fucking do."

"You get that equipment, Rhyder. I don't care who you have to kill to get it. I don't care if you have to blow up the goddamn station. You get that equipment."

Dinnie jerked nervously, but Feldman did not come out of her office. Shortly, they heard his voice again, at a normal level this time. Dinnie sniffed, and realized there were tears on her cheeks. She wiped them away and turned to face her people.

No one was looking at her, or at anybody else. They continued to stare at the work before them, lost in their private dread. They'd seen it happen before when innocent employees learned too much. Entire departments wiped out, a few people at a time. Vehicle accidents. House fires. Burglaries gone violent. The press never connected the dots, never pursued it at all.

Now it was them.

Behind Dinnie, Mike spoke. She turned, but he was still watching the display. "I have a sister on NISS."

She stared at him, watching as his shaking hand touched his keyboard. She wanted to shout at him, or jump on him, *something* that would stop him. But she couldn't move, couldn't speak. His fingers danced a pattern and the display flickered. He continued to tap, feeding garbage data into the system, setting priorities.

The security guard raised his weapon. "Step away from the keyboard, Mr. Ontrera."

Mike ignored him, except to tap faster.

The guard fired, a long, sustained burst. Mike fell, his body jerking from the shocks. Around the room, the tension exploded as if a pin had pricked a balloon. People screamed or sobbed, backing into each other or against the walls or furniture.

Dinnie dropped next to Mike, ignoring the residual shocks as she lifted him in her arms. "Mike. Talk to me. Mike ... Mike."

His body had stopped jerking, and now his eyes opened. He smiled at her, the smile and eyes ghastly in his white face. "Oops," he said. She had to listen very carefully to understand him.

"They'll just restore it from backups," Dinnie said. "It won't stop them."

"Slow 'em down a wee bit."

"Yeah."

His eyes closed, but the smile remained. "Not just a data flunkie." He breathed out.

"No," Dinnie said, holding him close. "No. No."

∞

Moira was asleep. Sarah scrunched against the wall with her backpack on her lap and regarded her partner. Her eyes had long ago adjusted to the darkness, and she could see Moira's shadowed form, her head tilted to rest on the wall. Sarah couldn't see her face, but her breath was slow and even.

It was good that she slept, Sarah thought. It had not yet been a full day since her surgery. In fact, despite all that had happened, it was only four hours ago that Moira had been released from the infirmary.

They weren't taking very good care of her.

Sarah raised her head, as she did periodically, to listen for footsteps or voices. There had been guards out there a few minutes after Karen left, but she'd heard them running off. Since then, there was nothing.

Real success meant that Karen came out of it all right. Sarah checked the time, keeping her Pad on its dimmest setting. Twenty minutes. It felt longer. That meant the bomb was down to two hours and fifty-two minutes. That felt awfully short.

When the sound came, it was so soft, Sarah almost missed it. She just knew her body went still with the instinct of the hunted, and her ears were straining for a repeat of ... what? She held her breath, then realized her hand had moved to Moira's arm, and that Moira also lay still, not breathing.

Listening.

The door opened, light from the corridor blinding them. Sarah felt Moira's muscle flinch under her hand, but the girl remained still.

The door closed. "Okay," Karen said. "Let's go."

With a whoosh of breath, Sarah sat up and moved the box in front of her. Karen grinned up at her. "Sunnies are busy elsewhere for a few minutes, and I found us a safer place. Bigger, anyway."

"There's a bomb in here," Sarah said, and watched the grin disappear from Karen's face. That was too bad. It had been nice to see it.

"Where?"

Sarah pointed and Moira leaned forward so she could see Karen. "It's down to two hours and forty-eight minutes."

"It's *live*?" Karen slapped her hands together once, then reached up. "Hand me your stuff. Get down from there."

As soon as they were safe on the floor, Karen scrambled onto the shelf, craning her neck to peer into the bomb's corner.

"Shit." She tapped her ear. "Ned." Her voice was a whisper. Sarah nodded to herself. It made sense to whisper: they had no way of knowing what Ned's situation was. Calling was dangerous.

His answer came quickly, matching her whisper. "Here." No questions, no demands. That could all wait.

"There's a bomb at our coordinates. It's live. Two-and-a-half hours."

"Any Sunnies?"

"Negative."

"There's a corridor near you. Is it empty?"

Karen's brow wrinkled, and the look she sent Sarah and Moira was puzzled. But she pointed with her chin, and Sarah eased the door open a crack, then closed it.

"Clear."

Karen passed the word along.

"We're on our way. Out."

"Okay," Karen said to the closed line, and shrugged at her companions. "I suggest we don't wait for them."

She jumped down on light feet, then squeaked in alarm as the door began to open. Her taser was out before Sarah could blink. It was several seconds before they understood it was Ned, rather than a Sunnie guard, who was staring at them.

"How the feck did you get here so fast?" Karen demanded.

"They ported," Moira said, as if it were the most logical thing in the world.

How fast the young adapt, Sarah thought.

"Would ye mind," Ned said, "not pointing that thing at me?"

"Porting's a real timesaver," Pete said from behind Ned, and Karen finally put her taser down.

"So let's use the time we have." Ned waved the women out of the closet.

Sarah was surprised when Andy stepped in, holding CERBO. He aimed it at the bomb, tapped a few keys, and just like that, the shelf was empty.

"Had to lose a few supplies with that one," Andy said. "It was that, or part of the wall."

Moira's expression as she looked at Andy made Sarah turn away to hide her amusement. Moira looked like she couldn't decide whether she was impressed or jealous. But then Sarah caught Sam's eye, and her own emotions confused her: relief that he was all right, happy he was here, and furious that they were still trapped in this outrageous universe. He seemed to feel the same way, as he pulled her to him for a brief hug.

"We've got a pretty safe place we're using to reconnoiter," Ned said. "You may as well come with us."

Sarah kept hold of Sam's hand as Andy worked his magic. *He's pretty good with that thing,* she thought, and then they were in a room filled with plants. It took a few minutes for all the explanations, but at last, they were all silent, sitting on the floor in a comradely circle, while Pete ran a search for more bombs, and Ned brought Arkady up to date.

"I just went on the offensive," Arkady said. "Because you know that Sun will be spinning the news from here. I thought I'd beat 'em to it."

"How'd you do that?"

"Sent a flash out saying we'd found bombs up here, and showing the manifests that prove Feldman set you up. I said the Sunnies were restricting our movements, but we're trying to find the rest of the bombs."

Ned shook his head. "They'll just pull the flash, Arkady. No one will get the information."

"Don't sell me short, man." Arkady was cheerful. "I know a thing or three about getting past the firewalls. Sure, the official channels will just get a few seconds, but underground will be burning up with it. And when NISS is concerned, people pay attention. There's a reason we've got people up here from every country, right?"

Phil was nodding in vigorous agreement as they all listened. Ned shrugged. "Well it can't hurt, that's for sure. It should be obvious at some point, that we're trying to get rid of the bombs, while Sun is hindering us."

"People are getting antsy, up here," Arkady warned. "They know the lockdown is to keep the area clear for the Sunnies to do their dirty work. People are talking about charging them."

"Get themselves killed, is what," Ned said.

"Maybe. Some of 'em are willing to take the chance."

"All right. Give us a bit of time to clear some more bombs. Between that, and your news flash, maybe we'll have 'em on the run."

Ned signed off, shaking his head. "Quit grinning like a fool, Phil. We ain't won yet."

Phil shrugged. "Offense is what we need. Sun wasn't ready for us this time, and we got them on the run. I say we hit hard and keep it up."

"Okay." Ned spread his hands and tossed the ball to Pete. "How many bombs have you found?"

"All of them." Amid their exclamations, Pete tapped a few keys and his display lit up. The large number of red dots silenced everyone. Sarah wondered if they were all as shocked as she was.

Pete pointed at the display. "There are nineteen left," he said.

"Nineteen?" Ned leaned in, his finger tracing a path among the dots. "What are they doing? If that many bombs go off, there won't be a molecule left of the station."

"Can't figure it." Pete followed Ned's finger with narrowed eyes. "We haven't examined any of the bombs. Maybe they're all low-charge. Maybe Feldman's trying to limit damage, but he's covering all his bases by having them all over the station."

"The bastard's psychotic."

"No doubt." Sam said. "How many of them are live?"

"Three. No way of knowing what our time frame is."

"Fuck me." Ned whispered it as they all leaned in to examine the display. "Guess we do the live ones first, eh?'

"That'd be my advice." Pete tapped a key and three dots began blinking. None of them were near any others.

Sam entered the coordinates into CERBO. "Let's get moving, and hope our luck holds."

Chapter 35

The screams brought Feldman out of Dinnie's office. She knew he was coming by the sudden silence of her team, as if they were withdrawing into themselves. She didn't bother to look up, couldn't think past the sick knowledge that Mike was dead. She couldn't help him. She couldn't help any of them.

"What happened here?"

Dinnie did not look up to see if Feldman had addressed the question to her. The guard answered.

"Mr. Ontrera was sabotaging the Detector, sir. I ordered him to desist and to step away. He did not obey."

"Dr. Warner, what are you doing?" Feldman's voice was hard.

Asked a direct question, Dinnie struggled to respond, to think of something coherent to say. All she managed was, "He's dead." She still did not look at Feldman.

"Officer Carmichael, was Dr. Warner a partner in Mr. Ontrera's sabotage?" Feldman asked, and Dinnie held her breath. What would Carmichael say?

He took his time answering, but when he spoke, he sounded as if he was sure of what he said. "No sir. She appeared to be as surprised as the rest of us. In fact ..." he trailed off, as if he was now uncertain of his words.

"In fact, what?"

"Well sir, I had the impression it was a spontaneous act. There was no plan behind it at all."

"I see," Feldman said. Dinnie heard the message in those words. Feldman knew it had been his own shouting that caused Mike to snap. He began giving orders.

"Dr. Warner, get this Detector fixed. You, and you," he pointed to two of the nearest people, "take care of this body. The rest of you, back to work. I don't have time to baby you."

As they moved Mike's body from her arms, Dinnie saw that Feldman was already back on a call. She didn't want to be near him, but he was standing next to the Detector. Careful not to look at him, she slid into a chair to look over the damage. Feldman continued to give orders, this time to his henchman on NISS.

"I can't trace them anymore, but they're still there. I want you to turn off the computer."

Dinnie was so numb by this time that she did not stop moving at all at this statement, but around her, she sensed everyone pause. To Dinnie, Feldman's decision made perfect sense. Turn off the computer on NISS. Lose gravity, life support, and orbital maintenance.

Of course. One dead person is never enough.

Rhyder evidently asked for clarification, because Feldman's next words were as cold as ice. "Then you'll have to make certain you finish your job in time to start it again, Mr. Rhyder. I trust you understand that it's your problem, not mine."

∞

"We waste time with every bomb, trying to find a space big enough to hold six people. Everyone doesn't need to go. Send just Phil and Lisa, for protection." Sam rubbed a hand over his head, frustrated and tired of the argument.

"Maybe, if it were just you. But you insist that Andy go along, and I'm not taking chances with the only two people who run that machine." Ned rarely argued with people. He just gave orders and ignored anything he didn't want to hear. Sam supposed he was lucky that Ned was still responding.

"Sarah can run CERBO in a pinch." That was stupid, of course. Still true, though.

Ned poked a finger in the display. "Send us here. Do it now, we're losing time."

Sam glared at the display but pressed the button, then looked over his shoulder to see a vast expanse of space through a floor-to-ceiling window. He'd known this location was on the outer rim, but wow. That was some view.

Fortunately, his bodyguards paid attention to their jobs rather than the view. When Phil bashed into him a few seconds later, he knew they were under attack. He curled around CERBO, trying to keep it safe, while over and around him, tasers sizzled. A few terrifying moments later, Pete shouted in his ear, "Crawl left! Stay down!"

He'd never been in the army, but Sam could belly crawl with the best of them. It was harder with CERBO, but he managed it. He arrived at a console the same time that Andy did. Andy gestured for Sam to go first, and he didn't argue. Once they were both on the other side, they stayed down, arms over their heads, until they heard Ned yell, "It's clear! Go!"

There was still shooting going on, but they both half stood and raced for the corridor where the bomb was. Their guards, four of them as Ned insisted, were keeping the Sunnies busy in the other direction. They leaped over a body blocking the hallway, and followed the rim's curve until an inner door appeared.

Which was locked.

"Damn." Andy began picking at his Pad. "Hang on, I'll override this thing ..." Three seconds later, Sam heard the lock beep. At almost the same time, Andy jerked back and tapped the side of his Pad. "What the hell?"

"What is it?" Sam pushed the door open and peered inside.

"Don't know," Andy said. "Think I lost my connection. Do you see the bomb?"

"Yeah." The room was a private office, just a desk, virtual screen and a file cabinet. There were two chairs, and according to his locator, the bomb was attached under the seat of the guest chair. To Sam's great surprise, that's where it was.

Careless. It could have blown up at any time.

Andy flattened against the doorjamb. "Someone's coming."

Sam sent the bomb to oblivion and turned in time to see Andy relax. "Lisa," Andy muttered, and they stepped out of the office to meet her.

"All done," Sam said.

"Brilliant," she said. "Ned says there's something wrong with the computer."

The others turned the corner and joined them. Ned pointed his chin at Andy's Pad.

"Is that working?"

"No. It went down practically the same time I unlocked the door. Good thing I got that done first, or we'd still be trying to get in."

"Communications are down," Ned said. "I can't get any station interaction at all."

"Are they blocking us somehow?" Sam asked.

"No, it's worse than that." Andy was flipping through screens on his Pad. "I think they've shut the computer down."

Everyone went silent. Sam glanced around the group. "I'm waiting for someone to explain that."

"It's a fail-safe," Ned said. "Very last-try stuff, in a life-or-death situation. Which I guess they think this is."

"You mean the computer that runs the station's systems?" Sam asked.

Everyone nodded. "Exactly that," Ned said. "Systems run on automatic for six hours, but if the computer is not up and running by then, it all goes dark. Gravity, temperature, shielding, that sort of thing"

"I get it."

"We've got cached files," Andy said. He brought up their bomb display, which showed two live bombs still blinking. They'd destroyed one of them, but without the computer, there was no update to show the number of bombs left.

Ned nodded. "Let's get the last one, then go back to Hydro and figure out our next step."

Sam ported them to their selected spot, an exercise area. There were no Sunnies, but everyone surrounded Sam and Andy anyway, tasers out and watching for opposition. Andy, who was holding the bomb display, pointed to a door off to the left. Sam tried the handle, relieved when it turned. But there came a sound of scrabbling from inside, and Phil stepped between Sam and the door. Lisa motioned Sam and Andy to back off and she took up a position behind Phil, while Pete and Ned continued to guard the room.

Phil kicked the door, which slammed against the wall. But instead of entering, he dropped his taser and raised both hands. Behind him, Lisa did the same, her face twisted into a bitter scowl. Sam realized that whoever was in the room could probably not see anyone other than Phil and Lisa. That gave them an advantage. But to do what? He needed to see where the bomb was. Then from inside the room, he heard a voice, young and nervous, but filled with defiance.

"You're smart, aren't you? Not going to mess with me, right? Right, that's good. Let's just all stay still a while, eh?"

Phil nodded once. "We aren't moving, kid, I promise." His voice was soothing, as if he were talking to a frightened animal. Sam began to get a sick feeling of what Phil and Lisa were seeing. Phil continued. "Have you really thought about this, mate? It isn't necessary."

"Yes it is," the voice yelled back. "You're interfering with the government. You're stinking rebels, and we've got to get rid of you."

"No need for you to blow yourself up, though," Phil said. "You can take it off and let it do its damage without you."

"No, I can't. You'll move it off the station just like the others ..."

Sam stepped up next to Phil, and the kid stopped talking, snapping the gun he'd had on Phil to aim it at this new threat. He was around Moira's age. His face was colorless, except for his eyes, which glittered dark and terrified through beads of sweat falling from his forehead. He wore a Sunnie uniform, and wrapped around his ribcage was a belt of explosives. Near his hip, a clock counted down. Two minutes.

"Put that down," the kid demanded, pointing at CERBO. "Put your hands up."

"Do you know how we're moving the bombs off?" Sam asked. "Did your superiors tell you anything?"

"I don't need to know it," the kid said. "I do what's necessary."

"Then let me tell you," Sam said. "I press this button that my thumb is on, and the bomb is instantly transported into space, away from the station. Instantly. There's no way to take it back. If I could, I'd narrow the field to just the bomb, but I can't discriminate that much. It's wrapped around you, you go with it. Please don't make me do that."

"Fuck you. I'm willing to die for what's right."

"Right doesn't want you dead, kid." Sam stole a glance at the time. One minute, 25 seconds. The hand he kept poised over the button was visibly shaking. "What's your name?"

The kid's bloodless lips tightened and he renewed his grip on his gun.

"Mine is Sam. In the next few seconds one of us is going to kill the other. Can we at least exchange names?"

He could see the kid reasoning through it, trying to decide if his superiors would like it. Next to Sam, and behind him, his comrades stayed still, silent. Giving Sam a chance. One minute, five seconds. The kid's jaw twitched, and he finally spoke. "Benjamin."

Sam nodded. "Benjamin. Benjamin, I don't want you to die. You don't really want to, do you?"

"It's my part." His chin came up. "I volunteered. So you fucking rebels don't win."

"Nobody wins if you die, Benjamin. You're so young. You have your whole life to live. I know there are things you want to do." Forty seconds. Sam began to choke on his words. "Please Benjamin, take it off. Just put it on the ground and I'll get rid of it."

The gun wavered, then leveled. "No."

"Please don't make me kill you. Take it off. You'll live. We'll make sure you're okay."

Thirty seconds.

"Please Benjamin. I'm begging you, don't make me do this. Please. Dear God, please."

Twenty seconds.

Benjamin was shaking as hard as Sam was, the gun he held jerking in uncontrollable directions. Sam felt the heat of his glittering dark eyes, staring right into him. He curled his fingers back, exposing the one finger hovering over CERBO's button. He yelled.

"Take it off!"

"No!"

"Don't make me kill you!"

"No!"

Sam jabbed the button. Benjamin disappeared before the final tones of his last word reached their ears.

"Nah!" Sam clutched CERBO to his heart and swung a vicious kick into the wall, then kept kicking, each one punctuated with his screams of rage. Then he put his back to the wall and sank down, sobbing into his knees.

No one said anything, until Andy knelt beside him, and with gentle hands, pulled CERBO from his grip. "Let me take us back, Sam."

Chapter 36

"I can't talk to Arkady with the computer down." Ned was tapping his Pad, as if he thought that would bring communications back. Moira thought he looked older than he had when she first met him a few hours ago.

"They've got some control in Security, don't they?" Andy asked. "Isn't the fail-safe designed to let the Sunnies handle an evacuation if it's necessary?"

Ned nodded, but it was Pete who answered.

"I think Security can handle doorways and escape pod ejections. Those also work on manual override, but that knowledge is limited to a few station personnel. Rather, they think it's limited. Arkady has trained everybody on how to do it, so that might work in our favor somehow. Security also has the ability to boot the system again, if it's a problem that can be fixed."

"Where do they have this access?"

"Their main office off the inner rim," Ned said.

"We can't deal with that," Sam said, his voice dull, as if he didn't care anymore. Sarah sat next to him on the floor, her arm resting on his knee. He was watching Ned's pointless poking. "We've still got sixteen bombs to get rid of. And the last few have all been armed when we find them."

Ned stopped poking and lifted his head to look at Sam. "All we've got is the cached display. If they move any of the bombs, we won't know where they are. If they arm anymore of them, we won't know that, either."

Sam shrugged. "We work with what we've got."

Moira traced a finger through her own display of the station until she reached the inner rim. "Why don't we port the Sunnies to Earth?"

The only answer she got was silence, so she glanced up. Everyone was staring at her, and her stomach fluttered in sudden nervousness. "Umm ... was that a stupid question?"

Ned's lip twitched. "What's stupid is we never thought of it." He looked to Sam. "At the least, we can port out any Sunnies we come to as we approach the bombs. Can you do that?"

"There are problems with it," Sam said, slowly, as if thinking about it. "I can program the destination ahead of time. But how do we get the guards to stand still in one place, so I can program in their location?"

"How much time do you need? It seems to take just a few seconds with the bombs."

"Yes, but the bombs aren't moving. And I have the coordinates partially entered based on the map location. I can do that for the guards too, of course. Assuming the guards are not moving around ... I'd need five to ten seconds."

"Sneak up on 'em," Ned said. "We'll have to port ourselves in a little farther away, but if we can reduce the number of Sunnies, the sooner Arkady can get this station under control."

"It will add seconds to every bomb search we do," Sam said. "I'll have to reprogram for the bomb every time."

"Can you port out the guards in the main office?" Pete asked. "You can use the coords for the whole office so that you get them all."

"That would port out the equipment, too," Andy said.

Ned held up a hand. "Let's do this another way. Send the ladies to Arkady's location. I think it's time we called out all the troops. With computer control gone, they're going to be hopping mad, anyway. Karen can tell Arkady that we need lots of distraction. They can keep the guards busy, isolate and strand them, if possible. We can send them off-station later. Here." He motioned to Karen, while bringing up his bomb display.

"We'll follow this path, going from lower to upper levels at each location." They all watched his finger move through the display. Karen nodded as if committing it to memory. "Tell Arkady I want people at each location, causing a ruckus."

He turned to Andy, indicating a corridor on the map. "Send the women here. Arkady's location is over here," a green light blinked a few doors down. "I doubt there're any guards in the area. Arkady would never stand for it. You should be able to just walk down there." The last was to Karen as she loaded up with weapons, but Moira nodded too. Finally, something useful to do.

She saw Andy press the button, but still experienced a shock to find herself someplace else. They were in a corridor with several closed doors in both directions. Karen turned in a circle, then picked a direction. "This way."

They followed her to the third door down, next to a window covered with a shade. Karen knocked and called out, "Arkady, it's Karen. Ned sent us down."

The voice Moira was used to hearing through Ned's Pad answered. "Hang on. We have to do this manually."

A whirring sound came from the wall for a few seconds, then the door slid open. The tall and skinny man who stood in the doorway gave Karen a big grin and pulled her into a hug, weapons and all.

"Karen, me love! You're a sight for me tired eyes. That husband of yours still treating you right?"

"Still is, Arkady."

"All right. You let me know the minute I have a chance, now."

Karen released herself from his grip and introduced Moira and Sarah. There were several other people in the room, which Moira recognized as the communications center she'd seen on the screen before they came up here. They all waved in greeting, but didn't interrupt. Karen explained what they wanted.

"Pfft," was Arkady's first response, but he elaborated. "I can't keep 'em down. People are plenty mad, let me tell you. Hang on and I'll get the troops started." He scooped a walkie-talkie from his belt, and began making calls. Moira could hear the relief in the voices of the people Arkady talked to. As she listened, she realized that they were scattered all over the station. It was called a lockdown because people were literally locked into their rooms when it went into effect, but as Pete had mentioned, they all knew how to override the locks. They were disciplined enough to wait for information before doing it, knowing that they needed to make the most of the ability.

The walkie-talkies were something else they weren't supposed to have. "There's one in every room of the station," Arkady said when she asked him. "I couldn't abide the idea that we couldn't talk to each other. In a real emergency, communication is essential."

The bomb display showed an active location on their level, about five corridors over, so he sent his own people there, letting Karen lead them. Karen insisted that Moira and Sarah stay with Arkady, who remained to coordinate the uprising. Moira fumed, but knew she'd just be a liability. Sarah seemed almost grateful to be left out.

"Whatever happens," Arkady said as the room emptied, "it won't take long. We've got five thousand pissed-off people, and they have only a couple hundred Sunnies."

∞

Andy had ported out three of the remaining bombs. Sam was still quiet, and made no effort to do any of the porting, although he did keep an eye on Andy's work. The next bomb was nearby, so they were walking, with Phil and Ned taking the lead. Pete and Lisa followed, walking backwards so they could see anyone coming from behind.

The noise hit them first, and Ned pumped a fist in the air. "Arkady's got the troops out."

There was no doubt about location, so they hurried, but the action was over by the time they got there. Ten people milled about the anteroom, trussing up the three unconscious guards. They greeted Ned with exuberance. "They never knew what hit 'em," one said. "They had no idea we weren't still locked away."

Andy and Sam slipped through the crowd while Ned talked to the group's leader. "Stash the guards in a defensible room and have a couple of your people keep an eye on them. We'll come back for them after we get rid of the bombs. The rest of you, join up with the next group. Remember, word will get to the other Sunnies that you're out. They won't all be easily surprised."

That was true, Andy realized, suddenly nervous. Some of these people could die. He sent the bomb out, and Sam nodded, satisfied. They returned to Ned.

"I don't think we should port to anymore locations," Sam said. "The people are helping with the guards, but we've lost the advantage of empty corridors."

"I agree." Ned rubbed the back of his neck as he peered at his bomb display. "Randy here says that Arkady sent groups to every bomb location, so there should already be a crowd at the next one. I say we just hoof it over there as fast as we can."

He turned to look over his burgeoning team. "Form a circle. These are the guys you're protecting. They stay in the middle. If we run into guards, cover them at all times."

As the group closed around them, Andy saw two of them take up station near a closed door. That must be where they stashed the Sunnies. He wished they had time to send them off station. But it would have to wait.

Chapter 37

Feldman closed the door to his office and leaned against it, letting his burning eyes close. This exacerbated the pounding in his temples, so he opened them again and stared at his desk, which seemed to float at the end of a long, narrow tunnel. He wondered, for just a moment, if he were having a stroke.

He dismissed this idea. Death might come today, but it would not be so easy.

"Ari, mute the window," he said. In the more welcome gloom, he added, "Have Dinnie Warner report to my office." He proceeded to his desk and the work waiting there.

This involved little more than calling up a display of the carnage that was NISS. In the last hour, communications with Rhyder had gone sporadic, then stopped altogether, as station civilians rioted, interfering with signals and distracting his security team from its mission of apprehending Sam Altair.

Feldman was reduced to getting his information from the news services. The prime minister, and other government heads, had honored Feldman's request to black out most of the more damaging reports, but reporters the world over were gleeful as they showed short takes of Arkady's second announcement that NISS was now under civilian control. There were hints of a radical new technology developed by the rebel alliances, and a few minutes ago, Feldman heard the first reports that Sun's security officers on NISS were mysteriously appearing on the wide expanse near Stonehenge, with no idea how they'd gotten there.

Ari sent him a ping. "Dr. Warner has arrived, sir."

"Send her in."

He watched the news display until she reached his desk. He raised his head then, happy to see her flinch from his gaze. Usually, her penchant for dark clothes contrasted with the spiky blonde hair to give her a tough, competent bravado. Now she looked like a pale wraith dressed in mourning.

There was a price for everything, and Dinnie Warner knew it.

He stood, brushing his fingers over his desk before addressing her. "Has your research revealed any correlation between Andrew Green and Sam Altair before they met yesterday in our laboratory?"

She stood stiff, not quite looking at him. "No sir, I could not find anything. However, based on Mr. Green's access to neutrino detection, I am certain that he saw the first occurrence in March. He and Moira Sherman both had unusual search requests centered on Belfast in the days immediately following."

"You did not think to look for this when you were vetting Mr. Green for employment?"

"No sir." He could see that she wanted to protest it wasn't her job to do that. He hoped she understood that it wasn't the point.

He turned from her, to pace a few steps behind his desk, thinking. "Altair's appearance came at a crucial juncture. I am curious as to how he, or the rebels, obtained information about the NISS Project."

He glanced up at her silence. "Can you enlighten me, Dr. Warner?"

"I?" Her jaw was hard as she lifted her chin. "I'm afraid I can't."

"But I think you can." He wandered back to his desk, unhurried, to bring up a hologram. "You know this man?"

He liked the hate in her eyes.

"He's my brother."

"He's assigned to the Western Brigade in Galway?"

"Yes."

"He provides you with information?"

"No sir. We seldom talk. We ... are not close."

He resumed his pace. "There is always a chain, doctor. A chain of information that grows as it passes from person to person, until it reaches the one person who is in the right place, at the right time, to make use of it. This particular chain wends its way from the spaceport in Galway, to this building, to this department, then on to a traveler from another dimension, to a notorious rebel, and hence, to the space station."

He stopped and smiled at her, his hands relaxed in the pockets of his pants. "This particular chain travels through you."

Her jaw moved as she swallowed, but she said nothing.

"In my career," he said, "I have crossed paths with many traitors. Some of them caused significant damage to Sun's mission, and to me personally. But you, Dr. Warner, are the best of them. You are the one who succeeded in bringing me to ruin."

Her eyes touched on his at last. For a brief moment of truth, he read her joy. "If that is true, sir," she said, "I can only say it was a happy confluence of events that allowed it to happen."

He was glad for her spark. It made her a more worthy adversary, and took some of the sting out of losing. He nodded and brought his hands out of his pockets. One hand reached inside his jacket. "Thank you, Dr. Warner. That will be all."

It was his favorite bullet gun, and it took Warner a few moments to realize she'd been shot. Her body reacted with immediate recoil, and her face registered the first shock of pain. But he saw the realization dawn in her eyes as she watched him. She fell backwards, living long enough to bring her bloody hands in front of her face, and count the cost charged to her account.

∞

After the last Sun guard vanished from sight, Andy turned and presented CERBO to Sam with a little bow. "That's the lot," he said. "NISS is officially a civilian station, thanks to you."

Sam grinned. It had taken a while, but he'd finally gotten into the spirit of the thing, as the Sunnies were sent packing in groups of twenty. He was especially tickled with the idea of sending them to Stonehenge. They'd chosen it for practicality, since in this world, no one was allowed at the site, and the area was large and flat. But Sam felt there was some kind of cosmic justice playing out, and he let it relieve his soul a little.

A crowd had gathered to watch, and now they broke into applause and cheering. On the public screens surrounding them, the video of Arkady's declaration of their independence was playing over and over. Several people were already talking about making this date a colony holiday, to be celebrated with pomp, speeches, and picnics on the outer rim.

Arkady came over and shook his hand. "We owe you big, Sam. Thank you for getting involved."

"I have a feeling our worlds will have to work together in the future," Sam said. "I think we're off to the right start, here. Although how you're going to hold onto it, I don't know. I have the impression that none of your governments are open to granting people freedoms."

"They aren't. But Sun is a bitch even to their friends, and there's a certain cache that comes with beating them. I intend to use it."

"Good luck to you."

"For now," Arkady said, nodding to the approaching Ned, "I understand we have another mission to do."

"Yep," Ned said. "Feldman's holding on to some stuff that ain't his, there's a big surprise. I promised Sam we'd help get them back, and I don't think we should be waiting around for long."

"Don't want to give Feldman time to lose them," Pete said, from behind Sam.

Sam raised a brow. "How many are planning on going?"

"We've had to beat the volunteers back," Arkady said. "Everyone wants to see Feldman eat shit."

Sarah shook her head. "This is not a joy ride. It's probably the most protected place on your planet. We'll be lucky to come out alive."

"Exactly," Sam said. "In fact, I think it's best if I go alone."

Ned held up a hand to silence the babble of questions this brought. He fixed Sam with a thoughtful stare and crossed his arms. "Explain."

"My first concern," Sam said, "is that I don't have a plan for forcing Feldman to return our items. He knew the original Sam well enough to know that I won't kill him. There's no point even threatening that. We've nothing to use for blackmail, as he's already lost a very public battle. He's essentially ruined, although I wouldn't put it past him to have a contingency plan."

"Basically, I don't know what we'd accomplish if a large, armed group of us shows up in his office. But say it's just me, with an open comm line broadcasting video and audio of our meeting. I'll make sure he knows our meeting is being broadcast. If he refuses to return the chip, the whole world will know that Sun has stolen it."

Ned shrugged. "The whole world might not care. People will want that technology."

"*People* will not get the technology if Sun has it," Sam said. "I've already given it to the people of your world, by giving it to you. In fact, I'm considering not going home until you've got an actual prototype built, because frankly, CERBO is the only advantage you have over Sun."

Everyone was silent as Ned thought it through. His frown showed he wasn't happy with the plan, but finally, he nodded. "I want to go with you, though. You need at least one person to watch your back. I can handle the recording too, so you can concentrate on handling Feldman."

Sarah nodded emphatically at this, and Sam smiled as he squeezed her hand. "You're on," he said. "But that brings up another point. I think it would be foolish to take CERBO back into Sun HQ, and give Feldman another chance at taking it. Andy can operate CERBO from here, to drop us off and pick us up. I have a blood marker that CERBO can trace. Andy already knows how that works. If you're coming, I suggest we put a marker in you, as well."

"So no matter what happens down there, Andy can always bring us back?" Ned asked.

"That's it."

"So where," Karen asked, "are you going, exactly? None of us know where in the building Feldman's office is."

"I do," Sarah said. When this brought several blank stares, she raised an eyebrow. "Well, I do."

"How?" Sam asked.

She brought up a display of Sun Headquarters. "While I was a prisoner in that little room, I wrote a bunny to help me build a map of the building. I hate not knowing where I am."

"Wait." Ned shook his head. "You wrote a bunny? What does that mean?"

"It's a piece of computer code. We call them bunnies, because we can send them hopping through a system for us. And because if you're not careful, they can multiply." Amid snickers, Sarah zoomed her display out to show a grid of Sun Headquarters. She pointed. "Feldman's office is right here. Eighty-fifth floor, east end of the building."

"If you ever need a job ..." Arkady shook his head.

"Don't work for the other guy!" Karen said.

Ned clapped his hands together. "Let's get moving. What do you need for this blood marker?"

"Just your basic chemistry lab," Sarah said. "I can do it for you."

"This way," a man called out, and they followed him around a corner. People began talking about cleaning up the station while they waited for the action to start. Arkady assembled a team to work on the video feed and prepare to once again hijack the public broadcast frequencies. Sam watched as Andy worked out the coordinates for Feldman's office.

"Are you really thinking of staying around a while?" Andy asked.

"Haven't discussed it with Sarah yet," Sam said. "I'm going to hear about that later, I can promise you."

Andy laughed. "I bet."

"But it's your biggest advantage, and you won't have it for long. Feldman's been holding that chip for a few days now. I'm sure he's had a team looking at it."

"No doubt."

"Provided we can access all the components, we can build one of these things in a few days."

Andy glanced up. "What was your original time frame for this mission? When are you expected back home?"

"I was hoping we'd be gone for one day. We allowed for three."

"You've been here five."

Sam nodded.

"What is your team doing?"

"Waiting. We do have a fail-safe in place, that retrieves us after seven days. We have our own problems with secrecy, you see. Only five people in our world know about the two universes."

Andy whistled, and Sam propped himself onto the table, giving in to the need to confess.

"The truth is, we're going to be in a lot of trouble when we get back. Just one person knew of this mission, Sarah's uncle, Jamie Andrews. He's a Nobel laureate, and quite respected. The three of us head a research consortium, somewhat similar," he shuddered, "to Sun. Without the drama and control, I hope."

"But given what's happened here, and the reality of the political climate, I'm afraid we've put our world into terrible danger. Sun's leaders will not ignore us, now that they know how to find us."

Andy rubbed a hand over his mouth. "Blimey. You do have a mess on your hands."

"We won't be able to ignore it. When we get back, we'll have to go to our world leaders. I don't know what they'll do."

"You have to protect your world from us," Andy said, his voice deep with conviction. "Sun is the greatest danger, but not the only one. What if they try to invade?"

Sam stared at his hands, rubbing them together in slow circles. He didn't answer.

"How can you keep helping us, knowing we might destroy your world?" Andy asked.

Sam looked up, then. "Because you're the reasonable voices in this world. You're our biggest hope, Andy. You have to save your world, for our sake, as well as yours."

"The stakes are higher than ever then, aren't they?" Arkady said from behind Sam. "I couldn't help overhearing." He pulled a chair over. "Your video feed is ready. I'd like to wire you. Ned, too, in case you get separated."

"Okay."

"Sam, you're doing the right thing," Arkady said. "Secrecy is a killer on this world. Everything we do needs to be out in the open. Full public knowledge will be our most powerful weapon. Even more than CERBO."

"It will have to be that way on our world, too," Sam said. "We are both going to have stunned populations when all this comes out."

"They'll live."

"That's the idea."

Chapter 38

Sam didn't know what to expect when Feldman's office appeared around him. He tried to be ready for anything, but he was not prepared for the bloody body on the floor in front of Feldman's desk.

Fortunately, Ned kept his wits about him. He aimed his taser squarely at Feldman's heart.

Feldman did not seem concerned about it, but he did sit back in his chair and scowl at them. "I can see this invention will require new standards of etiquette," he said. "You might have called first."

Sam shifted his gaze from Dinnie Warner's body to Feldman's cold eyes. "What did you do?"

"Don't be naïve, Sam. It's obvious what I did." He waved an indifferent hand. "Dinnie Warner was a traitor. The penalty for that is death."

"In cold blood? Without judge or jury?"

"Expensive time-wasters. Is there a reason for this visit?"

Sam gave himself a moment. When he thought he could trust his voice, he said, "First, you should know this meeting is being broadcast in real-time. We've hijacked the public channels."

"Impressive. But the company you've been keeping are known for their lawbreaking tactics."

"If the people of your world know their history, they'll remember there are sometimes lawless regimes, which require lawbreakers to change." Sam sensed Ned shift behind him, reminding him to stay on topic. "But we aren't here to discuss morality with the amoral. You have items which belong to Sarah and me. I've come to collect them."

Feldman rolled his chair back and Ned moved the taser with him, stepping forward as he did so. Feldman stopped, and raised both hands. "I need to open my safe."

"Where's the gun you used to kill Dr. Warner?" Ned asked.

"In my inside jacket pocket."

"Take it out. Slowly. Put it on the desk."

Feldman did this, his expression somewhat amused.

"Sam, go pick it up."

Sam walked forward, glad that Ned came with him, the taser still on Feldman. Sam shuddered when he stepped around Dinnie, careful to avoid her blood.

Ned kept control. "Please stand up, Mr. Feldman." When Feldman did, Ned moved around the desk, and frisked him. "I'm sorry about that," he said. "But you understand, we have to be safe."

"Of course I do, Mr. O'Malley. Do you understand that there are weapons in this room, as well as surveillance, which I do not control?"

"We can be pulled instantly," Sam said.

"Yes, I see that you don't have your CERBO with you. I assume Mr. Green is operating it? How is his young girlfriend, by the way?"

Sam looked upward and shrugged. "The chip, please. And the journals."

After first obtaining Ned's permission to move, Feldman led them to a small statue near the wall. He twisted its head in a complex pattern, and a shelf on the wall moved aside to reveal a small door with a keypad. Feldman entered a code and the door opened. He reached inside the small space and pulled out three journals. He handed these to Sam.

"Where's the chip?" Sam asked.

"I don't have it."

"You're lying."

"Oh, come now, Sam. Surely, with the events of today, you don't think my superiors would let me keep such a valuable item? The fact that the two of you have remained alive in my office for this long is a sign of how far I've fallen. Regardless, I wouldn't have the chip anyway. One of our science teams has it. Before you ask, I don't know which lab it's in. If I did know, I wouldn't tell you." He stood straight, as if proud. "I've made unpardonable mistakes, but my loyalty is not in question."

Sam heard Arkady's voice in his ear. "Guards are coming. I'm pulling you out." He didn't have time to argue, or even take a breath, before the walls of NISS formed around him. Behind him, Ned sighed.

"Sam," Arkady waved a hand from his seat in front of the comm unit. "We still have the broadcast channels. Will you make a statement?"

They had talked about this before leaving. It would be important to tell people what was going on. Sam supposed that, if Sun still had the chip, it was even more important to warn the world.

He met Sarah near Arkady's station and handed her the journals. She rubbed a hand across her grandmother's book, then brushed a tear from her cheek. "Thank you," she whispered, and kissed his cheek. Then they each took a chair, and began to explain.

∞

The next morning, Andy found Moira gazing in quiet rapture at the view outside the outer rim. The view was virtual, as the need for radiation protection prevented the luxury of windows. The station was wrapped in a sphere of water, which was encased between thick walls of RXF2 shielding material. The interior side of the outer rim was lined with floor-to-ceiling vid screens, for the enjoyment of the colonists.

Andy knew the view was virtual, but when he finally found Moira at the wall the next morning, it mattered not at all. He joined her, lost in the wonder of the planet below them. Above and beyond the planet, stars filled the view.

She smiled up at him. "All the time I was here yesterday, I never saw any windows. It wasn't until this morning at breakfast that I got to see the view."

Andy nodded. "I kept thinking of that, too. Some of the bombs were planted on the outer rim, so I did see it. Couldn't stop to admire it, though."

"I imagine not." Her gaze turned back to the window. "I looked for you this morning, but you were in a meeting."

"Yes, and when I got out of that, you were in a meeting. Arkady tells me he offered you a place on NISS. But the Swiss offered you asylum, too, didn't they?"

She nodded. "They did." She paused to take a deep breath before saying in a rush, "But I've decided to stay here." Her eyes flashed back to his face, revealing her worry that he would be upset with her decision. "I talked with Hans Greigan, who heads the physics department. He said they could offer me a research position while I read for a degree. Arkady said I could attend school here, to finish any courses I need for the sixth form, and start my college courses. There are several students here."

He turned to face her, crossing his arms and leaning against the railing. "That's wonderful. It's everything we hoped you'd be able to do with the rebels."

"Yes. I'm very excited about it." She stood close to him, her eyes on his face. "You're going to Switzerland, aren't you?"

"Yes. It seems our best bet for neutrality, and for the facilities we need to build another CERBO. The fail-safe in their CERBO will take Sam and Sarah home sometime tomorrow, but I'll continue to work on the project. The Swiss government has offered to assist us as we try to get the charges against us dropped. There's also the mess at Strickert to clear up. Evidently, Feldman teamed up with your stepfather to create that news report. The Lioness doesn't deserve what's happened to her reputation."

"And Grace," Moira said. "Please check on Grace."

"That is one of my first priorities, I assure you."

They were both silent, their shared burden felt without words.

Then Andy smiled, and reached a finger to touch her hair. "I will miss you. But I know you'll be in good hands here. It really is for the best."

"Yes," she said, animated again. "Everyone says that. They have all told me how much better off I'll be when I'm away from you. That I need time. Fortunately," and she gave a short, bitter laugh, "they don't quite say that I need time to grow up. Rather, they say I need time to learn who I am, so that I can know what I feel for you."

"It's true," he whispered. "I've said it myself."

"I am tempted to stamp my foot, and declare that I am old enough to know my own feelings." She struck a pose, hands on her hips, and a foot pounded the floor. He smiled, enjoying the picture she made. After a moment, she smiled back and relaxed. "I can't argue with the logic. But mostly, it occurs to me that you deserve someone who knows herself. Someone who is a whole person, who brings as much to the relationship that you do." Her voice cracked, and she looked away, swallowing hard. When she spoke again, she sounded normal, although she did not look at him.

"That isn't me, not yet. I have so much life to live, first." Her brows twitched upwards. "Arkady says I'll be on my own, here. Essentially an adult, although I'll have a counselor to assist me."

"This will be good for you," Andy said. "You're a very sensible young woman, you know. You'll make good decisions, and find good friends, and you will have the time of your life." He smiled because at last, she looked up at him again. "Do that, Moira. Have fun. Be at peace. When you're ready, date a few fellows. Find out who you are, and while you're doing that," he held up a finger, admonishing, "be sure you stay in touch. I expect daily reports, at least."

She laughed, but there were tears in her eyes. "At least. I would go insane if I thought I couldn't talk to you."

"We are friends, more than anything else, Moira." His Pad buzzed and he silenced it, his expression remorseful. "It's time for me to go. We're meeting the Swiss consulate in Bern at half past."

Her hand shot out and gripped his. "I'm suddenly terrified. How do I live without you?"

"We'll talk again in just a few hours," he said. "You'll settle in here, and soon, you'll be fine. I promise."

"Okay."

He pulled her hand toward him and held it against his chest. She had to lean toward him to keep her balance. "You have my heart, Moira. Take care with it."

"Always." A whisper.

He turned away, and left her there, knowing she watched him until he was gone. And he smiled, knowing that once he was gone, her gaze would return to the stars.

SECOND UNIVERSE

Epilogue
Dublin, Ireland
Two days later

Jamie Andrews watched the swirls as his spoon moved through the teacup. If the answers he sought were there, they weren't obvious. He brought his gaze back to Ireland's president, who was rubbing her forehead as if she had a headache.

She did this for a few moments more, then turned her attention back to him. "I wish you'd seen fit to bring us in on this several decades ago." Her glance included Sam and Sarah in her disapproval, even though both were far too young to have anything to do with decades-old decisions.

"Are you suggesting," she continued, "that I contact the heads of state of every other nation, and tell them we must prepare for an interdimensional war? I would be laughed out of the room."

"They have the right to know," Jamie said.

"It may not come to war," Sam said. "The most powerful force on that world was badly discredited. While a few megalomaniacs may harbor a desire to take over our world, I don't believe they have the power to accomplish it. A few of the more liberal governments were already working together to prevent aggressive use of the CERBO. I'm hopeful they will be successful."

"Hope is not how one protects one's country, Dr. Altair."

"No, of course not. But I do think it's important that we consider what the nations of that world will want from us."

"Which is?"

"Resources."

"What resources?"

"All of them," Jamie said. "Or any of them. That world is becoming toxic to humans. They will want water, food, air ..."

"How can they steal our air? In fact, how can they steal any of these things? Can't you create some kind of barrier that will keep them out? Or is there a weapon that would destroy their ... bridges, did you call them?"

"Bridges," Sam said. "And the answers are no and no, I'm afraid. As to how," he shrugged, "they port in, set up a base somewhere, and begin mining whatever they need. When a large quantity is ready, they simply port it back to their world."

"This is the kind of thing we need to be watching for," Jamie said. "They could be here, and we might not know for years."

The president stared at him, her mouth opening, then closing a few times.

Sam cleared his throat. "The Sun Consortium already had my chip, which was programmed with the neutrino shape of our universe. The fact is, Madam, they may already be here."

"We need to offer them alternatives, in my opinion," Jamie said. "For instance, they have the ability to travel through time, which will create a new universe. If they go far enough back in time—before humans existed—they can have an entire planet to mine."

"That is feasible," the president said. "Then we have only the megalomaniacs to deal with."

"Exactly," Sam said.

The president placed both hands on her knees and stood. The others scrambled up, exchanging uncertain glances. "You'll be happy to know," she said, "that we do have an emergency world-wide alert system in place. I can be in contact with every head of state in a few hours. I'm going to ask you all to remain here. I am certain there will be questions."

She turned a sharp gaze on Sarah. "You did not go back in time to find your great-grandparents, did you? Do you plan on trying again?"

Sarah shook her head. "No ma'am. We have discussed it, and we are certain that my grandmother would be against it, given the circumstances."

"I knew her," the president said, as a faraway look entered her eyes. "It explains so much about her, to know that she came from the future." Her lips twitched. "I always thought she was remarkably far-sighted."

Her visitors smiled at this, and she continued. "I've tried to emulate her in that regard. I suppose I should continue to do that, while I encourage the other world leaders to do the same."

She turned to the door, but paused, and looked from one to the other of them. "Second universe," she said, shaking her head. "None of them are going to like that idea."

She opened the door. "They won't like it at all."

Made in the USA
Charleston, SC
14 April 2013